ALSO BY CAROLE L. GLICKFELD

Useful Gifts

Swimming
Toward the Ocean

Swimming Toward the Ocean

A novel by

CAROLE L. GLICKFELD

ALFRED A. KNOPF   NEW YORK   2001

THIS IS A BORZOI BOOK
PUBLISHED BY ALFRED A. KNOPF

www.aaknopf.com

Grateful acknowledgment is made to Warner Bros.
Publications U.S. Inc., for permission to reprint an
excerpt from "They Can't Take That Away from Me"
by George Gershwin and Ira Gershwin, copyright
1936, 1937 (copyright renewed 1963, 1964) by George
Gershwin Music and Ira Gershwin Lyrics. All rights
administered by WB Music Corp. All rights reserved.
Reprinted by permission of Warner Bros. Publications
U.S. Inc., Miami, FL 33014.

Library of Congress
Cataloging-in-Publication Data

Glickfeld, Carole L.
Swimming toward the ocean : a novel / by
Carole L. Glickfeld. — 1st ed.
p.   cm.
ISBN 0-375-40892-4
I. Title.
PS3557.L514 S85 2000
813'.54—dc21   99-059640

Manufactured in the United States of America
First Edition

In memory of the loving-kindness of my family:
my parents, Blanche and Robert Lieber;
my sister, Myrna; and my brother, Stanley

Acknowledgments

*A zillion thanks to all those who kept
me going through the dark times,
especially Kathy Christman, Nancy Thomas,
and Bill Ogle, wherever you are, and the
staff, past and present, of Starbucks on Broadway;
and to Harriet Wasserman, who rescued me.
Also, my deep appreciation to the National
Endowment for the Arts for its early support.*

Swimming
Toward the Ocean

Part One

I imagine my mother straightening the decks of cards, then lining up the Parcheesi game with the Chinese checkers board before she takes my sister's jump rope off the closet shelf. She doesn't lock the apartment door when she leaves. In her backless slippers, she walks up two flights, clopping with each step. The door to the roof is heavy. She has to pull hard to open it. Only a few pyramids of snow remain from the storm a few days earlier, in recesses that the sun fails to reach. My mother wears a cotton dress, short sleeves, no coat, although it's November. Thanksgiving, almost. It doesn't matter that she's cold. It might help, she thinks.

She only wishes she had changed into regular shoes. She leaves her slippers by the door and, in her bare feet, mounts the cracked marble stair. Stepping out onto the tar, she sucks in her breath from the shock of cold. Like ice, she thinks. And then, So what?

In an open space between the wash lines, she takes the jump rope by its bright red handles, one in each hand. She snaps an arc of twisted hemp over her head. Jumps and lands on two feet. Her wrists rotate, and the rope flies up behind her, over her head again. She jumps and jumps. Her soles sting. When she tires, she lands on one foot, then the other. She doesn't notice the brilliant blue sky, the roof of the building across Brighton 8th Street, the Parachute Jump in the distance. She snaps the rope over her head, lets it graze the tar before her feet lift and land. Again and again. Faster now. Faster. Faster. From her half-open mouth come cloudlike puffs of visible cold. She tries to ignore the sharp pain in her chest. The cold sears her lungs. Gasping for air, she lets the rope drop from her hands. She bends over, one hand on her belly, the belly where I've been growing for the past five weeks.

It is two days later. My mother empties a tin of mustard powder into the stream of hot water flowing from the faucet. As the bath runs she removes her nightgown. She hangs it on the hook behind the door and catches sight of herself in the mirror over the sink. The gray streak in her light brown hair. Old, she thinks. Forty-five. She gathers the hair from her neck into a hair net, uses three hairpins to secure the net to her crown.

I have no hair yet. My head is huge. I am just beginning to form a face—eyes, nose, mouth. My mother asks the face in the mirror, "Why did this have to happen?" She thinks of the boy up the street who sits by the window, twirling a straw, day after day. A late-born child. She calls him a boy, but he is large like a man, full-grown, and all he does is sit and twirl.

My mother steps out of her backless slippers and plunges one foot into the tub. "*Oy!*" She yanks it out. Her leg is a rosy pink. It burns. She shuts off the tap and drains the water to a depth of six inches. With one hand on the tile wall to brace herself, she lowers herself slowly into the steamy bath. It stinks of mustard. She spreads her legs out before her and, with both hands, scoops the cloudy water toward me. I am immersed in a bath of my own: amniotic fluid, at just the right temperature. I have a tub of my own, an amniotic sac within her belly. I float.

Sometimes when my mother is in the kitchen, her body shakes. She cries. She asks God questions, out loud. I cannot hear her. I have no ears yet. No skull bones. I cannot answer. She thinks of words such as: *too late, split second, mistake.*

She remembers the night my father came home early from playing cards: He zips around so lively she can tell by his cockiness he's won some money. He won't tell her how much. He never does. She's awake when he reaches for her, his determined fingers sliding under her nightgown, up inside her fleshy thigh. She rolls onto her back. His mustache grazes her upper lip, and then they're joined, one to the other. Usually he pulls out of her and ejaculates on the sheet laid over a quilted pad. This time he spills partly inside her. Right away she goes to the bathroom and bears down hard, as if to expel me into the toilet. Then she tries to flush me out with a douche, extra hot.

Now she takes the red rubber bag from the cabinet one more time, fills it again with boiling vinegar, hangs it from the shower curtain rod.

I have been gestating for six weeks when my mother goes to the doctor. My father is with her. He asks her how much it will cost. "*Nu*, if I could tell the future," she says, "would we be sitting here?" The nurse calls her in. Her heart beats faster. Mine beats twice as fast as hers, little butterfly flutters.

In the waiting room my father studies Rocky Marciano in *Life* magazine, the boxing gloves poised midair. In his office the doctor assesses my mother's charms: good legs, good skin, clean. He likes the scrubbed look in women. Though she smells of garlic, she isn't dirty like some immigrants, and she understands English, even if her Yiddish accent is thick. She says "tink" for *think*, and "vot" for *what*. "Got" for *God*. He listens to her speak now, a prepared speech.

"Doctor, you told me last week, 'Think it over.' Okay, now I tell you and God what I think. What I think is no." She waves both hands in front of her. "No baby," she says.

The doctor tilts his head and says, "What's more beautiful than a baby?" He's thinking, Betty Grable in *When My Baby Smiles at Me*. He studies her small, silky face, her huge, heaving bosom. "You're married. You're healthy. What are you worried about?" he asks.

Plenty, she thinks, but doesn't say.

Inside her is a litany of reasons. She has two children already, one of each sex. There's hardly money enough for them as is. At long last they're in school, and she's too old to start over. Close to fifty. And what if the baby is retarded? That's all she needs. Lately she and my father aren't getting along so good. Not because he never helps her around the house. When wasn't that the case? But now he goes out all the time and leaves her home. To play cards, he says. To make a little extra money. They can't afford a baby-sitter, he says, and anyway he doesn't trust them.

"Doctor, to tell the truth, I'm very exhausted," my mother says. "You have no idea."

"Eat more red meat," the doctor advises. She also reminds him of Lana Turner, the ivory skin, the way she wears her shoulder-length hair in a net bag, though it's light brown, not blond.

"I can give you an injection," he tells her. "It'll stimulate a miscarriage." He can't bring himself to use the word *abortion*. He's risking his medical license as it is. "You know you'll suffer a lot when you're old," he tells her. He means physically. "Is that what you want?"

She doesn't waver for an instant. "Please, doctor, let's get it over."

While he prepares the needle, my mother imagines herself half a mile away, swimming toward the ocean. The sun is waking up over the horizon. She cuts a graceful figure, breaking the waves like a torpedo. With my paddlelike hands, I row clumsily in an ocean of darkness.

My mother tries not to think about what I look like now, what parts of me are already formed. But as the needle goes into her buttock, she imagines a teeny doll. She closes her eyes. My eyes are pits in the skull.

Afterwards the doctor says the injection can take up to twenty-four hours to work, sometimes longer. My father smiles when my mother emerges, looking pale and serious. He kisses her on the cheek. "We're much better off," he says. She walks with him to the elevated where he takes the BMT to Manhattan, to his job in the garment factory. Already he's lost half a day's pay.

My mother walks along Mermaid Avenue. She glances at the barrels of pockmarked fruits and vegetables, the ice beds of fish with eyes staring at nothing. Her hands are dug deep into her coat pockets, cradling my yolk sac. She walks and walks, exhaling contrails of frosty air. From time to time she glances at her watch, her engagement present from my father, twenty years before. She has to be home when my brother and sister return from school.

Checking her watch again, she realizes it has stopped. She finds a clock in a candy store. Two minutes to three. She starts to run. What will they do when they ring the bell and nobody answers? she thinks. *Gevalt!* They don't have keys to get in. Terrible, to lock out her own children. She runs and runs.

At Coney Island Hospital she has to stop to catch her breath. She looks up at the brown brick facade as if it's a warning to her. She hopes the pain won't be too bad.

My sister and brother are sitting on the stoop when my mother arrives. My sister is crying hysterically. "Where were you?" she asks. "I thought something terrible happened."

"*Kholilleh!*" my mother says. God forbid!

My brother looks calm but relieved.

"I had to go with Papa to the doctor," my mother says. "His upset stomach. Men are such babies. Come, we go for a *nosh.*"

At the ice cream parlor, she lets them get expensive malteds. So what if she has to cut back a little on groceries, she thinks. Feeling reckless, she orders a banana split.

At home, my mother gathers together a pile of rags, washcloths, and towels. She hopes she won't have a hemorrhage.

My sister asks what she's doing with all the rags. My mother says, "If you must know, it's that time of month." She doesn't say she's waiting for the bloody end of her baby.

That night my mother is awake when my father comes home, but she pretends to be asleep. In the morning she examines her *pish* in the toilet bowl, looking for blood. Nothing.

For a week after, my mother wakes up each day and puts her hand on her belly. *Please*, she thinks. *Make something happen.* She lifts her knees to her chest, boosts her hips up with her hands, and extends her legs into the air, one at a time. She does a hundred bicycle kicks, hoping to shake me loose.

Nothing happens.

I'm hungry all the time now. I suck more and more nourishment from her placenta. Her umbilical cord is my straw. My mother is also hungry all the time. She knows she should starve me, but she devours pints of cherry vanilla ice cream. She drinks quarts of milk. She finishes all the spinach and peas my sister won't eat. Waiting for my father to come home, she makes herself a midnight sandwich of American cheese. She becomes addicted to Ritz crackers with peanut butter, banana slices topped with raspberry preserves. In the morning she squeezes halves of oranges, turning them clockwise around the green glass juicer. She strains out the pulp and picks out the seeds. Sometimes she puts the seeds into the dirt of the snake plant, hoping they will sprout.

Every day my father asks her, "Anything?" and after she shakes her head no, he makes clucking sounds of regret. Else he doesn't speak.

One night after dinner my father puts on his good suit.

"You're dressing up to play cards?" my mother says.

He grunts.

"What kind of answer is that? You could talk to me at least."

He grunts again.

"I want to know," she says. "Where are you going?"

"None of your business."

"None of my business?" Her voice rises. "You're not my husband? Excuse me, what's between us certainly it's my business."

He slaps her so hard she stumbles back and falls onto their bed. She sits up slowly, her hand on her cheek.

In front of the mirror my father knots his tie.

My mother flings a pillow at his back. "What kind of man are you?" she yells to his image in the glass. "A *paskudnyak*! To hit a woman, to hit me, your wife with a baby here." She covers her belly with her palms. "Only a *parech*—" A lowlife.

She flings the words at him and pretends to spit, *ptooh*, *ptooh*, until he turns and raises his arm as if to strike again, but all he means to do is silence her. Just now he wishes he were elsewhere, in the arms of Trudy Fleisch.

With one hand on the cheek where he struck her, my mother hurries to the bathroom, her open slippers clopping as she goes. She hunches over the sink. How can she have this baby? she asks herself. Her husband doesn't love her. She opens the medicine cabinet and surveys the shelves: Colgate tooth powder, Pond's Cold Cream, Vaseline, Ben-Gay, Milk of Magnesia. There are only six Bayers left in the bottle. She could never swallow the Prell. Or the Mercurochrome. When she comes out of the bathroom, my father is gone. She cries herself to sleep.

The next morning, after my brother and sister leave for school, my mother goes for a walk on the Boardwalk. It's her favorite thing to do in the summers, to take in the salt air. To take in the life that bustles along the length of the wooden planks: Old people coming and going from the Brighton Baths. Mothers with strollers. Teenagers heading with their love blankets to the beach. Children stuffing their mouths with sticky cotton candy or balls of caramel corn. Gawking tourists, lured by the Bearded Lady. Laughing sailors, happy to be back after the war in Korea, trying their luck in other ways. As they aim feathered darts at balloons, she thinks of the mothers whose sons never came home. *"Tsores tsezhegen di hartz,"* she says out loud to herself. Trouble cuts up the heart.

In front of the sky-high Parachute Jump, she never tires of watching the soldiers egg each other on. Two by two they go, strapped into a little swing, two strips of canvas for a back. Overhead is a canopy of folded-up silk. Each swing is attached by cables to the latticed steel tower. It reminds my mother of oil derricks she's seen in newsreels. At the top, its girders fan out like a flower. Wherever she is in Coney Island, she can always see the Parachute Jump. To her it's the Empire State Building of Brooklyn.

Soon the soldiers rise to the very peak, maybe fifteen stories up, their feet dangling in open air. There's a popping sound as the parachute bursts open, and the men plummet to what seems like certain death. She stays until the soldiers are safely back, the seat bouncing hard from the sudden stop. Afterwards she treats herself to one paper cone of Nathan's crinkled French fries. That's all she can afford.

Now it's almost winter, but so warm! The crowds are gone, but today more people are out than usual, their coats wide open, wool scarves loose around the neck. Faces tilt skyward, eyes closed. The glare of sun off the Boardwalk is blinding. For some, life is good when the sun shines. Old men without hats—widowers, she decides—sit on slatted benches facing the ocean and doze, Jewish newspapers open on their lap. The eyes of the Steeplechase man, high over the Boardwalk, are laughing.

She crosses the Boardwalk, her eyes on the herringbone-patterned boards. This is the only way out, she thinks. What else can she do? She almost collides with a woman wheeling a perambulator, its blanket folded back. She can see the scrunched face of a newborn in a hand-knit cap. Yellow. Before she can help herself, she wonders whether she is carrying a boy or a girl.

Slowly my mother descends the stairs to the beach. In front of her is the warning: NO LIFEGUARD ON DUTY. Up ahead the waves crash into the shore, spewing foam that reminds her of semen. *Too late. Split second.* She heads diagonally across the beach, toward the water. With each step, the one-inch heels of her laced-up oxfords sink into the sand. Under the tongues, sand rubs against the instep. If she stops to remove her shoes, she might change her mind. She plods on. She blames me for how heavy she feels. I'm barely an inch long.

Along the surf she steps over white shells embedded in the coarse wet sand. The foamy edge of a wave swirls around her soles. She watches the wave linger before it washes out to the horizon, merging with the inky blue ocean. The tide is way out. Her wet shoes squish as she takes a step forward, and another.

She crouches down to unlace them, then rises to yank them off. She ties them together and returns to the dry sand to deposit them. Good, solid shoes. Maybe someone can use them. She takes off her coat, folds it lining out, lays it on the sand. She leaves on her kerchief. In her cardigan and dark skirt she looks like my grandmother in a faded brown picture, taken in Russia before the First World War. The baby swaddled in my grandmother's arms is my mother.

Now my mother walks straight on toward the ocean. Frigid water washes around her feet, splashes her nylon stockings. She's numb to the cold. All she can feel is a blinding drive to end the pain. The pain of my father's smack. She hugs her wool sleeves, embracing herself for the lonely journey. My little appendages can't reach around me, but I keep myself company. I am growing like crazy. Nerve cells. Blood cells. They multiply and divide into millions and millions. My mother takes a deep breath. The salt air wafts up her nostrils. I breathe in my mother's oxygen. She is my lifeline.

Just now I am not in her thoughts. If she could just sail away in the large ship sitting on the horizon . . . With each step she struggles to keep her balance. The ocean floor is jagged with pebbles and shells.

She has a flash of my curly-headed brother, his gangling torso hunched over the table, studying for his bar mitzvah. And my sister, pudgy fingers to her face, as she stamps her foot in fury. She imagines my father losing his temper with them when she is not there to step between. She can hardly stand to think of it: two children motherless. A fate worse than being pregnant.

A huge wave almost knocks her over. Scrambling to right herself, she staggers backwards, her heel coming down on a sharp stone. The pain jogs her out of her trance. The wind whips at her kerchief, lifts it clear off her head. She struggles to twist around, to watch the white chiffon soar above the sunlit beach like a seagull. Buffeted by the wind, my mother staggers toward the shore. I paddle about in calm waters.

Back on the beach, she crumples, shivering and exhausted, onto the dry, sun-warmed sand. She spreads the coat over her as if it's a blanket. Only her little head is visible. Her temples throb.

A man in a green fedora stops to ask if she is okay. She smiles wanly. "I only look half dead," she says. "A dizzy spell, is all." He helps her up. He is very handsome. Her husband is handsome, too, for all the good.

"I saw you from the Boardwalk. This is no day for swimming," the man scolds. "You could drown out there." His dark eyes search her face. She knows he knows what she was up to.

"Thank you. You're very kind." She's thinking, Maybe he's the devil in disguise, because for certain someone has given her the Evil Eye. She is cursed. Doomed. "I'll be all right," she says. "*Alevai.*" Would that it were so.

She watches the man walk down the beach. He looks back and waves. Her arm wants to lift and wave, but she just stares, as if she is in the midst of a strange dream.

Holding her shoes by the laces, she makes her way back across the sand. Her footsteps are heavy with resignation. *Evil Eye. Evil Eye.* Instead of going up the steps to the Boardwalk, she walks around behind them.

Under the Boardwalk it's damp and dark. Though she's barely five feet tall, there's no room to stand under the low concrete beams, all in shadow. She walks with knees bent. Like that comedian, Groucho Marx, she thinks. Some comedy, this! Whoever has it in for her must be laughing themselves sick.

She kneels on the cool sand between the pillars. Her body shakes as she sobs, her head nested in cupped palms. She wonders if I'll be born deformed. Crippled, maybe. Her body shakes and shakes. It feels as though she is rocking me to sleep.

The night before she goes into labor, my mother dreams she is giving birth. The doctor says, "Stop! The baby isn't ready." She tells the doctor, "It's too late."

Cradled in her hand is a porcelain doll, a young woman with little breasts and a matted mop of long red hair. The features are exquisite. Long, silky eyelashes. There is nail polish on the tiny toenails. "How many ounces?" my mother asks.

A woman in the next bed says to her, "Don't worry. They'll keep her under glass." Unseen people are screaming "Hooray, hooray!"

My mother realizes she is at the Steeplechase, and she is part of the show. The audience has watched her give birth. The baby is behind the glass now, lined up with the others. My mother bangs on the window. "Forget it," a man says. "She'll be safe here."

My mother wakes up in a sweat, feels for her belly, which is still huge. She hears my father whistling through his nose. In the dark she lies on her back, trying to figure what the dream is telling her. Is the baby dead?

Then she recalls the Incubators. She had wandered in, off the Boardwalk. Everyone was talking about them after the World's Fair. This wonderful doctor, saving the preemies. Maybe it's worth twenty cents, she thought. She didn't know then she was pregnant with her first child.

She was surprised when she saw them, lined up in rows of incubators. She thought *preemies* meant *freaks*, but they looked exactly like ordinary babies, only much smaller. Two pounds, most of them. The place was like a little hospital, with nurses in uniforms. The lecture they gave was very interesting, how they put oxygen into the preemies' lungs, how they filtered the air every couple of minutes. They told how they nursed the babies and fed them, sometimes with an eyedropper.

Now as my mother lies in the dark, she remembers the rumor that was going around at the time. People used to say the *Kinderbrutanstalt*, the baby hatchery, was actually part of the circus. They only pretended to grow normal babies. The real purpose was to breed freaks for the sideshows.

She knows now why she had the dream. She is certain it is an omen.

As they wheel her into the delivery room, terrible pain cramps her insides—like her worst period ever—but I imagine my mother is serene. She has prepared all these months for doom. Even while drinking milk and orange juice, eating an apple a day, bunches of carrots, she was sure the damage was already done. If the worst happens, she thinks now, she's brought it on herself. The mustard baths. Jumping rope. Painting the four-room apartment single-handed when she was eight months along. And just the week before, she went with my brother on the Human Roulette Wheel at the Steeplechase, her loose topper hiding her huge stomach. One last hope against hope.

Now her mind is made up.

If I am deformed, she will throw me away. Or she will ask the doctor to.

She bears down on her pelvis. Like moving your bowels, she thinks. She strains. Not hard enough. It hurts too much. "Come on," the nurse urges. My mother tries and tries again. She screams and screams. She spits and curses in Yiddish. Day turns to night. Finally, the doctor injects an anesthetic into her spine. Soon the pain is gone, but not the fear.

"Come on." The nurse looks hopeful. My mother bears down. Again and again. It feels like hours. She is soaking wet. The ceiling fan turns and turns, but the air doesn't move. All right, she thinks. She will face the worst. And then the doctor says, "Here we go."

I am coming down the birth canal. My own Coney Island ride of terror. My adrenaline surges. The doctor reaches for the forceps, but before he can touch me, my mother makes one heroic push, and I'm out.

At two a.m. the doctor holds me up. "A girl," he says, and hands my slimy, blood-covered body off to the nurse. Groggy, my mother studies his face, looking for signs. Will he tell her the baby is a freak?

She makes an enormous effort to ask. "The baby, it's normal, Doctor?"

The doctor nods impatiently. "A beautiful baby. Perfect."

My mother doesn't believe him. Certain they're saving the bad news for later, she drifts off to sleep. In the recovery room she wishes she had thought to bring garlic with her from home. She can hardly believe it's a girl. *Alevai.* It should only be. Girls are not wild like boys. In the snap of a finger, boys turn your hair white.

She remembers how last spring the police caught my brother and his friends joyriding. They were going to put the car back, my brother said. My father whipped him anyhow. My mother remembers how she screamed and screamed till her throat was raw.

When they bring me to her on the ward, she casts a wary glance at me. "Isn't she cute!" the nurse says. "*Kineahora!*" my mother yells, to protect me from the Evil Eye. "So ugly!" she adds, then spits. *Ptooh.* The nurse looks askance at her but helps me to her breast. At first I resist. My mother thinks all her worrying has soured her milk, but soon I suckle away.

After the nurse leaves, my mother inspects me, the way she examines merchandise in a store before she takes out the money to pay. She peers under my little nightgown, stamped with tulips. She peers into the diaper, front and back. She checks the number of my fingers and toes. She rubs her finger gently across the three wrinkles in my forehead. She examines both ears.

"*Oy.* So homely," she says, to fool her nemesis. "Such a weakling." She raises her voice so the Evil Eye can hear. "The smallest breeze will blow you over," she tells me. She looks up and down the ward to see who is listening, who might have it in for her. In my ear she whispers, "A miracle, thanks God."

She holds me to her nipple.

My mother runs the hose from the Electrolux canister back and forth over the living room rug. As she gets close to my father, she nudges his foot. "Lift!" she says.

"Why are you bothering me now? Can't you see I'm reading the paper? I'll give you later," he says, about the money from his paycheck.

"I'm bothering the dust, not you. Lift. You want the baby should get an asthma?" Then my mother realizes her mistake. She lets go the hose and hurries to the kitchen for a piece of matzoh, places it under the mattress of my crib, to protect me from harm.

When she returns, my father gives her the weekly allowance for the household. She puts it in the pocket of her smock and runs the hose around his feet until, finally, he lifts them.

From the money he gives her she removes a few dollars to pay on the bill from the hospital. It was cheaper when she had my sister and brother at home. Before she puts away what's left, something, she doesn't know what, makes her count it out. She counts it again, but still she is two dollars short. Afraid my father will accuse her of being careless, she doesn't say anything.

Later that week when her sister comes to visit, my mother asks if she can borrow the money. My Aunt Ruchel stuffs an extra bill in her hand. "Buy yourself a *nosh*," she says.

"You already gave me, for the baby, the blanket, the nightgowns, that dress and hat—*oy*, so adorable—how can I thank you?"

"Just don't stink up the dress with garlic," my aunt says. "Devorah reeks to high heaven."

My mother frowns. *"Takeh?"* Really? "I only pin it to the diaper." Then she laughs. "Better if it's strong, *nu*?"

My aunt laughs too. She thinks her sister is so Old World, but then Chenia didn't have much schooling.

All that week my father is cranky. My mother is sure he resents having another mouth to feed. Then she sees him put his pinkie in my little fist. From time to time he pulls the sheet up over me. Once he scolds my mother because there is spittle all over my mattress. Relieved he doesn't have it in for me, she hums while she changes the sheet.

Still, his mood doesn't improve. At dinner, he growls, "Why do we have meat so often? At those prices—"

"To keep breast-feeding," she says, "I need it. The doctor told me." Already her milk is starting to dry up. She wonders if it's from worry. She worries when she sees my father fidget and pace. She suspects he is losing money at cards. Even so, she doesn't say anything when he goes out after synagogue on Saturday, before the end of Sabbath.

My brother tells my sister, "There's a hypocrite for you."

"*Pisk! Shveig!* Don't talk bad about your father," my mother says.

All afternoon she imagines the worst: a debt they couldn't make a dent in. What if they can't pay the rent? *Gottenyu*, what if they're thrown out on the street? She recalls how their friend Arthur Vogel got in bad with a loan shark. He got his nose broken, and then he had to sell the silverware to pay, not even the debt, only the interest. She thinks of what there is in the apartment to sell. Only her body, stretched out like a used prophylactic. She noticed one on the street once. At first she didn't know what it was, till she saw the disgusted look on my father's face. Now she laughs, remembering.

When my father comes home, he looks happy. His luck has turned, she thinks, until he tells her he slipped in a grocery store. "Stupid," he says. "Careless." My father means the store owner. For not cleaning up the filberts.

That night he calls his brother from the neighbor's. He hates to admit his brother knows anything, but after all he's a businessman. "Tell me," my father asks, "you know a good attorney?"

"An honest one or a shyster?" his brother answers.

"Someone with *Hoden.*" Testicles.

The next morning my father limps around the apartment. He hugs his arm and shoulder as if he is in constant pain. He shows my mother his eyeglasses, how both lenses and the frame are cracked to pieces. She is positive she saw the glasses the night before on the highboy. They were in perfect condition then. My father pushes away the Cream of Wheat. He tells her he feels too sick to eat.

"Where were you?" she thinks to ask now. "Which grocery store?"

"Why? What difference does it make?"

"How often are you going to the grocery store?" she says.

"Are you calling me a liar?" He gets up halfway out of his chair.

She leans back. He hasn't hit her since that one time, but she no longer feels completely easy with him. "For what were you in a grocery store?" she asks. "To get roach spray?"

He stomps off. She sees he isn't limping.

On Monday morning, my father calls the factory from the drugstore. He tells the boss he has a toothache and will be in later.

To save money, he walks to Sheepshead Bay, and anyway it's a beautiful autumn morning. It's such a mystery, how the maple trees change color. There's so much he doesn't understand. Maybe if he could have finished school . . . become a lawyer, made good money. He wonders how much the lawsuit will bring. If it's enough, they'll move to Manhattan, he decides, near where Trudy Fleisch lives. A nice neighborhood, near the park. It'll be good for the baby. Coney Island is getting too crowded, anyway. Hoodlums lurk on the street corners. And there are muggings. A bad influence on the children.

A woman brings him out of his reverie. "Hello, Mr. Arnow! What a day!"

"Glorious as your dimples." He tips his hat to the neighbor

from downstairs. Although they look nothing alike, she makes him think of Trudy. Maybe it's the scarf. Stylish, he guesses. He works in a factory making ladies' clothes but he knows he's no expert.

Trudy, Trudy, he says to himself. *You're no beauty. Trudy, Trudy, you make me feel like a king.* So clever when it comes to sex, he thinks. She knows how to please him. Sometimes he worries how she's gotten her experience. Not from her husband. That fairy! One punch and he'd knock him out for good.

As my father nears his destination he worries that his brother has steered him wrong. The attorney is probably some *balmelokhe.* That's all he needs, an expert who is no expert. My father begins now to limp. His eyes narrow, his lips go crooked. The first thing he will do is ask the lawyer for Empirin, to kill the pain.

M y mother wheels me in the perambulator down the Boardwalk. With a nod to the ocean, she says to me, "*Nu,* I survived." What is Brooklyn but a place for survivors? she thinks. For whatever washes up on the beach. Immigrants—people who've been through *tsores.* Troubles. She can never go on the Boardwalk without her insides stirring. Even before she tried to get out of the whole thing. It's a wonder, she thinks, how the ocean tugs on her, why she has to stop on the Boardwalk over and over to watch. The waves go in, they go out. So simple. Yet to her there is no greater mystery.

Now it's Indian summer in late October. The top of the carriage is up, to shield my eyes from the sun. In the distance, she sees a man with a fedora coming toward her. In the brilliant light his hat looks black or brown. So it isn't him. Or is it? Then, squinting, she sees his dark eyes. It's him, she's sure of it.

She looks away. She feels ashamed of what she did, what she tried to do.

"Hello, hello!" the man calls out. "Remember me? You look shipshape." He walks right up to her and peers into the carriage. "Your baby?"

She nods. She can see the surprise on his face. She's no spring chicken. His dark lashes are long, his eyebrows strong. She can't tell his age. He glances from me to her and back again, says, "She looks like you. Beautiful."

"*Kineahora!*" my mother says. "So ugly she could scare away bats."

The man nods. "The gods have reason to be envious."

My mother doesn't quite understand but finds this interesting. His eyes smile at her. Chills go through her body. She starts to push the carriage, expecting the man to continue on his way. But like an old friend he walks along with her, beside the perambulator, his tie flapping in the light breeze.

"You must live near here." He points past the Cyclone. "I work over there. I'm taking my morning constitutional. Better than letting the pressure build up."

Dumbstruck, she only nods. "Such a beautiful day," she says at last. And then, "Where do you come from?"

"Ah, you knew I wasn't a native." He doesn't wait for her shrug. "Rumania. I came as a boy. I wasn't a boy for long. You?"

"Russia. Poland. My family, we come after the first big war. I was a young girl, sixteen. I never lose my accent. My English is bad, no?"

"The sun is in my eyes," he jokes.

"A diplomat," she says. The warmth comes now from inside, a kind of contentment.

He walks with her toward the Steeplechase. From time to time their eyes meet. She cannot say what it is about him, what's different from the dozens of men they pass, in suits and coats and hats. His complexion is darker, maybe suntanned. He's about her husband's height, five eight, but he looks stronger, full of zip. Like Burt Lancaster in *The Flame and the Arrow*.

When they get to the end of the Boardwalk, he says, "My name's Harry. Not Truman. Taubman. And your name?"

"Chenia." She hesitates to give him her last name, and then it's too late.

He makes a clucking sound. "Like music," he says. "Ah cha Chenia, ah cha Chenia . . . ," he sings to the tune of "Dark Eyes." He expects her to smile or laugh, but she stares, as if looking through a microscope. This woman is so guarded, he thinks. What is it she fears?

He shakes her hand and says he's pleased to make her acquaintance. "Be seeing you," he says. "Be well."

Harry. Not the name she would have chosen. She waves good-bye. Inside something swells and crashes inside her. Unstoppable, like the ocean. She forces herself not to turn her head, not to watch as he walks away.

At home my mother cannot get Harry out of her mind. He is beside her whatever she does: If she grates potatoes or scrapes the carrots. If she airs the bedding out the window. When she fusses over my formula, when she sterilizes the bottles and the nipples, when she tests the temperature of the milk. As I drink from the bottle, she wonders what kind of children she would have now if she'd met Harry first.

Every hour she looks at the clock and wonders where he is just then, what he is doing. Then she scolds herself.

All day she is pushing him out of her mind. It makes her so tired.

What is it with me? she asks herself. Never before has she been attracted to trouble. And now, with a new baby, she thinks maybe she is going crazy. *Meshugge ahf toyt.* Crazy to the death. Wanting what she must not have.

In the evenings she takes warm baths. She's heard they use warm baths to cure the insane. She asks my sister to keep an eye on me while she bathes. Soaking in the warm water, she closes her eyes, hoping to blot out everything, but there he is, under her eyelids. He's leaning over her on the beach. He's coming toward her on the Boardwalk. He's walking beside her, his arm encircling her shoulder . . .

When the water cools, she runs the hot water tap. Like oars her arms push through the water, circulating the heat. The memory of him churns.

Weeks go by. She is winning the battle, she thinks. Not a single day has she ventured onto the Boardwalk. Not even during the nice days of November. She wheels me along Surf Avenue, where many of the places are boarded up for winter. She aches to see the ocean, but it's not worth it, to risk what security she has: a husband with a job that pays regular.

She has struck a deal. She allows herself to think of Harry as much as she likes, so long as she doesn't put herself in the way of temptation. Right now she is all too susceptible. She is mortified by my father: how he lies and cheats to get money not rightfully his. And she is angry because there is nothing she can do. The least kindness from a stranger can bowl her over. It already has.

As the lawsuit progresses, my father's mood improves. For her birthday he buys my mother a set of rhinestone jewelry, a heart dangling from a collar of rhinestones, a bracelet and heart-shaped earrings. My brother baby-sits me when my father takes my mother to the Paramount Theatre to see *From Here to Eternity*. It's the first time they've been out since I was conceived. He seems for a while like his old self, the man she fell in love with when she was twenty-one, her own Burt Lancaster. In the balcony he nuzzles her neck. Walking home from the trolley, they have a snowball fight. He laughs when she manages to stuff snow down the back of his collar.

In bed that night, my father climbs on top of her. Without meaning to, she thinks of Harry. For once her body starts to move on its own. She doesn't know how it happens or even what she's doing. Something in her loosens, lets go. My father gets excited from the way her hips swivel, as if she's doing the hula. He spills inside her.

"You! You!" my mother screams. "*Zhlob!* Moron!" She pounds him with her fist. Her chenille robe isn't even tied properly as she runs to the bathroom. Cursing my father, she prepares the douche and thinks, For all the good. She vows that if she gets pregnant, she will do it this time, she will kill herself. As she sits on the toilet, she realizes it's one year to the day since she first saw the man, his kind face leaning over her on the sand. The green fedora. She imagines them in each other's arms, tumbling over and over, like one wave rolling into another.

The next day it's brisk. The wind cuts like ice. The sun looks like a metallic disk, a cold platinum ornament on a pale silk backdrop. Over my flannel rompers, I have on two sweaters. My mother ties an extra sweater around my neck for a scarf. I am also wearing wool booties and a wool hat. She tucks the blanket under the mattress of the carriage and wheels me onto the Boardwalk. There she takes deep breaths. How she loves the strong salt air! As she pushes the carriage, she fixes her gaze on the waves rolling and rolling into shore.

From time to time she surveys the few people coming and going on the Boardwalk, all in a hurry. Each fedora makes her heart lift and then sink.

Twice she walks from 8th Street to 37th and then back again. Exhausted, she sits on a bench and stares into the surf. In the wind her kerchief flaps hard around her ears. The surf roars. When I cry for my bottle, she doesn't hear.

A t five-forty p.m. my father rings the bell of Mr. and Mrs. Barney Fleisch. It makes a lot more sense to come directly from work, he thinks, only a half hour from downtown to her place. From Brooklyn it's two hours. Trudy opens the door wearing a red silk kimono, like someone in a movie.

"Fancy, shmancy. You should live on Park Avenue," my father says.

"Closer to Brooklyn," she jokes. "Is that what you'd like? Do you like this?" She twirls in the kimono. "My nephew brought it back from overseas. Tonight I'll be your geisha girl." She hangs his coat and puts his hat on the shelf, then leads him into the living room, where they always begin.

Before they even sit down, my father feels an inexplicable desire to touch the red silk. At the same time he doesn't want to look like a pansy. Embracing her, he runs his hands up and down the silky material over her back, her *tokhes*, only dimly aware of the flesh beneath. "Some imagination," he says in her ear. "Where do you get such an imagination?"

Her answer is to nudge her bare knee between his pant legs. "May I undress you, sir?" He is so cute, she thinks, the way he stands like a stick, like a guard outside the queen's palace.

She starts with his shoes, places them and his socks under the dinette chair. She knows he doesn't like to throw his clothes around, especially the suit. She folds the pants, places them over the seat, the suspenders dangling. She hangs the jacket on the seat back. Soon they are in the bedroom, lying crosswise over the Jacquard bedspread. Her hands roam over his body, his private parts. He is excited as a seventeen-year-old and as much in a hurry, but she doesn't let him enter her. Clutching his hands, she brings them to her breasts, which are small and pointy. She kisses him again and again. Enough already, he wants to say. He can feel himself on the wane.

Then she rolls him onto his back and, like magic, caresses him to attention. He is strong and ready when she mounts him. By the light from the living room lamp he can see the excitement on her face, the tightly closed eyes, the oddly pursed mouth. Best of all, he doesn't have to worry about getting her pregnant, because her tubes are tied. He lets himself go.

After his heart slows, he realizes she is studying him. "What?"

She props herself on her elbow, her hair draped over her arm. "You could have waited a little."

He always feels uncomfortable when she wants to talk about what they did or should do. At the same time he wants to keep her happy. "For what?" he asks.

"For what?" Her voice rises. "Tell me you're joking."

He wonders if she's the one who's joking. He doesn't always understand her, though usually he pretends otherwise. "For what should I wait?"

"Till I'm ready."

"Ready? I thought you were like that hard-boiled egg."

The egg is a joke between them. Once when he was there she put on an egg to boil, and then forgot, till it exploded.

"Ruben," she says. "Don't you know that women climax?"

"So?"

"Ruben, you're not getting my import. If you climax too quick, then I don't get to finish. You have to learn to pace yourself."

He searches her face in the dim light. She is looking at him the way a teacher looks at a child. He feels very confused, afraid to jeopardize what's between them. She gives him her body and asks for nothing. He will never find another woman like her.

"Do you know what I'm saying, Ruben?" She strokes the curly hairs of his chest, reddish mixed with gray.

"A woman can't finish like a man," he says. "You don't have semen. The egg stays inside you."

"It's true!" she shrieks. "I knew it. I knew it. Finally I figured it out." She slaps the bedspread and starts to laugh. She laughs and laughs and laughs.

Is she out of her mind? he wonders. Or is the joke on him? Feeling sheepish, he goes to the toilet to relieve himself. Then he puts his clothes back on, everything but the suit jacket. He helps himself to a tall glass of water in the kitchen. He hears her footsteps. The inside of his stomach burns.

She sings, "'Ru-ben, Ru-ben, I've been think-ing.'" Then she says, "How long've we been with each other? Two years? I'm sorry, I should've told you sooner. But you never want to talk about sex." She sees that tightness in his face, the embarrassment. So different from Barney and his foul language in bed . . .

"Told me what?"

"How women are. Your wife, she doesn't finish?"

"I don't know," he says. "I never asked."

This time when she laughs he gets angry. He flings what's left of the water in her face.

After my brother is suspended for setting off firecrackers in the schoolyard, he is whipped with his own belt. But first, my father makes my mother and sister leave the apartment. Mimi goes to her girlfriend's downstairs. My mother wheels me around the block, feeling sick to her stomach. She walks around and around the block. She thinks if she crosses the street, she will simply keep going and never come back.

For the next two weeks, Sheldon is forbidden to leave the apartment. My mother asks him to baby-sit me while she takes long, solitary walks, always away from the ocean. It isn't easy to fight the pull of the Boardwalk. She feels like a *shikker*, a drunk, resisting temptation. One day she's about to give in, when she runs into the doctor who delivered me.

"Mrs. Arnow! Everything okay?" he says. She can barely bring herself to nod. "Good, good," he says. "You made the right decision."

She doesn't ask him what he's talking about. She thinks maybe the shot he gave her was fake. And he had the nerve to charge her! Maybe he should pay the bills which are still coming from the hospital. Bills that my father tells her to forget.

With the settlement from the lawsuit he could easily pay them off, she thinks. He's bought himself a new suit, a new coat. He even agreed to increase her household allowance. "Ignore the letters," my father tells her. "They'll stop coming. Let the rich people pay." The more he says it, the more she feels like a worm.

One afternoon she stops in a bank and tries to open a savings account. From the extra that my father gives her now, she's saved ten dollars. To put them in the bank, though, is not so easy. She has to get my father's signature on the paper, the man tells her.

"How come?" she says. "My husband, he didn't ask me to sign nothing for the bankbook he got himself."

The man smiles. "That's our policy, I'm afraid. A woman shouldn't have to handle financial matters." His chin juts toward me—I'm resting in her arms. "I'm sure you have plenty to take care of."

"You have children, Mister?" my mother asks. He nods. "Tell me, which would you rather? To wipe their *tokhes* every hour or to count money?"

"I wouldn't have the faintest idea how to—how to diaper an infant," he says. He's thinking, Maybe things are different in the country she came from.

At home my mother copies my father's handwriting onto the form. She is pleased with her imitation, although she worries a little when she brings it back. They don't even give it a good look. They make her up a passbook, which she will hide in a shoe box. It's good to have savings, she believes. You never know what can happen.

As she walks out of the bank she has the feeling that Harry must be close by. She looks around but doesn't see him. You have to stop dreaming, she tells herself. Then she thinks if she stops dreaming, *mechuleh*. She's done for, destroyed.

On the weekend before his suspension ends, my mother asks my brother to baby-sit me one last time, so she can take my sister to get shoes. "I don't mind," Sheldon says. "Devorah's such a character."

"What means this?" my mother says. "She's only a baby."

"She likes me to sing 'It Had to Be You.' Wanna see?"

"Not now."

"I'm teaching her words," Sheldon says. He says the word *bottle* to me five or six times until I say, "Ba." He squeals. I squeal. "Ba, ba, ba," he says. "Bottle."

My mother's heart is bursting with affection for her son, but this she doesn't say. "Why do you get into trouble?" she asks.

"Ma, it's not the Evil Eye," he answers.

"Then what?"

"I don't mean to."

Tears well up in her eyes. "Please, do yourself something. Be a good boy."

"Mama, when are we going?" my sister yells. She wants them to leave before my mother remembers the garlic. Her and her silly superstitions, my sister thinks. How can garlic protect you from the Evil Eye? "Ma!" she yells.

"We're going, we're going," my mother calls out. She blows my brother a kiss.

Before walking into Magic Shoes, my mother studies the display in the big window. Three or four dozen pairs, each on a stand of its own. My sister wants a red pair with ankle straps. My mother has in mind the sturdy brown-and-white oxfords. "Why can't I have both?" my sister whines.

My mother loses patience. She bops my sister with her pocketbook. "*Shmegegge*, you know why. Those flimsy things, they won't last a minute. And then what? You get the oxfords or nothing."

My sister can tell when my mother's mind is made up. She trails her into the store. "Look what's crowded!" my mother says. Her voice gets louder and louder. "Some racket! All the shoes what's bought in the fall, they're no good, and spring it's hardly here. They do it on purpose."

"Mama!" my sister hisses. She moves away from my mother, who sits down to wait for the salesman nearby. He's helping a customer, a blond woman, maybe thirty. My mother counts the open boxes at this woman's feet: twelve. She listens as the woman says she'll take this one, this one, and that one, but she's not sure about the other two. The shoes are all for dress. Gold straps. Silver straps. My mother studies the woman's clothes: a two-piece suit, silk. The coat on the seat

between them has a mink collar and cuffs. The salesman jokes
with the woman and finally brings five boxes up to the register,
piled high from his crotch to his head. When he comes back to
wait on my mother, she is seething.

"Get!" she screams out to my sister. Reluctantly my sister
returns from X-raying her feet a few dozen times in the fluoroscope machine.

The three of them go outside. My mother points to the
black-and-white oxfords, but inside, the salesman brings
brown-and-white. Then he goes back and brings the wrong
size. My mother raises her voice. "If you don't have, better you
should tell me. For what you play games? Because we're not
rich?"

"Madam, I'm doing my best," the salesman says.

"Listen, I got an accent don't mean you treat me like a piece
of dirt."

"Madam, if you would—"

"Mister, don't 'Madam' me. This is no *oysvorf* you're talking
to." My sister doesn't know this word and imagines the worst.
My mother is flushed with anger. "Can you bring me the
shoes, size 6 double A, or not?"

"Madam, I'll have to get the manager."

My mother looks pointedly at her watch. "*Vantz,*" she says
under her breath. Bedbug. She slaps my sister on the upper
arm. My sister's head is practically tucked inside her blouse.
"What, are you a turtle?" my mother says. "You have nothing
to be shamed."

She looks up and sees the salesman coming with a man behind him. At first she doesn't recognize the manager. Then,
when she sees the dark eyes light up, her jaw slackens.

"Hello, hello," the manager says.

"Without the hat I didn't recognize you, Mr. Taubman."
She stumbles over his last name. To her he is Harry.

"With or without a hat I'd know you anywhere," Harry
says. "What can we do for you?"

Pointedly she says, "A salesman goes deaf when a poor woman speaks."

Harry is unperturbed. She's not the first immigrant in his store with paranoia. His own mother, in fact . . .

"And what's your name?" he asks my sister.

"Mimi," she says guardedly. She doesn't know why the man is being so nice to her mother. She feels suddenly protective, thinking he is going to take advantage of them.

The manager brings the shoes. My sister puts them on. My mother pokes. At the toes, the left ones, the right ones.

"Walk!" she commands. Back and forth she makes Mimi walk. "Stand by the mirror," my mother says. "In the mirror they look different," she explains to Harry. Finally the three of them agree: the shoes fit. Still, no one makes a move toward the register.

"Do you know where they get the word *oxford* from?" Harry asks. My mother says, "Tell me." "Mama!" my sister says, but my mother hushes her. "You can learn yourself something," she says.

Finally the manager rings up the sale. Expecting him to overcharge them, my sister is puzzled. He's given them a discount. Harry meets my sister's surprise with a wink, and gives my mother his business card. Between them, an unspoken question hangs in the air. Then he answers. "I didn't know your family name," he says. "I couldn't call." He notices the cashier looking. "To see how you were feeling," he adds.

My mother debates. To tell or not to tell. She smiles and follows my sister out. When they are on the sidewalk, she says, "Wait for one moment." She runs into the store. The manager is already on his way to the back. She walks after him. "Yoo-hoo, Harry! Mr. Taubman!" Her arms are flung out to her sides, like a bird coming in for a landing.

Harry feels his spirits lift. What is it that draws him so? he wonders. She's pretty enough, a simple woman, and yet there's something hidden, something mysterious. "What can I do you for?" he says.

"Arnow," she says. "A-R-N-O-W. We don't have a phone yet but soon." He nods. She points to the fluoroscope. "The way you look at me, is like that machine."

"I can see into the center of your heart," he says. "Beautiful." He grins. "However you say it in Yiddish—no Evil Eye."

When my brother returns to school, and life is back to normal, my mother brings up the subject she has turned over and over in her mind. "We have to have a telephone," she tells my father. "Not only for emergencies. The children have to talk to their friends, *nu*? It's not like before, when everyone, they live on the same block."

"We can't afford it." He's thinking, How will he explain calling from the drugstore when he wants to talk to Trudy? Why should he pay for a month of phone calls and for extra calls besides? He sees her looking at him with a new intensity. Maybe she suspects.

As for my mother, she is only fighting the cramp in her pelvis. A welcome pain. Thanks God, her monthly is here.

Then he says, "All right, if you pay for it out of the household money."

My mother thinks she can find a little work, a few hours here and there. Baby-sitting, maybe, where she can take me along. Her hopes lift. Just to hear Harry's voice once in a while, what a difference it would make.

Then my father says, "You shouldn't go to the bother, though, until we move. They charge you each time to make the installation."

"We're moving?"

"I told you. To Manhattan."

"When?" she asks. The floor beneath her wobbles as if in a fun house.

"As soon as I find a place."

"I want to go with you to look," she says.

"That's not necessary."

"It's necessary. If I don't look with you, *azoy*, I won't move." When he doesn't challenge her, she says, "For what are we moving? I like it here."

"Coney Island is for misfits," he says. "Hoodlums and freaks. Manhattan, they have a whole different class of people. You said it yourself, Our children are growing up. We have to think about these things."

"I'm already missing the ocean," she says. "And the Boardwalk. What will we do when it's summertime?"

"We can take the subway here," he says. "The same train I take to work."

She sighs but she doesn't fight anymore. Maybe this will save her from certain trouble, she thinks, even though in her heart—*my beautiful heart*, she says to herself, ironically—she doesn't want to be saved.

A thick envelope arrives in the mail from the lawyer's office. "From the settlement?" my mother asks my father, but he doesn't answer. Later she sees my brother's lanky body bent over a stack of forms on the table. His tongue sticks halfway out, he is concentrating so hard. He writes and writes and then he blots with the blotter. He reads what he wrote and blots again.

"For Papa?" she asks.

"His lawsuit."

"It's finished, no?"

"A new one," Sheldon says. "Dad bit on a cherry pit in a pie. In Horn and Hardart's. He says he cracked his tooth."

"The same tooth he cracked on the chicken bone?"

"Yeah. He's suing."

"This is not right. I don't want you to be part of this funny business."

"Ma!" My brother tilts his chin toward my father standing behind her.

"Don't mix in," my father tells her.

Later my brother starts to explain to her how he didn't really want to help my father. My mother cuts him off. "That one. Is enough to make me vomit. Don't grow up like you know who. *Ich darf es vi a loch in kop!*" I need it like a hole in the head!

In bed with my mother, my father notices things he never noticed before. First of all, he is the one who makes all the overtures. He is the one who does all the touching. He touches her breasts, her ass, her thighs. She hugs him but she never caresses him, never *there*. When he is inside her now, he opens his eyes to observe her. Her eyes are closed. Her face looks calm. Who is more typical of women, he wonders, her or Trudy?

My sister gets her first period. Excited, she tells my mother, "Now I'm a woman." My mother smiles. A woman at twelve, she thinks. "Don't let any boy touch you," she tells my sister. "Boys want only one thing."

My sister knows what, but she wants my mother to say it. "What?"

"Sex. They can't help it," my mother says. "A boy your age

tells you he loves you to get his way. Believe him, and you're a fool."

"How come?"

"You'll get pregnant. *Azoy,* your life will be ruined. Believe me, you have to wait till you're married."

"When you got married, how old were you?" my sister asks.

"Twenty-six."

"That's so old."

"For four years we went steady. To save up the money. What, you think marriage is free? *Oy,* does it cost! For furniture. For the electric. For rent. Then when babies come, *ai yi yi!*"

Having her period makes my sister feel she is on a more equal footing with my mother. She dares to ask, "That's why you didn't want Devorah to be born?"

"*Nisht getoigen!* You make no sense."

"I heard you and Daddy. That's why you went to the doctor."

"Listen!" My mother yanks the front of my sister's sweater. "What is, is. What was, was. *Farshtaist?*"

T he first time, my mother wheels me past Magic Shoes, only to look. She doesn't expect Harry to be in front or to see her, but there he is. Like a jack-in-a-box, he springs out the door. "May I buy you a cup of coffee?" he asks.

"I think so," she says.

It becomes their routine. Weekdays, when my sister and brother are in school, and my father is at the factory, she shows up at ten-thirty. Harry comes out of the store, and they walk, wordlessly, to Manny's Luncheonette. He gets coffee for himself and cocoa for her. They sit by the window. On the green-painted ledge is a tall aspidistra. Carefully my mother separates the chintz curtains so she can watch my carriage outside on the sidewalk.

She never knows how the conversation will go, not like with my father. Harry says to her such interesting things, she thinks about them the rest of the day. Once, he explains to her about nuclear fission. Atoms and molecules. Chain reaction. She can hardly believe it. "How you know this?" she asks.

"From books. Not to be a scientist, that's my greatest regret." Someday, he thinks, he'll confide his second greatest regret.

She's never known a man to talk about what his life is missing. Or what he dreamed the night before. Or what he reads in the *New York Times*, which is for educated people. After he tells her about the Supreme Court decision for Negroes, she thinks all day about *inherently unequal* and why it is wrong. Lately Harry is very concerned about the Russians building spy satellites.

"And you tell me, no such thing as an Evil Eye," she says.

"*Touché!*" Arms waving, he explains how *touché* came from fencing.

"I love it how you become excited over *taiglech*," she says.

"*Taiglech?*"

"Small pieces of dough. *Crumbs* maybe is better," she says.

He laughs. "My parents forbade us to speak Yiddish. They wanted us to blend in at school. I went a couple of semesters to college—at NYU."

She sighs. "For me, so little school. I go work in the factory. What you learn me is an education. Like my own professor, you are." Admiringly she views his wide forehead, which she didn't notice with the hat. A sign of brains.

Besides wanting to know what Harry knows, she wants to know about him. She spaces out her questions. One day she finds out his father is dead. Another day, that he has no sisters or brothers. And then she manages to ask, "Why you never get married? You don't like children?"

For once he tells her a little. "I was married at twenty," he says. "My two sons are already grown. One just graduated from Brooklyn College. He's a schoolteacher now. The other boy, he thinks he's an artist."

Her mind reels. Harry is married? The disappointment sits in her stomach like too much *kugel*. She should have known. To tell her like that—he could just as well stab her. Now for sure she must end it between them. If not today, soon. At the end of the week, she decides. She struggles now not to show the turmoil within her. "So," she says calmly, "your son, he's a painter?"

"Another kind of artist," Harry says gently. "A writer. He gets it from his mother. We divorced ten years ago."

My mother exhales. How can life and death hang on so little? she wonders. A word, for instance.

F̲ive days a week, week after week, my mother and Harry, they meet for coffee and cocoa. One morning he touches her hand, which is resting on the table. She looks down at her lap. She cannot meet his eyes. Another morning he says, "If only I could kiss you . . ."

A day comes when instead of walking him back to work, she wheels me down the alley between apartment buildings. He follows behind. When they are away from where anyone can see, he hugs her. Something happens inside her. Like when the anesthetic in the hospital wore off. But instead of pain, it's a sensation for which she has no words. They clasp each other— one long embrace—until he has to go back to the store.

Then, as the weather gets warmer, a day comes when they don't go to the luncheonette. They sit on a bench on the

Boardwalk. The first time, he kisses her on the temple. The next time, at the top of her ear. From time to time he raises her hand to his lips. Then one day he kisses her on the mouth, firmly, but he doesn't expect anything. The kiss is quick. Gradually his kisses go longer. It's the long ones she likes.

My mother worries the whole time that someone will see her and tell my father. One minute she pushes him off and the next she is kissing him back, with a passion that frightens her. Sometimes Harry's hand slips under her coat, even under her sweater. It makes her feel faint.

O n Valentine's Day Harry brings her a huge box of candy, so wide it has to tip to fit into my carriage. When my father gives her a valentine's card that night, she shows him the candy and says it's from her sister. She proffers the open box and watches him as he chews a truffle. Such a strange pleasure it gives her! She holds out the box of candy again and again, and when my father finally hesitates to take any more, she says, "One last!" and hands him a chocolate heart wrapped in gold foil.

M y mother imagines telling someone—my Aunt Ruchel, maybe—what she and Harry talk about. *What don't we discuss*, she says, though she knows so many subjects are taboo. *The family, for instance.* To Harry she doesn't ever talk about my father or my sister or my brother. With Harry it's as if she is free from the only life she knows. She thinks it must be that way too with him.

In her imagined conversation, my mother says, *Never are we talking about the two of us, not how we are now, never how we will be tomorrow, almost never what we were yesterday. Not even how we met. Each one waits for the other to bring it up. What is there to say, after all, when you're married? From that, everything and nothing follows,* nu?

The one thing she would like Harry to know is why she was on the beach that day. And what it meant to her, to see his kind face at such a dark moment. One morning, when he cannot come to Manny's Luncheonette because he has to go to the city on business, she writes a letter to him. Not to send, but for him to read someday if she should die before him. Carefully she puts down her thoughts, and then recopies them onto lined paper from my sister's notebook. She hides the letter under my mattress.

Later, when my sister offers to change the sheets in my crib, my mother says not to bother. "Don't you think I know how?" Mimi screams. My mother says, "If I should need your help, the sheet will be over my own head." After that, my mother reluctantly tears her letter into tiny pieces. She stuffs the pieces into the bottom of the garbage. Anyhow, she realizes, how could such a letter even get to Harry? Who would think to tell him she died?

My mother gets a burning wish to give Harry a compliment, but she feels shy. He is always complimenting her. Her eyes. Her skin. How she makes him laugh. She looks for opportunities to say something, but they never seem right. Then one morning, when the temperature soars and he buys her a plain seltzer to drink instead of her usual cocoa, she blurts it out: "I'm sorry the weather is too warm for your hat.

I'm crazy for your hat, the green one. When I saw it on the beach—"

"The fedora," Harry says. "I'm glad you like it. You were so unhappy then. May I ask how come?"

"Mr. Diplomat, you're asking why I should want to end my own life. *Khas vesholem*. God forbid."

Here is her chance at last, but she cannot tell him the whole truth, that my father smacked her. She points to my perambulator. "I learned I was expecting. Another child! *Oy*, it was too much for me." She sees he looks puzzled.

"But you've recovered fully, haven't you?" An aberration, he tells himself. She's perfectly stable now, if a little volatile in temper. The immigrant character, so quick to feel wronged. He touches her cheek. "Serene as a Madonna," he says. He has to explain *Madonna*.

My mother thinks he is sweet to worry about her.

O n the first day of spring Harry brings my mother yellow and orange daffodils. "Say you found them," he suggests, when she hesitates to take them. "We'll rough them up." He squeezes some petals till she begs him to stop.

That morning they head for the ocean. Such luck, she thinks, when they find an empty bench. She turns my perambulator toward the water but away from the blinding sun. "Like diamonds," my mother says about the glitter of the waves.

"You're my diamond, my jewel of the Boardwalk."

"More like rhinestone," my mother jokes.

After a while, Harry says, "Why don't we go down to the beach?" Unperturbed by the panic in my mother's eyes, he says soothingly, "No one will see. We'll go under the Boardwalk."

She thinks of her clothes getting all sandy. She makes a daring suggestion: "Maybe we should go instead to your place?"

Then he tells her, "My mother, God bless her, lives with me. Ever since her stroke, a year ago."

"*Alevai*, my own son should be so good," my mother says.

Harry picks up the end of the perambulator. She holds the front. They carry me down the stairs. On the concrete platform that rests on the beach, they leave me lying in the carriage as they duck under the Boardwalk.

Harry spreads his suit jacket over the cool sand. Side by side they lie, their legs sticking past the makeshift blanket. When he reaches under her clothes, my mother thinks of me, just yards away. She feels ashamed, even as she can't help herself. Up above me, seagulls circle and honk. I shake my pink and white rattle.

"So many clothes," Harry mutters. "A fortress." He tugs on her panty girdle. My mother starts to resist. "Don't you want me?" he asks.

"And what if I get pregnant, *kholilleh*?" she says. "One little drop, I'm done for."

"I had a vasectomy," he tells her. "I can't have any more children." He yanks the panty girdle down to her knees. "Don't worry."

The lovemaking is awkward, hurried. The garters that are still attached to her stockings press into her thighs. She hardly feels any pleasure, except for his warm kisses on her neck. Afterwards Harry says, "This is terrible. I promise you that next time will be better."

My mother says nothing. She is thinking, *Next time?* There cannot be a next time. What's between them is done. Finished. Now she will feel guilty for who knows how long. And for what? *A shandeh un a kharpeh!* A shame and a disgrace!

After she walks him back, she intends to throw away the flowers, the evidence of her *aveyreh*. Her sin. They are so cheerful, they mock her. Although she wheels me past one garbage can after another, the flowers stay draped across my blanket. Finally she is home. She will put the flowers in a vase, she thinks, and watch them die.

For the next few days, my mother walks around the apartment talking aloud to herself in Yiddish. Sometimes my sister and brother think she is talking to them. "What?" they ask. "I didn't say nothing," my mother answers.

"You did." My sister turns to my brother. "Sheldon, didn't she say something?"

"I heard you, Mama," he says gently.

"*Takeh?*" she says. Really? Then she mumbles something else in Yiddish.

Standing at the stove, stirring the barley soup, she talks to herself the whole time. Only my father doesn't seem to notice.

On the fifth day there is a thunderstorm. Sheets of water drench the windows. The thunder makes me cry.

"No one's angry at you, *bubbeleh*," my mother tells me. Though she believes that picking up a crying baby will spoil it, she lifts me out of the crib, holds me while she sings a Yiddish lullaby. I stop crying and listen.

The storm ends, she returns me to the crib. "*Oy!*" she says. "I forgot the flowers."

As she changes the water in the vase, she notices the yellow petals are firm yet silky. The green stems are strong and crisp, like straws.

My sister says to her, "Mama, you look so much better today."

My mother clutches the pouch of garlic in the pocket of her smock. "I looked to you sick?"

My brother says, "Mimi thought you had a fatal disease." Mimi nods.

"What? Me?" my mother says. "*Kineahora!* Say it. Three times, both of you." She reaches for the salt to shake over her shoulder.

My sister and brother look at each other, daring the other

to laugh while they chant. *"Kineahora, kineahora, kineahora."* Then my sister says, "Whoever gave you the Evil Eye, Mama, it was last Friday, right? I remember when I came home from school your face was grayer than this frying pan." She turns to my brother. "Right, Sheldon?"

My mother doesn't answer. She knows her daughter gets it from her, the ability to see under a person's skin. "Congestion of the chest," she tells them now. "I'm a whole lot better. *Kineahora.*"

It's true, my mother thinks, the guilt has gone poof! Flown up and away like a bird. Why is this? she asks her face in the mirror. Is it the devil tempting her to sin some more? All week she hasn't dared to look at herself, but now she scrutinizes. If anything, she looks younger. Forty, maybe. She wonders if she should touch up the gray streak in her hair.

M y father leaves the factory one night and is shocked to see Trudy Fleisch standing on the sidewalk by the lamppost out in front. Something's happened to her husband, he thinks. Then he realizes he's being foolish. "What are you doing here?" he asks.

Her smile is cunning.

Now he asks if Barney has gone out of town, but to that Trudy only says, "Don't hold your breath."

"So what, then?"

"An apartment. Three bedrooms. Two blocks from where I live."

"Three bedrooms? It must cost an arm and a leg."

"Don't you want to live near me?" she says.

"Of course, of course, but I have to be able to pay for it, no?"

"So you'll rent out a bedroom," she says.

"I have to buy furniture for it."

"I thought you'd be happy."

"I am happy," he lies. All of a sudden, he feels overwhelmed by the prospect of moving. He is used to how he lives, why does he have to change?

"You have to take a look at it. Right away," she says.

"Okay, okay."

"Tonight," she says.

"Tonight?"

"It's a gift from heaven. You think it's going to go unrented? My nephew, the one who came back to Philly from overseas, he would grab it in a minute."

My father's head is full of excuses as he takes the A train with her, up to Washington Heights. He'll tell her his wife has to see it. Then he can tell her his wife doesn't like it. He'll be off the hook.

The apartment is spacious, with cross-ventilation from the street and the alley. The basement has a washing machine, a new one. There's a carriage room so they don't have to *shlep* the carriage up the steps of the stoop.

"Give the super a deposit," Trudy suggests. When my father says he has no money with him, she takes a twenty-dollar bill from her purse. Maybe it's not such a bad idea, he thinks, Trudy just two blocks away.

On the subway home he can't think of a single reason not to move. By the time he arrives at the West 8th Street station in Brooklyn, he's already living in Manhattan.

"I have big news," he tells my mother in the mirror. She is sitting at the vanity, rubbing cold cream into her face. From his look of excitement, she's sure he's gotten a settlement for the cherry pit, but she won't give him the satisfaction to ask. "You got a raise?" she says.

Deflated, he answers, "In a way, yes," his mind formulating a plan. He tells her about the apartment. He cannot read her reaction. One minute she seems impressed, the next minute she looks at him blankly.

Finally she asks, "How much?"

"We'll rent out one of the bedrooms," he says.

She waves her hands. "From where do you get such an idea? A stranger living with us?"

"Temporarily."

"What about meals? This stranger will eat with us?"

"I don't know," he says. "What do you think?"

She shakes her head. "We have to have a phone," she says.

"Okay, a phone."

"Which you pay for."

"Okay, I'll pay for the phone," he says.

"I have to see the apartment first. If I don't like it, we don't move."

"Okay, okay." He thinks, If it's meant to be, it's meant to be.

All night my mother lies awake. *It's for the best,* she thinks. And then, *It will kill me.* Back and forth she goes. She cannot make up her mind. Maybe if she sees Harry again. Or maybe it's better if she doesn't see him. Since that morning she has kept away from his store. Every day, she wheels me down Ocean Parkway, away from the beach. She doesn't care if he worries. If he doesn't worry, it means he doesn't care about her. Only one thing she's sure of: They can't do it again, not like that. Not there, in the shadow of the Boardwalk.

"It's too dark," my mother says about the apartment in Manhattan.

"It's only temporary," my father says.

She senses he is desperate to move, though she cannot figure why. Maybe there's someone in Brooklyn he owes money to.

He shows her the big park in the new neighborhood. "Good for the children, no?"

She sees a couple walking up a grassy slope, hand in hand. "Parks are dangerous," she snaps. "You want a young girl should walk in the trees?"

He shows her the Chinese restaurant on the main thoroughfare. He insists they have dinner there. He orders the expensive combination plate. My mother asks for lobster rolls. "No lobster roll," the waiter tells her. "Order something," my father says. "Something on the menu. Something more kosher."

In bed that night my father reaches for her. She is lying on her stomach. She doesn't turn over. His caresses become more insistent. She moves toward the edge of the bed. He retreats to the other edge. "What do you want from me?" he hisses. "What's the matter with you?"

My mother turns on the light. "I don't want to live in the city," she says. "You can't make me."

"We'll see about that. If I move, the children come with me. If you don't want to move, don't trouble yourself." He reaches over her and snaps out the light.

When my mother arrives at Magic Shoes, Harry is talking to a woman up in front. His chin lifts when he sees her, and he walks backwards out the door. My mother thinks he left a customer hanging, but she doesn't scold him. To make a *tsimmes*, a fuss over nothing, she cannot do this now, not when she has to refuse to go again to the Boardwalk.

At their usual table in the luncheonette, my mother yanks open the curtain and says about me, "See how she sleeps." The aspidistra on the window ledge looks brittle. *Dying of thirst.* She pours her glass of water into the rock-hard sand.

"I'm sorry," Harry says out of the blue. "That wasn't a good idea."

"You're telling me," she says.

He whispers. "I just wanted you so much. I lost my head. I hope I haven't destroyed your faith in me."

"My husband wants to move to the city," she says.

"You don't have to make up stories."

She snickers. "I thought you were a diplomat."

"I thought you were the one being diplomatic, pretending you're moving."

"*Touché!*" She smiles, pleased to show him she's learned the word. "Listen, this is no *bobbe-myseh* I'm telling you. He wants to move us."

"And you? Is that what you want?" He puts his hand over hers. He wonders if there's some way to stop her from moving away. Her skin is so soft. He's never known anyone with skin so soft. Silky as talcum.

"If I could have what I want . . . ," she says wistfully. He looks so handsome in his brown suit, though the back of his hair could use a trim.

"When are you going?"

"The first of the month." For once she unburdens herself to him: "My daughter, she goes crazy to change schools at a time like this. My son, he looks forward. He hopes in a different class his marks will go up. Me, I don't know which is better. Either way is too hard."

"'April is the cruellest month,'" he quotes. "A poet wrote that. He must have lost someone he loved in April."

"Spring is cruel," my mother says. "Hope is cruel. You gave me hope. I should hate you."

"Meet me tomorrow," Harry says. "Promise?"

E ach morning at the luncheonette it becomes harder and harder to leave Harry when the time is up. Sometimes my mother doesn't walk him back to the store but sits there, drinking a second cup of cocoa. Sometimes she remembers herself as a girl in Russia, how simple life was. And how the trouble started when the soldiers came and knocked apart the wooden fence. There's nothing an individual has, she thinks now, that cannot be taken away.

"What crazy god makes such a life?" she says to the overweight woman at the next table who is drinking tea, her pinkie crooked.

"You bust out laughing or you cry," the woman says. Daintily she touches the cherries on her broad-brimmed hat. "I found this masterpiece laying on the Boardwalk. Someone lost it. I found it. It evens out."

"Is that so?" My mother smiles skeptically.

"God bless, you keep your baby so immaculate!" the woman says. "I seen her before. Looks real healthy, that one."

Ptooh. My mother spits on the linoleum.

"Lady," the proprietor calls out. "This ain't no saloon."

"You're telling me," my mother says. In a saloon she could order something to kill the pain.

Two weeks before moving day, Harry tells my mother he is planning something special for them. "Can you get away for a whole evening?" he asks.

"An evening? Never."

"How about an afternoon? A whole afternoon? Without the baby."

"Yes, maybe. I think so." In her brain the wheels turn. Next to adultery, what do lies matter?

For the special day with Harry she wears her best dress, polka dots, black on white. She doesn't put on earrings, afraid she'll lose them somewhere. She wears high heels. She doesn't want to wear the watch, my father's engagement present, but she has to know the time. She leaves a folded note on the door for my sister and brother: KEY NEXT DOOR — 3E. She takes me to the neighbor's and reminds her not to say anything to my father, to anyone.

"You look so pretty, where you going, Mrs. Arnow?" the neighbor asks.

"Lunch with my sister, in a fancy place. My husband don't like her, so I have to keep it secret." She hands her the key to the apartment.

"Enjoy your lunch, Mrs. Arnow."

My mother spits three times as she descends the stairs.

They meet at the luncheonette. Harry proffers a white rose wrapped in green paper. Roses should be red or pink, she thinks. Maybe yellow. But white? It's like a mistake.

"We're going to the Half-Moon," he says. "I arranged everything."

"The hotel?" The idea scares her. Like a white rose, it seems unnatural.

"Do you know why it's called the *Half-Moon*?" She doesn't, so he tells her. "Henry Hudson sailed up here. He anchored his boat out there in the bay. The boat was called the *Half Moon*."

"Who's this Henry fellow?" my mother asks, but it's just to make conversation. To go to a hotel with a man who isn't your husband—the worst sin, she thinks, almost as bad as murder.

He tells her about the English explorer as they walk, but she doesn't listen. They walk and walk. The hotel is so far away. "I wouldn't have worn high heels, if I knew," she says.

"Do you want me to carry you?"

"Sure. I call your bluff."

He picks her up, right in the middle of Surf Avenue.

"Put me down. *Meshuggener.*" Both of them, she thinks.

Although she's passed by it before, she's never really noticed the hotel. All brick, it looks serious, like a hospital. Her steps slow as they go through the door.

"It's okay," he says. "I already have a key."

They go right into the elevator, up to the sixth floor. My mother stands for a long time at the window, looking beyond the Boardwalk to the ocean. Harry hangs up their coats and stands behind her with his arms around her midriff. She has a fleeting thought, to open the window and climb out.

Then Harry brings out a flask of whiskey and she takes a sip, and then another. "The taste of lye," she says.

"A pun. Rye is a kind of whiskey," he explains.

"You always learn me something," she says.

Slowly Harry undresses her, kissing her, caressing her in the bed between the starchy sheets. At first she feels self-conscious, but soon she feels light-headed. She is not used to drink. It's a good feeling, carefree. This time he is in no hurry. After a while, she loses some of her shyness. His kisses make her shiver. She is trembling as he touches her down there. She has never been touched *down there* except by midwives and doctors.

Then Harry takes her hand and puts it over his *thing*. At first she thinks there's something wrong with it, because it's curved. Maybe that's why he can't have more children. But when he's inside her, she has sensations that are, *oy*, so out of this world. She can't get over it. She discovers how to move against him. Why did she never know such feelings were possible? She pushes the thought away. Now is no time to think of Ruben.

"My Chenia," Harry says. "Chenia."

To hear her name like that, she can hardly bear the pleasure. She is floating somewhere. Later when she recalls this time, she doesn't know where her mind went. But now she opens her eyes and sees Harry looking at her. A strange pleasure fills her insides and seems to shoot out in all directions. She wants to tell him what's happening to her but he is in the throes of his own ecstasy. By the time his pleasure fades, she is sobbing.

In their last hour together, they alternate taking swigs from the flask. "A radio and everything," she says. She fiddles with the knobs. On one station a woman is singing, "'I'm just wild about Har-ry.'" Such a coincidence, she thinks.

Harry sings along with the next line. "'And Har-ry's wild about you!'"

They laugh. He nuzzles the soft flesh of her upper arm. Soon they are kissing, again and again. Such kisses! Like butter melting into a toasted bialy.

The song ends, and the news comes on the radio. "In midtown Manhattan today, a raging fire in the garment district," the announcer says.

She's sure it hasn't affected my father, but what if? *Kholilleh*. She should choke on the thought. A tiptoe on the sand, she thinks, and soon you are burying the dead. *Khas vesholem*.

If Harry sees her distress, he doesn't let on. He tells her about the hotel, about William O'Dwyer. "He was the D.A.— District Attorney for Brooklyn—trying to convict a group of gangsters called Murder, Inc."

"This movie I think I saw," she says. "With Humphrey Bogart."

"The witnesses stayed right here in this hotel," Harry tells her. "They had cops guarding the place around the clock. But you know what happened?"

My mother shakes her head. She takes another sip of whiskey.

"The main witness was found dead on the roof over the kitchen, right downstairs. The cops fell asleep on the job. You know what they said about this guy?" My mother shakes her head again. " 'The pigeon can sing, but he can't fly.' Get it?"

"I think so," she tells him. "I have to fly now."

They leave the hotel separately, but together they walk the long way back toward Magic Shoes. *I'm just wild about Har-ry.* Slowly, they walk, arm in arm. *And Har-ry's wild about me.* "See, a half-moon," Harry says, pointing to the sky, which is not yet dark.

"Half a moon, this has to be enough," my mother says. She tries to smile. Each step is so heavy, she could be walking in heels through sand. It's five-thirty, rush hour. People spill out of the elevated, jostling them again and again. She glances at the commuters fanning out from the station, so eager to get home. She feels a stab of envy.

And then, in the midst of so many strangers, she sees a face she knows, staring right at her. No mistake. My mother can hardly believe her eyes. She tries to tell Harry, but she chokes on the words: *my husband.*

Part Two

With a loan from my father's brother, we move to upper Manhattan. Even though rivers border our neighborhood to the east and west, and there are sprawling parks, I imagine my mother feels hemmed in. There are no houses, as there are in Brooklyn, only apartment buildings, squished together without space in between. Sometimes she thinks she cannot breathe.

"Come to Jersey, I meet you at the bus stop," my Aunt Ruchel tells her.

My mother cradles me on her lap as we ride the subway to the Port Authority. On the bus that goes over the George Washington Bridge, I stand on my mother's thighs, staring out at the Hudson River. "Give a scream, give a look," she says to me. "This ain't no ocean."

As soon as she brings us home from the bus stop, my aunt sets out the herring, bagels, walnut cream cheese, and something my mother never tasted before, a quiche, which she calls *kish*. "Is an egg and cheese pie, no?" my mother asks. "From where you get such an idea?"

"I can't fool you," my aunt says. "Our new housekeeper made it. All I had to do was heat it up. The chopped green is scallions. I wouldn't let her put in bacon. Millie used to work for these millionaires, till she lost her job."

"She stole something?"

"They caught her with the head chef in the pantry, making love." My aunt rolls her eyes. "She tells me right out: 'I've nothing to hide.'"

"He got fired, too?" my mother asks.

My aunt shrugs. "I think the chef was white."

"So how's by you?" my mother asks, and my aunt tells her, "Knock on wood, everything is fine." "So how's by Isaac?" my mother asks. My aunt says my uncle's company is busy manufacturing pen holders for desks. "The kids?" my mother wants to know. My aunt says they're busy with school, with horseback riding, with tennis, with the organization for Zionists to help the young state of Israel.

"What, *bubbeleh*?" she says to me as I pull on her skirt. She hands me a paper napkin, which I tear to shreds all over the rug. To my mother, she says, "And what's with you? I don't smell the garlic. You forgot?"

My mother tilts her head one way, then the other. "So much has changed," she says. "For better, for worse. The fire in the garment factory, it was lucky and unlucky. Lucky for Ruben, he has now a better job. Unlucky for me," she says, "he bosses so many girls, I think his head is turning."

"Tch," my Aunt Ruchel says.

My mother longs to tell her sister about Harry, what happened when they ran into my father. How her heart stopped. To this day she isn't sure it's still beating. The morning after, she only called her sister to say, "Ruchel, you do me this one favor. If Ruben should ask, we were for lunch yesterday, together." So what does my aunt say? "I wish." She doesn't ask my mother where she was, or what happened. She knows when my mother is ready, she will unburden herself. In this way, two sisters could not be more different. My mother is already famous with her new neighbors for her questions.

"Yes, lucky and unlucky," she says again to my Aunt Ruchel. "Soon the loan from Ruben's brother will be finished." She means paid off. "But money don't heal the heart." She starts to cry. She tells my aunt she cannot get used to where they live now. "The Irish, they stick to the Irish," she says. "The Italians, the Jews, they stick to their own families, *nu*?" If she had the ocean, she wouldn't be so lonely, she says. She only looks at the four walls.

"The *pisherkeh*, she don't keep you busy?" my aunt says, meaning me. I tear up newspapers now because my mother says napkins cost too much.

"Busy you can be and still lonely," my mother answers. And then it spills out, about Harry. "This man in Brooklyn—but I should begin at the beginning. From the Boardwalk."

My mother doesn't spare the details. An hour later, when the phone rings, Harry and my mother have just arrived at the Half-Moon. The phone keeps ringing. My aunt doesn't answer. "Go on, go on," she says.

My aunt interrupts only to ask if my mother wants more coffee or crumb cake. She herself takes a slice, but the fork stabs the plate sometimes while she stares at my mother. My mother sighs.

She describes the furniture, the tiny flowers inside the glass knobs of the wood chest, the fringed lamp shades in the hotel room, as if she is right there, looking at them. Green and ocher swirls coming and going on the bedspread, wine, with drapes to match. The scalloped shades. She explains how the ocean was straight out from their window. "I never drank so much whiskey in my life," my mother says. "Five, maybe six, big swallows. Believe me, I was tipsy."

My aunt, who up until now doesn't know what to think, is starting to form an opinion. A man who would take a married woman to a hotel and get her drunk, this is the *khazer* her sister, her sensible sister, got involved with?

"I could use a schnapps now," my mother says, and laughs. "What you think of me, think a hundred times worse. Wait till you hear."

Finally she gets to where she and Harry are leaving the hotel. "My head, whoosh, so noisy like the ocean," my mother says. "To run into the street and let a truck run me over. If I could explain you, better I would understand it. The white rose from him, I leave on the table in a glass of water. I don't want to look at it after. Why should I? Only to remind me of what isn't, *nu*?

"So we meet, me and him, on the corner behind the hotel. Not a soul I look in the eyes. On the whole street. Number one, my *aveyreh*, the guilt from which. Number two"—my mother puts her hand on her chest—"*oy*, how it hurts! To know that never will I see this man, ever again. The murder in the hotel, the one Harry explained me, *gloib mir*, believe me, it wasn't the only one.

"We walk and walk. A walk like to the electric chair. At this moment, is still light out, but for me like the darkest night when I look up into the faces." With her hand, my mother makes an arc overhead. "All the people coming down and down from the elevated. Rush hour. You know how it goes. A thousand people coming home, but *in mitn derinnen*, only one face jumps right out."

My aunt's mouth hangs open. "Ruben?" she guesses.

My mother snickers. "Imagine!" she says. "That was the day the factory burned up. I forgot to tell you, we heard it on the radio in the hotel. They didn't say which place. A factory burns in midtown. I think, *Gevalt!* What if? Then Harry is talking. Like a history professor he tells me about the murders, how they were trying to get the gangsters. That part I told you. So, *nu*, I forget about the fire."

She sighs again. "*Azoy*, at the fateful moment, Harry and me, we're together, his arm in my arm. This *meshuggeneh*, she's arm in arm with one, and suddenly, she sees the other. I see Ruben. Ruben sees me. I *plotz*. I go like this." My mother makes a very loud sound as she sucks in her breath. "Harry, he knows right away the problem. 'Leave it to me,' he says. 'Introduce me to your husband. Wave at him.'

"He don't let go my arm," my mother says. "I try to get it away. He grabs tighter. We go right up to where the people come down, a whole flood. Wave! Harry says. I wave. Smile! Harry says. I smile. Inside I am thinking, *Mechuleh*. This is the end. Absolutely. Either Ruben will kill me or he will kill Harry. Right there by the elevated."

My mother sips on the cold coffee. Over the rim of the cup, her eyes meet my aunt's. If my aunt's eyes were magnets, they would pull the rest of the story right out of her, she thinks.

"Talk about bad luck and good luck," my mother continues. "Bad luck, the factory burns up. Good luck, Ruben is all *tse-dreyt*. He don't know if he's coming or going. 'This is my husband,' I say to Harry. Harry grabs his hand. 'Pleased to make your acquaintance,' he says. Then he says, 'Your wife wasn't feeling so well. She fainted on the sidewalk. I gave her a sip of whiskey, and'—he points to his head—'I think now she's okay.'

"'Thank you so much, Mister,' I say. Like an actress. Like I'm rehearsing this part for a month.

"'You're so welcome, Mrs.—' He says it like a question.

"'Mrs. Arnow,' I say. 'Thank you a million.'

"Out of the corner of my eye I'm looking at Ruben, but I can tell he's someplace else. First I think, is because we meet like this, suddenly at the station. Then it sinks in. 'You're home so early?' I say.

"'The factory burned down,' he says. 'No insurance. We're done for.'

"Bad luck and good luck. He don't ask for what I fainted. He's like a chicken's lost its head. I feel like I lost my *kishkes*. One good thing—the white rose I left behind me. Thanks God, I hope someone enjoyed it."

My mother sighs. Her head bobs slightly. She says, "Some story, huh?"

I imagine my aunt goes to the kitchen to catch her breath. Later she'll try to make sense of it all. She doesn't keep secrets from my uncle, but right now she wouldn't bet a plug nickel that she is going to tell him a thing.

After services, my father leaves the synagogue, goes up to Broadway, the yarmulke in his pocket. He walks on the cobblestones, along the outer edge of the park. Autumn leaves crunch under his feet. He is thinking again about mysteries: How the trees shed their leaves, how bare they are through the winter. Then one day, there are buds again, and then new leaves and flowers. The trees grow taller. The cycle makes sense to him as never before. The day the factory burned, he was a dead man. And now he is more alive than he has ever been.

No longer is he a nobody at work. At the new place he's a floor boss, over thirty-four girls. They make ties for department stores, not *shlock* like the other factory. He has more money in his pocket now, even after making his weekly payment to his brother. And the boarder pays in cash. As if all those blessings aren't enough, there's no more two-hour subway ride to see Trudy.

The only thing that bothers him, and he knows it's a small thing, is the television. He bought it for Trudy and for himself, to watch when they are together. That part is fine. But he can't stand to think of Barney also enjoying himself as he watches. Such a *shlemiel*, to believe his wife is making the payments.

My father rings Trudy's bell now, and she lets him in. "Like clockwork," she says. "You're always here, Tuesdays and Thursdays at five forty-five. Saturdays at noon." She follows him into the living room and stands while my father sits, as he always does, on the sofa.

"You want I should be late?" he asks.

"You could be late, if you stopped to buy me candy."

"You want candy?"

"Forget it," she says. "Listen, I'm hot to trot." She stretches with her elbows up by her ears. "Maybe we could go somewheres instead of staying cooped up inside."

"Where?"

"You know, out. To a movie maybe."

"For what did I buy you a television?"

"Listen, you don't have to remind me." Trudy plops on the sofa, a cushion between them. My father motions with his head for her to move over, but she shakes her head no.

"It's that time of month?" my father asks.

Since he's given her the idea, she nods. "My daughters are coming home for Thanksgiving, for a week. My nephew and his wife might come and bring their new baby. A girl. Hannah. There's something wrong with her eyes . . ."

Trudy talks and talks and my father falls asleep. Stabbing the heel of her shoe into his calf, she jolts him awake. "So, are we going out?" She runs her hands through her hair, which hangs loose on her neck.

"I don't mind," he says.

"Say it. All you want to do is poke me with your pee pee. Stab me with your *shlong*. Am I right?" She laughs. "You're blushing, you little devil."

"We'll go to a movie, Trudy, but please, not here in the neighborhood." He knows it's dumb, but he feels a deep disappointment, like a kid with a brand-new toy that got stolen. Maybe not so brand-new, he jokes to himself.

M y mother sits and stares at the telephone. When it doesn't ring, it makes her sad. When it rings and it's not Harry, it makes her sad. Sometimes she wants to yank the cord out of the wall and throw the phone into the garbage. Does he ever think of her? she wonders. Can she ever stop thinking of him?

My mother gets in the habit of wheeling me to the park. She isn't one for trees, she thinks, but in Fort Tryon Park she's away from the stink of the street, the cars, the trucks, the garbage. The playground is as large as a whole block, with rides for children, swings and slides, seesaws and monkey bars. There are trees all around. She sits on a bench near the large, shallow pool, my stroller to her left so as not to block her view of the big fountain.

She likes to watch the water shooting from the brass spigots into the air. She makes wishes when she sees rainbows in the spray. The toddlers in tiny bathing trunks, so cute, she laughs when they shriek under the downpour. She marvels at how the little girls, so dainty in their two-piece swimsuits, have big sisters willing to take care of them. Her own daughter is always too busy to baby-sit.

Then one day my mother realizes the big sisters with the bobby sox and pedal pushers are the mothers. Girls, not even twenty years old, twenty-four tops, with two kids, even three. Like kids themselves, they sit on the edge of the pool and dunk their feet, two or three girls together, pink rollers showing under their kerchiefs. They chew gum and talk while their children splash around them.

Sometimes a young girl sits on the same bench with her. "You shouldn't have the blanket over the whole carriage," my mother might say to her. "The baby will only breathe dust." The girl says, "Oh yeah? It don't seem to bother Billy none." Or my mother will say, "You shouldn't put the baby on its stomach to sleep. It can choke to death, *kholilleh*. God forbid." Always she warns them against kissing a baby, even their own. "You give it germs," she says.

Soon the girls move away from her. She sighs. She remembers how headstrong she was when she first met Ruben. "He's not for you," her father said. Did she listen? Her stern father. *Olov hasholem.* May he rest in peace.

One day a young girl in a white blouse with a Peter Pan

collar and a plain skirt sits on the bench with my mother. Her two babies are dressed alike, but one is chubby with brown hair, one is skinny and bald.

"They don't look even related," my mother says.

"They're fraternal twins," the girl says.

"What is this, 'fraternal'?"

"Two different fertilized eggs. Identical twins come from one egg that splits and divides."

"This I never knew. Are you a nurse?"

"I learned that in biology. Funny you should ask me. I was just thinking of going back to school"—the bubble gum in her mouth pops—"in a few months. When I don't have to breast-feed them anymore. My little cannibals," the girl says, and pats her breasts.

Is she something! my mother thinks. She has to remember to tell her sister. "Someone takes care of them while you go? Someone you trust?"

"My husband's ma passed. Mine's in California."

The skinny baby cries and the girl picks him up. She opens her blouse and pulls down her bra on one side. My mother can see the white skin of her breast. Only after the girl starts nursing the baby does she cover it up. My mother can't get over it, nursing like that in public.

My mother is about to tell her she'll spoil the baby, feeding him whenever he cries, but she stops herself. She doesn't get to talk to so many people, besides the neighbors. The young girls, they have their own ideas. She can't keep her eyes off the suckling infant. "Your mother," she says. "Maybe she could help you. She could visit, *nu?*"

The girl shakes her head. "She won't even admit she's a grandmother. Maybe you'd like to be their grandma," she says. "Just joking. Is that your daughter's baby?"

"You thought I was her grandma?" The girl nods. "To tell you the truth," my mother says, "she was an accident. Two I had already. Thirteen and fifteen now."

"I couldn't imagine having a kid at your age," the girl says. "What is she, a change-of-life baby? Pardon me for asking."

This time it's my mother who ends the conversation. "I'm late for meeting my son," she says. "You should excuse me."

Change-of-life. Grandma. The words linger in her mind as she wheels me out of the playground. Not ready to go back out on the street, my mother takes an uphill path winding through a forest of trees. After a while she has no idea where she is, but she doesn't care. She keeps pushing me, up and up, until she finds herself at the very top of the park, overlooking the Hudson River. The water seems as gray and dirty as the low stone wall in front of us.

"Some scenery!" she says to me. "We're so high up. Like on Empire State." She sits down to take a longer look. Across the water is New Jersey. "Look"—she points to our left—"the George Washington Bridge. I took you. Look, the river, so quiet. Teensy little waves. *Mit shnai ken men nit makhn go-molkes.*" From cheesecake, you can't make snow.

She forgets the view as she chews on the girl's words. It's true, she tells herself, she is old enough to be a *bubbeh*. She'll be decrepit—a decrepit hag, by the time the baby grows up. Who will want her then? What was it her sister said? "Whatever you're thinking, Chenia, you can't divorce him. He'll prove adultery on you and you'll lose the children. You're trapped."

Without the baby, my mother thinks now, she could be free in five years. By then her daughter will be out of high school. By then the baby will be in school already. But how could she leave a five- or six-year-old kid?

My mother stands up and leans over the low wall. Right below her is a wilderness of trees and rocks, a steep drop to the very bottom. In a matter of seconds, she thinks, she could be free. *I don't know how come I dropped her. It was an accident.* She glances at me in the stroller.

I have my arms out, ready for her to pick me up. "Mama, out," I say.

She lifts me up and holds me tight to her bosom as she sits back down on the bench. I squirm around in her arms until I am facing the water. "You like the river?" she says to me. "*Feh*, boring."

After a while I too am bored. As she reaches for my bottle of orange juice, I wriggle out of her arms and down to the ground. My mother bends over a moment to look in the bag. I scamper. By the time she notices, I am yards away. My mother chases me. I giggle and run some more. I run along the wall but suddenly the wall ends. I look down.

"Nooo!" I hear my mother scream.

Then arms scoop me up, lift me into the air. "Gotcha!" the voice says, but it isn't my mother's. It's a man I don't know. I'm too surprised to cry.

My mother is beside us now. She is panting. Her hand is on her chest. "Thank you, Mister. God bless."

"She could train for the Olympics," the man jokes.

"What's that?" a little girl says. She has reddish hair, like mine, and blue eyes.

"My daughter," the man tells my mother. "Here you go." He lifts me in the air before lowering me carefully into her arms.

"Your wife is here?" my mother asks.

"Visiting her folks. Cara and I have our special afternoon. Right, Cara?" The girl nods.

"Wonderful you take your daughter out," my mother says. "You don't work?"

The man laughs. "Swing shift. I start at four."

"Oh," my mother says. She watches as the man and his daughter clasp hands and disappear around the bend.

What if she got the divorce and Ruben took the kids? she wonders. They wouldn't starve. He would find someone to marry, if only to take care of the baby. Her son would be the same, working on cars, chasing the girls. Her daughter wouldn't miss her, the way she acts lately, ever since they moved. The baby wouldn't even remember her.

I drink my orange juice from the bottle. My mother is elsewhere, with Harry in California, where she's never been. She imagines a backyard with palm trees. They're drinking tall glasses of iced tea. Harry is smiling at her, but she is not smiling. "What's wrong?" Harry says. "My baby," she answers. "I can't get her out of my mind." *Trapped.*

She puts me back in the stroller and hooks up my safety belt. She starts down the winding path. "Think we can find the way home?" she asks.

"Home," I say. "Home. Home home home home home."

My mother stops pushing the stroller and does something she has never done before. She kisses her hand, and presses it to my forehead. *"Mmwah,"* she says, very loud.

I don't see the tears in her eyes.

My father is listening to the Dodgers game on the radio. Twice my mother tries to talk to him, but he waves at her to stop. During the seventh-inning stretch, he says, "What?"

"Next Saturday, is before Labor Day. We could go to Brighton Beach."

"The water is polluted. You want the kids to get polio?"

"For the fireworks, I mean."

"Who?" my father says.

"Who? All of us. Before the children go back to school. We didn't go even one time this summer. Not even Fourth of July."

"Two hours going, two hours coming. You want to see the fireworks? Go! Take the children," my father says, wondering if Barney Fleisch is working that night or not.

My mother's bosom heaves. "Just an idea," she says. She doesn't tell him the idea was to run into Harry, somewhere in the crowd of thousands of people. Of course he will go see the fireworks. Who in Coney Island doesn't? And if luck is with her, she would see him. At least a glimpse. She wishes now she had a snapshot of Harry, something she could look at outside her own mind, something she could touch.

"You know what?" she says to me as she puts me on the potty. "You can't kiss a memory. And that's a fact."

"Fat?" I say. "Fat?"

In the telephone book my mother tries to find Magic Shoes. She goes patiently through the different listings for Magic: magic carpets and magic nails and magic swimwear. My brother comes in and sees her with a magnifying glass, poring over the page.

"Why don't you get glasses? What're you looking for?" he asks.

"The shoe store from home."

"Magic Shoes?"

"That's it."

"That's Brooklyn, Ma. This is Manhattan."

"Oh," she says.

"You can get it from Information." Knowing she doesn't know how, he tells her, "You dial 4-1-1 and ask the Operator."

"Oh."

"You want me to do it?"

"No, it's okay."

"I'll do it, Ma."

"No, I was just wondering, that's all."

Later she writes down "4,1,1" on a piece of paper and sticks it in the drawer under her brassieres.

On Tuesdays and Thursdays, when my father comes to Trudy directly from work, he brings takeout from the Chinks on Dyckman. More and more, though, Trudy wants to eat out. He tries to tell her it's not a good idea. Once he brings expensive steaks over, but Trudy says, "What do you want me to do with these?" "Cook them," he tells her. She puts them in a pan, and then they burn. That's when he finds out that Barney does the cooking. That fairy! he thinks. It occurs to my father that Trudy is a little lazy, not making dinner, but he doesn't dwell on the thought.

Now that he's with her three times a week, they don't always have sex. That, too, he would never have believed a few months ago. He hardly has sex at all anymore, and he's not an old man. Not yet, he thinks. He doesn't know what's wrong at home, why his wife mopes around, why she's moved into the other bedroom with Mimi and the baby's crib. The boarder sleeps in the third bedroom, my brother sleeps on the couch. "No more babies," my mother tells him. "I've had it."

"You should get your tubes tied," he says. "I'll pay for it."

"You can go fix yourself. Why not?" And then, to rub it in, she says, "And you can take it out of the household money." He has an urge to smack her fresh mouth, but he controls himself. He wishes he could confide in Trudy. He carries a lot inside him. It makes him feel old.

On a Monday, not his regular night to see her, he gets a craving for Trudy's company. Instead of going home for dinner, he goes to the Sun Luck Restaurant. He orders himself

Subgum Chicken Chow Mein from Column A and Beef with Pea Pods from Column B, and Chicken Fried Rice, which costs extra. But with all the food on the table, he's hungry only for Trudy. He has the food put into takeout cartons, even the almond cookie, and hurries out of the restaurant.

Tonight he will go to bed with Trudy. He's been patient long enough.

Waiting for Trudy to answer the bell, my father hears the television. He rings again, keeping his thumb on the bell. Finally the peephole opens. "It's me," he says. "Who were you expecting?"

She opens the door only a couple of inches. She has on the red kimono. "I'm not feeling very well. I have the curse."

"Sorry to hear it. I brought you some Chinks."

She's still standing with the door mostly closed. "Thanks but no thanks," she says. "I'll see you tomorrow. I should be better then."

All of a sudden my father gets suspicious. He pushes the door open, making her stagger back a couple of steps. He storms into the living room. *I Love Lucy* is on the television, but no one is watching it. He looks into one bedroom, then the next, then the bathroom. When he returns to the hallway, Trudy is standing with her arms crossed. "Satisfied now?" she asks.

"You should be flattered that I'm jealous."

"If you're so jealous, you shouldn't let me go alone to Las Vegas."

"What? When are you going?"

"Over the Christmas holidays. With a group from Temple. Why don't you come with me?"

"Trudy, make some sense. This job, I have it for five months. How can I get time off?"

"Where there's a will, there's a way," she says. "We'll get rooms next to each other. Think of it. Five nights together, all night. Like honeymooners." She watches him stroke his mustache. Coward, she thinks. With or without him, she's determined to go. She feels in such a rut.

"What about Barney?" my father asks.

"Newspapers don't have holidays. Anyway, Christmas and New Year's, he gets overtime. Think it over. I'm taking a nap now, so if you'll excuse me—"

Kissing Trudy good-bye, my father recalls she had the curse just a couple of weeks before. While she's in his arms, he loosens her sash, puts his hands inside the kimono. When he feels her sanitary belt under the slip, he lets go. He ties her kimono and tries to kiss her again, but she turns her head. "I told you, I don't feel so hot. And you stink of onions."

"What's Chinese food without onions?" he jokes.

Her smile is weak. She reminds him to take the leftovers with him.

On his way home, he puts the bag in a garbage can. Then he stops in the pharmacy to buy a bottle of Listerine. It could come in handy, he thinks, to hide the odor of a partial denture. Besides, it don't cost that much, he tells himself. Reason after reason he gives himself for buying the mouthwash, so as not to feel like a marionette dancing on Trudy's string.

All the time now my mother finds herself thinking about sex. About Harry, yes. About that time in the hotel, yes. But it goes beyond. In her love pocket, as she calls it, she feels something continually *mutching* her. It's a torture, all right, worse than a *kitsel*, a tickle. At the same time, the stirring within her is pleasurable: a flame that won't burn out.

What's wrong with her? my mother wonders. One day she knows from nothing. The next day, it's all she can think of. She recalls stories of men with urges, men who molest and rape. A sickness. It's not like that, she tells herself. She doesn't want to hurt anyone. She has a craving she can't help. *Di tayve*, she thinks. Passion. Lust. Then she recalls a word so close, *der tayvl*. The devil.

Sometimes at night, she returns to my father's bed and snuggles close to him, so he'll get the idea to make love. But when he's inside her, it's not the same as with Harry. Not even a *bissel*. Maybe because his *thing* isn't curved. And also, because he doesn't even try to make her feel good. He is only putting out his own little fire.

Restless, she looks at men everywhere with a new yearning. The man who scoops her ice cream cone. That smile! The long, slim body of a man leaning against the deli. The good thing about the park, she tells herself, is that there are only women there. Still, one day she sees a man sweeping up the trash. A handsome fellow, with big shoulders and a strong back.

On Dyckman Street, she stops to watch the television in the store window, with the stroller beside her. She falls a little in love with Edward R. Murrow. *Oy*, what would it be like to be in his arms? she wonders.

For all the pain, she doesn't mind knowing what she is missing. She was dead for so long. She will be dead again. Now, at least, she can feel.

My mother sits at the kitchen table on a Saturday afternoon, drinking coffee. It's more than two years, she thinks, since she first met Harry. She can still see his eyes, the way he leaned over her crumpled body on the beach.

Mr. Mangiameli, our boarder, limps into the kitchen.

Leaning on his crutch, he says, "So where's your hubby, Mrs. Arnow?"

"Playing cards. From this he tries to make a living."

Mr. Mangiameli laughs. "I thought he was the *gantser macher* of the garment district."

"How come an Italian guy knows Yiddish?" my mother asks.

"As a kid in Chicago, I was a *Shabbes goy*. I kid you not. I lit ovens for the old ladies. I turned on their lights. I learned a little of the mother tongue."

"This you never told me." A year he's lived with them and she's asked all the usual questions, but never did my mother think to ask if he speaks Yiddish. She marvels that he could keep such a thing to himself. She wonders if maybe he's understood things she's said to my father or my father to her.

As if reading her mind, he says, "I know *bubkes*." Mere trifles. "What I wanted to say, Can I bring you something? I'm going out for smokes."

"Thank you but no. I appreciate." A nice fellow, she thinks, but the rent money isn't worth it. Though she feels sorry for him on account of his wooden leg, he makes her feel a little strange in her own home.

In a moment he comes limping back.

"Mrs. Arnow, I hate to ask. Could you do me a very big favor?" Her stomach churns, thinking he is going to ask for money, but that isn't it at all. He asks if, Monday, she could go to his bank on Dyckman Street and get a money order. He'll give her the money. "I can't get there during work," he explains, "and my friend in Indiana, she's in a jam."

"Why not? On my way to the park I'll stop in, *nu*?"

"You're an angel," he says. "A Hebrew angel."

Just then her little bank account pops to mind. What has she done with the bankbook? After Mr. Mangiameli gives her the cash, she searches the closet. She goes through one shoe box and the next and the next, till she finds the passbook. Sixteen dollars and thirty-two cents. By now it's a few cents more.

How could she have forgotten? Inside, a voice answers: *You've only been sleepwalking.*

Now she makes a plan.

Two days later she sets out with me in her arms. She wishes she didn't have to take me. I'm too heavy now for her to carry comfortably, but my sister can only baby-sit me after school, when the bank is already closed. Anyhow, to get to Brooklyn and back, my mother has to start early in the morning so she'll be home before my father. She's not even sure she knows how to go.

She asks the snub-nosed man in the change booth for directions. "Lady, you won't believe this—my relief is here and guess where I'm headed?" he says. Another man slips into the cagelike booth and this one steps out. "Let's go," he says. His face is like an upside-down triangle, broad at the forehead, pointy at the chin. Odd. An accident of birth, she tells herself.

Her mind reels ahead. So long as they stay on the subway, what's the harm? As they wait for the train, the man tries to give me a penny Suchard from the vending machine. "She's too young for chocolate," my mother says. "She might choke, *kholilleh.*" May it not come to pass. She almost spits, and then she remembers, she no longer believes in the Evil Eye.

"How come a petite broad like you has such a bruiser for a kid?" The man is a *grobyan*, a coarse individual, but it's not such an easy job, she thinks, standing all day in the booth, making change. All the questions he gets, the aggravation. Still, she's almost sorry she asked him for directions.

"I like your dress. Hubba hubba. Fits real good." His glance lingers on her right breast. She is holding me over the other one.

On the train he talks and talks and doesn't notice that she's elsewhere. She studies the different women sitting around them. What are their lives like? she asks herself. What are their secrets?

At Times Square, they change trains. He leads the way and she follows. Carrying me on her hip slows her down. She lags behind, tempted to simply get lost in the crowd, but she loses her nerve. "Hey, Mister!" she yells.

He stops till we catch up. "What'd you feed her?" He pokes me with his finger. "Lead? It's not normal when a kid's so mum."

My face scrunches up. My mother shifts me to her other side, away from the *grobyan*.

By the time the train gets to Brooklyn, all she wants to do is look out the windows. The red brick houses, the scrawny trees, the wash lines in the boxy backyards, so *haimish*. To her, Brooklyn will always be home.

"What're you going to Coney for?" the man asks. "To ride the Cyclone?"

"Visiting a friend."

"Lucky fellow."

"Mister, I'm a married woman." She points to her wedding ring.

"Hey, I didn't mean nothing by it. It's just my way of joking, see."

"It's okay. I don't take offense."

"Lady, you just took offense, but I don't take no offense, ha ha."

Now the man is really on her nerves, but what can she do? Say, Excuse me, Mister, and go into another subway car? Suppose when they get there, she runs into Harry with this awful man. So common. She would never get over it.

"Cat got your tongue?" the man says.

She puts her hand to her head. "Excuse me, my head is splitting."

"Oh, you came to the right place." He digs into his pocket and comes up with a tin of aspirin.

"Thank you, I'm allergic. I just need to be quiet a while."

"Dragging a kid around is tough, huh?" he says. He sticks his tongue out at me and makes a raspberry. "I feel for you. Criminy."

She doesn't answer.

He says it again, louder.

"Mister, if you say one more thing to me, so help me, I'll scream."

He makes faces and waves his hands around, as if talking to her in sign language.

The man must be a mental case, she tells herself. He will kidnap them and . . . Shaking inside, she hoists me up toward her shoulder and gets ready as the train pulls into the Avenue X station. She counts to three while the doors stay open, and at the last moment, she darts out. Through the windows she sees the surprised look on the man's face. His index finger points at his temple and makes little circles. He's trying to tell her *she's* crazy. Waiting for the train to leave the station, she feels her heart pound.

Outside the Stillwell Avenue station, she looks around, worried the man is waiting for her, but she doesn't see him. She goes straight to the bank, and after she explains that she and my father have moved to Manhattan, they let her close the account. The day will be all right, she tells herself, but as she strolls along the avenue, she feels someone behind her. She turns and there he is. He pretends to be looking in a store window. "Hey, Mister!" she screams. "Stop following me!"

The man disappears into the store. She hurries around the corner and then waits right there, her clothes wet now and clinging to her body. Minutes later, he comes around the corner, surprised to see she expects him. She points and yells, "The devil, he's following us." People give her strange looks.

The man tells the people passing by, "My wife—she's wacko." Before crossing the street, he blows her a kiss. "See you at home, darling."

She stands there, her chest heaving, but he doesn't go away. As loud as she can muster, my mother screams, "He-elp! Police!" The shrill sound pierces my ears. I let out my own wail.

Now the man takes a few backwards steps, throwing a very evil glance at her. He skips off, turning around from time to time, but he keeps going.

My mother is still breathing hard when she gets to Magic Shoes, not where she was planning to go. She peers through the glass door but doesn't see Harry. She steps into the store and plops me on the counter. When the cashier asks if she needs help, she says, "*Oy*, do I! Tell me, is Mr. Traubman here?"

"Mr. Taubman?" the cashier corrects. "Today's his day off."

"Oh," my mother says. It's too much, she thinks. *Too much.*

"Can I give him a message?"

My mother spots the business cards on the counter. During the move to the city she lost the one he gave her. "I just take one of these, thank you," she says. She takes three. She should have called him, she realizes now, but she wanted him to be the one to call first.

M y mother holds my hand as we walk to Manny's Luncheonette. The aspidistra is still there. It looks even drier than before. First she waters it, then she gives me my bottle from her bag. Then she remembers. She pours some salt from the shaker into her hand and throws it over her left shoulder. For what the man said about her baby. *Too quiet.*

I start to babble. "It works!" my mother tells me. She points. "Salt."

I reach for the shaker. "Sol, sol," I say. I kick my heels gleefully on the cushion of the chair where I am sitting, next to her, like a grown-up.

After a time she opens the curtains to see the lamppost, the trolley, all what she used to see when she was with Harry. A bittersweet reminder. Slowly she sips a cup of cocoa. Outside, the bare branches of trees are shaking. She feels the wind blowing in through the cracks around the window. Funny how she completely forgot how much colder it feels by the ocean.

When her cocoa is gone, she doesn't know what else to do but go back to Manhattan. She fights the urge to walk on the Boardwalk, first because she's afraid we'll both freeze to death. Then she has an image of herself, with me in her arms, walking headlong into the water.

"Hey, didn't you used to come in here?" the proprietor calls out to her. "With the manager of the shoe store?"

"You have a good memory."

"Yeah, especially for ladies who spit." And those great gams! he thinks.

My mother laughs. The man laughs. The couple at the next table gives her an odd look. Feeling in a crazy mood, she says to them, "Do you want I should demonstrate?" And then she hears a knocking on the window beside her table. Outside, his face peering in at her above the aspidistra, is Harry.

He's wearing a cap with a wide visor, like the Sheffield milkman, but it's black-and-white check. In a short suede jacket, he looks dashing, like Stephen McNally in that movie with Barbara Stanwyck. He waves. Her stomach lurches. She waves. She doesn't know why he continues to stand there instead of rushing in, instead of grabbing her in his arms.

It seems like hours before he comes inside. The tension builds up in her. "How are you, Manny?" he says first to the owner. Finally, when he is standing beside her, she cannot even say, Hello, how are you? or Hello, I missed you—the words she later thinks she should have said. Instead she bursts out with "You don't want to see me? Better you should go right away."

"Chenia!" he says reproachfully. "Is this how you greet an old friend?" He bends down to hug her, to kiss her on the cheek. How can this be? she thinks. A hug and a kiss so polite it hurts. He starts to kiss me on the cheek, but she holds up her hand like a stop sign. "Germs," she says.

He orders a coffee for himself and another cocoa for her. "I was just checking on the store. We have a second one now, on

Bushwick Avenue. I go back and forth. I can't stay long," he says. "My mother, she's not well."

"I'm sorry to hear it."

"She had another stroke."

"My sympathies."

"How've you been, Chenia?"

"For what are you asking?"

"Chenia's all thorns today," Harry says. "Like a rose." Then he tells her about a poet named Burns. " 'O, my Luve is like a red red rose,' " he quotes.

"So why did you bring me a white one?"

He looks puzzled until she reminds him of that day at the Half-Moon. "White for your purity," he says. "Your innocence."

"Don't make with the jokes." Inside her now there's a pain worse than being away from the ocean. Is that how he sees her? *An old friend!* Does she look so terrible?

"No joke, Chenia. That's how you were to me. Inviolate." He has to explain the word.

"And now?" When he doesn't answer right away, she says, "Now you would bring for me a red rose, no?" On her face is a smile like a wince. She aches to put her hand on his cheek, to feel the scratchy stubble over the flesh.

"Sorry, Chenia, I have to go." He stares at her. "I hope you believe me."

"The eyes reveal what's in the heart," she says. "Yours, they're like ice, they burn me."

His jaw is clenched as he says the words: "You left *me*. I didn't leave you. You just, poof! disappeared." He's too angry to tell her how he walked the Boardwalk, the streets all around, searching for her. One day he rode around in a checkered cab. No Chenia. He worried she had done something rash. This he doesn't mention. "Isn't that so?" he prods. "You left *me*?"

Even as she knows this is true, she feels he is being unfair. "You are not my only concern, Mister. I have this one"—she clops her hand on my shoulders—"and two more at home."

"Shhh," he says quietly.

"Don't *shhhh* me, Mr. Traubman. Whatever your name is. Don't you dare!" She takes a breath and glares at the couple who is staring at them. She hisses, "I risked for you everything, and for what? What do you have to give me?"

He gets up. "Chenia, really, I have to leave. When are you coming back?"

"For what should I come back?" she asks.

"I can't speak for your heart," he says.

It takes us three hours to get home. My mother spends an hour getting us lost while trying to change trains. I get very cranky. I wail. I fuss. At home I spit up my food. My mother hums a melancholy tune as she bathes me and dries me. She sings some words of a song she's heard on the radio: "'. . . Your lips may be here, But where is your heart?'"

As my mother puts me to bed, I flail and cry. "I don't blame you," she says. "Not a *bissel*."

An hour later, Mr. Mangiameli arrives home from work. "Thank you so much, Mrs. Arnow. You did me such a favor."

"The money order!" My mother slaps her head. "*Gevalt!*"

"You forgot?" Mr. Mangiameli says.

"The money, it's right here," my mother shows him, lifting up the doily from the dresser. "Tomorrow, so help me. I am so sorry." She can tell from his face how disappointed he is. He nods and limps out. She runs after him. "Would you like some veal cutlets?" She's never invited him to dinner before. She only makes him breakfast.

"That's okay," he says. "I'm just concerned for my friend in Indiana."

"I understand. I feel terrible." My mother is so exhausted from the long day, she starts to cry.

"Please, it's *bubkes*." A trifle. "Please don't cry," he says, but tears dribble down her cheeks. While Mr. Mangiameli tries to console her, my father comes home. He finds them in the bedroom, the boarder's arm around her.

"What's going on?" my father asks.

"Nothing," my mother says.

"Don't nothing me. You're not crying for nothing. What happened here?"

She tries to explain to him about the money order. He looks at her, at the two of them, suspiciously.

Later, before my mother goes to bed, my father says to her, "I don't want you running errands for the boarder."

"I never. Just this one time."

"Don't ever do it again," my father says. "Hear?"

Long after my mother and Mr. Mangiameli are asleep, my father ponders. Is something going on between them?

T he whir of the sewing machines is loud in my father's ears as he squeezes into his boss's small office at the rear of the factory floor. Through the glass he can keep an eye on the seamstresses, especially that Rosalie who would rather gab than work.

"Make it quick," the boss says. "I have to leave for *Shabbes*."

"Can I take off a few days over Christmas? Without pay, of course."

"You have a good reason?"

"Can we talk man to man?" my father says. "I don't want to lie to you. I have a lady friend—"

The boss cuts him off. "I don't want to lie to you either, Mr. Arnow. You're a married man, yes?"

"Yes."

"You see my yarmulke?"

"Yes."

"I'm an old-fashioned guy. Don't ask me to condone anything illicit."

"I just want a few days off," my father says.

"Request denied," the boss says. "Tell that Rosita if she doesn't start producing, to look for a pink slip."

"All right," my father says.

At Rosita Flores's station, my father doesn't try to compete with the loud whir of machines, he just waggles his finger. Angrily, Rosita shoves the navy fabric to one side and goes with my father to his cubicle. She plops down on the wooden chair, her legs wide apart. Not that she reveals anything under the cotton skirt, which sags between her thighs.

This is what he has to contend with, my father thinks. This new breed. Girls who don't want to work to get paid. He doesn't mind laying them off, but he likes to think he can teach them a little something first.

"So, Rosalie, you know why I call you in here?" my father asks.

"Rosita."

"Rosita," he corrects.

"Because you got nothing to keep you busy," she says and laughs at her joke.

He studies her, wondering how careful he has to be. Some of these girls, they have boyfriends who'd just as soon pull a knife on you as look at you. "I don't get it," he says. "The less you do, the less you make."

"What are you picking on me for?" She puts a hand on the front of her neck, as if she feels a choking from him.

"How many times I warned you? As many as there are pencils in this cup. Again this morning you're gabbing with Lena and Flora in front of Mr. Gershenfeld. You don't do your work, you distract the others. Tell me, what am I supposed to do?" He's tried everything, he thinks. Being nice. Being gruff. Hinting she could get an increase. Threatening she could get fired. He looks now into her laughing eyes. "All over the city," he says, "we're losing factories. In the south they can pay the workers peanuts. The working conditions, they're terrible." He has no idea if this is true. He embellishes his fib. "And for overtime, no extra pay. If you can't help me meet our quota," he tells Rosita, "then I'll get a replacement."

"I can help you." Pretending to stretch, she throws back her shoulders, and thrusts out her breasts. Her eyes are saying, Come on, I know what you really want.

My father explodes. He pounds the desk so hard the pencil holder flies off. The pencils shoot out in all directions. "Go!" he yells. "Empty your locker. If you want to sell your body, go to Times Square." He fishes out a dime from his pocket. "For carfare." He slaps it on the desk in front of her. "Here I need a seamstress, not a *kurveh*, a whore."

To soften the blow, my father takes Trudy downtown to the Tip Toe Inn. If they should run into someone they know, he has an explanation all prepared.

"Order what you like," he encourages Trudy. "Have soup. Have salad."

"Darling, have the whole *shmear*," the waiter says.

Trudy orders veal parmigiana with a side of creamed spinach. He orders flanken and chews and chews, but he can hardly swallow. Finally he gives up, so preoccupied he doesn't tell the waiter to pack up the leftovers. He studies the paper place mat, trying to work up the nerve to bring up Las Vegas.

Trudy beats him to the punch. "Did you send in the deposit?" she asks.

His boss won't give him time off, not even without pay, he tells Trudy, then the waiter sets down the footed glass cups. My father is about to yell that they didn't order dessert, when the waiter says, "Things go down easier with pudding." With a wink, he puts the bill on the table.

"You charge for the advice?" Trudy says. She and the waiter laugh.

"You can leave it in the tip," the waiter answers.

My father hears, but doesn't smile. As soon as the waiter is gone, my father says to Trudy, "I'll make it up to you. In the summer we'll go somewheres. Wherever you want."

"What will I tell Barney?" she says calmly.

"That you need a vacation."

"He'll ask for his two weeks then and come along. So what then?"

"Trudy, don't be angry. This isn't something I can help." He sees her thinking it over. "Trudy, in a minute I would go with you. Why not? You're very special to me, you know."

Silently she eats her chocolate pudding with a spritz of whipped cream in the center. When she's done, she asks, "Aren't you going to eat yours?"

"Here." He pushes it toward her. "Frankly, I don't need it." He pats his middle where lately he's gained a little weight. He looks at her, expecting a smile. "Are you sure *you* need it?" he teases.

"I owe you this." She picks up a glass and flings the water at him. She looks very attractive to him as she walks to the coat-rack, her high heels hammering the floor. Even as people stare, and the water runs down his head, he doesn't altogether mind. He feels proud that he has such a good-looking woman for his mistress.

For Thanksgiving we go to my Aunt Ruchel's. My mother wears her Persian lamb coat and the muff to match. My father has on his new suit. My brother wears his only suit, my sister her best dress. I am in a corduroy jumper, with a matching hat, a present from my father's boss. My mother has brought a bottle of Manischewitz cream sherry. Aunt Ruchel says, "You shouldn't have."

Except at bar mitzvahs and weddings, my mother has never seen such a fancy dinner. Silver and crystal on crisp pink linen. At each place, two gold-rimmed plates under a matching soup bowl. Two of everything: knives, forks, spoons, glasses—water and wine with a pink cloth napkin inside, folded like a fan. In the center of the long table, a spray of odd flowers, pink and purple and white. Where do you get such flowers in winter? my mother wonders. They must cost a lot of money. My aunt reads her mind. She whispers, "The business is going good, knock on wood."

My Cousin Rhonda alarms my parents by making the drinks at the bar, even though she is not allowed even to taste them. As I sit in an old playpen nearby, my Cousin Sandy hands me painted wooden blocks, exclaiming over each one. "This is an A. This is an apple." "This is a B. This is a banana."

"Nana," I say. "Eat."

My mother can't get over all the food. Besides the turkey with little paper crowns on the drumsticks, there's a huge roast beef. There are regular mashed potatoes spritzed into spiral towers, and sweet potatoes scooped into hollowed-out oranges. There are string beans with almonds, little carrot pies in a real crust. The shredded-beet salad is on a kind of lettuce my mother's never seen before. "Watercress," Cousin Rhonda says. The bread and rolls are served hot.

What a waste of money! my father thinks. They're just trying to show him up.

My mother remembers her sister in their youth, burning the Wheatena, burning the tapioca. The Thanksgiving before, the pepper in the potatoes made her eyes water. The turkey wasn't quite done when it came out, so it had to go back in. By the time they ate, everyone was starving. Still, when her sister asked her to come, she couldn't say no. "Since when you cook like this?" my mother asks now. Then she remembers the *kish* that the housekeeper made.

"Tell her," my Uncle Isaac says. "If you don't, I will." My aunt insists she's not trying to hide anything. "Millie!" my uncle calls out. "Millie!" A hefty Negro woman about twenty-five years old comes out of the swinging door that leads to the kitchen. "What, Mr. Pies?"

"Hear what she calls me?" my uncle says. "Mr. Pies. What a gal!"

"He just loves them pies," Millie says, "so I don't call him Mr. Peisner, I calls him Mr. Pies."

"Millie is our secret," he says. "If I weren't already married, I would run off with her."

Millie laughs, my aunt and uncle guffaw. "Oh, Daddy," Cousin Sandy says. Cousin Rhonda lowers her eyes. My mother smiles. My sister and brother give each other looks. My father stares at my uncle, shocked.

After Millie leaves the dining room, my aunt tells my mother how lucky they are to have found Millie. She lowers her voice to say Millie's husband is a *shikker*, a drunkard, and Millie has to support him.

"Liquor isn't *billik vi borscht*," my uncle says. "Cheap as borscht," he translates.

Aunt Ruchel continues to sing Millie's praises. "And she's so good with the girls. I let her drive my car to take them to the riding academy."

My mother has this fleeting thought that she knows is foolish, but she can't help herself: When the time comes, she will leave me with her sister, and Millie can help raise me.

"Did you ever hear of such a thing?" my father asks Trudy. "How my brother-in-law can talk like that in front of the children! It's disgusting."

Trudy runs her tongue over the curly hairs on his belly. "Is this disgusting?" she says.

"What are you doing?" he asks.

"Relax. Close your eyes."

He closes his eyes, and two seconds later they pop open. He's heard of women doing that, prostitutes, but a nice woman?

"Relax," Trudy says. "Close your eyes. Now!"

He closes his eyes. Soon he is no longer thinking about anything but her mouth and tongue on his flesh. He is about to burst when she pulls away and climbs on top of him.

"Remember," she says, "take your time." She leans down to kiss him. He can smell himself on her breath. He feels a little nauseated. He starts to shrivel.

"Oh you!" She caresses him back to full strength and puts him inside her. Then she starts to move against him. To keep from climaxing, he thinks about baseball. *Duke Snyder. Jackie Robinson. Gil Hodges.* He feels her hipbones grinding against him, harder and harder. Then she stops and lets out a sigh of pleasure. "Good boy! Now let's take care of you."

The stopping and starting has diminished his appetite. She grinds away on top of him, but not much is happening. Not until he recalls my aunt's housekeeper, Millie, standing in the doorway. Millie with her big breasts. His buttocks rise a few inches off the bed as he bucks into Trudy's body.

As he lies on his back panting, Trudy says, "You never thought about it?"

"What?"

"What it would be like to make love to a Negro?"

"What's wrong with you?" he says. "You have a sick mind."

At home, before he falls into a deep sleep, he wonders if he could ever do such a thing, have sex with a Negro. No, he thinks at first. But then a voice deep within him says, *What if you could be sure that no one would ever find out?*

O ne night, while my father sleeps beside her, my mother presses her legs together. This feeling, it's driving her *meshugge*. She reaches under her nightgown. A crazy old lady, she thinks. She squeezes the outside of her love pocket together. She doesn't know exactly what she's doing, what she's trying to do. One part rubs against another. Something strange starts to happen, but then she drifts off to sleep.

The next time is after my father has been inside her. She waits for his snore before she starts squeezing. The little cheeks, she calls them. There's a little spark of pleasure between them. She tries not to make a sound, not even of breathing. Her face in the pillow, she imagines someone— who?—some faceless man touching her breasts.

The sensation is not what she would call pleasing. Pleasing is when she gets her hair brushed in the beauty salon. This is like scratching an itch. She scratches and scratches, and then it happens. That miracle. Unbelievable, she thinks, how ignorant she was. Her whole life.

T he radio is on, I imagine, as my mother puts away the blouses she has carefully ironed. She sings along with Doris Day. " 'Once I had a se-cret love, he lived with-in the heart of me . . .' " When she comes across a rolled-up paper bag in my sister's drawer, she doesn't hesitate a second to open it. She shakes out the contents on the bed: a cape and a paper crown.

My sister walks in, screaming, "Mama! What're you doing with my costume?"

"For what is this?" my mother asks, unruffled.

"The school play. I play the queen."

"You never told me," my mother says. "When are you playing?"

Mimi shrugs. "Oh, in a couple of weeks."

"You have to tell me a day so I can come."

"You don't have to come." Mimi looks down at the floor. "It's not that important, Mama."

"*Nisht gefonfet.* Don't double-talk me, you! It's religious, this play?"

Mimi winces. "It's not religious."

"What, you think I wouldn't want to see my own daughter on the stage?"

"You're making a whole thing out of it. It's no big deal."

"So what then? You're afraid you'll make some mistake? That don't matter," my mother consoles. "Who wouldn't make a mistake?"

"I know my lines. Mr. Glover says I'm very good."

"Oh, I get it." My mother thwacks my sister on the head with the empty paper bag, once, twice. "What, you're shamed to have me to school?" Her voice rises. "Why? Your mother she's an immigrant? An ignorant foreigner?"

"If you want to know," Mimi says, "yes! Yes, yes, yes! Because this is how you act. You don't act normal, like my friends' parents." My sister snatches the bag and throws it on the floor. As she runs into the bathroom, she passes my father.

"What's going on?" he asks.

"Don't mind her," my mother says. "It's that time of month." She goes to the radio and turns up the volume, but there's another song playing now, one she doesn't recognize.

"Mimi's got a fresh mouth." He doesn't add, Maybe she

gets it from her mother. He wonders why everything with women has to do with the curse.

At Sunday dinner my mother stares out the window, into the alley, at a wash line strung with clothes, all frozen, looking like headless paper dolls.

"You can save your arguing for summer," my father is saying, but my brother and sister continue their battle.

"How can you like the Dodgers?" Mimi taunts. "They're in Brooklyn."

"Because they're the best," Sheldon says. "Wait till next year! The Yankees stink like Mr. Mangiameli."

My sister sticks out her tongue. "Pee-you, they don't stink like your feet," she says. "Or like people who don't wear deodorant."

So that's how she looks in the eyes of her American kid, my mother thinks. Is that how Harry sees her? The way he acted, like she gave off a stink. Why? Now that he's had her, for what does he need her? To embarrass him? *Fool.* That's what she is. *A big fool.* To think that he ever loved her.

My mother tries to make it up to my father. She cooks his favorite dishes: stuffed cabbage, halibut baked with sour cream and corn flakes on top, kasha varnishkes. She buys the Ivory soap, what he likes. She squeezes out enough money from what he gives her to buy his favorite, a lemon pie, from the A&P. She buys him two shirts instead of one, for Hanukkah.

One night she waits up for him to come home, without cold cream on her face, which he hates. That night, after they make love, she sleeps with him in the double bed. At dawn when my sister wakes and sees the bed next to her empty, she goes to the other bedroom to take a peek. My mother is lying in the crook of my father's arm, his hand over her breast. That's so disgusting, my sister thinks. They're so old to be *doing* it.

At first my father doesn't notice the change in my mother. Then one day it occurs to him. For a long time she hasn't complained about his staying out three nights a week. He begins to notice other things, how when he tells the children something, she backs him up instead of being sarcastic. Or how when he asks for a glass of water in the living room, she doesn't say, "The exercise will do you good," but hurries to bring it to him. This is how she was when they first married, in every way but one, a perfect wife. Not that all of it made up— can make up—for his disappointment with her in bed.

One evening, when he comes home from work, he sees she is wearing a dress, not one of those ugly smocks. "Where are you going?" he asks.

"Nowhere. I thought I should put on a little something for you."

"For me?"

"For who else?" There is a twinkle in her eye as she says it. Later he remembers the look. It keeps coming back to him. What does it mean? he asks himself. Is she making fun of him?

In the middle of the night he wakes up after a bad dream. A wolf had clamped its jaws onto his leg . . . He lies there, sweating in the dark. Now he hears a thump, thump, thump. Mr. Mangiameli walking without his wooden leg. He is going to the kitchen. Soon my father hears voices. The boarder's and my mother's. He puts on his robe and creeps into the hallway outside. For a long time he listens as the faucet is turned on and off, the Frigidaire door is opened and shut. He can't quite hear what they are saying, but as long as they talk, he thinks he shouldn't worry. Then suddenly the light is snapped out, and my father hurries, as quietly as he can, back to bed.

He strains to hear where they are going. Now he worries my mother is in the boarder's room. When he goes to see, there is a light under the door. He presses his ear to the door, but he hears nothing. Then he goes to the bedroom my mother shares with my sister and me. Quietly, he turns the knob.

"Who's there?" my mother yells.

"Shhh, it's just me."

"You're not feeling so hot?"

"I thought I heard a mouse," he says.

"What!" she screams. She turns on the light. My sister wakes up. "A mouse!" my mother shrieks. Now she and my sister are standing on the beds.

"What is it?" Mr. Mangiameli calls out. He comes hopping in.

"Maybe I was mistaken," my father says. "I heard some creaking. I thought a mouse."

"The way she keeps house," Mr. Mangiameli says, "so spick-and-span, the mouse would starve."

Over breakfast my father keeps an eye on them, to see if anything special passes between. My mother makes some little joke about the French toast, and Mr. Mangiameli laughs. When my father asks what's so funny, my mother says, "Don't bother yourself." That day at work, the girls at the factory give him a new name, Mr. BowWow, for all the barking he does.

To check on my mother when he isn't there, he asks her at night what she was doing during the day. Then he asks my sister or brother, to see if he gets the same story. He creeps up on my mother and the boarder whenever he knows they are in the same room together. So far he has not been able to catch them.

One night he decides to leave work early. He tells his boss he has a toothache. As quietly as he can he slips his key in the lock of the apartment door. Mr. Mangiameli is in his own room, but my mother is in the bathroom, which is nearby. When she comes out my father asks, "What were you doing in there so long?"

"My business," she says. "What else?"

"I don't believe you."

"Zei nit kein nar."

"Who are you calling foolish?" he says.

"You don't believe me, go smell," my mother says. *"Gevalt!"*

She's only bluffing, my father thinks. But as soon as he gets to the bathroom door, he concedes she was telling the truth, at least in part. He doesn't even have to inhale.

The images in my father's head torture him. His wife in the arms of a *kalikeh*, a cripple. He tries to get them out of his mind, but they are so vivid. He see the two of them kissing, embracing. He can even imagine the *shtupping*, with Mr. Mangiameli on top of my mother, the stump resting outside her hip.

After the first time, my mother returns to the top of Fort Tryon Park, again and again. Usually the wind is brisk but not worse than the wind off the ocean in Brooklyn. Today, though, it makes my face look raw. Trying to find a warmer place to sit, my mother takes a good look at the strange building she's barely noticed earlier. It pokes up in the middle of nothing but trees. She can hardly get over it. So big, like a mansion, with stones shaped like bricks, large ones and small ones. The windows are scooped out in the shape of long, skinny gumdrops. There's a round tower and a tall square one. Each part has the same kind of wavy roof, like red clay. What kind of place is this? she wonders. Could a family be living in the park? Or is the building for offices? Why do the couples going in act like they're visiting?

She looks around for someone to ask. There is only a woman who is walking her Chihuahua. My mother usually avoids dogs because they carry germs, but she goes up to the woman anyhow. "Could you tell me, please, what this place is?"

"The Cloisters," the woman says. "A monastery they brought over in pieces from the Middle Ages."

"Oh," my mother says, but she hasn't the faintest idea what the woman is talking about. She hardly notices that the dog has jumped on her leg until the woman says, "Down, Mitzi!"

"*Oy!*" my mother says, seeing the run in her stocking. "Thank you for the information, but it wasn't free."

"She was just being playful," the woman says. "Weren't you, Mitzi!" The dog barks sharply, twice. The woman looks my mother up and down. After she gives me a once-over also, she hands my mother a five-dollar bill. "For your stockings."

"I don't have change," my mother tells her.

"Keep the change. Let's go, Mitzi." The dog pulls the woman away.

My mother wants to fling the money after them, but her practical side takes over. She will put the five dollars into her new savings account.

At home she asks my brother if he knows what a monaster is.

"A monster?"

"Monaster. Up on top of the Fort Tryon. A building."

"That's the Cloisters, Ma."

"And what is a Cloisters?"

"Beats me," he says. "Ask Mimi."

"She's not speaking to her *mameh*."

"I forgot," he says. "I'll ask her."

Later, as my mother darns the run in her hose, Sheldon tells her a monastery is a place for nuns or monks. "They're in seclusion from the world. All they do is pray. Mimi says, but I don't know if it's true, that they're not allowed even to talk to each other."

"Nuns and monks in the park?" my mother says. "She must be telling you some *bobbe-myseh*." Some fairy tale.

Not since her obsession with Harry has anything taken hold of my mother like the Cloisters. Every day now, she wheels me up the winding paths until she finds out she can go to the subway tunnel at 190th and take the elevator up. From there it's a short walk into the park and to the stone building.

She stares at the outside, trying to figure who's going in, who's coming out. Then we sit on the bench. Before we go back, she studies the building again. Depending on the time, we take the elevator down or walk the long way.

One day, she sees a group of mothers and children enter the Cloisters. It's more than she can stand. She unhooks me from the stroller, parks it out in front, and takes me inside. Nobody stops her. Nobody asks her anything. She goes up the marble steps, past a doorway flanked by statues, and finds the mothers and children in a large hall. The paintings on the wall are in dark colors, black and red mostly. Like in a dream, nothing connects with anything else. A room. A garden. Another room.

She follows the group to a courtyard, and as they walk one way around the outside, she walks the other. She stops to look at the animal heads carved into the columns, and when she glances across the garden, the mothers are gone. She tries one door and then another, but she doesn't find them. Now she and I are on our own.

In other large rooms, there are rugs on the walls, and a chandelier, like in fancy living rooms. There are statues every-where, and a half-naked Jesus Christ. Such surprise on his face! she thinks. How can this be God? With all the crosses around, she concedes maybe nuns and priests have something to do with it, after all. There's even a little church inside, with a huge cross and chairs for the congregation. A church in a park! She can't get over it. She wonders if there are parks with synagogues.

She puts me down from time to time, but when I start to run in the wrong direction, she picks me up again.

Each garden has different arches, pointy, round. Beautiful. We sit for a while on a backless marble bench as she watches the people come through. They don't all look Catholic. Some even look Jewish, she would bet on it.

Finally she is tired. "Enough already!" she says to me. It takes her a long time to find the way out. Outside, she looks for my stroller but it isn't there. She is sure someone stole it, a hundred dollars when it was new, my aunt told her. My mother leans back against the wall. *Gevalt!* How will she explain it to Ruben? She doesn't want to tell him where she was. She's dis-covered a little world she wants to keep for her own.

I wriggle in her arms, and she puts me down. At the end of the driveway I see a little boy pushing a stroller. I run toward him.

"Wunderkind!" The word bursts from my mother, and she runs after me. She thinks maybe her eyes are going bad that she didn't see it herself. She talks to the little boy, but he won't give up the stroller. His grip tightens. My mother laughs as she tries to get his fingers off the handle. Then from nowhere the boy's mother comes up to us. She smacks the little boy.

"For what are you hitting him?" my mother says. "He's just playing."

"He's not supposed to play with someone else's belongings," the woman says sharply.

"Lady," my mother says, "he means no harm. He's just a little kid."

"I hope your daughter doesn't grow up to be a thief," the woman says.

My mother decides that the woman isn't going to spoil her afternoon. She makes a rude sound with her tongue half out, then plops me in the stroller.

She looks at her watch now. Was she really inside the Cloisters building for over three hours? It went like a minute. In the subway elevator, the operator, an elderly Negro man, says to her, "You been up to the Cloisters?"

"How did you know this?" she asks.

"This time of year, middle of the day, that's all we get up here. A mighty interesting place, the Cloisters."

"You been there?"

"I go during lunch."

"Can you tell me, Mister, what is this place? A church?"

"A what?"

"Church." She pronounces it *choych.* "You know, where they go to pray. Church."

"Gotcha. Some of the things, they came from churches from all over Europe. They put them into this museum." The elevator stops. "Watch your step."

She smiles to herself. A *museum.* She's never been to one before. Paintings, she thinks now. The statues. She should have known. My mother wheels the stroller down the hill to Broadway. "The man learned me something," she says to me.

She can't wait to go back. *Museum.* She loves the sound of the word. For the first time since we moved to Manhattan, my mother feels as if she has some reason to get up the next day.

My father tells his boss he has to leave early on account of his stomachache.

Mr. Gershenfeld narrows his dark eyes. "Your girlfriend's giving you a pain?"

"The tuna fish, I think it was old," my father says.

"You'll come in early tomorrow?"

"Certainly," my father says. "An hour early."

When he emerges from the Dyckman Street station, he stops at the newsstand outside a candy store and reads about a nuclear submarine. He'll give the boarder time to hang himself.

Behind him, he hears a familiar laugh. Trudy's? He looks around, and there she is, passing right by but looking toward the street. He doesn't recognize the man walking beside her who's waving his arms.

He forgets about the boarder at home and follows Trudy and the man, staying far enough behind so he won't be seen, and close enough not to lose them. He wishes he could hear what they're saying. They walk directly to her building. From outside the vestibule, through the leaded glass, he can see them wait for the elevator. A moment after they enter the car, he runs into the lobby, to see on what floor the elevator stops. Trudy's floor. Only one stop.

He punches the button and takes the elevator up, rings her bell. When she opens her door, he charges in past her. He will kill this man. He will beat him to a pulp.

"What's the matter?" Trudy asks. "What are you looking for? There's no one here."

My father searches the entire apartment. "Where is he? I saw you with him," he yells.

"Where?"

"Don't give me where. Outside. On Dyckman Street, and then you came home."

She rolls her eyes. "Ruben, I don't know what's gotten into you. That's my neighbor down the hall. I ran into him at the deli, then we walked back together."

It's too much for my father. He crumples onto the sofa, his head in his hands. For what is he being tortured? he asks himself. He doesn't know anymore who to believe.

"Something happen at work?" Trudy asks. "Your boss give you trouble?" My father shakes his head no. "Then it's the girls. Too many women for Ruben to handle," she jokes. "Ooh la la!"

"That's it." He looks up at her. She seems concerned, as if she cares for him. "Let's forget it," he says, "and go out to eat."

In the Sun Luck Restaurant Trudy winces as my father dips his egg roll in the sharp mustard. "Doesn't it make you sneeze?" she says. "Ha-choo!" she pretends. She laughs. He dunks the egg roll, bathing the crust with creamy pale mustard. His sinuses burn as he chews, but he shrugs, as if he feels nothing, and looks away when his eyes tear.

He sees the owner of the restaurant seat a group of raucous teenagers at a long table in the center of the room, girls on one side, boys on the other. The girls face the booth along the wall where my father and Trudy are. He tries not to look at their tight sweaters, but he can't help it. He takes a forkful of chicken chow mein, steals a glance, then another. Even from a couple of yards away, he can see the sweater of the blond girl is angora. Soft. Her pageboy bobbing, she jokes easily with the girls next to her, and the boys across the way. It's a whole different world now, my father thinks. If only he could do things all over again . . .

"You're not listening," Trudy says. She's holding out a picture now of her nephew's daughter, Hannah.

"Very nice." He sucks the red and green Jell-O cubes off his spoon.

"But look at her eyes. They're not normal."

"Too bad." He glances at the blonde across the way. She and the boy at the end are having a mock duel with chopsticks.

"Still thinking about work?" Trudy says.

"If you had to do it over, would you marry Barney?" he asks.

"Knowing what I know? I think so. He was a good provider. He was good to the children. He's a good cook. Ruben, don't sulk. I'm not finished answering. But once our daughters went to college, I should have divorced him. After twenty years, he became like a brother to me." She doesn't tell my father what Barney has to do in bed to get excited.

My father doesn't know where it comes from when the question pops out. "Why don't you divorce him now?"

"And then what?"

"And marry me."

She looks up at the ceiling and sighs. "By the time we go through the whole thing, we won't want each other anymore."

"I don't know." He tries to imagine what it would be like, to have her in the same bed, to have her whenever he wants.

"Pop?"

My father and Trudy look at the gangling teenager standing over them.

"What are you doing here?" my brother asks.

"What for you're asking me?" my father says brusquely.

"This is your son?" Trudy says. "Nice to meet you. Sheldon, isn't it?" With that curly hair, he doesn't resemble Ruben, she thinks.

My brother ignores her. "What are you doing here, Pop? Mama thinks you're out playing cards."

My father gets up. "Let's go outside," he says to my brother. He sees now that the chair opposite the blonde with the tight sweater is empty. Was Sheldon there the whole time? Did he hear anything? All this flutters through his mind as he walks up the aisle. He will tell his son to mind his own business. But when he turns around in the vestibule to speak to him, my brother is not there.

Everything in the Cloisters my mother finds fascinating, but she doesn't know why. The carvings on every doorway, every arch, she could study for a year. Bearded men. Children. Women with crowns. Whole bodies but often with noses or fingertips missing. Because of juvenile delinquents, she thinks. So mean! Sometimes the carvings are heads. Many are of strange animals. Some seem both animal and human. She can't get over the faces. As if they're screaming or they want to scream. On top of the stone coffins the faces are peaceful. She wonders if there are real bodies inside. She wonders if it's a sin for a Jew to be there.

Each room is full of treasures. Stained-glass windows. The furniture. She loves the chairs with backs taller than she is. The gold plates. The tall candles and metal candlesticks. The atmosphere is very strong. Most of all she loves the varieties of stone. Large stones and small ones, on the walls, the floors, the arches. Some are smooth, most are rough. Some are gray, some brown or yellowish. She could never explain how they make her feel. Sad, as if she's in a real prison. Yet quiet and calm. In each room the clack of her heels is very loud. My babble is very loud.

I like the echo. I babble louder. For once my mother doesn't tell me to be quiet. The echoes to her are an eerie music.

She imagines trying to explain the fascination to her sister. She imagines my Aunt Ruchel saying, *So for you it's an escape.*

Yes and no, she would tell her. She would say, *In the Cloisters I am in a world away from everything. At the same time I feel there more like myself, when I see the beauty all around me.*

She laughs when she thinks how the place also makes her feel like a nun. A very peaceful nun. "See that?" she says to me. We're beside a silvery statue of a woman with a little baby in her arms. "Look how the woman smiles. *Alevai*, I should be so happy."

My brother threads a needle for my mother because she cannot see to do it herself. "Get yourself some glasses, Ma. Why do you keep putting it off?"

"Because your *mameh* is vain. Getting glasses, *oy*, I'm so old."

"You're not old," he tells her. They both know he is just being kind.

The optometrist on Dyckman Street tests my mother's eyes, then she picks out some frames, black with a couple of rhinestones at the corners. He tells her to return in a week, he'll have them ready. When she comes back, he slips the glasses on her. "Bifocals take getting used to," he tells her. He hands her a newspaper. She can't get over how big the print is.

"Come outside," he says, and in front of his store, my mother is amazed she can read the signs across the way. As we go up the street she says the names of all the stores opposite us, until she comes to one she has never seen before, not even from up close. *Vey iz mir!*" she says in a half whisper.

She pushes my stroller out into the middle of the street. A car honks, but my mother doesn't even hear it. A taxi narrowly misses us. On the sidewalk, my mother wheels the stroller by the curb so she can see farther up the block. So she can decide if what she thinks she saw is really there. *"Nit gedacht,"* she says aloud. It shouldn't be.

Her footsteps slow as she surveys the sheets of plywood, some pipes. There's a new store going in, all right. And the sign is already up, clear as anything she's ever seen in her whole life: MAGIC SHOES.

Mr. Mangiameli starts eating dinner with us in addition to breakfast, for which he pays my mother extra. It is my father's latest scheme to make money. Behind his back my father calls him The Cripple. "I wonder what The Cripple does in that store," my father will say, meaning the fruit and vegetable store near the George Washington Bridge.

"A wooden leg don't take away his brain," my mother answers.

"How can he serve the customers with a limp and a crutch?" he prods.

"How should I know? Go to the store, see for yourself."

My father is only testing her. She is so secretive lately, humming to herself all the time now. He wishes he could be in Las Vegas, instead, with Trudy. He gave her ten dollars to bet for him. He asks my mother, "What does Mr. Mangiameli do in his room at night?"

"*Nu*, he listens to the radio, what else? Sometimes he goes up to the corner to get cigarettes. You see him. Why are you asking me?"

One night after supper, my mother gets me ready for my bath. She takes off my clothes and starts the water in the tub. I run into the living room past my father napping in his chair. The phone rings. I run into the foyer and try to open the outside door, but it's locked. I drag over a chair so I can reach the lock and turn it, as I've seen my mother do a hundred times. With both hands I pull the door open. The chair tips over but I'm not hurt, just startled. I scamper down the three marble steps and open another door. Exhilarated, I run down the stoop and into the street.

I run into Mr. Mangiameli coming back from buying cigarettes. He sees me on the sidewalk, naked. "You naughty! You'll freeze to death!" He picks me up in his arms and carries me home. I am laughing because he rocks me back and forth. He doesn't do it on purpose. It's because of his bad limp.

My mother answers the phone—a wrong number—then goes to look for me in the kitchen, under the table where I like to play. She sees the chair by the open door. She thinks I've been kidnapped, maybe taken to the roof. Things happen up there, always at night. She runs up the five flights, losing one slipper along the way. Expecting to see my little body sprawled on the concrete below, she sidles to the edge of the roof and looks down. Then she sees us coming up the stoop, Mr. Mangiameli with me in his arms, but we don't see her.

Mr. Mangiameli carries me into the apartment. He walks all the way through, looking for my mother in every room. Soon he hears her at the door. He goes to meet her. My father wakes from his nap. He hears my mother say, "Oh my darling, how can I ever thank you!"

He creeps up on the hallway where we are. When he pokes his head around the corner, he sees me clasped in Mr. Mangiameli's embrace, his palm spread over my naked buttocks. He sees my mother with her arms around Mr. Mangiameli.

My father snatches me out of his boarder's arms, sets me down, and pushes me toward the living room. Then he punches Mr. Mangiameli in the head and face. "You keep your hands off my family!" he yells. "What kind of ungrateful monster are you?" He punches Mr. Mangiameli some more. "You cripple!" he shouts. "I took you into my home."

My mother is screaming. I run back to see what is happening. I am screaming, too. There is blood everywhere. My mother tries to get between them, but my father pushes her out of the way. My mother picks me up and carries me to the bedroom. Soon I hear a loud bang, bang, bang. My father is hammering Mr. Mangiameli's wooden leg to pieces.

After Mr. Mangiameli moves out, we move again, to a smaller apartment on the fourth floor, no elevator.

Part Three

On a humid Saturday morning in July, I imagine my brother is lying on the sofa, thumbing through *Collier's* magazine. My sister is in the bathroom, plucking her eyebrows with her new tweezers. Sitting on the floor in the bedroom, I am teaching a stuffed cotton doll to walk. My mother is at the sewing machine, the electric fan blowing on her legs. My father knots his tie in front of the mirror.

"You're going out?" my mother asks him. "It's too late for synagogue."

"All I do is work, work, work. Can't I go play cards?" In truth he is taking Trudy to the Brass Rail to celebrate her birthday, one day early.

"With a tie in this weather?" she says. "It's ninety-five degrees. Maybe I should turn off the fan, *nu?*"

"So I'm wearing a tie. Are you looking for trouble?"

"Trouble, it finds me. Who has to look?" She thinks of my sister, who was caught shoplifting. "You're not having lunch?"

"Put it away for me. I'll have it tonight."

"It's the little one's birthday," she tells him. "You forgot already?"

"What do you want me to do?" he asks.

"*Alevai*, stay home, have lunch with your *mishpokhe*, sing 'Happy Birthday,' help blow out the three candles. Plus one for good luck."

"You told me I don't sing on key. So, blow the candles without me."

My mother snaps off the light on her sewing machine and marches to the kitchen. She removes the lid from the big pot simmering on the stove and dumps the potato soup into the sink. She eases the blintzes from the frying pan into a casserole dish, covers it, and puts it in the Frigidaire. She stomps to the bathroom and knocks loudly. "Come out of there!" she yells.

My sister slips the tweezers into the front of her bra. She saunters into the living room, expecting to be interrogated over something she's done.

"We're eating out," my mother announces. "At the Lucky Sun. Get dressed!"

Flanked by my mother and sister, my brother pushes my stroller along Dyckman Street. When we are nearly opposite the restaurant, my mother refuses to cross over. We go up to Broadway to cross, and we come back down the other side. With her eyes to the ground, my mother strides ahead of us.

"It's Magic Shoes," my sister whispers to my brother. "I bet she thinks it's unlucky to pass right in front of it."

"It's a new store," Sheldon says. "What's it ever done to her?"

Mimi tells him how my mother threw a fit in the store in Brighton Beach. "Every time we're on this block," she says, "Mama takes off her glasses. Look, she's not wearing them now."

In the restaurant it turns out my mother left her glasses at home, so she can't read the menu. My brother starts to read it to her but she clops her hand over it. "Order me something. The little one can eat from my plate."

"Ma, you finally buy glasses, then you forget to wear them," he says. "They look fine on you." My sister concurs.

"*Sha!*" my mother yells. Shut up! The other people in the restaurant stare. My sister cringes.

Sheldon is dying to tell Mimi about the last time he was in the Sun Luck, but he doesn't. He recalls how he walked away from my father and went back to his friends at the table, his insides churning. He couldn't help telling his girlfriend. Lenore said, "What does your father see in her? She's not nearly as attractive as your mom." It surprises him that anyone would think his mother attractive. But then, Lenore has only seen her from a distance."

From her combination plate, my mother makes me a little plate of my own, with vegetables cut into tiny pieces. When we're done, she says, "No dessert, we have the birthday cake at home. How old are you?" she asks me.

"Three," I answer.

"How old am I?" she asks.

"Ten!" I scream. It's the biggest number I know.

"I'm telling you, she's a genius," my brother says.

"Don't get carried away. She's just a little precocious," Mimi says.

"'Genius.' 'Precocious.' Don't make her out to be a freak," my mother says. "*Alevai*, she's a normal kid." My mother cannot tell them she is bowled over by the things that come out of my mouth from time to time.

After we leave the Sun Luck, my mother says, "Walk me to the corner. I want to have a look." Mimi elbows Sheldon. We walk back up to Broadway. When we get there, Mimi says, "What did you want to see?"

"I forget," my mother says. "Let's cross." We cross the street and walk back down on the other side.

"Ma," Sheldon says, "what are you avoiding? Magic Shoes?"

"For Magic Shoes, *a deigeh hob ich*. I don't give a hang. For what you ask?"

"The way you act when we get close."

My mother taps her head as if to say he has it all wrong. With eyes like that, she thinks, he'll never need glasses.

Later, my brother consults his girlfriend. "My ma acts as if the store is poison," he tells her. "She's such a character!"

"Maybe your dad's girlfriend works there," Lenore speculates.

"You think my ma knows what's going on?" Sheldon says. "It would kill her if she knew. All hell would break loose."

My brother isn't with his girlfriend when she noses around Magic Shoes. The shoe clerks are all men, the cashier a mousy-looking woman around thirty. She'd be very pretty, Lenore thinks, if only she would fix herself up. This she reports to my brother as they lie on the big lawn in Fort Tryon Park.

"My ma's weird," he says. "All that old-country stuff. According to her, anything could be unlucky, even dropping a knife." He tells Lenore about the Evil Eye. "She used to embarrass us every time she spit in the street."

"Used to?"

"That was in Brooklyn. She's different, ever since we moved. Mimi and I tried to figure it out."

"Have you asked her?"

My brother turns on his side and chucks Lenore under the chin. "I love how you think." Lenore is not sure how to take this. He puts his arms across her waist, leans down, and kisses the tip of her nose. "Grrr," he says, but she gives him a warning look. She's already told him she doesn't like making out where other people can see. He goes on talking. "My ma's the opposite of you. A lot goes on in her head that she'll never tell you."

"Have you asked her?" Lenore repeats.

"Mimi's asked her about the garlic she used to keep in her pocket. We used to stink something awful when she made us go to school with it. Then we got smart enough to stash it under the milkbox."

"So what did she say? About the garlic."

"She said, and I quote, 'If the Devil has it in for me, I must deserve it.'"

"Wow! She's probably got a guilt complex."

"You think so?"

Lenore turns on her side and searches my brother's brown eyes. Even though he's always working on cars or listening to ball games, he's the only boy she knows who also talks about emotions. "What's your mom so guilty about?"

"I don't know, unless it's not having enough money to give us things we want. Or the education to keep up with us. She flies off the handle, if you get on her nerves. Her family, they went through a lot in Russia, or maybe it was Poland. She's not sure which. She's got a really good heart, though."

"I'd love to talk to her." Lenore's strawberry-colored lips pout.

My brother thinks she is so beautiful, lying there like that, hair the color of corn draping her cheek, her round breast pushing against the blouse. He cannot tell her he has the feeling my mother won't like her.

Each time she sees Sheldon now, Lenore *nudzhes* him. "When do I meet your mom?"

"Tell you what," he says one day. "I'll take you to her favorite place, if you bring your swimsuit and pack us a lunch."

"What should I pack?"

"Anything. Salami and pickles." The heck with the lunch, he thinks. He's dying to see what she looks like in a bathing suit.

They go on the sweltering subway to Brighton Beach. As soon as Lenore sees the million people lying towel to towel on the sand, she says, "You kidding me? She likes this better than Far Rockaway?"

My brother grins. "I swear to God. I told you she was weird."

As Lenore removes her blouse and skirt, my brother is nervous with anticipation. He pretends to be busy folding his shirt and pants into a makeshift pillow, but he watches out of the corner of his eye. When she has stripped down to her bathing suit, my brother gives her a quick once-over. "Mamma mia!" he says, and whistles.

"I got it at Orbach's," she tells him, meaning the satiny black suit.

"Snazzy!" he says, although her hips could be bigger. He wishes he had brought the camera. She is so gorgeous he can hardly bear to look. "Race you," he says, and sprints straight toward the ocean. Later he rubs suntan oil into her back. "Ooh," she says, "you do that so nice." They eat salami-and-pickle sandwiches and sunbathe for a while, till she complains she's frying.

"French-fried Lenore. Can I have her with ketchup?"

"You silly."

"There's only one place that's got shade," he tells her, and takes her under the Boardwalk.

In the cool shade, as long as the Boardwalk itself, they lie on towels and French-kiss, again and again. Too late, my brother realizes he should have brought a blanket to cover them with. He shields her body with his own as he pulls down the straps from her bathing suit. The warmth of her breasts on his bare skin sends a hum through his body.

A line from a song he never appreciated before comes back to him: "When the moon hits your eye like a big piz-za pie, that's a-more." *A-more. A-more. A big pizza pie.*

My brother is in love.

I imagine my sister running her hand along the cotton tops hanging on the department store rack. *Eenie, meenie, miney-mo.* Her pulse races as she plucks off three tops in her size, solid, polka dot, and striped. It's true she needs clothes. Soon school will start again, and my father refuses to buy her anything new. "I'm still paying off your Uncle Yakob," he says. "Moving to Manhattan costs a lot of money." It isn't the need for clothes that brings her back to Alexander's, though. It's the thrill.

In the dressing room she tries on the tops, slowly. The anticipation makes her shiver. She buttons each blouse completely, tucks it into her skirt, turns this way and that, as she gazes in the three-paneled mirror. Finally she decides on the black-and-white striped. She leaves it on, tucks the price tag into the sleeve, tucks the collar under, and buttons her blouse up over it. She studies herself from the front, from the side. She is building to that moment of tension, a fright like she's only had on the Cyclone, as if her life could end right there, on a dime.

Her pulse pounding, she strolls leisurely onto the sales floor. She pretends to have an interest in the pedal pushers on a rack against the wall. She looks up. No one seems to be lurking around, waiting to catch her. She walks slowly, casually, to the escalator, steps onto it, and turns sideways to see who has followed her. Only a prim-looking woman with a tight, curly permanent.

On the main floor my sister takes a circuitous route, through handbags, through men's shirts. Now is the moment. She steps into the revolving door. For a couple of long seconds she is captured within the glassed partition. Her adrenaline surges as the door moves, then opens onto the street. She blinks in the brilliant sunshine splayed over the Grand Concourse. Not breathing, she waits for the clop of an arm, for what feels like Death to come to get her, and when it doesn't, she knows she has survived. Again.

At home she stuffs the tags from the striped blouse into the bottom of the garbage. She waits a week before wearing the top. Right away my mother asks, "From where you get the zebra?"

"My friend Suzanne," Mimi says. "I'm just borrowing it."

My mother pleads with her to stop stealing. "Number one, it's a sin. Number two, if they catch you again, they send you to reform school."

"I told you, I borrowed it," Mimi says defiantly.

My mother feels she has no choice but to tell my father.

My father watches as my mother goes through my sister's dresser drawers. She pulls out anything she doesn't recognize. When my sister comes home, my father yanks her by the sleeve to the bedroom. There he points to the pile on the bed. "Never did I ever think," he says. "Tell me, am I looking at stolen goods? Admit it!"

My sister shoots my mother a look as if to say, You betrayed me. My mother feels terrible, but she cannot let her daughter steal.

"Tell me!" My father shakes Mimi by the shoulders and keeps smacking her face till she admits she's been shoplifting. Then he gives her one more smack, backhanded, for good measure. He tells her, "For one month you're staying home. Period. No going out with friends. No allowance."

My mother thinks this is a good idea until my father says, "If you have to stay here with her, you make sure she don't go nowhere."

Later she says to my father, "For what should I be cooped up? I have shopping to do, I have to take the little one for fresh air."

My father gets angry. "Which is more important? We have to teach Mimi a lesson." When my mother doesn't agree right away, he says, "Of course you can go out, but not all day."

At night, she tosses and turns in her bed. Less time for the Cloisters, my mother thinks. Why does this have to happen? She feels resentful, panicky even. The Cloisters is her one happiness. Then she remembers the woman whose boy took the stroller. *I hope your daughter doesn't grow up to be a thief.* From where does her daughter get the idea to steal? my mother wonders, but the answer comes to her the following week, when my father announces he is suing the Transit Authority.

The wicker seat in a subway car tore a hole in his pants, he says. This time my mother says something back. "Those pants, they were so thin already, I think they tore themselves."

"What do you know about it?" he answers. "You have a Ph.D. in textiles?"

M y mother still takes me to the Cloisters every day, except when it's closed, but she feels too guilty to enjoy herself. We don't stay as long as before. Then one day she says to my brother, "Do me a favor." He agrees to baby-sit me the following Saturday and gives her subway directions to Brighton Beach. Then she informs my sister that they are going. "You do me this favor, I'll talk to Papa to let you out of the house sooner."

My sister doesn't mind. She is going stir-crazy. She's read all the library books twice. My mother, who's never used a library, doesn't know how to pick out new books to bring home. Rereading all the magazines, my sister has become an expert on Hollywood gossip. She experiments with my mother's makeup. She teaches me new words. *Powder puff* is my favorite.

"Powder puff," I say, watching my mother pat her nose. "Where we going?" I ask.

"Not you. You're staying with your brother."

"Why?" I follow her to the kitchen, where she packs a lunch. "Because why?"

"Me and your sister, we have to go to Coney Island."

"What's Coney Island?"

With her finger my mother pushes the egg salad off the knife and into my mouth. "Where you were born," she says.

"Can I go? I want to go."

"Another time. Don't chew with your mouth open. I wonder what your brother will learn you today. Maybe something too hard for you."

"No!"

"We'll see," she singsongs. "We'll see."

At the subway station my mother suddenly recalls the crazy man from the change booth. She doesn't want to know if he's in there now. She throws a dollar at my sister. "You get," she says, and waits by the turnstiles, the shopping bag between her legs. On the platform she looks all around.

"What're you so suspicious of?" Mimi says, trying to hide her annoyance.

My mother tells her how the man from the booth followed her and the baby in Coney Island. She doesn't mention the bankbook, or Harry either.

"What were you doing there?" Mimi asks.

"*Oy*, how I miss the salt air!"

"Does Papa know what happened?"

"Crazy your mother isn't. *Kholilleh*, he'd kill this man and go to jail."

"Why are we going to Coney now?" Mimi expects my mother to say something like, Maybe the salt air will cure your sickness. Something cuckoo.

"You wouldn't believe me. Anyhow, is hard to explain."

Unlike my mother, my sister finds the long ride boring. Still, she's glad to be out of the apartment. She reads and rereads the placards overhead. I'D WALK A MILE FOR A CAMEL. She wonders what it's like to be Miss Subways. She would never say it, but she is also glad it's just the two of them together.

As soon as she sees the crowded beach—sand hardly visible in between all the bodies, a million bodies it looks like—my sister says, "We should have brought our bathing suits."

"I have right here." My mother rattles her shopping bag.

"So what did you want to show me?"

"First we go change," my mother says. "Then we'll see."

One at a time they go into the bracing ocean while the other one watches their belongings. They eat egg salad sandwiches and drink milk from the thermos. While they lie on towels under the hot sun, my mother says, "I did a foolish thing once. More than once, but it's once I want to tell you."

My sister thinks my mother is going to confess that she stole something. She closes her eyes. She hears seagulls honk above the din of voices. The heat from the sun feels like the blast from an open oven. Her body tingles.

"Remember I was expecting with your sister, I went to the doctor's?"

"Yeah." Mimi yanks the straps off her shoulders.

"I was very depressed at that time. And then your papa and me, we got into an argument. He gave me such a smack—"

My sister's stomach tightens. Maybe she doesn't want to hear this.

"After I cried my eyes out, you know what I did? I went there, to the Boardwalk." She points behind them, but my sister's eyes are still closed. "I walked and I walked. I was thinking, 'Should I, shouldn't I?'"

"Should you what?" Mimi asks.

"Should I kill myself."

My sister opens her eyes. "You thought about killing yourself?"

"More than thinking. Sit up."

Mimi clutches the top of her bathing suit and sits up.

"See?" My mother points to a crowded area near the water. "There, I collapse after. At that time, deserted. The sun, so pale and cold. *Got shikt di kelt noch di klaider.* God sends the weather you need. I think I'm laying down to die alone, *nu?* but from nowhere this nice man comes, he asks me if I'm all right."

My sister is squinting from the horror. "You tried to kill yourself? But—but what would have happened to us?"

It's the question my mother was hoping for. "That's it," she says. "Why I didn't kill myself. At the moment I go in the ocean, all I'm thinking is me me me."

"That's so selfish," Mimi says.

"That's it," my mother says again. She waits a decent interval before saying, "When you help yourself to clothes they don't belong to you, all you think about is you. You don't think about your family. How it hurts me and Papa. And your brother and your sister. Your shame is our shame, *nu?*"

My mother speaks matter-of-factly, without reproach. "I tell you so you should know what this pain is, deep inside me." Her hand over her breast, she says, "*Azoy!* Now, we get ourself some *geshmak* French fries by Nathan's."

On the long subway ride home, my sister falls asleep. She dreams she is floating on water, content under a warm sun, until she overhears someone say she is going to get burnt to a crisp. She tries to go back for her blouse to put on over the swimsuit, but the tide pulls her in the opposite direction. "Help!" she calls out to the other swimmers. They smile and cheerfully wave her on. In the distance a woman in a white filmy dress appears over the water. She has dark hair to her knees and a glittering tiara. She tiptoes from wave to wave, coming toward my sister. Up close, my sister realizes the woman is as tall as a balloon in the Macy's Thanksgiving Day Parade. "Use the breaststroke, dear," the giantess counsels, but what she demonstrates is the backstroke, and soon she recedes toward the horizon. My sister thinks she says "Use the best stroke." Circling her arms wildly through the water, she flutter kicks like crazy, no longer afraid to be swimming toward the ocean. But when she lifts her head, she sees the beach coming closer and closer.

My mother makes them get out at 190th Street, to avoid the man at Dyckman. Just the thought of him gives her the creeps.

In the tunnel they pass the elevator operator who is in uniform but taking a break. "How are you folks today?" he asks.

"My older daughter," my mother says.

"Hello, miss. You been to the Cloisters again, ma'am?" he says.

"We were on the subway. From Coney Island," my mother answers.

"See you soon." He tips his brown cap.

My sister gives my mother an inquisitive look. "Sometimes I take the little one there." She shrugs, as if it's nothing. "You ever see this place, inside?"

"Our art teacher took us once. All those crucifixes and statues. Jesus and the Virgin Mary. It's all hooey."

My mother says, "People need something to believe in, *nu?* What's mysterious can be like a magnet."

My sister ignores this. "If you like art, there's lots more at the Met." My mother looks blank. "The Metropolitan Museum, in Central Park. Downtown."

"Is that so?" My mother gets the idea that museums are only in parks.

"It's incredible what they have," Mimi says. "I like the Egyptian part and the Impressionists. There are Rembrandts, too. And metal armor the knights wore for fighting. Everything. Whole floors of paintings. A cafeteria. It's fifty times, a hundred times bigger than the Cloisters."

"So big?"

"I swear, Mama. I've been there ten times, and I haven't seen half of it."

"Imagine! This I didn't know."

"There's a lot you don't know," my sister says.

"We must be close to home," my mother says. She means it ironically. "So, please, tell me. I'm all ears."

The receptionist for the factory flings open the door of my father's office. She aims her pencil at the phone. "I think it's your wife."

"Thank you," my father says stiffly. He's never given my mother the number, because Mr. Gershenfeld has warned them about personal calls. He picks up the receiver now, warily. He's hoping it isn't the baby.

Hearing Trudy's voice, my father lets out a big breath. "You nearly gave me a heart attack, telephoning here."

"The worst thing happened," Trudy says.

My father thinks Barney has found out about them. His mind reels. Is Barney on his way to the factory? Is he divorcing Trudy?

"My nephew," Trudy says, "the one I told you who was overseas—"

"Something happened to him?"

"And his wife." Trudy starts to cry. "They were killed in a car crash."

"My condolences. That's a terrible thing." He takes another big breath.

"They left their little girl with the baby-sitter. G-d in heaven, now she's an orphan."

"The poor kid. She's going to an orphanage?"

"Not if I can help it," Trudy says. "Right now the baby is with my niece, but she's only a schoolgirl. In college."

"What can you do?" My father sees his boss walking down the aisle between the seamstresses.

"I'm taking the train. To Philly. It may be a few days. Okay?"

"You're asking me? You have to go to the funeral, no?"

"Not just the funeral. I have to see about the kid."

My father wants to tell her not to mix in, but he knows he has to get off the phone. "Call me when you come back. A safe trip."

"Thank you. I love you."

"Likewise," he says as Mr. Gershenfeld steps through his office door.

Sometimes when my mother and I leave the house, I remind her to take her glasses. At first she thinks it's very cute. She takes the eyeglasses in a case. Or puts the glasses on, but if we go to Dyckman Street, she takes them off. She thinks that if Harry should happen to come out from the Magic Shoes store, if he's just visiting there, say, it would be better not to see him.

One afternoon when she tells me we're going shopping, I say, "Glasses, Mama." Her eyebrows lift up. She looks like Olive Oyl in my sister's comic book. "Stop *tchepping* me!" she says. "Three years old, already you're a nag."

This is the first time I've ever heard her angry at me.

At the kosher butcher's, she parks the stroller and I go inside with her. "Don't play on the floor," she says. When she turns her back, I put my hand down on the sawdust. I like how it clings to my palm. The butcher gets aggravated when she asks him to read her the prices on the board behind the counter. Twice. "Missus," he tells her, "you broke your glasses? Get them fixed. I'm not the Lighthouse for the Blind."

At the bakery, she points to me. "You," she says. "Not a word from your mouth since we left. Talk your head off, but don't tell me about my glasses, *nu*?" She takes a number, and we wait with the other customers. Overhead [1] [8] becomes [1] [9]. I want to ask what makes it change, but I don't.

"*Oy*," my mother says, "you break my heart with those eyes." I go to the case where the fancy cookies are and peer in, my hands on the glass. She's told me before that sweets are not good for me. Today she says, "Half a cookie you can have. This one time."

"A whole cookie!" I say. "I want a whole cookie."

"She knows from halves?" a customer says.

"A whole, a half, that's not much to know." The number changes to [2] [2]. "Right here!" my mother yells. After she orders a pumpernickel, sliced, my mother asks the lady with the organdy apron and hat, "Can I get one little cookie, if you please?"

"A quarter-pound minimum," the lady says brusquely, before she sees my hopeful stare. "For her?" she asks.

"She just turned three," my mother says.

"Here." The lady hands my mother a cookie on a piece of waxed paper. It has a cherry in the center. "How much?" my mother asks, but the lady waves her hand dismissively.

Outside the store, my mother breaks the tiny cookie in half. She keeps the part with the cherry. "Don't get a cavity from this," she says, giving me what's left. I know my mother is saying she's sorry for getting angry, but I don't ever ask her again about her glasses.

"Mr. Arnow, you're getting so popular." The receptionist tilts her head toward the phone and backs out the door.

Now what? my father thinks as he picks up the receiver. "Mr. Arnow speaking. How can I help you?"

"I have some ideas," Trudy says.

"Trudy! For God's sake, don't call me here. The boss don't like it."

"You could at least say, Welcome back."

"Yeah, what is it?" He fans himself with the order book.

Her voice bubbles as she says, "Can you see me tonight?"

The heat wave is still on, and my father has decided to take my mother and me to the movies, where it's air-conditioned. Now he wavers. Trudy sounds so eager, she must have missed him. Since he hasn't mentioned the movie to my mother, he tells Trudy, "Okay, we'll take in that James Cagney picture." Just then Mr. Gershenfeld comes up the aisle. "I have to go," my father says, and puts down the receiver.

For once Mr. Gershenfeld comes into the cubicle without his jacket. When it's a hundred twenty degrees in the factory, my father thinks, hell freezes over. He mops his forehead, waiting for his boss to read him the riot act on personal calls. Mr. Gershenfeld only explains about the new wonder fabric they're going to try. Polyester.

The receptionist pokes her head in the door. "Telephone, Mr. Arnow. It's the same lady."

"Would you tell her I'll call her later?"

Mr. Gershenfeld puts his hand up. "Take the call. It must be something urgent for her to interrupt you at work, right?"

"I'm very sorry," my father says. "I'll ask her not to call me again."

Mr. Gershenfeld nods. He can tell my father has gotten the message.

Alone in his office now, my father picks up the receiver. "Hello?"

"Don't be angry," Trudy says. "I just had to tell you."

"Didn't I say, Don't call me?"

"Yes, but—"

"My boss was just in here," my father says, his voice rising. "Do you want me to lose my job?"

"No, I only—"

"Trudy!" he screams. "Never, ever call me here again, understand?" He looks to see if anyone outside the booth heard him, but the girls are working away, even Flora, her long hair falling on the fabric near the needle. He'll have to tell her to comb her hair back before there's an accident.

"You don't have to get apoplectic. I only wanted to let you know I can't go tonight to the movies. I have my nephew's daughter here."

"For how long?"

"Ha!" Trudy says. "That's a good one. Let's see, I would say, uh, fifteen years. Barney and I are adopting her."

On the factory floor my father feels at sixes and sevens. What is Trudy talking about? What has gotten into her? If she wants company, she should get a dog, he thinks. What does she need with a kid?

When he arrives at Trudy's place, three-year-old Hannah is running in circles around the living room. She bangs together two wooden horses.

"Isn't she cute!" Trudy says. "I'm taking her to a doctor next week for her eyes. They go in different directions."

"Can't you tell her to be quiet?" he says.

"She'll calm down. She just got here. Sometimes she asks for her mother. It breaks my heart."

The last thing my father wants to see at Trudy's is a baby. For that he already has a home, but what can he say? "Why should you be the one to adopt her?" he says. "You could be her grandmother."

"Hannah," Trudy says. "This is your grandpapa. Say hello." Hannah stops running for a minute and stares. Then she squats under a chair. From there she clops the horses together, over and over, as if they're at war.

"We could go to 181st, is better for the variety," my mother says.

"I told you, what I want is in the Magic Shoes window," my sister says.

My mother is pretty sure Harry is still in Brooklyn, but why take the chance? "In that case," she says, and hands my sister the money.

"You're trusting me to buy shoes?" Mimi says. "Chicken Little, the sky is falling."

"Make sure they fit, or I'll give you a *loch in kop*." A hole in the head.

While Mimi is gone, my mother waits. *Zitsen ahf shpilkes*, she thinks. On pins and needles. Finally my sister comes home with a plain pair of pumps. "Put them on," my mother orders. "Walk back and forth." She pinches the toes to check if there is room. "We'll see how long they're good for. Tell me, you see someone in there we know?"

"The shoe store?"

"No, the dairy farm. To whom am I talking, please?"

"I didn't see anyone, why?"

"It's nice in there?"

Mimi shrugs. "Like the one in Brighton Beach but smaller."

"The salesman was nice to you?"

"Why shouldn't he be? I didn't yell at him. I didn't insult him."

"All right, all right," my mother says. She figures if my sister saw him, she would remember him from the other store and say something. My mother feels calmer but not altogether easy. She wishes the store wasn't there. She can never go now on the main shopping street without thinking of Harry.

I imagine my mother is surprised when my father agrees to go with her on Friday nights to Temple. In Brooklyn they went regularly, but in the city she goes only on the High Holy Days. Lately she feels the need for some uplift.

At first they argue over which synagogue to attend. Though my father prefers the Orthodox or Conservative, my mother refuses to sit with the women in the balcony like some outcast.

My brother and sister don't want to go at all, which aggravates my father, so he makes them take turns baby-sitting me.

The Reform Temple is a makeshift building next to a garage, but my mother feels it's *haimish.* Homey. The rabbi clasps her hand in both of his. "Mrs. Arnow, how good to see you again!" He reminds her a little of her late father. She reminds him of his mother.

At the services my mother sees some of our neighbors and others from around the area. The Hebrew is foreign but familiar, and the English cadences move her. *Thou createst day and night; thou rollest away the light from before the darkness, and the darkness from before the light; thou makest the day to pass and the night to approach, and dividest the day from the night* . . . Like the ocean, she thinks, meeting the shore. Dark against light.

One evening she says to my father, "A book like this at home for the little one, her brother could read to her."

"You'll make a fairy out of him," my father says. "The kid's too small."

"Look, that one isn't too small." My father looks and sees Trudy and Barney Fleisch with Hannah sitting between them, asleep.

After services, though my father doesn't want to stay for the social hour, the Fleisches troop up to them and my father has to make the introductions. "Join us for a *nosh*," Barney says, and my mother says, "Why not?"

In the other wing, which is the Community Center, they drink punch and eat rugelach. My father is on edge, but the danger excites Trudy. She sizes up my mother, surprised she is so tiny, and at the same time, full-figured.

"From where do you know each other?" my mother asks Barney.

"My old handball adversary," he says. "Brighton Beach, off the Boardwalk." He pinches my father's cheek. "I see him at the Jewish Club sometimes, playing hearts."

Trudy recalls to herself how she and he met there that time, an instant attraction. One moment they were introduced. Moments later, she kissed him by the water fountain. She thinks he's hilarious now, looking bored, as if he wants to escape. She knows he is afraid.

"Since when did you start coming here?" Trudy asks my mother. She really wants to ask what kind of night cream she uses on her face. Not a wrinkle anywhere.

"A few weeks. I didn't see you before."

"We used to come all the time, before we got our little Hannah. We're adopting her." Trudy tells my mother the story.

My mother cringes to hear her use words such as *died* and *orphan* in Hannah's presence. "Some *mitzvah*," she says, "to take her in." Too bad, she thinks, about the kid's eyes. Such thick lenses.

Hannah points to my father. "Grandpapa."

"No, that's not Grandpa," Barney says.

"Grandpapa," Hannah insists. She looks to Trudy for confirmation. Trudy smiles feebly. My father scowls.

"Cute," my mother says. She has to stop herself from saying, *Kineahora.*

It's a whole different situation now, my father tells himself. Whenever he visits Trudy, they can't just fall into each other's arms or go to bed. He watches television until Trudy tucks the kid into her crib at seven o'clock. Even then they wait until the kid is actually asleep before they make love—if Trudy isn't too tired by then. Afterwards, all she talks about is Hannah this and Hannah that. He's given up going there on Saturday afternoons because the kid is awake the whole time.

Discontent runs through my father's head as he sorts the orders at his desk in the factory. When he sees Flora and Ida gabbing once again, he storms down to their stations. "Both of you," he yells, "if I have to tell you one more time—" He runs his index finger across his throat. He thinks he'd hate to fire Flora, she's such a beauty. Her unpainted lips are the color of red grapes.

As he walks back up the aisle, the sewing machines come to a sudden stop, and he hears barking sounds behind him. He whirls around, but he doesn't see who's doing it. The machines are running again. He starts walking. *Urh urh. Urh.* The barking follows him, but he keeps going.

Returning from his break, he finds a piece of paper taped to his office door: MISTER BOWWOW. He can feel the eyes of the girls on his back. He forces a laugh. "Ha! That's a good one." He turns around and, sure enough, two dozen pairs of eyes are on him. "That's me," he says jovially, "Mr. BowWow." Then he screams at the top of his lungs: "NOW GET TO WORK!"

After Mr. Gershenfeld leaves for an appointment, my father calls Trudy. "I can't see you tonight. I have to work overtime."

"It's for the best. Hannah has a bad cold and an earache. She's all cranky, aren't you, Hannah? Poor Hannah," Trudy coos.

"Can't you talk about anything else?" my father says.

"I never liked kids before, but now that my own are grown, I get such a kick out of her." Trudy squeals, a new laugh since the kid arrived. "You should have heard her when we had the T.V. on—"

"See you Thursday," he says, and puts down the receiver.

He flips a page of his desk calendar to get ready for the next day, surprised by his sudden sense of loss. Where did the time go? It was just yesterday when he was in an undershirt and shorts after a handball game, and a girl—what was her name?—waited for him outside the courts. That night was his very first time, with her under the Boardwalk. So quick he didn't know why everyone made such a big deal about sex. But the more he did it with her, the more he wanted to. Still, she was just a girl. She didn't know what Trudy knows. Why does Trudy have to slip away from him? he asks himself. Before his eyes she is becoming a grandma.

Through the glass now, he watches Ermelinda bent over her machine. The way her skirt is bunched under her, he can see her leg to the knee. A pretty caramel color.

My mother and I are sitting on a low wall around a court-yard in the Cloisters, near the wavy columns. In the garden is a fountain no taller than I am. My mother won't let me poke my finger in the water that bubbles from the center. "Here, look," she says, writing with her fingernail on the little magic slate. She brings the slate now on all our outings, ever since my brother taught me the alphabet. "What is this?" she asks.

"I know," I say.

"Tell me."

"You tell me."

"I don't think you kno-ow," she says in singsong.

"I do too. *Mama*," I say.

"*Mama*. That's right." She lifts the cellophane that makes the letters disappear. "Now you."

With the little stick I write LOVE. The letters are very crooked because there are no lines, like on the loose-leaf pages my brother gives me.

"*Love*," my mother says. "Very good."

"What a smart little girl!" I hear someone say. A man is standing behind my mother. Her eyes get very strange. Frightened, I think. Slowly she turns her head. "You," she says.

"Chenia," the man says. He has dark eyes and a green hat with a tiny yellow feather. "Hello, hello," he says to me.

"You've grown so much I hardly recognized you. How old are you now?" I look at my mother.

"It's okay, you can talk to him," she says. "He's somebody I know from Brooklyn." She's told me many times not to talk to men.

"Three!" I tell him.

"Just three?" He looks at my mother. "She's reading and writing?"

"A *bissel*."

He leans over her shoulder to draw a figure on the slate. "What's that?" he asks me.

"I don't know," I say.

"You know," my mother prods. "A heart. A valentine."

"Valentines are red," I tell him. "We have a valentine box." My mother flushes, almost the color of the box. It's the one he gave her, with all the candy, only now it holds her necklaces. Sometimes she lets me play with them.

"So, Chenia, how have you been?"

"*A sach tsu reden, vainik tsu heren.*"

"You know my Yiddish is wanting," he says.

"A lot to tell, but too little to hear," she translates.

"Write me," I say.

She writes PAPA with her fingernail.

"That's too easy," I say.

She lifts up the page to make PAPA disappear.

"Write my name," I say.

"What's the first letter?" she asks me.

"D."

"That's right." She prints DEVORAH. "Such a hard name for a little girl to spell." Handing me the slate, she says, "You can copy it."

"So," she says to Harry, "here we are." She sounds calm, but inside, she is in great turmoil. He looks to her smoother than before. Maybe it's the silky gray suit. She remembered him taller.

"I thought you would be by the river," he says.

"That?" she say. "Big enough only to spit in. We see the whole *megillah* from outside there, then we come in here, where I like it. *Oy,* the little one will think she's a Catholic." My mother makes the sign of the cross.

He laughs. "Fascinating, huh?" She looks to him a little different. Standoffish, maybe. He liked her hair longer. In the net. "Have you seen the Nine Heroes Tapestries?" he asks.

"The tapestries I saw. Such skinny thread. You could go blind."

"You know there are Jewish heroes among them?"

"Really?" She thinks to herself, How can this man know so much? Does he make it up? She wants to tell him to go away, before she falls back in love with him. With his mind.

"Come," he says. "I'll show you." We follow him until he stops at a doorway. "Fifteenth century. Limestone." He takes off his hat before we enter the room. "Here are the Greek heroes," he says.

He points at a huge tapestry on one wall. "There's Julius Caesar, the great Roman conqueror. Those men are famous Christians. And on this wall, the Hebrews' tapestry. *Voilà!* There's King David—see his harp? There's Joshua with a dragon on his shield. And Judas Maccabeus. These tapestries are from the fourteenth century, more than six hundred years old."

My mother is standing with her mouth hanging open. I am climbing on the big chair under the funny window that doesn't look out on anything. Harry comes to lift me off the chair. He plops his hat on me. I laugh. "I have to get back to work," he says. "It's a long walk from here to there. Like from one end of the Boardwalk to the other. You know I'm on Dyckman Street now? I asked for the transfer." He doesn't tell her why.

"From your mouth to God's ear," she says. "What should I know? No one ever rang my telephone to tell me."

"I did call you once. I think your daughter answered. I hung up."

"Your finger broke? You could dial again."

"Chenia!" he jollies her. "Your fingers, they don't look broken to me."

Harry's hat falls off me as I run around the table in the middle of the room. "You!" my mother says to me, but I know not to touch the plates or the pitcher on it.

"You must have seen our store. Did you bother to come in?" Harry says.

"Why would I? The way you acted last time."

"Chenia, my mother was ill. By the time I returned, she was on the floor, crawling on her belly to get to the phone. I've been more than punished for the few moments I spent with you." He stoops to pick up his hat.

"This I'm sorry to hear." She pauses, thinking, Is it true?, then she says, "But you acted like we never knew each other. Hello, how are you, good-bye."

"Let's hash this out, Chenia. That there should be no misunderstanding. When and where can I meet you? This is too far from work."

My mother's chin juts toward me. "Big ears grow bigger every day."

"I realize. I'll think of something, I promise. Bickford's on Dyckman?"

"When?" She looks very sad. She's thinking, Maybe it's better not to start again.

"Tomorrow. Two o'clock. I'll take a late lunch."

"Who's that?" I ask, after he goes.

"A man from the shoe store in Brooklyn."

"What's his name?"

"*Bubbeleh*," she says, "I have such a headache. Let's go outside. Do you want an ice cream?"

Outside the Cloisters my mother buys me a Dixie cup, half chocolate, half vanilla, from the man with the wagon. It's so frozen she has to help me dig in with the wooden spoon, until the ice cream starts to soften. When I can't eat any more, I say, "What's his name?"

"Peter," she says. "Peter the Wolf. Did I ever tell you that story? Your sister has the book someplace." We sit on our bench and she tells me about how Peter almost ate Red Riding Hood. "If Red Riding Hood didn't go to school," she says, "she wouldn't know about wolves and how dangerous they are. But she went to school and she was a smart little cookie. She knew how to spell her name, and it was a much longer name than yours."

My mother writes on the slate board RED RIDING HOOD. "She had red hair like you," my mother says. "And red shoes."

"My shoes are red." I point to my hair. "This isn't red."

"There's different kinds of red," my mother says. "You're right. Life is, *oy*, so complicated."

Ever since she went with my mother to Brighton Beach, my sister has resisted the temptation to shoplift. Now school has started, and every day she resents having to wear Cousin Rhonda's castoffs. The other girls wear plaid skirts and sweaters with dolman sleeves, all the latest fashions. In spite of her resolve, one afternoon my sister boards the trolley to the Grand Concourse.

A few stops later, an old woman on the sidewalk is yelling "Hey! Hey!" Her shopping cart, loaded with a tall cardboard box, is too heavy for her to boost up the high step. The conductor is gruff. "C'mon, lady, this ain't the pony express. I'm already running late."

My sister rushes to the rescue, taking the handle of the cart and yanking it into the car. The woman climbs on and says something to her in a foreign language. Thank you, maybe.

Her face is brownish, the color of old makeup, with deep pockets in the flesh. It reminds Mimi of a sponge.

"Are you going far?" she asks the woman.

"By Alexander's." She taps the box in the cart. "This kind of cabinet you can't get there." Her arms are so thin, her wrist bone looks like a tumor.

When my sister pulls the cord, the woman says, "I get out, too."

"I'll help you," Mimi says. She carries the cart down to the sidewalk. "I hope you live in an elevator building."

"You couldn't get me in an elevator—" the woman says.

"Maybe I should walk you home," Mimi suggests.

"It's not necessary," the woman says. "But if you want . . ." Slowly they walk two blocks off the Concourse, my sister pulling the cart. The building doesn't have an elevator. My sister lugs the cart up the three flights.

"There you go," she says.

The woman opens her purse and says, "Wait, I give you."

"You don't have to tip me. I just wanted to help," Mimi says.

"Then you come in, have a cup of tea."

My sister is curious. As far back as she can remember, my mother has warned her against strangers—all the more reason to say yes now.

The dark apartment smells like an apple core left out too long, but it's not exactly repulsive. The foyer is full of dark furniture and glass and china knickknacks. In the kitchen, she and the woman manage to slide the cabinet out of the carton and stand it up by the sink, next to several bags of garbage.

Mimi loads the garbage into the empty carton. "I'll take it down for you."

"It's not necessary. But if you want . . . Then I'll have your tea ready."

The basement is darker than my sister expected. When a large man steps out of the darkness, she shrieks. "What the hell?" he yells. He's unshaven, with overalls that are too tight.

He yanks the carton from her and plops it down by the garbage cans. "Visiting someone here?" he asks.

The way he looks at her—too happy to see her—gives Mimi the creeps. To be polite, she answers him. "Yes."

"You come here often?"

"This is my first time." Maybe she misjudged him, she thinks, then she sees him looking over his shoulder as if to check whether they're alone. She goes back as fast as she can, taking the steps two at a time.

The table is already set. Yellowish tea—like *pish*, Mimi thinks—sits in two glass cups. "How we have it at home," the woman says. Mimi doesn't have the heart to tell her she doesn't drink tea. On a chipped plate are ginger cookies covered with powdered sugar. My sister fills her mouth each time with a big piece of cookie before she sips.

The old woman asks her about school, about where she lives. She asks the old woman if she has a family, where she came from. An hour goes by. "Have some more tea," the woman says. "I have to go now," Mimi says. The woman looks very sad. Maybe she is missing her son who died at Pearl Harbor, Mimi thinks. She has only a brother who lives in Queens.

At the door the woman slips a rolled-up bill into my sister's hand. Mimi tries to refuse but the woman says, "Please, you can come visit me, anytime. I tell you my name." She points above the doorbell. "Sofie Vrebolovich."

"I'll never remember it."

The old woman gives her a used envelope with her name and address. Slowly she prints her phone number. It seems to take forever. "You come anytime for lunch."

On the landing below, my sister opens her hand. In her palm is a twenty-dollar bill. For some reason, she thinks of the woman in her dream, the giant with the tiara. She feels there's some connection with the old woman, but she doesn't know what.

. . .

At Alexander's my sister buys herself two outfits, a blouse, a sweater, and a felt skirt. She has money left over, which she will put toward shoes. When she gets home, she leaves everything in the bags and waits for my mother. "Mama," she says, "the most amazing thing happened today." She shows her the receipts and the envelope from the old woman. She tells my mother about helping her with the cabinet, about the tea and the money. She doesn't mention the man. "I'm happy for you," my mother says, "but tell me this, what were you doing on that trolley to begin with?"

While Mr. and Mrs. Gershenfeld and their five children vacation in the Poconos, my father calls Ermelinda into his office. "I want to compliment you. You're our best worker. Did you know that?"

She gives him a shy smile. My father isn't sure if she understands. Her English is only so-so. "Would you like to have dinner with me tonight?" he asks. When she looks a little puzzled, he pretends he's spooning something into his mouth, then points to her and himself. "Tonight," he repeats.

Ermelinda says something, maybe in English, but he can't make it out. He thinks he hears the word *baby*, which sounds like "behbee."

"Baby?" He makes his arms into a cradle and swings them back and forth. She nods. "*¿Casado?*" he asks. Married?

She reaches inside her blouse and takes out her gold wedding ring, which is on a chain around her neck. Most of the girls wear their rings around their neck so they don't get caught in the machines.

Through the glass, he sees the girls who sit by Ermelinda watching them. Ida says something. Flora gathers the hair at her neck and laughs.

"That's all," my father says. "You can go back to work."

"Know you're very nice boss," Ermelinda tells him. "*Gracias.*"

Although he pretends to read a production schedule, my father sees the girls question Ermelinda when she is back at her station. The three of them eye him and make faces at each other, their eyes rolling and bugging out.

The next night my father leaves work as usual. As he rounds the corner to go to the subway, someone comes up behind him and jabs something in his back. "Over here," the man says, prodding him toward the alley.

My father swings his fist behind him, like a mallet, catching the man in the solar plexus. Then my father runs. In the subway station he feels for his wallet, which is still in his back pocket. Not so bad for an old man, he thinks, his heart racing.

At home he tells us about the attempted robbery.

When Ermelinda doesn't show up the next morning for work and doesn't call, my father puts two and two together. That night, he walks the long way around to the subway.

Ermelinda doesn't come back to work. After a week, my father cautiously resumes his normal route to the IND. Three days later, two men grab him by the arms and force him into the alley. They take his wallet, his watch, and land a few punches before he breaks free.

"Oh, my poor Ruben!" Trudy says when he gets to her place. "What happened?" She puts ice cubes in one of Barney's socks and gives it to my father to hold over his swollen cheek and bruised eye.

At breakfast the next morning my mother learns what happened. "*Oy,*" she says, "I thought we moved to the city because it was safer."

My father takes it as a criticism. "A mugging can happen

anywhere," he yells. I start to cry. "Don't cry," he says. "There's nothing to cry about."

"Papa, hurt," I say.

He carries me into the other room and sets me down. From his pocket he fishes out a small handful of change. "Here, you pick two." I pick the biggest coins, a half dollar and quarter.

"Good girl!" He lowers his voice. "Don't get high-strung like your mother. There's nothing to be nervous over."

"Noy-vus?" I say, which is how my mother says it.

"Nervous, not noy-vus. Okay?" he says.

"Okay," I say, but I wonder who is right.

B y November, Harry has everything worked out. He rents a furnished room on Broadway. He locates a former school-teacher who now teaches French to little ones at home. My mother and Harry arrange their meetings to coincide with the lessons.

The first time they take me to Madame LePage, I scream when my mother tries to leave. Madame gives my mother permission to stay. My mother sits on the sofa and worries about the dust on the rug where the rest of us sit, six children and Madame, whose slender legs fold easily under a gathered skirt. Madame teaches us a song in French while she plays her xylophone. Enthralled, my mother forgets the dust.

That night my mother sings, "'*Frè-re Jac-ques, Frè-re Jac-ques.*'" Soon I am singing with her. "Where'd you learn that?" my brother asks. My mother tells him about the class. He tells my sister. Mimi gets very jealous. "You never gave me any classes," she says to my mother.

"If we had the money, I would've given you," my mother says. "I would have given myself." She wishes she could take the French classes with me.

Each time she picks me up from Madame's, she asks what I learned. At three years old, I am teaching my mother French. Numbers, colors.

When my father asks how this came about, my mother is glib. "A woman in the park. Her kid goes, too. Only twenty-five cents," she lies.

"Maybe it's not good to put so much into a child's brain. I don't want her to get sick. She can't wipe her *tokhes*, and she's learning a foreign language?"

"Don't be old-fashioned," my mother says. "It's the new thing, to start when they're so little."

The first few times alone with Harry, my mother is uneasy. "This ain't the Half-Moon Hotel," she jokes. Their rented room in a retired man's apartment is dusty, with a blue chenille bedspread on the single bed, and no curtain on the window, just a yellowed shade. The light from the uncovered fixture overhead is harsh. My mother won't let Harry turn it on, so he buys a little lamp with a muslin shade from the Five and Ten. The retired man always hovers by the door to the apartment, whether they come in or go out.

And then she worries about me.

"Madame has the phone number here," Harry says. "Don't worry."

Finally Harry gets the idea to bring a bottle of schnapps. He says he can't drink because he has to go back to work and they'll smell it on his breath. "Take a sip," he tells her. "It'll do you good."

"*Honik-lekech*," she says ironically. Honey cake. Still, she has to admit, the liquor helps. Once she stops her worrying, she finds making love with Harry is *ganaiden*, Paradise. What was good before is now even better.

In between their meetings on Tuesdays and Thursdays, my mother drives herself crazy with guilt. How can you do this? she asks herself in the mirror above the vanity. What kind of person are you? A *bummerkeh*, she answers. Lowest of the low. She resolves never to see Harry again. An hour before she brings me to Madame LePage, she swears to break it off with him. She has no idea what the classes cost, but she will scrub floors to pay for them.

Then she sees him again, and her knees weaken. After they make love and they lie squished together on the narrow bed, she thinks, *Whatever God is going to do to me, it was worth it.*

For New Year's Eve, my parents go to a party given by the Vogels, friends my father knows from Brighton Beach. The Vogels live now in Manhattan, in a co-op on the East Side. "Arthur hit it big with the horses," my father tells my mother. "A few bets, and he's rich. Is that fair?"

"He suffered plenty," my mother reminds him. "They lost everything, *nu*, after he was beaten up by the bookies."

Snow is falling as my parents cross Lexington Avenue. The Christmas lights are still strung up high across the street, with five-pointed stars, as far as the eye can see. Windows in the grand buildings are lit golden and orange, some with stars or menorahs. Tiny bulbs in all different colors wink around the frames. *Oy*, to live in such a place! my mother thinks.

Stationed in the middle of the circular driveway, a doorman in a long maroon coat tips his cap and asks my parents their name. "Chenia Arnow," my mother says and the doorman checks his list. "I don't see it," he says, looking under the Ch's. "I'll have to call upstairs."

My father scans the list from upside down. "Here," he says. "Arnow."

"I'm sorry, sir," the doorman says. "I misunderstood you."

In the elevator, my father says, "He did it on purpose."

"Shhh." My mother hitches her shoulder toward the elevator operator.

"The doorman should go to hell," my father says.

"You'd think he'd recognize you, so often you come to play cards."

The elevator operator casts a glance at my father, who does not look at all familiar.

"*Paigeren zol er,*" my father says. He should drop dead.

"It's New Year's Eve," my mother says. "*A leben ahf deir.*" You should live and be well.

The Vogels' foyer has green-and-gold-striped wallpaper. Fancy, my mother thinks, but she doesn't know if she likes it. Vera Vogel presses her cheek against my mother's and takes her Persian lamb coat, which smells of mothballs, and my father's checked coat. Arthur Vogel shakes my father's hand, slaps him on the forearm, and asks what he'd like to drink. "Nothing," my father says, but my mother says, "Me, I'd like a little something."

"That's the spirit." Arthur takes her arm and leads her to the bar, past two couples, clinking their tall glasses.

While my father talks with Vera, another guest arrives in a full-length mink. Vera introduces them. "Ruben, this is Bertha Landau. Her husband passed last year, God rest. Did you know him? Myron Landau was a first-rate poker player. Bertha, this is Ruben. Fifty girls he has under him—at work. You better watch out."

Bertha smiles. "I didn't catch your last name."

My father says, "Arnow," but he hardly notices Bertha, except for her buckteeth. He wonders if Trudy will come to the party. She wasn't sure Barney would get the night off. "I don't want to be alone on New Year's Eve," Trudy said, "when everyone has someone."

"Are you a teacher, Mr. Arnow?" Bertha asks. "A gym instructor?" she banters. She likes his mustache, neatly trimmed. He looks like the writer Robert Benchley, but with lighter coloring.

"He manages a factory," Vera tells her, and goes to deposit Bertha's mink on the bed in the guest room, away from the Persian lamb.

"I'm just the floor boss," my father says. "We make ties for all the big stores. LVG Fabrics."

"What a coincidence! The building you're in, it's one of ours."

"Excuse me," he says, "maybe I didn't hear right. You own the building?"

"Technically, Myron Landau Estate owns the building."

Now my father takes a good look at her. With the buckteeth, she reminds him of Eleanor Roosevelt. Even the hair, short and a little curly, looks like her. He wonders if the jewels around her neck and all over her fingers are real. "Too bad the elevator needs repair," he says.

"You're telling me!" Bertha smiles as if unaware of her buckteeth.

My mother is back now with a glass of punch. "Something strong," she says. There are introductions, and then the doorbell rings.

"I'm here," Trudy Fleisch announces as she steps in, her beaver coat over her arm. She is wearing a silky green dress my father has never seen and green high heels to match. She stares right at him as she hands her coat to Vera. "Sorry Barney couldn't make it," Trudy says. "And it was so hard to get a baby-sitter, until the last minute. My neighbor took the baby—"

"Come in, come in," Arthur says. "Who needs Barney when you look like a million dollars?"

"Tell us your secret," Vera says.

"It ain't from bicycling," Trudy jokes. She elbows Arthur.

For the moment my father has forgotten Bertha Landau. He tries to remember now how Arthur knows Trudy. Finally it comes to him that Arthur used to work with Trudy's husband at the newspaper, before the bookies chased him out of town. They still play poker together, he thinks.

"We should try the canapés," my mother says, "after all the trouble Vera made." My father nods, but he doesn't move. The vodka punch makes her feel better at first, but after she drinks some more, my mother gets melancholy. She strikes up a conversation with Mrs. Landau. She doesn't have to ask a lot of questions. Mrs. Landau is only too happy to let her know that she owns several apartment buildings and all they give her is grief. "It's a shame, this city is not geared for business. All the regulations! And the expenses are enormous, you can't imagine."

"Is that so?" my mother says. She doesn't recognize anyone in the room, except Trudy from Temple, who's talking nonstop, with Arthur hanging on every word. Trudy's pointy chin and big eyes remind my mother of a goat.

Finally she can't stand it. My mother goes to the sideboard and helps herself to the canapés, two each of half a dozen different kinds, and five gefilte fish balls with toothpicks. When she returns, Mrs. Landau is saying, "Our sojourn on the *Queen Mary*—" She stops to peer at my mother's plate. My mother thinks it's because she's hungry.

Watching Mrs. Landau and Trudy go to the sideboard, my mother says, "It's good, two women alone to stick together." My father doesn't answer. He helps himself to the herring off her plate. Not long after, they follow the women to the buffet. My mother heaps her plate again, wondering why Mrs. Landau has only one tiny sandwich on her paper plate, the size of a half dollar.

"You're fasting, Mrs. Landau?" my father jokes.

"I'm sure they won't run out of food," she says. "Please, call me Bertha."

"So, Bertha," my mother says, "you get your exercise going back and forth."

Trudy laughs. A big horse laugh. Her belly shakes. My mother wonders why Trudy isn't wearing a girdle under the silk dress, even if she has no *tokhes*. She herself is tightly corseted. Her soft, rounded flesh is in one piece, firm as a marble statue at the Cloisters, even while she does the samba with Arthur Vogel to a phonograph record.

"You're some dancer!" he tells her. Is he flirting with her? Anyhow he's too eager, not reserved like Harry. She wonders now if Harry's good manners come from growing up rich. She knows so little about him.

Back from dancing, she finds Trudy and Bertha have my father cornered by the grandfather clock. She edges in and puts her arm through his, as the Vogels announce the rules of the first game, Short Straw. A man is blindfolded and spun around, then he's supposed to use his mouth to get the short straw into the mouth of his wife. Other women try to confuse him by grabbing onto the straw with their own lips.

Is she imagining things? my mother wonders, when it's my father's turn. Bertha and Trudy are elbowing each other out of the way to line their lips up in his direction. A second later, Trudy yelps and points to her foot. "Oh, I beg your pardon," Bertha says, her voice dripping like honey. My mother doesn't hear what Trudy says back, but Bertha looks shocked. There are more words. People stare. Arthur steps between them. "Come with me, you beautiful creatures." My father takes off his blindfold and asks what's going on.

"Me-ow!" a woman tells him. "Two women fighting over you." She gestures toward their backs as Arthur spirits them to another room.

My father glances at my mother. "One of them I never met before in my life."

The woman baits him. "And the other one?"

"My mistress," my father says. There's a howl and then a larger one after my mother says, "You wish." In fact, my mother cannot conceive of my father's being attracted to Trudy Fleisch, not just because she looks like a goat and laughs like a horse. A very aggressive type, my mother thinks. Trudy would scare my father to death.

Just before midnight, champagne glasses clink together. My mother yearns to call Harry, to hear his voice. When she suggested it to him, he told her his mother goes to bed early, even on New Year's Eve. She realizes now she doesn't even have his number. She's not even sure where he lives exactly.

While the ball drops in Times Square, my mother's eyes are closed as she kisses my father. She is thinking, *Alevai*, the goat should run off with him.

My father's eyes are open. He and Trudy are staring at each other. "I love you," she mouths. From across the way, Bertha catches Trudy's eye. She mimics her, mouthing, "I love you." Trudy flushes. She doesn't care if Bertha knows, so long as Barney doesn't find out.

After the kissing, a conga line forms. The dancers use one hand to maintain contact with the person in front of them. The free hand twirls a noisemaker. In the street, horns are honking. The dancers snake around the room, through the French doors of the dining room, into the kitchen, and back again. Someone shakes a cowbell. The dance gets faster and faster. *One two three kick.* People drop out. My father drops out when Trudy does. Bertha keeps on. *Onetwothreekick.* So does my mother. They are the last two dancers. My mother kicks off her shoes. Finally Bertha drops out, panting. My mother is declared the winner. A man she doesn't know hands her a glass of champagne. "I should pour it into your slipper," he jokes. My mother is about to ask his name when my father steps between.

She sips the champagne, thinking, Another year. Let it be

healthy and happy for the kids. Then she thinks, *Harry, Harry, Harry*. She gives the glass to my father to finish. "So, I beat the lady who owns half the buildings in New York," she says.

With Bertha a safe distance away he tells my mother she also owns the building he works in. "Do you think those are real diamonds she's wearing?"

My mother glances over her shoulder. At Bertha's gray silk shoes, at her gray silk purse, at her gray silk dress with just a little extra fabric draped over the breast, at her short finger-nails shiny with colorless polish. "I don't know," my mother says, "but only a very rich lady would look so plain."

A few days after the party, Bertha Landau troops into my father's office at the factory, with Mr. Gershenfeld behind her. "This is our landlord," the boss says. "She wants to look around."

My father stands up.

"Good to see you again," she says. "Please, sit."

My father doesn't see Mr. Gershenfeld narrow his eyes. In her mink coat, Bertha makes a show of examining the ceiling and the walls. "You can leave me here to putter around," she tells Mr. Gershenfeld. Once he's gone, she says to my father, "We're thinking of selling this building. I want to be sure it's in top condition." Her perfume makes him want to open the door.

"Of course, if there's anything I can do to help . . ." he says.

"Tell me, is there a nice place around here for lunch?"

He tries to think where Mr. Gershenfeld might go, then re-calls his boss goes only to the kosher deli down the street. "Schrafft's is on the next block."

"What a good idea! Now, how would you like to join me?"

My father is too embarrassed to tell her he brings his lunch and doesn't have enough money with him. He decides to go with her anyhow. Later he'll act as if he forgot the money at home.

The restaurant is too dark for my father. He starts to apologize for his mistake, but Bertha says, "*Au contraire!* I'm fond of dark wood and subtle lighting." My father looks at the little brass lamp on the table, which gives practically no light. Beyond it, Bertha is practically all in shadow. Suddenly my father understands her preference.

She orders a club sandwich and tea. My father has the least expensive item, a grilled cheese, nothing to drink. They talk about the party, the predicted snowstorm. Bertha asks if he grew up in the city, surprised when he says he was a boy when his family emigrated from Berlin.

"That's why you have no accent," she says.

"I enjoyed learning English. My parents—may they rest in peace—they didn't know what my brother and I were saying. You have no accent either."

She tells him how she learned English in Austria, and when her family fled to England, she improved her accent. She tells him stories about their life in Vienna, where her father was a confectioner, then orders a layer cake, with two forks. When the waiter leaves, my father says, "They don't mind?"

"I'm the customer. It's their job to please me, not the other way around."

My father laughs nervously. He thinks, She must be rich, all right. When the cake arrives, he digs in only on his side, but Bertha guides his hand to where she's been eating the jelly between the layers. He thinks she wouldn't even mind if they had only one fork. "Don't be shy," she says.

That's what money does for you, my father thinks. It gives you *Hoden.* He excuses himself to go to the rest room. When he returns, she says she is ready to go. "We didn't get the bill yet," he says.

"I took care of it."

"How much?" my father says. He makes a show of digging into his pocket, but she puts up her gloved hand.

"Please, don't embarrass me," she says. "It's nothing. Allow me to treat. Another time you can buy me a cup of coffee."

The day before Valentine's Day Trudy gives my father a blue tie dotted with large red hearts. "Say you got it at the factory. I cut out the label."

"You're so clever," he says. He thinks Bertha would never go for such a loud tie. He'll keep it at work and wear it once or twice to Trudy's before throwing it out. He gives Trudy a two-pound box of Barricini's candy in a pink heart-shaped box. She offers the first candy to Hannah.

For Valentine's Day my brother and Lenore have dinner in an Italian restaurant on Fordham Road and go to the Loew's Paradise to see *Trapeze* with Burt Lancaster and Gina Lollobrigida. They sneak into the loge and make out so heavily, they see very little of the second movie. Sheldon takes Lenore home, and on the marble floor under the stairwell, she loses her virginity.

For Valentine's Day my sister makes Sofie Vrebolovich a pink paper heart, which she delivers along with a rose. She climbs up on a chair to change a lightbulb for Sofie and sorts through her mail. Sofie feeds her a bowl of borscht, the kind my sister never had before, with meat in it instead of just beets. Before

Mimi leaves, Sofie insists on giving her an old rolltop jewelry box filled with costume jewelry. "I'm cleaning out," she says. "To make less work for whoever finds my body."

My sister is horrified. "But you're not sick."

"I'm old. Eighty-one. I could go any minute."

At home, my sister paws through the garish earrings and necklaces and finds a hundred dollars in tens, rolled together. She calls up Sofie to tell her. "That's for you," Sofie says, "my little angel." My sister cries.

For Valentine's Day my mother gives Harry an umbrella with a wood handle. "So you think of me when it rains," she jokes. Harry gives my mother a little gold heart on a chain. He fastens it around her neck before they have sex in the narrow bed. My mother wears it home, not the least concerned that my father will notice it. On the way she picks me up from Madame LePage's.

Right away I notice the heart. I point. *"Coeur,"* I tell her, and poke my finger at the middle, which is missing.

"Coeur?"

"That's right, Mama." I show her the valentines I made, one for her, one for Papa, one for Sheldon, one for Mimi. On each one I've printed JE T'AIME. *"Je t'aime* is 'I love you,'" I say. *"Je t'aime, Maman."*

"Je t'aime, Mama," my mother says.

"Je t'aime, Devorah," I correct. "You're *Maman."*

"Excusez-moi," my mother says.

For Valentine's Day my father gives my mother a large, store-bought card inscribed TO MY DEAR WIFE. Inside is a fifty-dollar bill. For Valentine's Day my mother gives my father an argyle sweater vest and a medium-sized, store-bought card inscribed FOR MY HUSBAND.

. . .

A few days after Valentine's Day, my father gives Bertha a five-pound box of Barricini's candy in a red heart-shaped box. Although they've only had a few lunches together, I imagine my father considers it an investment. His hopes are buoyed when Bertha gives him gold cuff links. One is a baseball, and one is a bat. "I had them made for you. I wish I could have them engraved." He only wishes she had ordered a pair that matches.

At the Rainbow Room, he insists on picking up the check, and is shocked by the tab. Short on money, he stints on the tip. As they walk back to her place, Bertha thinks she will have to teach him about taxis, but later. All night my father has been planning their first kiss, so when they arrive at her building, he is crestfallen to see the doorman right there, holding the door open. Seconds later, when Bertha invites him up for coffee, he feels on top of the world.

The living room is like a hotel lobby, with its baby grand and two sofas, each with two facing armchairs. Too nervous to make the first move, my father stands by the window for a while. Is he really looking at Central Park? He wants to pinch himself for his good fortune, meeting Bertha Landau. Whatever happens, he thinks that this could do a lot for his future.

Soon, he sits primly on the tapestried-brocade sofa, the china cup and saucer on his lap. He is conscious of not knowing how to behave.

"I gave the boy the night off," Bertha says.

"The boy?"

"He cooks my dinner, makes the fire. It's good to have a man around the house."

"I don't cook," my father jokes. "I've never made a fire, either."

"Then we'll have to find some other use for you," she says.

"I'm at your service," he jokes back.

From the other end of the sofa, she holds out her hand. As my father takes hers, his cup and saucer tip over onto the carpet. The coffee splashes on the pleated skirt of the sofa. My father is mortified, but Bertha says, "Good! I needed an excuse to redo the room."

L ove is such a funny thing, my mother thinks. Once upon a time she thought she loved my father. Now she only wishes him away. Whatever she is doing, darning his socks, washing the clothes, ironing them, she tries to imagine what Harry is doing. Once as she lies in his arms, she asks Harry to tell her what he does after work. "I want to know, minute by minute."

"Oh, I read. Listen to the radio. Then I have dinner—"

"Who makes it? Your mother is sick, *nu*?"

"Since when is a Jewish mother too sick to cook for her son?" Harry says.

"But she had two strokes—"

"Her speech is a little affected, but she gets around okay."

"She's a good cook?" My mother doesn't wait for the answer. "I would love to cook you something. My *kugel*. My potato pancakes. I would bring you some, but warmed up is not the same as fresh."

Each time they're together now, the minutes go like nothing. She thinks someone is turning the hands of the clock ahead faster and faster. One afternoon, when it's time to leave, she says, "A year from September the little one will be in school. Then I can see you more." When he doesn't say anything, she says, "I know, you have work." He nods.

"But on your day off—"

"I do the shopping, the laundry."

"Such a good son! But maybe you could help on some other day?"

For a long time Harry has expected the balance to tip, for Chenia to become dissatisfied with the status quo. He only wishes the moment weren't upon him just yet.

"What are you thinking?" she asks.

"How grateful I am for these few moments of perfection! It's dangerous, Chenia, to ask for too much. Let's not be too greedy, all right?"

My mother is quiet. The way he acts, she thinks it must mean he doesn't love her as much as she loves him.

The next time my mother is supposed to meet Harry, she drops me off at Madame LePage's, but she doesn't go to the rented room. She walks up Broadway in the opposite direction, until she reaches the George Washington Bridge. She gazes at the steel towers, which remind her of the Parachute Jump. Just for an instant she thinks of going off the bridge. She doesn't really want to die, only to escape.

Digging her hands into the pockets of her suede jacket, she walks back, chewing on why Harry hasn't brought her home. His mother wouldn't have to know she's married. She chews on how she and Harry should be going places together, doing things, something besides making love in that skinny bed.

Outside Madame LePage's, he is leaning against the arch that leads to the courtyard. His head tipped back, he looks for a moment like Robert Taylor, full of the devil, but also tired. He turns slowly toward her. "I thought something happened to you," he says, his eyes full of self-pity.

"We don't have a future," she says. "Not like this."

"Chenia!" He takes her hand, but she pulls it away. "Chenia, when your daughter's in school, I promise, I'll rearrange

my life. These past two hours were the worst I've had since—
since you disappeared on me, in Coney Island."

"A day here, a day there, there's no future," she repeats.

"I can't bear the present without you, Chenia. Don't you
love me?"

Love. It's the word she's been yearning to hear. But she can't
give in so easily. "What am I to you?" she says.

"What are you to me? My beautiful Chenia! Let me count
the ways—"

Now the children and mothers spill past them, from across
the courtyard. My mother edges away from Harry, looking
around for me, my reddish hair.

"Thursday," he says. "Please come. We'll talk."

She averts her eyes. When she looks back, she concentrates
on his ears, which are a little long, his protruding Adam's
apple. It's over, she thinks. *Es iz ois!* Finished. Done.

The first time my father has sex with Bertha Landau, I
imagine he has no trouble with his erection, getting or
maintaining. The bedroom is dark, and anyhow, the novelty
propels him. Bertha is only his fourth woman, not counting
the two with whom he petted heavily before he was married.

The second time, Bertha leaves on a little night-light. Even
without his glasses, he can see her face. He gropes under the
sheet covering their bodies. Even without seeing, he can feel
that in the parts where Trudy is firm, Bertha is flab. As his
erection withers he feigns a sneeze. "Ah-ah-choo! Too much
perfume," he mutters. "I should have told you. I'm allergic."

"Oh, my dear Ruben," she says. She doesn't say that her
husband also used to complain.

What saves him is Bertha's expertise. Deftly she takes hold
of his soft member and tugs on it, knowledgeably, as if she

possessed one of her own. He responds. Though she isn't wet, like Trudy, he enters her easily enough, but then he struggles to maintain. "Bertha, sweet Bertha," he mutters in her ear, surprised when her hips counter his bucking with their own. The mechanics propel him to a climax.

During the fifth or sixth time, when Bertha switches on a lamp, saying, "I want to see your handsome face, Ruben," he is in trouble. He pushes and pushes inside her, but he doesn't feel excited. He slips right out. She caresses him until he can re-enter her, and he thrusts violently till she tells him to take it easy. He thinks of Trudy or even of Ermelinda to keep himself going, but it's too complicated. Finally he thinks of Millie, the Negress. How dark, how soft, how she embraces him, clasping his head between her breasts . . . He comes.

Not seeing Harry, my mother suffers. She misses glimpsing a world larger than her own. She misses making love. It's crazy how she can hardly bear not to see him, but to see him would be too painful. What made her think he ever loved her?

At night, after my father falls asleep, she touches her *knepl.* What she calls her love button. She needs the comfort of sex, even a poor substitute. To quell the fire. It takes no time at all now for her to have a climax. Still, she feels cranky all the time. Unfulfilled.

More and more my father gets on her nerves. As he leaves for work one morning, she says, "Tonight you can't have dinner with your *mishpokhe*?"

"It's Tuesday. What do I always do on Tuesday?"

"This card playing, is it a *krenk* with you?" A sickness. "Monday, Tuesday, Wednesday, Thursday, Saturday afternoon, now Sunday afternoons."

"There's a big game tonight. Special odds."

"Where are you playing?"

"Where else? At Arthur's," he says. "If you think I'm lying, call him."

"I'm only asking. Vera don't mind the company? Cooking and cleaning?"

"They have a maid. Anyway, it's not her business."

"Listen," she says. "This cannot go like this. I want you home. The little one, she never sees you."

"Tomorrow," he says right away. He knows Bertha is going to the opera with her lady friends. He was planning to see Trudy instead.

"One day from seven," my mother says. "Yes, Friday night we go to Temple. Two from seven. *Tu mir nit kein toyves.*" Don't do me any favors.

"Saturday," he says. "We'll go someplace."

Now my mother wonders why he's giving in so easily.

Sex with Bertha is all right, my father tells himself, but the more he thinks about his conquest, the better it becomes in retrospect. Though he seldom has sex anymore with my mother, he finds ways to keep her from thinking his attentions are elsewhere. He offers to paint the bathroom ceiling, which is peeling. "You want I should faint?" she says. He suggests new linoleum for the kitchen floor. My mother and I spend days in the linoleum place, deciding on a pattern, squares within squares. Yellow, red, and green. Then, wonder of wonders, my father orders a television set from the appliance store on Dyckman Street.

"I can't believe it," Mimi says.

Now my mother's sure my father is making up for something. Or that he's won a big lawsuit. Even so, she thinks it's the best thing, to have the family around the T.V., but soon everyone starts arguing over what to watch.

"Stop it!" she screams one night. "You make me crazy with

the fighting!" When Sheldon and Mimi start again, she hurls a vase across the room.

Even before it shatters, I run behind the sofa.

"You scared the wits out of Devorah!" my father says, pleased to have something against my mother. Something tangible. "Devorah, come here," he cajoles. "Your papa loves you. Come here. No one will hurt you."

But I stay put. Finally I let my brother coax me out. I sit on his lap for a few minutes and stare at the screen. I don't know why he is laughing. I go to get my book of ABCs. I read it for at least the hundredth time.

On the first day of spring we're at the top of Fort Tryon Park, but my mother doesn't take me into the Cloisters. "I change my mind," she says, and wheels me around. She feels she's losing her mind, thinking of Harry. Maybe if she changed her routine . . . Down we go, all the way to the bottom of the park. "Wheee," she says, as she pushes and runs.

"What did you forget, Mama?" I ask.

"My head. I don't even know my name. Tell me."

"Chenia," I say.

"What's Papa's name?"

"Papa."

"Papa and what else?"

"Troublemaker."

She leans over to see me better. "What did you say?"

"Troublemaker."

She makes a sound I've never heard before, kind of a short shriek. Then she laughs. "You're a one-person act, like in vaudeville."

"Poison?" I say, because that's how she says *person*. She's told me not to touch the poison in the kitchen cabinet, which is for the roaches.

"*Oy*," she says. "Person, not poison."

"*Poyson*," I say.

"That's it. Person. All by yourself you could be on the stage. I'll take you to the Roxy when you're older."

O ften, when they see each other, Bertha gives my father a gift. The gifts are expensive: a mahogany clock, a silver razor, a silver-backed brush, a silver mustache comb. My father scolds her, but she says, "I like to spoil you." Each time he rings her bell now, he wonders what she will have for him. If he could wish for anything, besides a million dollars, he would wish her smile didn't remind him so much of Howdy Doody.

O ne afternoon, my mother parks my stroller outside Magic Shoes. "Holler if anyone touches the carriage, hear?"

Inside the store she asks for Mr. Taubman. The cashier's bangs flounce as she says he's not available. "Can someone else help you?"

"No. Is he here?"

The girl tilts her head. "Can I tell him what it's concerning?"

"So he's here?"

When the girl doesn't say anything, my mother says irritably, "What's with the big mystery? He's here or he ain't here."

"He's tied up," the girl says.

"Can you go untie him?"

"I'm sorry, I can't. Can I give him a message?"

"I don't think you'd like it." My mother slams the door behind her.

Outside the store she releases the brake of my stroller, sees the *funfeh*, the double-talker, smirking. My mother has an urge to slap her. What is this new crankiness in herself? she wonders. Is she getting her period? Now she wonders how long it's been. If she's pregnant . . . She doesn't finish the thought.

She asks me where I'd like to go, and I tell her, "On the swings!"

In the playground she lifts me into a little metal seat with a bar across, like my old high chair. She pushes me, but I know how to pump my legs. "Not too high," she yells. "High!" I yell. "Higher!"

"Well, lookee who!" a woman says. Trudy Fleisch plops Hannah into the swing next to mine. She pushes Hannah's swing as she looks my mother over. She likes the suede jacket, the suede gloves. She wonders why my mother wears shoes with thick heels. "You come here often?" she asks. Push push.

"Not anymore," my mother says. "How's about you?"

"Every afternoon." She forgets to push, and Hannah starts to wail.

"Push her," I say.

"Okay, okay," my mother says. "Don't tell Trudy what to do."

"Trudy?" I say.

"Mrs. Fleisch, to you," my mother says.

Later my mother and Trudy sit on a bench while Hannah and I play nearby. "How old is your kid?" my mother asks.

"Four. At my age I'm ready for grandchildren, then my nephew had the accident . . . And you? You wanted another child?" Trudy says.

My mother glances at me. "This one, she understands too much for her own good."

"Mrs. Fleisch," I call out. "Spell your name. Please?" I say it to show off. Anyway, it's hard to play with Hannah. She doesn't talk. She just wants to hold her teddy bear.

"Why don't you go chase pigeons?" my mother says.

"I want to listen," I say.

"I want you to go chase pigeons. Show Hannah."

"C'mon, Hannah," I say. "I'll learn you to chase the pigeons."

"I'll *teach* you to chase the pigeons," Trudy says to me.

"I know how," I say. My mother can hardly keep a straight face.

Trudy doesn't seem to notice. She opens a compact and powders her nose. "Your husband, he's okay?" she asks.

"How should he be?" my mother answers. "The same. How's by yours?"

"Barney's always working overtime." Trudy snaps the compact shut.

"Extra money, it couldn't hurt. Ruben, he never gets a day of overtime."

"Is that so? Never?" Trudy wonders if my mother is trying to worry her. Overtime is the excuse Ruben gives for only seeing her once a week now.

"Six kids his boss has," my mother says. "Orthodox. He don't believe in overtime. Why? You like your husband not to work so much?" With her sad blue eyes, Trudy looks more like a goat than ever, my mother thinks.

"I never see him," Trudy says. "We lead two separate lives."

"Who sees a husband? With Ruben it's cards, cards, cards. Monday, Tuesday, Wednesday, Thursday, Saturday, Sunday . . ."

Trudy stands up. "I have to run some errands."

"Maybe we could meet here again sometime?" my mother says.

"Oh sure," Trudy says, but then she hurries off. My mother tries to figure out what she did to drive her away. Maybe she's jealous of the little one after all. Next to Hannah, even a blind person could get the picture.

"Now what do you want to do?" my mother asks me.

"I want to go to the library."

"Let your sister take you."

"You take me."

"I can't."

"Why?"

My mother sighs. "Why? Why? Why? I don't know where it is."

"You could ask."

"It's too far. I'm tired," she fibs. Actually she feels like running. She is so restless.

When we get to our building, my mother races me up the stairs. For once she doesn't let me win. With so much energy, she thinks, she couldn't possibly be pregnant. Taking off her hat in the apartment, she catches sight of herself in the mirror. Her skin seems dry, lined all of a sudden. Now it dawns on her, why her monthly is late. She is beginning her menopause.

"What's?" my mother asks my brother again. He is slumped over a newspaper he has spread across the kitchen table.

"Nothing. I told you."

"Nothing, you didn't tell me," she says. "You look like the sky is falling."

"It is."

"You're in trouble at school?" she asks.

He shakes his head. "I need money. A lot of money."

"For what?"

"I don't want to tell you."

"Is so terrible?"

"Pretty bad, Ma. I'm sorry." His eyes are sunken into his long face. She wonders if he's losing weight.

"Your *mameh*, she's heard many things in her life. You can tell me." She sits down next to him and puts her hand on his wrist.

"I have to have the money."

"You broke something? What? A friend lent you his car and you smashed it up?"

"That would be a lot simpler, Ma."

Now she starts to worry. "*Gevalt*, you got a girl in trouble?"

His eyes flash. "My friend Donny knows someone who will take care of it, if we could just get the money."

"Take care of the baby?"

"Take care of it," he says. "You know—"

Get rid of it, my mother thinks. She feels suddenly queasy. "This individual, he's a doctor?"

"No. It's illegal, Ma. You can't go to the doctor."

"How much?" she says.

"A hundred fifty."

"Dollars?" My mother sits down next to him. "Her mother knows?"

"Of course not. She'd kill Lenore."

"Lenore? Have I met her?"

"No."

"What kind of girl is she? You love her, or you were just taking advantage?"

Sheldon flashes her an angry look. "She's a nice girl. Her father's a chemist."

"If she has brains, she should have used them," my mother says. "She must be pretty."

"She's no dummy. She was planning to go to college."

"Oh yeah? She don't want to get married so young?"

"If her parents find out, they'll make her." He puts his hands over his gaunt face. "What am I supposed to do?"

"I don't know," my mother says. "Let me think."

My mother aches to talk it over with Harry. He would know
what to do, she tells herself. He wouldn't get angry, because it
doesn't involve his own son. That afternoon she leaves me
with my brother and goes back to Magic Shoes. The same
cashier is there and recognizes her.

"I'd like to see Mr. Taubman," my mother says.

The cashier flashes a quick, phony smile. "He's in a meeting."

"You worked here so long you have X-ray eyes from the
machine?" my mother jokes. "Listen, darling, tell Mr. Taubman there's someone to see him."

"I can't."

"What's your name?"

"Jilly."

"Jilly, go get Mr. Taubman. Now. Go!" My mother smiles
to herself. She can hear how she sounds like a boss.

Jilly stares for a second, then picks up the phone. "A
woman here to see you. I told her you're in a meeting." Jilly
hangs up. "He's coming."

"Mrs. Arnow!" Harry strides up to her with his hand extended. They shake hands. "What can I do you for?"

"There's a little matter I need to talk over," she says.

"Jilly, I'll be back in a half hour." He winks at her.

As they walk up Dyckman, my mother says, "You were in a
meeting?"

"That Jilly, she's always trying to protect me."

"From what?"

"Customers. They get angry. They buy shoes that don't fit,
then they blame us." He takes her arm and squeezes it. "Chenia! I've missed you. God, how I've missed you!"

His breath is warm, familiar. She aches to draw him close
to her.

In Bickford's they spend ten minutes staring into each

other's eyes before my mother remembers why she's there. "Harry, can I ask you something?"

Harry tenses the muscles in his solar plexus. "You can ask."

She tells him about my brother and the girl. He asks how old he is. "Seventeen," my mother says. "The girl I don't know."

"I hope she's of legal age," Harry says. "Her parents could put him in jail."

"Jail? *Gottenyu!*" Her eyes get wild, she comes up out of the seat, but Harry tells her he was just thinking out loud. "What do you think is best for him, Chenia?"

"All I know, my son, he wants her to get fixed."

"An abortion? Very dangerous," Harry pronounces. "Sometimes the girl bleeds to death or gets an infection, a bad one. After that she might not be able to bear children."

My mother sips the cold coffee.

"How many weeks along is she?" Harry asks.

"Not so many, I think."

"That's good news. It's not a baby yet, just a lot of cells, like a tadpole."

"What is this, *tadpole*?" she asks.

On the napkin he makes a little sketch. "That's how big it is. In the Torah, the zygote is considered to be only water for the first forty days after conception. The fetus isn't a human being until it can exist independently."

"So small?" she says. She can't get over it. The torture she went through . . .

"But tell her not to wait, Chenia. It's a sad situation none-theless. I'm sorry. Is that why you came to see me?"

"Just part."

"You missed me?"

"A *taigel*," my mother jokes. "Half a *taigel*."

My mother dreams that she is lying on the operating table. Her belly is huge, and encased in limestone. It looks like an igloo. The doctor uses a hammer and chisel on it until it cracks open. He lifts me out. I am wearing a gingham dress, red-and-white-checked, with a matching bonnet, and papery white shoes, the kind dolls wear. "It's either you or her," the doctor says. "You have to decide!" My mother feels herself shriveling. Her belly collapses, and her body is folding up, into itself. She knows she will have to live the rest of her life as a dwarf.

She wakes up sweating and moaning.

All the time now my mother daydreams different ways to get my brother out of his difficulty. Maybe he should go in the Army. Maybe she should meet the girl's mother. In the daydream my mother puts on a housecoat and a kerchief. She puts garlic all over herself and carries two shopping bags. She talks only in Yiddish. The girl's mother decides she doesn't want her daughter to marry into a family of foreigners.

In another daydream my mother tries to borrow money from her sister, but in reality she's too ashamed to tell her what my brother did.

One day, as she imagines asking my Uncle Yakob for the money, the phone rings. I pick it up. "Hello," I say.

"Let me talk to your mother," the voice says.

"Mama, a man."

My mother takes the phone. "Hello?"

"Chenia? It's Harry. I've missed you."

Her stomach flutters. "Me, too."

"When can I see you?"

"Let me take care of this business with my son," she says, "and then my mind will be free again."

"I understand, but I miss you so much. I want to hold you, to kiss you."

"Me, too," she says. "The little one is right here."

"I understand. Give her a kiss for me."

My mother announces to my brother that she wants to meet Lenore.

"Why?"

"Why? Because something has to be done. You could go to jail for what you did."

"Lenore would never let her parents do that to me."

"*Yold!*" Simpleton. "Lenore cannot stop them."

My brother is instructed to stay away while my mother has Lenore to the house after school. My mother sizes her up, a nice girl, with a good figure, but a brain she isn't. My mother takes heart. She serves us milk and bananas, then the three of us go to the playground. She asks Lenore to wheel the stroller. Thinking it's my mother's way of inviting her into the family, Lenore relaxes.

They sit on a bench near the fountain. My mother doesn't say much.

"Do you miss Brooklyn?" Lenore asks.

"Sure," my mother says. "Why not?"

"You come from Poland or Russia?" Lenore asks.

"That's so."

Sheldon was right, Lenore thinks. His mother is very mysterious. Lenore stops asking questions for a while, but then she gets impatient. "What did you want to talk to me about?" she says.

"Don't be in such a hurry. Sit. This is what you'll be doing for the next ten years, sitting on this bench, watching your children." Lenore gives her a look. "What?" my mother says. "You think I make this up? Look around you." On all the benches are girls just a few years older than Lenore, with carriages and strollers.

No! Lenore thinks. *I'm not going to. I can't. I can't. God help me.*

They sit some more. Then my mother says, "Darling, is this a future for you? You're so young, so pretty, my son tells me you get good marks. You could go to college."

"That's what I want," Lenore says.

"So tell your parents. If they think better you should get married, my son is willing, but kids having a kid, it couldn't be much of a life."

"I don't know whether to have the baby anyway," Lenore says.

"You could have it," my mother says. "But if it's adopted, you'll only break your heart."

Lenore starts to cry. "I love him."

"What is love? You want him with you. That's one kind of love. A childish love. Grown-up love, you want him to finish high school. You give him a chance to make a decent living. Then you can get married, right? He's not going nowhere."

"My parents will kill me."

"I don't think so. You're a nice girl, I bet you have nice parents. You want me to talk to them?"

"No, I'll do it," Lenore says.

"Let me at least walk you home," my mother says. "You have to talk to them right away, before the seed starts to grow into a baby. Now is nothing. Did you know that?" Lenore looks doubtful. "*Emes*," my mother says. True.

On the way to her place, Lenore asks my mother, "Don't you go crazy, sitting in the park like that?"

"At your age, yes. Now, I don't mind so much. The little one keeps me company. Today she's all ears, but when we're alone together, she has plenty to say. Right, you?"

"Lenore," I say. "L-A-N-O-R."

"Almost," Lenore says, and spells it for me. I spell it for her, correctly. "My golly, Sheldon told me she was a genius."

"What's genius?" I ask.

"It's another word for *bubbeleh*," my mother says.

O n a bench in front of Central Park, Trudy waits. People walk their dogs. Limousines pull up to the awning-covered entrance of the building across the street. Taxi horns blare. She was here the evening before, but my father didn't show up. When she finally asked the doorman for Mrs. Landau, he said she was out. Now Trudy scans the windows, wondering which apartment is Bertha's.

Just as she gets discouraged, a crosstown bus stops across the street. My father gets off the bus. Although Trudy has planned only to spy on him, she darts across Fifth Avenue and catches up with him under the awning.

My father opens his arms. "Surprise! What are you doing here?"

"Waiting for a friend. And you?"

"I'm going to see Bertha Landau. She isn't feeling well."

For a moment Trudy is so thrown by his clever answer she believes him, then she decides to call his bluff. "Maybe I better go with you."

"Too many visitors," he says. "Better call her and come another time."

"Baloney! You've been having an affair with her all along, haven't you!"

"What are you talking about?"

"Either you come with me now, or it's over between us," she says.

"Trudy, don't be foolish!"

"Can I help you?" the doorman asks.

"No!" Trudy and my father say in unison.

"I mean it," she says. "Are you coming with me?"

"I have an appointment. I can't stand her up."

"You can call her and make an excuse."

My father contemplates. "Okay, where would you like us to go?"

L ate at night my mother wakes. Another hot flash. She wipes the sweat from her forehead. She wonders if my brother is asleep. He didn't eat his dinner. He tried to call Lenore after the abortion, but she hung up on him. Now my mother thinks she hears someone walking through the living room. She gets up.

The kitchen light is on. Funny sounds, like squeaks or hiccoughs, are coming from that direction. As she nears the kitchen she realizes it's the sound of sobbing. My brother's face is buried in his arm, resting on the table. His shoulder wings bob as he cries.

My mother goes back to get her bathrobe. He is still crying when she returns. She walks up to him and puts her hand on his back. "Darling, you did the best thing for all concerned."

He wipes his nose on his pajama sleeve and looks up at her. "We killed a baby."

"It wasn't a baby. Just cells. A tadpole," she says. "This big." She shows him with her fingers.

"Really? You're not just saying it?"

"Darling, one of the smartest men I ever knew told me this."

"Who?"

"I forget his name. How is Lenore?"

"She won't talk to me."

"Eh, she's upset, that's all."

"She says she hates me." Sheldon starts again to sob. My mother puts her hand on his hand, smoothes his pajama collar. "Listen," she says. "Right now you want to make it up to her, and she won't let you. Both of you, you make such a *tsimmes* from so little." My mother can hardly believe she's saying this, but she would say anything to stop her son from hurting. "Are you listening to me?"

He wipes his nose again. "Yeah."

"A few cells, they came out of her body, like she had her monthly. That's all it is. You have to tell her. She's built it up in her mind. *Farshtaist?*"

My brother nods. And suddenly a sob comes out of him, from way inside. He sobs and sobs. My mother stands there with her arms around him, tears streaming down her own cheeks.

Even before Harry says anything on the phone, my mother can tell he's excited. "My mom, she's visiting her sister for a week. I want you to come over."

"All right." My mother is very curious what kind of place he lives in, how he lives altogether.

"Can't you get away for an evening, for a week of evenings? I want to take you out to dinner, the whole *shmear.*"

"I have to figure," she says.

"Figure fast," Harry says. "She's leaving tomorrow."

My mother has me wait on the landing below as she rings Lenore's bell. Lenore looks very surprised to see her. "Sheldon sent you, didn't he!"

"I thought between you and him is over," my mother says.

"That's right."

"I want you to baby-sit my little one. Tomorrow night."

"Me? Why?"

"She's good company. Right now your mood, is sour. You need an uplift."

Mrs. Arnow's so strange, Lenore thinks. Her face is serene, like those on cameos, but she's a little bundle of nervous energy. Lenore wonders whether Sheldon takes more after his father, quiet and reserved. "I'm not sure it's a good idea," she tells my mother. "I want to forget everything to do with babies."

"Listen," my mother says. "Someone falls off a bicycle. They have to get right back on. Someday, *alevai*, you'll have little ones, when you're ready."

Lenore doesn't know what it is, the way Mrs. Arnow looks at her, the way she talks, piercing right through her. Even with her accent she sounds so smart. "What time? Can you bring her here? I'm sorry, I don't want to see your son."

My mother leaves me with Lenore and meets Harry at Bickford's after he gets off work. They take a cab to a restaurant way up Broadway, a place with blue-and-white-checkered tablecloths and candles in wine bottles with wax dripping down. My mother finds it very interesting, but the food is a little spicy. It's the first Italian restaurant she's ever been in. By the time the spumoni comes, she feels tipsy from the Chianti. She reaches across the table to touch Harry's cheek. "I love you so much. You have no idea."

They take a cab to his apartment, near the river, it turns out, on a tree-lined street that curves around. The building has a sofa in the lobby and an elevator. The apartment is on the fifth floor and smells of pine.

There are two bedrooms and a dining room, two bathrooms, and three steps down to the living room, with a fireplace that Harry says is real. Her eyes take everything in hungrily, but it's all so plain, beige upholstery, beige carpet. *Boring,* she thinks, before pushing the word out of her mind. On the mantel, there's a framed picture of his mother. She can see he gets from her the dark eyes, but her hair looks white now. They sit on the beige sofa and drink a little sherry.

"We're always in such a hurry," he says. "Tonight we have time. Tell me about you, where you grew up."

She loves how he hasn't touched her, how he leans forward now, his elbows on his thighs, his hands clasped, to listen. She tells him about her father who was a carpenter, how he never spoke anything but Yiddish. She tells him about her mother who always wore a wig because she was Orthodox. She tells him about her sister who got into trouble for loving a Russian soldier.

"Ruchel?" he says.

"No, the other one. She passed. *Oleho hasholem.*" May she rest in peace.

When my mother stops talking, it is ten o'clock. "*Gevalt!* I have to go home. If Ruben comes there first—" Then she remembers, the little one is with Lenore. "You devil," she says to Harry. "You can make me forget everything."

He insists on seeing her to Lenore's place, and waits outside. My mother is amazed I'm still up, but she doesn't scold. Lenore refuses money from my mother and gives me her *Look* magazine. Harry puts us in a taxi, where I fall sound asleep. My mother has trouble rousing me when we get home.

Upstairs, while I dream of Lenore pushing me on the swings, my mother stays awake. Tonight was one of the best nights in her whole life, she thinks. She can't get over it, how strange this is, because she and Harry didn't even make love.

Over dinner at Longchamps my father tells Bertha that Trudy showed up outside her building. Bertha says, "I doubt it was accidental on her part. Wasn't she your girlfriend?"

"Yes," he admits. He is counting on his frankness to disarm her.

"But you're not seeing her now, is that right?"

"That's right. But she's very jealous."

"That I can believe." Bertha looks approvingly as my father tears a piece off his roll to eat, instead of cutting it in half. He is making progress under her tutelage. Next she will get him to stop using his fingers to shove the peas onto the fork.

Why can't he find one woman who has everything? my father wonders. After their big fight over Bertha, Trudy went back to Philadelphia to sign the adoption papers, but now she is all lovey-dovey. As soon as he steps through the door, she throws her arms around him and starts to tear off his clothes. He knows to arrive later these days, when Hannah is already asleep.

Tonight Trudy pulls him down on the floor. "Always the bed," she says to him when he resists. "Let's do it here."

The floor is hard on his knees, but he goes along. When his head bends down to kiss Trudy's ear, he feels as if he is inhaling dust from the rug. Even so, he's glad to be with her, to be inside her. Their bodies mingle like vanilla and chocolate pudding swirl. He lets his mind wander to help him last longer. To keep from climaxing too soon, he thinks of his future with Bertha Landau.

Lenore has such a good time baby-sitting me, she calls my mother the next day and offers to do it again. "Tonight?" my mother asks. Lenore says okay. My mother calls the store and talks to Harry.

"I was just going to call you," he says. "A cousin of mine drove in without telling me. I'm so sorry, Chenia. How about tomorrow night?"

"I'll try." She calls Lenore back to ask, but Lenore says she has to go a party. "How's Friday?"

My mother calls Harry back.

"Friday is fine," he says. As soon as she gets off the phone, my mother remembers that Friday night she and my father attend services. She is heartsick. The whole week with Harry is going, and there's nothing she can do.

She feels out my brother, but Sheldon says he's promised to fix a girl's car. She doesn't have the heart to ask him to change his plans. He is starting to act normal again. She asks my sister, but Mimi says she has to study with her friend Suzanne for a test. My mother gets the idea to look for Trudy Fleisch in the playground, but when she doesn't find her, she calls her at home.

Hearing my mother's voice, Trudy is shocked. She believes that she and Ruben have finally been found out.

"You know, how one hand washes the other?" my mother says.

"What are you getting at?" Trudy wonders how she can persuade my mother not to tell Barney.

"I have to go shopping at Alexander's, but is too much with the little one. Maybe you could mind her tomorrow night when they stay late. Some other night, you need a baby-sitter, you call me, *nu*?" When Trudy doesn't answer right away, my mother says, "You're there?"

"I'm here, can you hold a moment? I have to see about Hannah." In truth, Trudy needs time to decide. She wonders if my mother is testing her. Thursday is her regular night with Ruben. She's afraid to say no to my mother. At the same time, she's afraid that if she makes an excuse with Ruben, he'll go see Bertha.

Trudy picks up the phone. "Okay, what time?"

M y mother and Harry go for dinner to a steak house. When they first enter the place, all she can smell is beer. "They couldn't save more on the electric," she says. "So dark in here. Are you trying to hide me?"

"Chenia! This is one of my watering holes." He explains *watering holes*.

Her eyes adjust soon to the dim light. The men at the bar seem to her coarse, with red noses and large pores on their faces. After the food arrives, she hears a woman singing, "'Gon-na take a sent-i-men-tal journey . . .'" She is across the way, on one of the bar stools. She has a feather in her hat, and her white blouse is unbuttoned down to her brassiere.

Harry sees my mother looking. "A regular," he says.

"To me is like a tavern here."

"Don't tell me you're a snob. Isn't the steak good?"

"Very good. You come in here often?"

"Twice a week." He gestures with his hands. "For the company, I guess."

Just then she sees a man coming toward them. He is limping. She puts her hand along the side of her face and bends her head down.

"Mrs. Arnow?"

She looks up.

"Oh, Mr. Mangiameli! How are you?" she says warmly. Inside she is cringing. To think what Ruben did . . . For months she couldn't get over it. It made her so sick. "This is my cousin, Peter," she says to him.

Harry gets up, and they shake hands. Her heart sinks when Harry says, "Would you like to join us?" but Mr. Mangiameli declines. He tells Harry to please sit down.

"You're looking very good," Mr. Mangiameli tells her. "How's your little daughter?"

"Getting big. You, too. You gained weight. You look good."

Mr. Mangiameli gives Harry a once-over, then he pats her upper arm. "Be happy," he says knowingly. "You deserve it."

Her eyes brim with tears. After he limps off, she tells Harry he used to be their boarder. She can't bring herself to tell him what happened.

"Why are you all teary-eyed?" Harry asks. "Was he your boyfriend?"

"What?" she says indignantly. "You are my first, my last. What do you take me for?"

"I'm sorry, I didn't mean—"

"He's a good man. Italian. I feel very sorry for him."

"Ah, Chenia, you have such empathy." Harry explains how empathy is different from sympathy.

For a few minutes they are quiet. She chews on what he told her earlier and says, "So, you come in here every week?"

"I have a beer, let off some steam, and then I go home."

"Your mother, she makes you nervous?"

"She's not the easiest person to be around."

"What about me?" my mother says. "Am I so easy?"

"You?" Harry slaps his head. "If you were, I wouldn't be so crazy about you."

"Since when are you crazy about me?" she asks.

"Since I saw you on the Boardwalk. You had that new-mother glow."

"The glow from the ocean wind, that's all."

"You were so beautiful. I didn't want to go back to work that day. Your hair's growing now," he says. "I like it longer."

"Then I let it grow."

As he traces her fingers with his index finger, they are both quiet. With his thumb he massages the back of her hand. She feels hypnotized, so completely in his power. What scares her also makes it thrilling.

The bedspread is gray plaid, a rough material. He pulls it down. *Harry's bed*, she thinks. They sit on the side and kiss for a long time, then slowly he undresses her. This time she starts to undress him. A first. "Go on," he encourages. Then they lie under the sheet, and soon he is inside her. Right away he has a climax. "Oh Chenia, I'm so sorry, I was so excited. In a few minutes we'll try again."

For my mother it doesn't matter. Just to lie there, in Harry's arms, to feel his naked body against hers, the hairs of his belly against her belly, is pleasure enough. He kisses her all over. When he tries to kiss her down there, she pushes his head. "What are you doing, Mister?"

"Relax."

"You make me nervous. How can I relax?" He kisses her hip instead, her breasts, her neck. Then he is inside her again. For a while she thinks nothing is going to happen, but when he takes her face in his hands and they look at each other, that sweet feeling floods through her. She loves hearing him moan with pleasure as he spills into her.

She has never felt so close with my father. Not in all their twenty-two years. "I love you, Mister," she says to Harry.

"My Chenia," Harry says. "My dear, dear Chenia."

"The bus, it never came," my mother tells Trudy. It's eleven o'clock, and the store closes at nine-thirty or ten, my mother can't remember which.

"What did you buy?" Trudy asks.

From her pocketbook my mother takes out a paper bag, an old one, from Alexander's. She has put an unused linen hankie in it, with a tiny gold sticker on it still, which she shows to Trudy. "Bedspreads I couldn't find. Thank you a million for watching the little one."

"Did you try on some clothes? Your zipper is halfway open." Trudy zips up my mother's dress.

"Nothing fit," my mother says.

Trudy has a fleeting thought that my mother is lying.

"The little one didn't give you trouble?" my mother asks.

"She followed me everywhere. Questions, questions. She wouldn't look at the television with Hannah. Your husband's out tonight? He must be, or you wouldn't be here."

"Playing cards. If he wins, he comes home in a good mood."

"How often does that happen?"

"I should know," my mother says, meaning she doesn't know. "Last night, midnight, he came home singing to himself."

"Is that so!" Trudy says. *Just wait*, she thinks. *There's going to be hell to pay.*

The next afternoon, as my mother gets me ready to leave the house, Vera Vogel calls. "I know this is short notice, but I'm practically in your neighborhood, and I need to talk to someone."

"Talk."

"Can you meet me at 181st Street? I'll buy you a cup of coffee."

"I have the little one with me, is okay?"

"This is the best news I've heard in a week."

My mother puts on her felt hat, which she only wears when she's visiting. As she wheels me up the hill she says, "We meet my friend Mrs. Vogel. She wants to talk, so you have to be quiet and read your library books."

In the coffee shop, which smells of chocolate, Vera pinches my cheek and hugs my mother. "I'm so glad to see you."

Before they even look at the menu, Vera says, "Arthur's in the hospital. Presbyterian."

"*Gevalt!* How come?"

Vera sighs. "The loan shark from Brooklyn, he found him. I told Arthur, 'Pay up!' but does Arthur listen? Arthur, he's such a damn fool, he says, 'A hundred percent interest, are you kidding?'"

Before I can ask, my mother says, "Vera's husband is sick. Mrs. Vogel to you." The waiter takes the order: coffee and apple strudel for them, milk for me. My mother gives me pieces of apple from her plate. I try to read my book, but the conversation is too interesting, even if I don't understand very much.

"So what happened to him?" my mother asks Vera.

Vera clucks. "His nose, his ear, several ribs, and they cracked his knee."

My mother puts her hand over her face. "*Gottenyu!* I'm so sorry."

"What can I do? I begged him not to get involved with those gangsters."

My mother is thinking it's a lesson to her, not to envy people with fancy apartments. "When did this happen?"

"Four days ago, he's walking down the street. Boom! From nowhere. When he doesn't show up for dinner, I get an inkling. By the time the phone rings, I'm out of my mind."

"He's been in the hospital since Monday?" my mother says. Vera nods. The wheels in my mother's brain start to turn.

"So how's Ruben?" Vera asks. "Everything all right between you? I haven't seen either of you since you were over for New Year's, except—"

A strange chill goes down my mother's spine. "Your husband, he don't play cards anymore?" she says.

"Thursday night poker, that's it. I put my foot down. Isn't this strudel delicious!"

"Delicious," I say.

"Chenia, maybe it doesn't mean a thing—" Vera begins.

"What?"

Vera swallows. She looks away as she speaks. "Arthur and I, we were in Longchamps Saturday night. On my way to the powder room, I saw Ruben. He was with Bertha, having a fancy dinner."

"Bertha?"

"You remember Bertha Landau. The widow who was at the party, bragging about her real estate."

"I remember," my mother says. "In Longchamps? Where the movie stars go?"

"Saturday night." Vera grabs my mother's hand. "I wasn't going to tell you—"

"Thank you. I could die of shame, but you do me a favor."

We finish drinking and eating, and then my mother hugs Vera. Vera hugs me. She takes something out of her pocketbook. It's a gold locket on a chain. "For you," she tells me. She tells my mother she bought it in the jewelry store next door while she was waiting for us to get there.

"*Coeur*," I say. "Like yours, Mama, but bigger."

"What?" Vera asks.

"That's *heart* in French," my mother says, and makes a face that I know means, Be quiet. "Besides, this one opens." She shows me how, then asks, "How do you say thank you? In French."

"*Merci. Merci beaucoup.*"

Vera claps her hands. "It would be wonderful if she could go to private school. Maybe she could get a scholarship?"

My mother nods, but she's too distracted to hear. Her head is full with news she has to digest.

Fancy dinner. Vera's words *tchep* at her. My mother waits up that night for my father. She drinks a glass of milk at the kitchen table, studying a sheet that Madame LePage gave us, with

drawings labeled in French. LA MAISON. LA PARAPLUIE. LA
FLEUR. Her heart thumps when she hears the key in the door.

"Can't sleep?" my father says.

"I worry how much money you're losing, all the cards
you're playing. Did you lose tonight?"

"Just a little."

"Who won?" she asks.

"Arthur. He's so lucky."

"*Takeh?* You played cards at his place?"

"What're you giving me the third degree for?"

"We never get to talk," she says. "I was just wondering."

"Yeah, we played at his place."

"What a coincidence! I saw Vera today."

My father changes his story. "Actually I didn't play cards
tonight. I was at the factory. We're having problems. Serious
problems. I didn't want to worry you."

"How can you have money problems when you're seeing
such a rich woman? Don't look so stupid at me. You know who
I mean. This Bertha Landau, she must be some cardplayer!"
My mother hurls the milk at him. The milk doesn't reach him
but plops on the table and runs off the edges.

"What are you talking about?"

My mother holds up her hand. "*Vemen narst du?*" Whom
are you kidding? "Go, go to your Bertha Landau. For my part,
I want a divorce!"

"Don't be crazy," he says. "You don't know what you're
talking."

"Liar, snake! You think I'm so stupid? You think you can
fool me? Playing cards five days a week! With a man who's in
the hospital. That's right. Your friend Arthur, he's in the hospital. I want a divorce. Now *gai avek!*"

My father looks at her, not quite understanding.

"Out, get out of this apartment! You have no right—no
right to be here!" she screams.

Awakened by my mother's voice, my sister comes to the
doorway. "What's going on?"

"Nothing, go back to bed," my mother says. "Go!" Mimi leaves the kitchen but lingers in the hallway where she can listen.

"If I leave, I won't come back," my father says.

"Es vert mir finster in di oygen." I am fainting.

"All right!" he says. "I'm going."

My sister retreats to the bedroom. As soon as my father steps outside the door, he hears my mother put the chain on. He should have taken a toothbrush with him, he realizes, but then Bertha probably has an extra.

In the morning my mother calls her sister to ask how to get a divorce. She tells her my father is seeing this rich woman, Bertha Landau.

"Are you sure?" my Aunt Ruchel says.

"All this time I think he is playing cards, but he is out with *her*, with all her money, in fancy restaurants. Imagine."

"I mean, are you sure you want to get a divorce?"

"Mechuleh! It's finished!" my mother says. "With all her money, *er hot nit kein zorg.*" He hasn't got a worry. "Now I'm free to marry Harry."

My mother stops by Magic Shoes. She leaves me outside. "I want to go in," I say.

"I'll just be a minute. Wait on this spot."

Inside she says to the girl, "Would you tell Mr. Taubman I'm here?"

"What's your name again?" Jilly looks annoyed for some reason.

"Mrs. Arnow."

"Mrs. Arnow, he's very busy. Really. We're doing month-end inventory."

"Tell him anyhow." My mother expects her to pick up the phone like last time. Instead, Jilly stomps across the floor. Then she stomps back to the register. Soon Harry comes out.

"Mrs. Arnow, what can I do you for?" he says cordially, extending his hand.

"I have to talk to you."

He looks at his watch. "Two o'clock okay?" Jilly is glaring.

"All right," my mother says. The door opens, and as a customer walks in, I run in beside her. "Are you buying shoes?" I ask my mother. "I want to see."

"You! I'm just talking to someone," she says.

"Who?" I ask. Harry hears us and turns around. "Peter the Wolf!" I say.

"That's right," my mother says. As she opens the door for us, she sticks her tongue out at the cashier.

For the big occasion my mother buys me a glass of apple juice and a black-and-white cookie. She sips her coffee and keeps looking at the big clock on the wall of Bickford's. She doesn't talk to me. I play with the locket around my neck. I wish I could see the tiny pictures my sister put in it, of Mama and Papa.

At ten after two, Harry comes in, handsome in his light blue suit, the dark blue tie. He doesn't order anything but sits right down, opposite my mother. "Hello, hello," he says to me. Then he says, "Chenia—" He is going to ask her not to come to the store anymore, but he doesn't get the chance.

"I have news," she says. "Ruben is having a A-F-F-A-I-R. I'm getting a D-I-V-O-R-C-E."

"Really?" Harry says. "It's all decided?"

My mother gazes at him expectantly. "Such a surprise for me, too. What I wanted all along. Now—now we can be together. Now you don't have to be shamed to bring me to your mother. I feel like I know her already."

Harry's dark eyebrows are knit together. "Chenia! What are you thinking?"

"What's to think? We're free now. Nothing goes in our way. Thanks God, we can be married." She can see by his expression, so perplexed, that something is not right.

Waiting for the big moment to arrive, my mother has imagined Harry embracing her. She has imagined he would lift her right off the floor the way he did that time on Surf Avenue. But all he does now is frown.

"What?" she asks. "What?"

"But Chenia," he says, "I have a wife."

"A wife? What are you talking? You told me you were divorced."

"From my first wife."

The way he looks at her, my mother feels very strange all of a sudden, as if she is in a fun house where everything is *moyshe kapoyr*, all upside down.

He raises his hand, a helpless gesture. "I'm married, Chenia. I've been married for eight years." Before she can ask, he says, "I can't leave her. It's too complicated to explain now . . ."

Inside she feels something moving, crashing against her insides, like the waves of the ocean. "Married? You never told me this."

"I'm sure I did, Chenia. Anyway, you had to know. You know I can never see you in the evenings."

"Your mother, you said."

"Shhh."

"Don't shhh me," my mother screams. "You!" she yells at him. "You! *A finsternish* on you!" A plague on you! "So I was your *tsatskeh*!" Your plaything.

She lifts the bottle of sugar high over her head and tries to bang it on his shoulder. He wrests it away from her and sets it back on the table.

I jump off the chair and pull at her skirt. "Mama, don't!"

My mother is screaming. *"A ruach in dein taten's tateh!"* You can go to the devil! Harry is saying, "Stop it! Stop it!" He tries to hold her in his arms, but she breaks away. She picks up my glass and smashes it against his chest. The glass flies everywhere. A shard cuts my cheek. I touch it and see blood on my fingers. Blood drips on my dress. I start to wail.

"Genaivesheh shtiklech!" she yells at him. You and your tricky doings. *"A brokh tsu dir!"* A curse on you! She catches sight of me, the cut, the blood, and she collapses to the floor. I am so shocked I stop crying and only stare.

When my mother comes to, one policeman is holding smelling salts to her nose, the other one holds napkins against my face. *Oy Got, such a fool,* she thinks about herself. *Yekl!* Greenhorn. Sucker.

Very calmly, Harry tells the cops that Mrs. Arnow got a little upset. He whispers in the policeman's ear that my mother caught him with another woman. The policeman says, "I gotcha." Harry gives him his business card and home address and says he'll pay for all the damage. The cops take my mother and me to the hospital in a police car. The stroller goes in the trunk.

As we wait in the Emergency Room, my mother looks strange to me, vacant. She looks as if she's gone blind. She doesn't say a word. When they give me an injection so I won't feel the stitches, she keels over again. I scream so loud they have to give me another injection to calm me down. I don't even yell when the second needle goes in.

"What happened?" the neighbors ask when they see us coming up the stoop, me with a big bandage over half my face.

"An accident," my mother says. "Ten stitches!" She gives me a look.

"Poor kid!" someone says.

"You're telling me," my mother says.

We go inside the building, but we don't go up right away. My mother plops down on the marble steps. "You!" she says to me. "*A glik hot dich getrofen,*" she says in her ironic tone. A piece of luck happened to you. "Today your mother went crazy," she tells me. "When you're older, I'll explain you everything. Now I want you to listen to me something."

"What, Mama?" I'm so glad to hear her speaking to me like normal, nothing else matters, not even the awful throbbing in my cheek, like iodine poured into a cut.

"I didn't mean to hurt you. That your mother could do such a terrible thing, I can hardly believe it. You hear me?"

"Yes, Mama. Why did you get so angry?"

She sighs. "You're almost four years old," she says, "but to understand, you have to be twenty-five."

"So old?"

Her head bobs. "To think that I hurt you—" She puts one hand on her chest, the other over her face.

"Don't cry, Mama. I'm okay. I'm okay."

"No more. Your mother will never hurt you again. Never again. Not today, not tomorrow." She takes my hand and kisses it, over and over. I lose count. "I'm not fit to be your mother," she says. I don't ask her what she means.

In the bathroom my mother stares into the mirror. Devil, she thinks. That devil! She knew when she first saw him. And still she was tempted. And now her child will be scarred forever. Why? she thinks. Why? It was *her* sin. She let herself be used. Like a *kurveh.* A whore.

When I tell my brother how Mama tried to hurt Peter the Wolf, he keeps asking, "Who's Peter the Wolf?" Then he asks my mother how I got the cut.

"For what you keep asking?" she says. "An accident! Is all! All I can do now is kill myself."

"Ma!" Sheldon says. "You're talking crazy."

My sister guesses there is a man in the picture, especially after she picks up the phone twice when it rings, and there's no answer.

Sheldon says, "That's ridiculous. Whatever's going on, it has to do with Papa. Since he left that night he hasn't been back. Maybe he's the one calling."

"Papa would never do such a thing," Mimi says.

"There's a lot you don't know about Papa," my brother answers. He wishes he could talk things over with Lenore. He tries not to think about her because it makes him ache.

After my stitches come out, my mother asks her sister to take me for a week. "The little one had an accident, ten stitches in her face," she says, but doesn't go into detail. "One *tsore* after another. I need a rest."

"Of course," my Aunt Ruchel says. She is glad my mother mentions nothing about a divorce. Maybe she's come to her senses, she thinks. She tells my mother she will send Millie with the car to get me.

Millie rings our bell. She is wearing a straw hat and a green dress with little white cherries all over. My mother invites her in and gives her juice to drink. "Hot enough for you?" Millie asks. My mother nods. She hasn't noticed the temperature.

Millie takes my suitcase. I don't want to go with her. I cry. I beg my mother to let me stay. "I'll be good, Mama. I'll be good. I won't talk about it nomore."

My mother comes down the stoop with us, her backless slippers clopping with each step. She blows me a kiss through the car window.

"Mama!" I scream. "Mama!"

As soon as Millie drives off with me, my mother puts her bathing suit on, a dress over it, and goes to the subway. She takes the train to Coney Island. *You fool, you fool, you fool.* The words chug to the rhythm of the train. When she gets out at Stillwell Avenue, she wonders if she should have left a note. She doesn't know what she would write, anyhow. She thinks of the bankbook. She wishes she had given it to my brother first. Now it's too late.

On the beach she removes her shoes and kicks them under the Boardwalk. Then she walks in her bare feet on the hot sand, a crooked path between a hundred blankets and towels, until she is at the water's edge. She takes off her dress and leaves it in a heap. She walks into the water. She keeps walking until the water is over her head.

Part Four

"I want to show you something," Sofie Vrebolovich says to my sister. My sister follows the old woman into the bedroom, which smells like stale sheets. She thinks maybe Sofie is going to show her more old photographs. I imagine Mimi never tires of looking at them. I imagine she can't get over how beautiful Sofie was as a young girl. She had a long neck then and regal bearing. Now she has practically no neck, and everything droops: her eyelids, her nose, her spongy skin.

The old woman points to a marble-topped chest, jammed in the corner behind a sewing machine. Mimi helps pull the machine aside to get a good look at the chest. There are red flowers and green leaves painted on the inlaid wood. Maybe cherry wood. Each of the three drawers has a large, brass keyhole. Mimi runs her hand along the edge of the cool marble. "Oh, that's so pretty!"

Sofie nods. "I was hoping," she says, pleased my sister likes it. She reaches inside her blouse and pulls out a large brass key on a string. She yanks the string over her head and puts it around my sister's neck. "You keep this for me."

"But if this is locked, how will you open it?"

"I have another key," Sofie says. "You hold this in case I lose it, yes? I get more and more forgetful."

"All right." Mimi glances at the top of the sewing machine, which seems to be covered with a light gray felt. "Do you have any rags? I'd like to dust this for you."

"It's not necessary," Sofie says. "But if you want . . ."

Diligently my sister dusts the furniture in the bedroom and living room. She wants to dust the knickknacks in the curio cabinet, but Sofie insists it's time for tea. Hot tea in the middle of summer! My sister can't get over it.

"The best thing to cool off," the old woman says, wiping her deeply furrowed brow with the cuff of her long sleeve.

When my sister is about to leave, Sofie says, "God forbid, anything happens to me, I want you to take that chest."

"You shouldn't think about dying so much."

"It's a very good chest. Then, they knew how to make furniture. More than fifty years ago, when I was married. Promise me you take it."

"It's not necessary," my sister says. "But if you want . . ." She says it with a straight face, but Sofie gets the joke. She howls.

Close to six o'clock, when my sister arrives home, the apartment is deserted. She tries to remember if my mother was going someplace. She recalls that Millie was supposed to get me. She wonders if my mother went along for the ride.

At seven my brother comes home. "Ma's not here?"

"She's hiding under the bed," Mimi says.

"Where is she? She didn't leave us dinner?"

"She ran off with Burt Lancaster."

"What's with you?" Sheldon says.

"Some people can't take a joke," she answers. "What do you want for dinner? I know how to make French toast."

"Okay," he says. "Let's put ice cream on it."

Just as they finish watching Ed Sullivan on *Toast of the Town*, my sister hears the key in the lock. "Thank God!" she says. She steps into the hall as the door opens. But it isn't my mother. "It's Papa!" Mimi calls out. Sheldon doesn't move from the sofa.

"I came to get some clothes," my father says. "Devorah's asleep?"

"She's staying in Jersey, with Aunt Ruchel," Mimi tells him. He wouldn't ask about *her* in a thousand years, she thinks. "Mama's not home yet."

"It's after nine o'clock. Where is she?"

"I don't know. Maybe she went to Jersey, too." Mimi notices his short haircut, parted on one side instead of in the middle. The ends of his mustache are longer.

My father strides through the living room. He and my brother glance at each other, but neither says a word. My father peers into the room where I usually sleep, as if Mimi was mistaken. From his wardrobe he takes out his summer suit and lays it on the bed. He makes a pile of short-sleeved shirts, underwear, and socks.

He should be happy to be moving in with Bertha, he thinks. To be living in the lap of luxury. Who would have predicted it! Still, he cannot help feeling angry. What right does Chenia have to throw him out? He gets a suitcase from the closet and packs.

My sister doesn't want to wait for my mother to come home to tell her my father showed up. In the hallway, she dials the Operator for long distance.

As Aunt Ruchel answers the phone, she hears me crying in her guest bedroom but says to my sister, "Devorah's fine. Tell your mother."

"She's not here. I thought she went with Devorah."

"Isaac!" my aunt calls out. "Come here! Hold on, darling," she says to Mimi, and confers with my uncle. Back on the phone she says, "Is your brother there? Let me talk to him."

"You can talk to me," Mimi says.

"Darling, please, I need your cooperation. Put your brother on."

My aunt doesn't tell Sheldon what she really thinks. She says, "Your mother, God bless her, she was very tired. Probably she went away for a rest."

"Without telling us?"

"When you're so exhausted—" my aunt starts. "Never before has your mother asked me to take the children. I know, darling, it's hard to comprehend. Do you and Mimi want to come here? You're welcome." She looks at my uncle as she says, "You can stay with us so long as you like." He nods.

"I don't know. Can we talk it over and call you back?"

"Please, darling. I'll wait up to hear."

My father hasn't heard the conversation, but as he walks through the living room with his suitcase, he gets an uneasy feeling. "Mama's on her way?"

Sheldon starts to say yes, but after what he told her, Mimi is too upset to remain silent. "Aunt Ruchel thinks she went somewhere for a rest."

"What?" my father says. "She went away? Where?" Mimi shrugs. He puts the suitcase down. "She leaves you here, just like that? Is she out of her mind?" His eyes go in all directions, trying to account for Chenia's absence. She's always been so responsible. "She left you money?" he asks.

"Nothing," Mimi says. Although she's always regarded my mother as somewhat peculiar, for the first time she considers the possibility that she might also be romantic. To walk off and leave everything behind . . .

My father breathes noisily through his nose. "I better stay. This is unbelievable. Unbelievable! She must be insane!"

"Don't!" Mimi says.

"You walk off and leave your kids. What, is that sane to you?"

"You left, didn't you?" Sheldon says.

"Don't get smart!" my father says. "Your mother, she threw me out."

My brother is about to say something, something provocative, but my sister saves him. "Maybe she went shopping and she's just not back yet," Mimi says. She doesn't say, Maybe she got kidnapped. Mimi is starting to feel afraid.

Even as my father works himself into a fit of anger, part of him thinks, This will help with the divorce, though he's not sure how. He doesn't want custody of the children. What would he do with them, the little one especially? He'll think about it later, he tells himself. Right now he has to call Bertha to let her know. He wonders if Bertha will believe him.

It doesn't take my Aunt Ruchel long to figure out that cookies are my weakness. "Eat your dinner and you'll get a cookie," she might say. Or she says, "If you go to bed right now, you can have a cookie tomorrow." If I refuse to brush my teeth, she says, "Uh oh. The Sugar Monster will make holes in your teeth, and without teeth you can't eat any more cookies."

When she's not going to riding lessons or the Young Zionists' Club, my Cousin Sandy reads stories to me, over and over, as many times as I want. They're all about a girl named Nancy Drew. She teaches me to play croquet. She puts me on her old tricycle, even though I can't reach the pedals. My Aunt Ruchel has a fit. "You want her to have another scar?"

I don't see my Cousin Rhonda very much. Mostly at dinner. Or in the mirror over her vanity. She asks me questions but in a way I'm not used to. "What's up, kid? Having fun, kid?" She doesn't always wait for my answers. She walks quickly through the house, usually with a tennis racket over her shoulder.

My Uncle Isaac likes to chuck me under the chin. His big hand hovers delicately near the puffy skin. I get the idea he wants to touch my scar. He doesn't seem to know how to talk to me, as if we come from different countries.

Millie is the only one who carries on a conversation with me, usually in the kitchen. I help her husk corn and hull strawberries. She shows me how to squirt little flowers out of the pastry bag. She doesn't mind if I make a mess. "You's a good helper," she says. "Soon we'll have you baking pies for Mr.

Pies." For some reason she thinks that's very funny. She teaches me how to use the flour sifter. "That day I drug you here, you was white as that flour," she says.

"White like you," I say. I laugh for the first time since I got there. She drops her jaw in mock anger, and then she laughs also.

She tells me how she used to cook in this big house she calls a mansion. "One whole room they's got for a Frigidaire, and one's for groceries. Ain't that something!" She says a lot of things different from what I'm used to. She says "right nice" a lot, which for a long time I think is "write nice." I find it very interesting. Just before she hangs up the phone, she says, "God keep you."

"What's that mean?" I ask her.

She starts to explain about the Lord, but my aunt interrupts. "Millie is a Baptist. We're Jewish. We believe different things."

Later Millie asks me, "What kind of name's Devorah? Is that Hebrew?"

"I don't know. What's Hebrew?"

She takes a salami out of the Frigidaire and shows me the Hebrew letters. "Hebrew is Jewish."

"What kind of name is Millie?" I ask her. "Is it Baptist?"

She shrieks. "That's a good one, girl." Sometimes she reminds me of Mama.

In the morning, when Aunt Ruchel watches Millie dress me, I ask her if we're going to see Mama.

Today she says, "I told you. She's where sick people go until they're better. Do you know what a hospital is?"

"Where I got my stitches?"

"That's right, a place like that."

"There's lots of them hospitals," Millie says.

"Did Mama cut herself?"

"No, she's sick," Aunt Ruchel says. She thinks, *It could be true. My sister, God willing, could be alive* . . . She looks at my scar and forces herself not to think.

"Does she have an earache?" I ask.

I imagine Aunt Ruchel trying to decide what to tell me. Which sickness. "Her ears are fine," she says.

"Does she have a cold?"

"Yes, a very bad cold," she says today. "You don't want to catch it."

When my brother goes with my father to file a missing-persons report, the police say they'll check the morgue. When no one turns up resembling the description of my mother, the police are nonchalant. "Thousands of people run away every year," they say.

"Why would she run away?" my father says.

I imagine the police zero in on certain facts. The outside door was locked. There was no sign of forcible entry. And my mother left her pocketbook at home, but her keys are gone. They ask if she ever leaves home without her purse.

"To do the laundry," Sheldon says, "but she doesn't lock the door." It turns out that the hamper is full of laundry, and anyway, her slippers are by the bed. Whenever she does laundry, she is always in her slippers.

"Anything unusual happen, before she disappeared?" the police ask. My father and brother silently recall my mother asking my father to leave. "No," they say. "Was she under pressure?" the police ask. "Did she owe money?" "Does she have a history of mental problems?" "No," they answer. "No."

I imagine my brother reports the conversation to my sister. She says, "What about Devorah's accident?"

"Silly, what does that have to do with anything?" Sheldon says.

"I don't know. I think it affected her," Mimi says. "A lot."

My sister likes her new freedom. Without my mother around, she can come and go as she likes, even in the evenings if she tells my father she has to study with her friend Suzanne. It surprises her, though, when fits of weeping suddenly come over her. "How could she leave us?" Mimi rails at Sheldon. She alternates between feeling angry and feeling scared. What if something terrible did happen to Mama? Maybe on the roof. Or in the cellar. What if she turns up dead, God forbid!

In the first week after my mother is gone, my sister rushes to the phone whenever it rings. As time passes without any word, she becomes pessimistic. Today she lets the phone ring and ring. She has the feeling that it's bad news.

When the ringing stops, she goes to the doorway of the bedroom. She kisses her hand and places it on the mezuzah, which is nailed to the doorjamb. "Please, God," she says out loud, "let her be all right. Even if she doesn't come back to us."

Kneeling before the shelves, my brother lines up the cans of peas—neatly, as the boss has told him. He stews over my mother's disappearance. If anything bad has happened to her, he will make my father pay, one way or another. He fumes over my father's demand for money to cover room and board. My brother has been saving up to buy a used car. He will have to cut down now on what he spends, going out with his new girlfriend, Joyce. *That S.O.B.*, my brother thinks, as he moves on to the canned spinach.

At Aunt Ruchel's, the phones ring a lot, especially after dinner. They have two phones upstairs and two downstairs. Millie talks a lot on the yellow phone in the kitchen, when my Aunt Ruchel is out playing mah-jongg. Cousin Sandy shows me how to dial their number, which makes a busy signal. She lets me dial when she calls her friends. Sometimes she lets me say something. Her friends ask me what grade I'm in, which I learn has to do with school. Cousin Sandy tells them I'm too young for school. "I'm not!" I say, but I know she doesn't believe me.

I try to make telephone calls by myself, but I forget which letters and numbers to dial. I make up new ones, but they don't work. Finally I notice my aunt and uncle using the phone book before they dial. Later I open the book and study it. Soon I am talking to a lot of people in New Jersey. They always tell me to put the phone down, or they ask if they can talk to my mother.

On the front lawn, Millie peels potatoes while Cousin Sandy and I play croquet. I ask her, "Why can't we telephone Mama?" Millie shakes her head. She sings, "'Don't know why, there's no sun up in the sky—'"

"She doesn't have a phone," Cousin Sandy says. Her mallet hits the wooden ball so hard it rebounds off the wicket and rolls down to the street.

"That's right," Millie says. "There's no phones for the patients."

I think she is saying my mother doesn't have a phone because she isn't patient. "Where is she?" I ask.

A man walking by picks up the ball and lobs it on the lawn, near me.

"Say, 'Thank you,'" Cousin Sandy coaches.

I don't tell her I'm not supposed to talk to strange men because they take you away and you never see anyone you know, ever again. "Thank you," I say.

"Devorah, you knows the answer to that one," Millie says. "You gonna tell me now? Tell me where's your mama."

"In the hospital," I say, because it's what she wants to hear. I have a new theory, though. I think Mama talked to some strange man. That's when he took her away. Now he won't let her see me anymore.

"Your turn," my cousin says. "Go on."

I look very hard at the wicket, and then I aim the little mallet. *THWOCK!* The ball goes right through.

A t night when I'm supposed to go to sleep, I climb over the chair by the side of my bed and sneak to the door of my aunt and uncle's bedroom. They talk about people I don't know. They also talk about Millie. I don't always understand what they're saying.

Aunt Ruchel says, "You tell her. She's twenty-eight. Old enough to know." Uncle Isaac says, "Me? You tell her." My aunt gets very angry. I wonder if she's going to try to hurt my uncle.

Sometimes they talk about Mama. One night I hear Aunt Ruchel say, "They haven't found her yet. How could Chenia disappear into thin air?"

Now I wonder why Mama is hiding.

I go to the vanity in my room. I turn on the tiny white lamp and look in the mirror. I open the locket around my neck that Mrs. Vogel gave me. I touch the pictures of Mama and Papa. "I promise I'll be good," I tell them. Then I poke the scar on my face until it hurts.

My mother chafes under the regimen of the hospital. The room is never completely dark, so she cannot sleep very well. She puts a pillow over her head, but soon it falls off and the lights from the corridor shine right in. Anyway, who can rest with so much noise? All the voices from the radio on one side of her. And music from the radio on the other side of her. Across the way there is talk and more talk. There is moaning from the bed in the corner. And coughing all around. Sometimes it sounds as though someone is choking on phlegm.

Trays and carts rumble down the hall. Bells ring. All the time they are looking for Dr. Levinson. "Doctor Levinson, Doctor Levinson, please call the operator." My mother thinks, Maybe he is lost, like her.

Day and night people are coming and going. Nurses. Doctors. Orderlies. They bring things, they take things away. They pull open the curtain around her, they pull it closed. They roll her on her side, they roll her on her back. They stick things in her arm, they stick things under her tongue, they jab her *tokhes* with needles. They ask her to swallow this pill and that. They slap a rubber mask over her nose and mouth and ask her to inhale. They stick her head under a little tent where the steam comes up. They talk in singsong.

Sometimes a whole group of young men come, wearing white coats, with stethoscopes outlining their collarbones. They push the cold metal disk up against the bottom of her breast. They ask her to breathe in, to breathe out. Strange words fly from their thin lips: *roentgen evidence, intramuscular paraldehyde, sodium phenobarbital.* The older doctor who is with them speaks slowly and simply to her as if she is a child. "How do you feel today?" he asks.

The social worker comes to the ward. She hovers by the bed. Her blue eyes look concerned. "I don't know what I'm going to do with you," she says. The fourth or fifth time she says it, my mother snaps, "Don't feel sorry for me!" It's the first sentence my mother volunteers.

"We all deserve compassion," the social worker says.

"How can you be so sure?" my mother answers.

Finally her fever is down. Soon she is out of bed and shuffling to the bathroom. Soon she is aware of the visitors who come twice a day, but never to see her. In the corridors they pace and light cigarettes. They ask questions in a cheerful voice. *Are you feeling better? How's the food?* They bring candy or flowers, they bring greeting cards, they bring things people forgot at home, toothbrushes and toothpaste, bathrobes and slippers. Once a priest comes. The nuns visit in twos and threes, draped in black from head to toe. Once she sees a man with bandages piled high on his head. She thinks he is not long for this world, but the social worker tells her he's wearing a turban. "A hat for a corpse," my mother says. Before, she never thought about how many people there are, dead people, walking around.

Sometimes the visitors stick their head in the door and ask for people who are somewhere else. No one knows where she is. She has a new name. Barbara Hayward. From her two favorite actresses, Barbara Stanwyck and Susan Hayward. She's told the lady who comes with the clipboard she has no relatives. "But what about this wedding band?" the social worker says, pointing to her finger. "You must live somewhere."

"You call this living?" my mother jokes. "Where I used to live, was all in my mind. There I was happy beyond belief, but for that I have no address."

The social worker doesn't want to call in a psychiatrist. She knows that if they take her to an asylum, it'll be the end for her. She likes my mother's sharp tongue. The residents who trail the important doctor on his rounds my mother calls *nuchshleppers*, hangers-on. The social worker can't get over it. She tells everyone in the office. Among the hospital staff my mother becomes famous.

She wonders why they come talk to her on their break, on their lunch, after work. They ask for her opinions. "You are really something!" they say. What do they want with a lady who doesn't care if she gets well? In a way, she is already dead, she thinks. She wonders if anyone is sitting *shiva* for her. Mourning her death.

Where can she rest? she wonders. In the hospital is too busy. She can only sleep while drugged. In the ocean is too cold. It wouldn't let her rest. From the cold she got pneumonia, and now she is in a place where you can't tell night from day. To rest, you have to know which is which. And anyhow, she cannot rest when she is so tired. She hardly has the strength to cough.

For the first time in twenty years my father sleeps alone. The first night, when he finds my mother is gone, he is not comfortable in the double bed by himself. He sleeps on the side he's used to. In the ten days he stayed at Bertha's, their only argument was over which side of the bed he should sleep on. Bertha prefers the side near the door, like him. He had room enough in her bed, which is queen-sized, but he wasn't comfortable sleeping on the side by the windows. Now he can sleep wherever he wants. Gradually he moves to the center of the bed. Soon he is stretching his arms in both directions. Most nights he falls into a very deep sleep. He thinks for the first time in his life he is really getting a good rest.

On my birthday, my sister and brother come to Aunt Ruchel's. At first I don't talk to them because I'm angry. But then my brother picks me up in his arms and swings me around. "*Oy gevalt*," he jokes, "she's so heavy I'm getting a hernia." He tells me what a hernia is. It makes me giggle.

They bring me some coloring books and crayons, and a watercolor paint set in a tin box. Mimi says, "You look adorable, like Shirley Temple." The night before, Cousin Sandy wound hunks of my hair with rags, and now my head is all in curls. I tell them what I got from my aunt and uncle: a pink pinafore, a pink pocketbook, and a bracelet of pink hearts. And what I got from my cousins: a big book of fairy tales with color pictures.

"Any news?" Aunt Ruchel asks. They shake their heads. They say my father wants me home. "He could have come with you," my aunt says.

"He has more important things to do," Sheldon says. My aunt and uncle give each other a look.

"Darling," my aunt says to Mimi, "you look fabulous."

"How much weight did you lose?" Cousin Rhonda asks.

"Ten pounds," Mimi says. "I just haven't felt like eating."

The pot roast Millie makes is so good, my sister cleans her plate. When Millie brings in the chocolate cake, they sing me "Happy Birthday." Millie sings the loudest. I blow out all the candles. I make a wish for Mama and Papa to stop being so angry at me. After we eat the cake, Cousin Rhonda goes upstairs. Uncle Isaac goes into the den. Millie goes in the kitchen. The rest of us go out on the back porch. My brother and I swing on the bench, and he croons, "'Some-where there's mu-sic, How high the moon . . .'" Then my brother says they have to go home.

"I want to go with you," I say.

"I wish you could," Sheldon says, "but there's no one to mind you. I'm working in a store all day."

"You could mind me," I say to Mimi.

"Not every day."

"Why?"

"I have to go visit this old lady."

"Why?"

"Because," she says. "Just because."

I scream when they leave. I lie down on the carpet and bang my feet. I start to bang my head, but Millie scoops me up and holds me in her arms. I bang with my fists on her back and I try to kick her, but she holds me tight. "You're too big to be behaving like a two-year-old," she says. "How old are you, girl? I thought you was four years old today."

"I want my mama!" I cry.

Millie carries me up the stairs. She sets me down on the bed, and then she kneels on the floor beside me. She puts her hands together and bends her head. "O Mighty Lord," she says, "hear our prayer. Bring Devorah's mama home to her, safe and sound." Millie teaches me to say, "Amen."

W hile my sister and brother ride the bus back to Manhattan, my father tries to find Trudy. He keeps calling her home, but there's no answer. He walks around the neighborhood. He looks in the playground where he knows she takes Hannah; she isn't there. Finally he reaches her on the phone.

"Oh, it's you," she says coldly, but she doesn't hang up. After their big fight, she lashed out at him. "You were at Bertha's every night, weren't you! That ugly beast! Get your glasses fixed!"

"I've missed you," he tells Trudy now.

"That and a nickel will get you on the Staten Island Ferry."

"You're right. But I have big news for you."

"You're getting a divorce," she says sarcastically.

"You heard?"

"Don't pull my leg, Ruben."

"Who's pulling your leg?"

"Really, a legal divorce?" Trudy thinks, *If he's just saying that to make up to me, I'll kill him. I'll go to Chenia and wreck his home.*

"Chenia threw me out," he says. "She got suspicious."

"Of me or Bertha?" Trudy asks.

"Not Bertha. I was doing her some favors, that's all. I told you."

"I heard a joke on *Jack Benny*," Trudy says. "A husband arrives home late and says to his wife, 'Can't you guess where I've been?' The wife says, 'I can, but go on with your story.' "

"Trudy, this is no story, but it could be. Chenia throws me out and what do you think? She goes and disappears. No one knows where she is."

"Wait a minute," Trudy says. "Give it to me slow."

My father wants to pinch himself. Here he is, back with Trudy, in her bedroom once more. She is kissing him all over. It takes just a few seconds when he is inside her until he spurts. "I'll be better," he promises. "I got so excited, being with you again. You smell so good, you feel so good—"

He has never been that expressive, Trudy thinks. "I love it when you talk to me like that," she says. She kisses his chest around the nipples. She slides her head down to his belly, and then she takes his member in her mouth. Right away he gets hard again. This time when he is inside her, he thinks of Mr. Gershenfeld, threatening to dock him for all the time the girls talk. He thinks how ironic it is, to be with one woman where he has trouble finishing and another where he finishes too fast. Then he wonders where my mother is.

"Ruben? Where are you?" Trudy asks.

"With you," he says. "You smell so good, you feel so good—" Although he pushes inside her, he knows he is having trouble. He cannot believe it. Why now? He tries to inhale Trudy's scent, like spring flowers. He concentrates on her nipples, but they feel wrinkled, shriveled like his member. He doesn't want to, but in desperation he falls back on his sure thing: He thinks of Millie, her big breasts in his face, his hands on her big *tokhes*.

"Oh Ruben," he hears. "I love it when you're so passionate." It's Trudy, he realizes, having a climax.

My father comes.

The day after my birthday, the city is sweltering. Even with the fan, the apartment feels like a furnace. My sister recalls Sofie's cool basement and the strange super. She gets goose bumps.

On the stoop she waits for her friend Suzanne. They are going to buy shoes. She hopes Suzanne invites her over for dinner. Her mother makes the best mashed potatoes. Mimi misses having real dinners. *Mama!* my sister says to herself. *Where are you?*

A neighbor rocks her baby carriage close to where my sister is sitting. "How's Devorah? I never see her anymore, or your mom. Are they still living upstairs?" Mrs. Kleeberg probes.

"They're in the country. On vacation."

"Tell me, how did your sister get her face cut up?"

"She fell over a bike," my sister says. "Why?"

"Just wondered." Mrs. Kleeberg forgets to rock. Her baby starts to wail.

"What? You think my mother did that to her?"

"No, of course not," Mrs. Kleeberg lies. "I didn't know your sister had a bike." The baby screeches.

"It was a little boy's bike, okay?" Mimi says. "On Dyckman Street."

"Sure, okay. You don't have to get so upset," Mrs. Kleeberg says. "Especially if there's nothing to hide."

In Magic Shoes, Harry is at the cash register when two teenage girls walk in, one lanky and awkward, the other small, with graceful arms. The little one reminds him of Chenia, with the tiny face, the intense eyes and pointy chin. Could it be? he wonders, moving toward her. He sees now her eyes are not as dark as Chenia's. "Have a seat," he says. "Someone will be right with you."

My sister does a double take. She recognizes him from the store in Brooklyn. The broad forehead, the deep pores in his cheeks.

"Coney Island," Harry says, and smiles. "You came in with your mother, as I recall. There was a, uh, little problem . . ."

"That's right," my sister says. She is dying of embarrassment. "My mother, she, uh, couldn't come today." She ignores Suzanne's quizzical look.

"Is she all right?" he asks.

"Fine," Mimi says. "Why wouldn't she be?"

"Give her my regards," he says. "I'm the manager here."

My sister feels a chill spreading through her. She waits until he is out of hearing range, then says to Suzanne, "Don't think I'm nuts. I just know there's a connection. Between him and my mom."

"Oh my God!" Suzanne says. "You don't think he kidnapped her? He doesn't look the type. Doesn't he resemble Perry Como?"

"A little," Mimi says. "You can't really tell what people are like." My sister studies Harry while he is at the register. He reminds her of my father, the medium build, how neatly he dresses, but the manager is more of a shmoozer, the way he handles the customers. "It can't be just a coincidence that he works here now," she says to Suzanne.

Suzanne whispers. "You don't think your mom was, you know, involved with him? He looks younger than her."

"She's the last person I'd ever—" my sister says, before the salesman asks what he can do for her today.

A t six in the evening, Bertha dials my father's home number. When my sister answers, Bertha disguises her voice to ask, "Is your mother home?"

"She's indisposed," Mimi says. "Who's this?"

"I'll call back later," Bertha says. The next time she calls, she speaks in a high-pitched voice. She asks the same question. She gets the very same answer.

Humming to herself now, Bertha puts on the blue dress that Ruben says is his favorite.

In the entryway of Schrafft's, Bertha bumps her cheek against my father's. "Ruben! You've shaved off your mustache! You look—less mysterious." She resists telling him that she's missed him, that a week has never felt so long.

"I don't like this business," he says. "Devorah is still at my sister-in-law's. Mimi is no cook. What she doesn't burn, she leaves raw. Last night the chicken—"

Bertha cuts him off. "Perhaps if they know we're waiting—"

Once they're seated at a table, Bertha recognizes an acquaintance nearby. She, too, is with a gentleman. Bertha glances at my father's hand, at the wide, gold band on his fourth finger. She can't see the hand of the gentleman across the way. She wonders if Ruben will ever notice she's taken off her own wedding ring.

After studying the menu, my father resumes where he left off. "The chicken last night was so raw—"

"Your usual?" the waiter says, and Bertha nods, not waiting for my father. Her acquaintance is leaning forward, forearms on the table. A romantic interest, definitely, Bertha thinks. Or maybe financial.

Bertha waits for the food to arrive before she brings up what's on her mind, but even then she doesn't rush into it. "Mmm, the prime rib, it's roasted to perfection," she says, and then, "Have the police made any progress?"

"Nothing," he answers, slathering more sour cream on the baked potato. "The neighbors, they saw her go downstairs with Devorah and the Negro maid, she works for my sister-in-law. After that, no one remembers."

"Maybe you should hire a detective."

"What does something like that cost?" he asks.

"What does cost matter? If she doesn't turn up, you won't be able to divorce for—I think it's seven years. That's too long to wait, isn't it?"

"It's unfortunate I can't see you," my father says. Bertha only nods because she is chewing. "Have you sold the building?" he asks.

Bertha swallows. "Not yet. They're claiming demand is down. The market is depressed." She splays her ringless hand over her chin. "How old is Mimi again?"

"Fourteen. Fifteen, maybe. I think fifteen."

"Certainly old enough for her to be home alone in the evening, Ruben."

"You're right. The worry, it's affected my thinking. At work the girls laugh at me. I can't make them listen." He slurps the seltzer through the straw.

"Please!" she says. "You're doing it again. Order another if you want."

His eyes flash, then he says, "Sorry."

What's wrong with her? Bertha wonders. It has to be more than the fact he looks so different now. "I miss your mustache," she tells him.

He shaved it off after Trudy said it tickled too much when he kissed her. Now he tells Bertha, "When it's cooler I'll grow it back. Just for you."

Finished with his seltzer, he starts to push the glass away till he sees Bertha's eyebrows go up. He removes his hand and balls it into a fist, resting it on the linen. "I have to go to the dentist," he says. "I'm having trouble with my partial. If he don't fix it right, I may get a lawyer."

Is he always so boring? Bertha wonders. "Ruben, tell me something new."

"The orders are coming in," he says. "We have to hire more girls."

She perks up. "You think the economy is doing better, then?"

Now that my mother is almost ready to be discharged, the social worker is determined to get more information from her. All the file says is that the patient was brought into Emergency with a high fever, blue lips, pains in her side. She's made a remarkable recovery, Mrs. Markham thinks, as she apologizes for the partitioned space that is her office.

"A broom closet is more interesting," my mother says. "The beige, it makes me yawn."

"Well, maybe you'd rather visit in the lounge."

"Visit who?" my mother asks.

"Each other," the social worker says. "All right?"

It doesn't matter, really, my mother thinks, but she nods. It's an effort to lift one foot up, then the other, as they walk, slowly, to the end of the hall. The seersucker robe flaps against her bare legs.

In the crowded lounge, they find two seats beneath the large clock. Everywhere people are talking, but my mother thinks no one is listening. "Here there is nothing to do," she says, "except wait for the news. Good or bad."

"What do you consider good news, Mrs. Hayward?"

"Good news? Maybe that boy, the lifeguard, didn't pull me out after all, and now I am dreaming only. 'Leave me,' I told him. 'Leave me.' 'Not if my life depends on it,' he says. Such a funny thing, maybe I dreamt it."

Mrs. Markham doesn't always understand what my mother means. Is she referring to a suicide attempt? "Mrs. Hayward, or whatever your real name is—" She winks. "Do you ever hear voices talking to you?"

"Inside my head, you mean?" My mother's head bobs slightly.

Mrs. Markham tenses, until my mother says, "Only my conscience. What makes me so tired. Why I wanted the water to keep me under."

Wanted, past tense, Mrs. Markham notes. "Why? What happened to make you want to stop living? It was either a man or a child. Am I right?"

With those large blue eyes and the wide, smiling mouth, the social worker seems to her a simple woman, but she's smarter than she looks, my mother decides. It's just that nothing terrible ever happened to her. And nothing so wonderful either that she would kill herself for losing it.

"So which is it?" Mrs. Markham asks. "A man or a child?"

"Both," my mother says. "It's a long story."

"I have time."

My mother tells her because she doesn't care. She tells her about Harry, whom she calls *This Man*. As she talks, she becomes oblivious to everyone in the waiting room, those talking too loud with relatives they haven't seen for a while, those sitting like stone, those wishing they could be somewhere else. She doesn't notice the clouds of cigarette smoke, the doctors in green coming fresh from surgery, masks hanging around their necks.

Two hours later, when my mother says, "*Nu*, that's it," the social worker says, "You know, happiness isn't a permanent state. Neither is unhappiness. There's a flow, back and forth. It sounds as if your daughter makes you happy. She must be a real kick. I'd love to see her."

"She has a big scar," my mother says. "Ten stitches on her face."

"That's not the end of the world." Mrs. Markham raises her own skirt up over the knee. Through the nylon stocking my mother can see a whitish, ridged scar. Like a short, fat worm.

"My father pushed me so hard I fell over a big flowerpot," Mrs. Markham says. "He had a violent temper, yet I knew he loved me." The social worker realizes she has my mother's rapt attention. "I needed at least ten stitches," she continues, "but see how the scar has faded?" She lets the skirt drop. "All kids have accidents—of one kind or another. That's life, isn't it?"

My mother's face scrunches up. She cannot believe it, how she feels. The fact that she feels anything at all. A pain worse even than missing *him*.

On the first day of August, when my Aunt Ruchel sees the return address on an envelope postmarked *Brooklyn*, I imagine her heart practically stops. At the top of the typed letter, she reads, "In re: Discharge of Chenia Arnow." My aunt thinks it's a notice of her sister's death. "Go outside," she tells me, and then she sits down to read.

It's the first time she's told me to go anywhere without her. Outside, I spank my teddy bear. "Bad boy!" I say, and stick him in the corner of the porch.

Inside, my aunt reads the letter twice to make sure she understands. It says the patient will be discharged on August 2. The hospital prefers that she be accompanied by a responsible party.

My aunt presses the letter to her breast. It's so hard to grasp . . . She has already been thinking of Chenia in the past tense. *My sister had such a sense of humor . . . My sister was such a good mother . . .* Now she has to alter her world again. She knows she ought to call Sheldon, but first she calls my uncle, and reads the letter to him.

"They're stingy with information," he says. "Shall I get in touch with them?"

"I was hoping you would offer."

"You don't have to wait for an offer. You can ask."

When my aunt tries to call me in from the backyard, I am not there. "Devorah? Devorah!" she calls. She looks for me. She goes out to the front and looks up and down the street. If it isn't one thing . . .

By now I am two streets down Elm, skipping on the narrow sidewalk. I don't like it when dogs bark. For a while I stop to play with two little girls. They pull me around the corner in their wagon. Then their mother tells them they have to come inside. I try to retrace my steps, but nothing looks familiar. I know I'm lost. I'm scared. I want to scare Aunt Ruchel for making me go outside. I wasn't being bad. Why did she tell me I couldn't stay with her?

I walk and walk. I start to cry. A mailman sees me. "Why are you crying?" he asks. "Where's your mommy?"

"I don't know." I cry even louder. I'm not supposed to talk to him.

"Where do you live?"

"I don't know."

"What's your name?"

"Devorah Arnow."

The lady in front of her house says he can use her phone. We go inside and he looks up Arnow in the phone book. He dials someone, but it isn't the right person. "I have to finish my route," he tells the lady. "Can you take her to the station?"

As soon as I see the police I think something terrible happened to my aunt. But after the lady tells them I'm lost, they take me to the office inside and give me ice cream and a clown doll. They give me sheets of paper and pencils in different colors. I copy words I see on a legal pad: CASE ROB I. SUSPECT. TRACE.

Outside it gets dark. There are different policemen at the desk now. I ask why they don't wear uniforms. I ask them to spell *detective*. One is blond and has a tiny nose, like my doll at home. "Stop your squirming," he says. "You have to pee?" I move to the bench against the wall.

The other detective is puffed out like my teddy bear at Aunt Ruchel's. He has red hair like me. He picks up the phone when it rings. He winks at me as he says, "Describe her." He puts his hand over the receiver and asks me if I know my aunt's name.

"Aunt Ruchel," I say.

"Bingo!" he says. "You're not lost anymore."

When Aunt Ruchel gets to the police station with Millie, the blond detective asks her where my mother is.

"In the hospital," I answer.

"That's right," my aunt says. She's wearing a necklace of white hearts and a lacy blouse with a square neck. I want to tell her she looks pretty.

"Well, we have a little problem here. I can't release her to you, being as you're not her immediate family. What's your name?"

"Mrs. Isaac Peisner."

"And what's the mother's name?"

"Mrs. Ruben Arnow."

"Peisner. Arnow. What kind of names are those?"

My aunt stiffens. She knows exactly what he's asking, but she says, "What do you mean?"

"Are they, uh, Italian?"

"No."

"Maybe they're Chinese. No? Well, they must be Hebrew. Are you Hebrew?"

"We're Jewish," my aunt says. "We came from Poland, but now we're American citizens."

"Yids, did you say? Imagine that! So where's the Yid's, uh, kid's father?"

"He can't be bothered," she says. By the way they look at her, she knows it's the wrong answer. "He's working," she adds, "in a factory in Manhattan. My sister asked me to care for her child, temporarily. Come, Devorah, let's go."

"Not yet," the blond detective says. He turns on the little fan that sits on his desk. The papers fly all over. "Goddamnit!" he says, and shuffles them together. "What took you so long to report her missing?" he asks.

"I called immediately," she says indignantly. "They gave me the other precinct. Our street is on the line between." My aunt's voice gets louder. Millie clears her throat. My aunt lowers her voice. "What if I show you the letter from the hospital?"

"That depends," the other detective says. He loosens his tie.

Aunt Ruchel sends Millie home to get the letter. "Tell Mr.

Peisner I'm here." She hesitates to call my father—why make things more complicated than they already are? "So warm," she says and wipes the perspiration off my brow.

"How did she get this?" The blond one points to my scar. "It looks new."

"An accident," Aunt Ruchel says.

Soon I am in a room alone with a lady cop. She talks to me about different things, then asks me how I got the scar, which she calls "a big sore."

At first I don't want to answer, but she keeps asking.

"From the glass," I say.

"What glass?"

"Mama threw the glass."

"Your mother threw the glass at you?"

"At Peter the Wolf."

"Who's Peter the Wolf?" she asks.

"A man," I say.

"What man?"

"He works in the shoe store."

The questions go on and on. I tell her everything I can remember. She asks me to wait while she goes back to the other room. I get the idea they know where my Mama really is.

In the other room they ask my aunt how I got the scar. "I don't know," she says. The blond one looks up at the ceiling. He starts to hum.

After a while they let me back in the first room, a lot noisier now, with two fans going and more people. I don't see the clown doll where I left it, on the bench. Soon Millie arrives with the letter. They pass it around. One reads it, then another. In between they answer the phones.

Fanning herself with an envelope, Millie tells my aunt that Mr. Peisner isn't home yet. There are wet blotches under her arms.

Finally the blond detective says, "Come back in the morning. If everything checks out, we'll release her into your custody."

Aunt Ruchel grabs my hand and yanks it over my head. "What do I tell her mother? That I don't have her kid any-more?"

"We'll take good care of her," he says. "Go on, there's nothing you can do here." My aunt doesn't move. When the policewoman tries to take me out of the room, I get hysterical.

"Please," Millie says to them. "Her mama's sick. Don't be torturing this child any further."

"Are you accusing us of torturing her?" the blond police-man says. The way he says it, I stop whimpering.

My aunt picks up a phone to call my uncle. She puts it down. Chenia wouldn't stand for this, she thinks. Softly she says, "You don't think I kidnapped her? Here, here's my identi-fication." She hands him her wallet. "Twenty years I've lived in the same house, ten minutes from here. I'm not moving away overnight. My husband, he's a respected businessman. We have two daughters of our own . . ."

"Ma'am, there are procedures we follow." He flips the wallet in the air. It lands on the floor. He looks up at the ceil-ing. Millie stoops to pick it up.

"If you think I'm a criminal, please, lock me up right now." My aunt wipes her forehead with the back of her hand. "I have to pick up my sister in the morning. Look at the letter."

Aunt Ruchel glances at me to see if I understand. I do in a way, but I think it's what my mama calls a *bobbe-myseh*. A fairy tale. I think my aunt is trying to fool them so they'll let us go.

They look at the letter again. They mop their brows with large white handkerchiefs. They confer among themselves. The redheaded one who winked at me says, "It's more trouble than it's worth." The policewoman says, "But it's probable abuse."

Probable, I say to myself. I wonder what it means.

My aunt mutters that this is crazy. Millie tries to calm her down. My aunt can't stand it. She yells out, "If you knew the mother, you'd know she'd take her own life rather than hurt her kid. What kid doesn't have an accident?"

The policewoman points to me. "She's the one who told us. Her mother threw the glass. Didn't you say that, Deborah?"

I'm starting to understand what I've done. I shake my head no.

"You told me that, Deborah," the policewoman says.

"No! My name is Devorah."

"How did your face get cut?"

"It was an accident," I say.

"She's been coached," the policewoman says.

After the redheaded detective answers the phone, he says, "There's a guy on the water tower, threatening to shoot himself." He glances at us. "Let it go," he says to the others.

Millie takes the cue. She shepherds me out the door. Outside in the cool night air, she says, "Forgive me, Lord. There be murder raging in my sinful heart."

"Amen," I say.

My aunt's eyes nearly pop out. Millie shrugs. My aunt hugs her with one arm and me with the other.

I am feeling so happy all of a sudden, but when I look at Millie, I can see something is wrong. She pulls out of my aunt's embrace. "Better be getting back. Don't want Mr. Peisner be thinking we is lost."

In the car going home, Aunt Ruchel says, "Darling, I have to ask. I want you to tell me the truth. Did your mother throw the glass at you?" When I don't answer, she asks Millie to ask me.

"At Peter the Wolf," I say. Before she can ask, Who's Peter the Wolf? I say, "He works in a shoe store."

"*Veys mir,*" Aunt Ruchel says. "No wonder she ran away!"

I think she is talking about me, but of course she is talking about my mother.

As soon as we step out of the hospital elevator—Aunt Ruchel, Millie, and I—we see a tiny, frail-looking woman in a wheelchair by the nurse's station. "Thank you, Jesus!" Millie says, and then I realize it's my mother. Her hair is all pushed back on the sides with hairpins. She has white socks on, like a girl's, and sandals I've never seen. Up close, she seems smaller than I remember.

She makes an effort to smile. To see her daughter after all this time . . . and her sister . . . It's too much. My mother steels herself. She doesn't want to feel a thing.

My aunt bends over to kiss her on the cheek, but delicately. She thinks that hugging her sister might cause her bones to break.

My mother keeps her eyes on me the whole time. I know she is looking at the scar on my face. "You've been picking at it?" she says, her first words to me.

"All the time," Millie answers.

"You're so big," my mother says to me. "How tall are you?" I don't answer.

My aunt starts to scold me. My mother says, "*Nu*, she's angry. She has a right. You!" she says to me. "If you think I forgot about you, think again."

"Do you want to rest?" my Aunt Ruchel says to my mother, when we get to New Jersey. "I never saw traffic that terrible."

"Resting makes me so tired," my mother says. "You have iced tea?"

I watch her change into one of Aunt Ruchel's housedresses. She seems familiar to me, but not completely.

Out on the back lawn, we sit on metal chairs that have bent tubes instead of legs. The petals of the pink flowers shiver in the slight breeze. Just as a bird flies into a big green bush, another one flies out. They're different from the purple and gray pigeons in the park. They're bluer than the sky. I look at them awhile and quickly back at my mother. I keep expecting her not to be there.

My aunt riffles through her mail. My mother presses the glass of iced tea against her cheek. "So much better than paper cups," she says. "Real glass. What?" she says to me. "What's the matter?"

"G-L-A-S-S," my Aunt Ruchel spells. "A-C-C-I-D-E-N-T."

"You have something to do inside?" my mother hints. I think she means I should go away. But then my aunt blows us a kiss and goes in the house.

"So quiet here," my mother says. "A bee buzzes, it sounds so loud. Tell me, what you find to do here?"

I tell her about going to the grocery store with Millie. "She lets me push the basket."

"You play with kids your own age?"

I tell her about the two girls with the wagon. I don't tell her how I met them.

"Comment-allez vous?" she asks. When I don't answer she says, "Listen to me. Your mother had to go away. I was sick. Too sick to take care of you."

"Why?"

"Why? Who knows how sickness comes? *Nor Got vaist.* Only God knows. Some say the devil brings it. This man I knew once, he believed the germs make us sick. Sometimes we make ourself sick."

"Why?"

"That's a good question. Why do you pick at your face?"

I shrug.

"We all do foolish things," she says. "Things that hurt us. That hurt other people." She sighs. "What do you want to do when we go home?"

"Can I go to school?" I ask.

"By Madame LePage?"

"Regular school."

"At four years old?"

"Cousin Sandy told me I can go when I'm bigger, but I want to go now."

"This is an idea," my mother says, "but how do we get them to take you? Oh, I know. A big girl doesn't pick at her face."

"I won't anymore. Can I go to school? I won't pick at my face."

"Only one month till September, when school starts. Now is August. That's thirty days."

"'Thirty days hath September, April, June, and November,'" I rattle off. "'All the rest have thirty-one.' August has thirty-one."

"I'm *plotzing*," my mother says. "Who learned you?"

"Don't you think it's strange?" Aunt Ruchel says to Uncle Isaac. "She hasn't called Sheldon or Mimi yet. It's been, what? five or six hours since we got home. Should I call them?"

"You can call them. Would she talk to them?"

"I'm sure. But it's so strange. Maybe she's—"

"Not right in the head?" my uncle says. My aunt nods. "If you ask me, the whole episode is strange. She disappears, God knows where. A week later they find her under the Boardwalk. How did she get pneumonia?"

My aunt has been thinking about this very question. She tells him, "According to Millie, that day she picked up Devorah, Chenia already looked peaked. Like she hadn't slept for a while. I think she was exhausted, frankly."

"From what? And where did she go? She had no purse, nothing, when she came into Emergency."

"Isaac, let's talk of something else. This is killing me." My aunt suspects my mother ran off with the man from the shoe store and then he dropped her. She imagines my mother was too ashamed to return home. But where did she go? She can't stand to think of her sister living in the street, like some bum on the Bowery.

There is lots of hugging the next morning when my sister and brother arrive at Aunt Ruchel's. We go downstairs to the rec room, where the big television is, but they don't turn it on. Cousin Sandy gives us all seltzers from the wet bar, and there is lots of talking, but no one talks to me.

Mimi says, "I can't get over it." She says it over and over.

Sheldon says, "You okay, Ma?" My mother nods. "Are you sure?"

Aunt Ruchel has warned them not to ask my mother questions. My mother does a lot of asking. Only in that way does she seem like her old self. Her hair is the way she used to wear it, with the pompadours on the sides, but she is different somehow. Not so peppy. She is surprised that Sheldon has a job. "Tell me," she says, "what you do all day."

While my brother talks about stocking shelves and fixing loose wheels on the carts, my mother appraises him as though he is a stranger. He's not bad looking, she thinks. A kind face. His ears are still too big, his nose a little long. She hopes he finds a nice girl, with *alleh meiles*, all the virtues. Then my mother notices my sister pouting.

"My toothpick!" my mother says, because my sister is no longer pudgy. "Your nails are fixed up nice."

"You're giving me a compliment?" Mimi says. "I should faint." My sister tells her she got the manicure at the beauty school in our neighborhood.

"How much this costs?"

"The old lady gave me some more money," Mimi says. "I put most of it in the bank account I got through school. I have a passbook and everything." Mimi doesn't say she had to forge my mother's signature.

"What old lady?" my mother asks.

"Mama! The one in the Bronx I helped with the cart."

My mother smiles weakly. And then it comes to her. "With the long name, *nu*?" Everyone looks relieved—my sister, my brother, my aunt.

We go upstairs for cold tomato soup and hot biscuits, which Millie serves. Everyone agrees the lunch is delicious. My mother looks surprised when my sister brags that she makes dinner every night. "We have salami and eggs a lot," Sheldon says. "I do the vacuuming, by the way. And I'm learning to iron."

"You'll make someone a good husband," my aunt says.

"Pop, of course, does nothing," Sheldon says. "Not even his wash."

"Papa . . ." my mother says vaguely.

My sister and brother look at each other. "He's back," Mimi says. "He doesn't trust us to be alone."

"Back where?" my mother says.

Now my aunt is getting worried. "Back home," she says.

"Did he go away?" my mother asks.

"Ma!" Sheldon says. "Don't you remember? You threw him out."

"I did?" She looks at her sister. "You're kidding me, no?" There is a long pause. She shrugs. "I forgot. So where is he today?"

"At work, Ma! It's Monday. I asked my boss for time off."

"Monday," she says vaguely. "In the hospital, you couldn't tell one day from the next. Except Sunday. On Sunday a lot of flowers came . . ."

Right away Aunt Ruchel changes the subject. "Congress might pass a big bill on civil rights."

"You can't force people to accept everyone as equals," Uncle Isaac says.

"I don't think segregation is right," my sister says.

"Why would someone want to go to a school where no one wants them?" Cousin Rhonda says.

"What if it's the best school in the city?" my brother says.

Back and forth they argue. No one even notices me. Finally I interrupt to ask Sheldon, "What time are you going home?"

He laughs. "We haven't had dessert. Why, you want to get rid of me?"

"You're not turning into a little brat, I hope," Mimi says.

"Brat!" I say. It's a word I don't know. I point to my sister. "What time are *you* going home? I'm staying here," I tell them. "With Mama."

My father divides his evenings between Trudy and Bertha. The nights he doesn't see Trudy he tells her he spends in New Jersey with me. He tells Bertha the same thing. When Bertha asks my father how much the round-trip costs, he says, "Are you testing me? Why don't you have a detective follow me around?"

While we stay at Aunt Ruchel's, my mother doesn't say much. "You're restless?" my aunt asks. "Go for a walk."

"Such a little sidewalk," my mother says. "And all you see are trees."

"Do you want to go home?"

"Not yet." My mother thinks she has to make a decision first: whether to keep living like a zombie or whether to end it all, the whole *megillah*.

"How can we entertain you?" my aunt says. "Shall we see *Blue Gardenia*? I know you like Anne Baxter."

Cousin Sandy is supposed to baby-sit me, but I tell my mother I want to go with them. "You have to sit quiet a long time," she says, "no matter what."

It isn't hard to sit still. The movie is very fascinating. When the woman picks up the poker and hits the man with it, my mother sucks in her breath so noisily the whole theater can hear. After it's over my aunt says, "That rat! He got what he deserved. Isn't Richard Conte a doll?"

"*Feh*," my mother says. "He needs oomph."

"What's oomph?" I ask. My mother smiles, the first real smile I've seen since she came from the hospital.

Before the second movie they take me to the bathroom. Then Aunt Ruchel buys me candy. "You spoil her," my mother says.

"Chenia, after what she's been through—"

"Don't make me feel any more guilty than I am!" my mother says.

Right after the second movie begins, I fall asleep. In the morning I wake up with a sore throat, but I don't tell my mother. I know she'll blame it on my staying up late. My throat hurts more and more each day, but still I don't say anything.

On Saturday Cousin Rhonda leaves with a little train case for a pajama party. Cousin Sandy gets my aunt to take us shopping for clothes for school.

"I want to go to school," I say. My mother looks helplessly at her sister.

"She's so bright," my aunt says. "Maybe a private school would give a scholarship. Talk to Isaac when we come home."

After ten minutes in the car my mother realizes I have a temperature. She asks my aunt to take us back. "You go on, go shopping. You must be sick to death of me anyhow."

Aunt Ruchel makes a dismissive sound. "My sister is welcome to stay as long as she likes."

Cousin Sandy blows my mother a kiss. "We like having you," she says. "You too," she says to me, "you little squirt."

I ask her, but she can't explain *squirt* to me.

My aunt drops us off at the house. "I'll buy a something for Devorah anyhow." She winks at me through the open car window.

My mother and I walk into the house, which is open. We don't see anyone downstairs. As we go up the stairs, I hear a funny noise. Then my mother hears it, like a dog crying.

I see them first. The bedroom door is open. My Uncle Isaac is lying on top of Millie. Below his shirt his heinie is bare. Millie has nothing on her legs. Her skirt is bunched up around her waist. My mother sucks in her breath and clops her hand over my mouth. We go back down the stairs.

"Lay down on the couch," she says softly. "I'll get something." She returns with half an aspirin and a glass of water. "Swallow, then I want you should listen," she says. She looks very serious. I think she is going to tell me she's going away again. I don't take enough water with the aspirin. I can taste how bitter it is but I don't care.

"Uncle Isaac and Millie are being very naughty," my mother says, practically in a whisper. "They're playing a game they're not supposed to play. *Farshtaist?*"

"Which game?"

My mother cannot think so fast. "They're trying to make a baby. Uncle Isaac is only supposed to make babies with your Aunt Ruchel. If Aunt Ruchel knew, *oy*, would she be upset! It would hurt her feelings. So you forget the whole thing. Hear? Forget we went upstairs."

"How do you make babies?" I think she's making the whole thing up.

My mother decides she's gone so far, there's no turning back. "The man's pee pee goes in the woman's and plants a seed which grows. That's why when a woman is expecting a baby, the belly gets so big." My mother shows with her hands how big. "You remember Mrs. Kleeberg from downstairs?" I shake my head no.

"That's okay. Just promise me you keep your lips zipped." She pretends she's pulling a zipper over her mouth. She strokes my hair, damp with sweat. She is wondering what to do. Should she mention something to her brother-in-law? To Millie? Should she tell her sister? Always there are problems. *Accidents*, the social worker said.

As I turn fitfully on the cushions, my mother hums the song from the movie we saw. "Nat King Cole," she says, "the way he sings, *se tsegait zich in moyl.*" It melts in your mouth.

Millie comes downstairs first, adjusting the belt on her shirtwaist. She looks shocked to see us.

"We didn't want to go upstairs," my mother says pointedly.

"I'm sorry," Millie says. She looks at her bare feet.

"Can I bring her up to bed?" my mother says. "The kid is not feeling so hot. You have a thermometer?"

Millie carries me up the stairs. My mother follows. We meet Uncle Isaac at the top of the stairs. He has pants on, but his shirt is outside. My mother was going to snub him, even though she knows that would make her a hypocrite. For her sister's sake, she thinks. But at the last second she remembers she's supposed to talk to him about private school. "The little one is sick," my mother says. "We came home early."

"Please—" he starts to say.

"Don't worry. What goes on, is none of my business."

My father gets upset when he learns that my mother and I are not coming home right away. My Uncle Isaac delivers the news to him by telephone. "We thought, a week in a bungalow—just the two of them. Chenia's still weak."

"From what?" my father says.

"The pneumonia." Incredible! my uncle thinks. Ruben's just now getting around to asking questions about his wife?

"How did she get this?" my father asks, wondering if he can sue.

"No one knows," Uncle Isaac says. "A cold goes into the lungs . . . She needs time. What's one week, anyhow?"

"Devorah's my daughter, not yours," my father says. He worries that I'll catch something serious from my mother.

"Look," my uncle says, "if you want to take care of your daughter, we'll send Chenia by herself." He doesn't tell my father he's also arranging for me to attend a private school in Manhattan.

"Where are they going?"

"To Atlantic City. The seashore will do them both some good."

The only thing I actually remember about Atlantic City is being with my mother in a Chinese restaurant. She orders chicken chop suey and lobster Cantonese.

When the food arrives, she slaps her own hand. "An *aveyreh*," she says. "A sin. Jewish people aren't supposed to eat lobster."

"Why?"

"It's not clean. Not healthy. But for me is out of this world."

She spears a chunk of lobster and reaches across the table.

I open my mouth. My teeth scrape the morsel off the fork. I chew it once, and then spit it out on my plate. "It's like an eraser."

"An eraser!" She looks at the ceiling. "What she doesn't think of. Listen, it's a grown-up taste, like cigarettes and liquor."

"You like it. Why? Why do you like it?"

"Human nature," she says. "Being attracted to what isn't so good for you."

I imagine we walk a lot on the boardwalk and watch the waves roll in. When we get tired, we take the covered choo-choo, as my mother calls the tram, all the way down to the end, then back again. My uncle is paying for everything. To have so much spending money makes my mother giddy. She buys cotton candy and fudge. She buys caramel apples and caramel corn. She buys taffy, but I can't have any. She pays for us to get into the Steel Pier.

Our *koch-alein* is a block away, a tiny bungalow with two tiny bedrooms and a kitchen.

On our second day, the owner comes to see if everything is all right. He has burgundy hair. "Dyed," my mother tells me after. There are palm trees on his shirt, which he leaves unbuttoned over his rust-colored pants.

"When's hubby gonna join you?" he asks.

"I'm not sure," she says.

The owner is picking weeds out of the grass when we come out of the house the following morning. "Beautiful day!" he says. My mother tries to smile. "Your hubby coming today?" he asks.

"I think so," she says.

On the boardwalk, she refers to the man as a *tsutcheppenish*, a pest.

"Why?" I say.

"I can tell he likes me." She thinks, An old lady with a kid, what does he want with her, except to take advantage?

"Aunt Ruchel likes you. Is she a pest?"

"He's not supposed to like me. Because I'm married. He's probably married too."

"Married people aren't supposed to like each other?" I ask.

"If one's a man and one's a woman."

I think about this for a few minutes. "You don't like Uncle Isaac?"

"He's my *shvoger*. Brother-in-law. We're related. Relatives are supposed to like each other. There's like and there's like. One is too much."

I think some more. "I know. Like Uncle Isaac and Millie!"

"That's it," my mother says. "There's a difference between friends and more-than-friends. That pest over there, he wants to be more than friends with your mother. Come, let's go to where your Aunt Ruchel recommends us."

From high up at the Steel Pier, we watch a lady get shot out of a cannon and land in a net. We watch swimmers and divers, girls in ruffled costumes riding horses—real horses. We watch seals and chimpanzees. We even see a movie there. In between we eat fried fish and French fries. We drink milk shakes.

When we get back to the bungalow in the early evening, the man is there. "I know a good seafood place. I'd like to invite you and your kid."

"Thank you very much, but my husband, he's due any minute."

We eat corn flakes and bananas for dinner. "I should cook you a real something," my mother says, "but, *nu*, I'm too tired."

The rest of the week we eat Chinese. During the day we never go on the beach. "I want to go in the water," I say. "Another time," my mother tells me. "Now is not a good idea. And don't ask me why."

She goes to bed when I go to bed. She turns on the radio and falls asleep. I make up stories until I fall asleep too. I wake up first. I read my big book of fairy tales. Every day my mother gets up later and later. First seven, then eight, then nine o'clock. "I could sleep all day," she says. "*Oy*, the more I sleep, the tireder I feel. I have two months of catching up. Too bad for you, your mother isn't so much fun. You should have someone to play with."

"Can Millie come here?" I ask.

My mother is too weary to tell me that Negroes aren't welcome by the shore. "No, Millie has to work."

"Where does she work?"

"You know. She works for your Aunt Ruchel. What she does for them, the cooking, the cleaning, the driving. They pay her for her time."

"For her watch?"

"For her time, *bubbeleh*. They pay her by the hour. The more hours she works, the more money she gets."

Sitting on the boardwalk, my mother teaches me addition, using Millie's hypothetical wages of a dollar an hour. She says Millie has to work because her husband is a *no-goodnik*. "He drinks and he don't work. If Millie didn't work, she and her children wouldn't have any place to live," my mother says.

"They could live here," I say, pointing to the beach.

"*Got zol ophiten!*" she says sharply, flinging up her hands. I guess she sees how she frightens me because she says gently, "To be a bum on the beach, is not such fun. At night—" My mother gets choked up. "At night, for a woman alone, is very dangerous." She points to a mound of sand showing only a girl's head sticking out. "There, like the coffins in the Cloisters, *nu*?"

We spend another whole day at the Steel Pier. This time we stay till after dark to see the show. There is a chorus line and singers, and then the comedians come onstage. I don't understand what they talk about, but I like it when they spray each other with water or honk horns that are hidden in their clothes. I've never heard so many people laugh at one time. My seat shakes.

Mostly, though, my mother and I walk. "I figured it out," she says one morning. "The difference. See all the couples holding hands? They're honeymooners. They just got married. No one goes to Brighton Beach on their honeymoon. People come for the day, then they go home. Here is supposed to be a vacation."

I know she wants to talk, so I don't say anything. She goes on and on about the honeymooners. "This couple looks happy. That couple, something's wrong—he's walking ahead of her. Over there, he can't keep his hands off her. I suppose he thinks he owns her. Look at them two, how they smile at each other . . ."

I see her wiping tears from her eyes. "Why are you crying, Mama?"

"The wind, it got in my eye."

Sometimes we walk off the boardwalk. Once we find ourselves in a Negro neighborhood. "Like Harlem," my mother says, "but not so interesting." I find it fascinating. Lots of little girls are playing on the porches of houses or on scrubby grass. Some are playing with tires. "How did they get brown?" I ask.

"They're born Negro," my mother says. "The Chinese people in the restaurant, their skin is in between. Auburn hair you got, your sister more like me. *Ver vaist?* Who knows?"

We browse in different souvenir shops. She buys a bell for my sister and a glass car for my brother. GREETINGS FROM AT-LANTIC CITY, they say. For herself she buys a salt and pepper shaker set. For my father she buys a box of taffy. I look at some dolls in a glass case, and when I turn back, I don't see my mother. "Mama!" I yell. "Mama!" Everyone turns to look at me. Then my mother comes running up to me. "With lungs like that you could be an opera singer." Before I can ask what an opera singer is, she says, "They're big, fat women, and they sing very loud."

"Like Millie," I say. "She's big fat and sings very loud. I'm not big fat."

"My skinny opera singer," she says. "Please, do me a little something. Don't let go my hand."

On our last night there, we go to a different Chinese restaurant, not the dumpy one we're used to. This one has rose-colored tablecloths and black-lacquered chairs. Fresh flowers in shiny black vases. Soon after we're seated, the waiter comes over and says a man wants to buy my mother a drink. He tips his head toward the bar. The owner of the bungalow is in a pink jacket and a flowery tie. He raises his glass as if toasting us. "That *tsutcheppenish*, I think he followed us," my mother says. "Tell him no thank you," she says to the waiter.

Soon the waiter brings drinks with purple parasols and cherries stuck on toothpicks. "This one's a virgin," the waiter says about mine. "No liquor," he explains. My mother thinks he's being vulgar. Before she lets me drink, she takes a sip, just to be sure. Her own drink sits on the table. She eats the maraschino cherry and gives me the parasol. "Wait here," she says.

She goes to the bar where the man is. She's thinking she doesn't want to make him angry because he has the key and he could come into the bungalow whenever he wants. "Thank you, Mister," she says. "You're very kind."

"Don't mention it. There's lots more where that came from."

"I just got out of the hospital," she says. "I'm not so well. For a month I didn't see my daughter, so you please excuse me if I don't have time to talk to you. She needs me."

"She stays up all night?" He waves to me. I don't wave back.

"I go to bed when she goes to bed." She smiles ingratiatingly. "You look like a nice man," she fibs. "You can find yourself a nice, unmarried woman."

He grabs her wrist and whispers in her ear. "You know you can't be without a man for so long . . ."

She pulls away. "If you touch me again I call the cops."

After the almond cookies come, we sit there a long time. The man sits there too. My mother is afraid to go back to the bungalow. It has no telephone. Finally she decides what to do. We go to the phone booth in the restaurant. I squeeze in, against the brown, lumpy wall. She dials the Operator. It takes a while for the Operator to understand she wants to call her sister, collect.

My uncle tells my mother to go to the Claridge Hotel. "It's right on the boardwalk. Stay there for another week, so long as you want," he says, but my mother says one more day is enough.

At the entrance to the Claridge, we stop while my mother looks up at the sky. "Some coincidence," she says. "A half-moon." The second time in her whole life she is staying in a hotel, she thinks, and the moon has to be the same.

"How does the moon get different?" I ask.

"Moving around the world." She walks around me. "Now you see me. All of me. Now you see a little bit. Now you don't." At least from *him* she learned a little something to tell her daughter, she thinks. "'It's a matter of perspective,'" she says, just the way he told her.

The clerk at the desk gives my mother a strange look when she says she has no luggage. The elevator operator says, "Something smells good," about the carton of chop suey my mother is holding. Once we're settled in the room, my mother turns out the lights and opens the window. We sit by the window for a long time, listening to the roar of the surf.

In the morning my mother is still by the window when I open my eyes. Her bed is still made up. Uncle Isaac and Aunt Ruchel come to get us. First we go to the bungalow for our things. The owner shows up just as we're ready to leave. He's wearing a maroon undershirt and shorts with palm trees. "Hope you enjoyed your stay," he says to my mother.

"Some parts more than the others," my mother says. "Last night, not at all. I think you owe us money since we didn't sleep here."

The owner starts to object, then he glances at my uncle. He takes out a ten-dollar bill from his pocket to give her. "That's all I got."

My mother takes it and gives it to my uncle. Quickly we all get in the car. Uncle Isaac drives us to Manhattan.

"Such a good rest I got!" my mother tells them. "How can I thank you?"

"You enjoyed Atlantic City?" my uncle asks.

"The ocean, it's very nice." To herself, she says, It ain't Coney Island. Not by a long shot.

To my mother the city looks familiar and unfamiliar at the same time. It looks grayer than she remembers, maybe because the sky is overcast. She can't believe that she misses being in the hospital. There she was free. No one knew who she was or where she came from. There she had no worries.

As soon as we get home my mother spends all her time putting the apartment in order. Then comes the day she's been dreading. She has to take me downtown to the Belevair School. My brother gives her directions. The subway part is easy, but we get lost on the Upper West Side. Finally a nice lady walks us there. Then we have trouble finding the subway back.

At the school, my mother doesn't know how to fill out the papers, so she brings them home. My brother writes in all the answers he can. "How much does Pop make?" he asks. My mother shrugs. "We have to tell them," Sheldon says. "Or she won't get financial aid."

My mother can hardly bear to think of it. "All I can do is ask your papa. If he says, 'None of your business,' we'll make something up."

She shows my father the form. "It's a very good school."

"How would you know?" he says.

"Isaac says. He's no *moyshe kapoyr.*" A person who does everything wrong. "Besides, the little one wants to go."

My father looks over the application. "It's none of their business how much I make."

"Okay, you tell her she's not going."

"I don't like it when you boss me around. You throw me out of the house and now—"

"I was sick then," my mother says. "I didn't know what I was talking. Can you believe me?"

My father doesn't know what to say. It's easier if she throws him out. Otherwise he'll have to prove adultery on her to get a divorce. He makes huffing sounds, sounds of aggravation.

"I have an idea," my mother says. "You fill this out. We put it in an envelope, we seal it, and I swear to you on the little one's head I won't open it."

My father nods grudgingly. The amount he writes in is what he made when Gershenfeld first hired him. He looks over the form to see if it's complete. "Why did you sign it?" he says. "I'm the head of the household."

"Please," she says. "Go ahead and sign over me."

The second time we go to the Belevair School, we bring the papers back and make an appointment for me. The third time, they ask my mother to wait while they give me the tests. My mother whispers in my ear, "Do whatever they tell you. They want to see if you're smart enough to go to school."

The tests make me forget I'm scared. I have to put blocks of wood into puzzles, which is easy. I have to count until the lady tells me to stop. I get to forty-two. Now I notice the big watch on her desk that has no strap. Sometimes she pushes down the little button on top, sometimes she pulls it up. Then she says, "I'm going to read some words to you. I want you to repeat them after me."

"What's repeat?" I ask. She smiles.

"When I say something, I want you to say the same thing. If I say 'chocolate,' what do you say?"

"Chocolate?"

"That's right." The lady gives me small sentences to repeat, and strings of numbers. The sentences and the strings get longer and longer. After I repeat them, she says, "Very good," and then I say, "Very good," and then she smiles. She shows me drawings of boxes stacked on top of each other and asks me questions about them. Sometimes I don't know the answer. "Tell me," I say. Now the lady laughs. A man with a red bow tie comes in, and she shows him the paper she's been writing on.

"Do you know what a school is?" he says to me.

"Where they learn you things," I say.

"Why do you want to go school?" he asks.

"To be a smart cookie," I say.

Now the man is laughing with the woman.

When we are not going back and forth on the subway, my mother is cleaning up. "Such a mess!" she says. Everywhere she looks, she sees dirt. Under, over, behind, in front of. Where does all the dirt come from? she wonders. She spends her days with the Frigidaire or the oven or the radiators. She spends her days on her knees, on the stepladder, on windowsills washing the windows outside and in. She spends her days with sponges and brushes and rags, with a broom, a mop, a vacuum hose, with Ajax and borax and Clorox, looking for dirt as if panning for gold.

We don't go anymore to the park. We don't go anymore to the Cloisters. She sends the *nexdooreker*, the boy who's our next-door neighbor, for whatever she needs from Dyckman Street.

For a few nights my father comes straight home from work. He teaches me to play checkers. He lets me win every game. On Saturday, while my mother washes the windows, he takes me to the playground in Fort Tryon Park. Mrs. Fleisch is there with Hannah. "Go play in the sandbox," he orders.

The sandbox is very boring. I get Hannah to sit down, and then I throw sand on her legs until you can't see them anymore. Soon the sand is up to her waist. I can see my father and Mrs. Fleisch from the sandbox. It looks like they're having a fight. I tell Hannah I'll be back. Anyway, she can't move. I run up to my father. "Don't fight!" I say.

"Where's Hannah?" Mrs. Fleisch asks.

"In the sandbox. I buried her."

Mrs. Fleisch gets hysterical. "What've you done?" she screams at me. She runs to the sandbox.

My father helps her dig Hannah out from the sand. "What's the matter with you," he yells at me, "putting all that sand on her?"

"I saw them on the beach. Mama and I saw them."

"Atlantic City," my father mutters. When Trudy's eyes pop, he realizes his mistake.

"You were in Atlantic City?" Mrs. Fleisch asks me. She is looking daggers at my father.

"With Mama," I say. "We stayed in a *koch-alein*, until the man gave us the drinks."

"What?" my father says. "There was a man there?"

"Who were you with in Atlantic City?" my father asks my mother.

"No one," she says.

"The one who bought you the drinks, that's the man you went away with, isn't it!"

"What are you talking? I was with the little one."

"Not Atlantic City. When you left here, when you didn't tell nobody where you were going."

"Believe what you want," she says, "I was by myself only."

I answer the phone when it rings. The woman's voice says, "Is your father home?"

"Papa!" I call out.

He takes the phone. "Hello?" He glances at the back of my mother's head. She is wiping the mirror over the credenza.

"Ruben!" Bertha says. "When are you returning?"

"Give me a little time. My daughter, she needs me."

"I need you too. I'm booking Labor Day weekend in the Catskills for us."

"Sure, sure! By then, everything will be straightened out." He fingers the cord and sees me staring at him. "I'm busy right now."

"I'll see you Tuesday, then? Shall I let Joe have the night off?"

My father hesitates. "All right," he says, and hangs up.

"Who's that?" my mother asks.

"Gershenfeld."

"And you told him you're busy?"

"The accountant from Gershenfeld," my father says. "A *nudnik.*"

My mother wipes the ceramic pitchers with the rag. So expensive and useless, she thinks. "Remember these?" she says. "From Yakob."

"They look just like—"

"What?"

He was going to say, What Bertha has on her buffet. "Like what they have in this store downtown. The Going Out of Business store."

My mother is still chewing on his conversation. Was he talking with Trudy Fleisch? "So, you had a fight with Trudy Fleisch," she says.

My father makes a who-me? face.

"The little one told me. In the park, *nu?*"

"It's all in her imagination."

"Listen," she says. "Ignorant I may be, but I know what I know. The kid has an eye like a camera."

"She don't always understand what she sees," my father says. "We're making jokes, she thinks we're having a fight."

"She's certainly one for laughing," my mother says. "That Trudy Fleisch."

In bed that night my father reaches for my mother. All he wants is some comfort. He feels more and more like the taffy she brought back from Atlantic City, pulled and pulled, stretched into bits and pieces.

You're his wife, my mother tells herself. She closes her eyes. *You're his wife.* She tries to empty her mind. She wants to push him away. She imagines pushing so hard, he falls out of bed. She wants to scream.

After he climbs on top of her, she puts her arms around him and raises her knees.

"Can I take Devorah to Sofie's place?" my sister asks.

"That's an idea," my mother says. "I can wash the kitchen walls."

"What are we going to do there?" I say.

"She's heard a lot about you. She wants to meet you," Mimi says.

"I want to stay home with Mama."

"Remember what I told you about trolleys? You can pull the cord to make the bell ring," Mimi says.

"Okay," I say.

On the trolley I make the bell ring. Then I want to stay on the trolley to do it again, but my sister won't let me. "On the way back," she says.

When a man answers Sofie's door, my sister thinks something's happened to the old woman. "Is she okay?" she blurts out.

"Oh yes," the man says. He looks to her about thirty-five, too young and too thin to be wearing suspenders. Because of his short-sleeved dress shirt and his tie, she is sure he works in an office. "Benjamin Farber," he says, extending his bony hand. "Call me Ben. You must be Mimi." They shake hands, and he says, "And this one?"

"Devorah," I say. "How do you spell Benjamin?"

We walk into the kitchen, and he spells his name for me. He asks me how to spell Devorah.

"Capital D," I begin. I spell my first name and my last name.

The old woman at the far end of the table claps. She points to her sunken chest. "Sofie Vrebolovich," she says to me. "Your sister can give you the spelling lesson later."

"Devorah got a scholarship to the Belevair School," Mimi says.

"Impressive," Ben says. He speaks fussy, as if he's English, my sister thinks. She wonders if he's a relative Sofie hasn't mentioned.

"If you're wondering who I am," Ben says, "I'm her attorney. Don't be alarmed. Mrs. Vrebolovich wants to be sure her papers are in order, that's all."

"I told him to give you the chest," Sofie says. "If anything should happen." She pours from a teapot and gives each of us a glass of tea. "Careful," she tells me. "It's very hot, the way I like it."

"You're not sick, are you?" Mimi says to her.

"No, but I've lived long enough. My brother is in hospital now."

"A serious heart attack," Ben says. "We saw him yesterday."

Sofie looks depressed, Mimi thinks. "I'm so sorry," she says. "I wish there was something I could do."

"Give Benny your address," she says.

My sister glances at me. This is different from what she had in mind. But I find it fascinating.

"You're about to start high school?" Ben asks Mimi. "Planning to go to college?"

She shrugs. "I don't think my father would give me the money."

"If your grades are good, you can go to City College. It's free."

"Really? I wonder if you can study art there."

"Benny," the old woman says. "You'll take care of it?"

"Absolutely, Mrs. Vrebolovich."

My sister gives her an inquisitive look. The old woman waves her hand, as if to say, Don't mind me.

"Vrebolovich," I say. "Vrebolovich."

"You're pretty good with words," Ben says. "Maybe you'll be an attorney."

"What's that?"

"When people have arguments, I have to help them figure things out."

"Everyone has arguments," Mimi says.

"I don't like it when people fight," I say.

Looks pass between Ben and the old woman. "You're right," he says to me. "Other people get hurt."

"That's the truth!" Sofie says.

"Ain't that the truth!" I say.

"Who taught you to say *that*?" Mimi asks.

"Millie. She learned me lots of things." I try to blot out the image of her, with her dress all the way up, and Uncle Isaac's heinie between her legs.

A s Labor Day weekend approaches, my mother fastens on the thought that my father will want us to go to Coney Island for the fireworks. First she thinks she won't go, she'll just refuse. Then she thinks she'll go, and if she sees *him*, she'll give him a snub. Then she decides it's impossible, she'll have to pretend she's sick.

The Wednesday before Labor Day, in the middle of dinner, my father says, "I have to go to Philadelphia, Friday, on business. I'll be back Monday night."

"Who's doing business on a holiday weekend?" Sheldon asks.

"If you stay this fresh when you're out of high school, you can go look for somewhere else to live," my father says. "Next summer."

"One minute please," my mother says. "Now is this year. You're going to Philadelphia?"

"Gershenfeld asked me to go for him. On account of the Sabbath. To see about our orders," he adds awkwardly.

My mother is sure my father is making it up. Still, she doesn't want to say anything. Not until after the weekend.

"I want to go with Papa," I say.

"Devorah, your papa has to work," he says to me. "I'll bring you back a surprise, though. What?" he says to my mother. "You don't believe me?"

"If you're telling me the truth, I believe you," she says. "*A sof, a sof.*" Let's end the discussion.

I imagine that Trudy Fleisch misses my father, even knowing he is two-timing her with another woman. What does he see in that cow but her money? Trudy thinks. *Big Bessie*, she calls Bertha, in her mind.

At night she lies awake till the wee hours, till her husband comes home from the printing plant. Lately she's been reaching out to him, to reassure herself she's still desirable. "What has you so hot?" Barney says in her ear.

Not hearing from my father, Trudy dials Bertha at all hours. The phone just rings and rings. How can she find out what's going on? Trudy wonders. She tries to see Mrs. Landau at home, but the doorman won't let her in. She tries to find my mother in the park, but my mother doesn't go there anymore.

Desperate, Trudy gives her a call. "Chenia, Hannah is throwing up and I can't reach the doctor. Can you recommend someone?"

My mother asks about Hannah's symptoms. Then she says, "Take her to the Jewish Memorial. Right away."

"All right. I hope you and Ruben are having a nice weekend."

The remark strikes my mother as peculiar. "Ruben's in Philadelphia, on business," she says.

"Oh, is that right? For how long?"

"Till Monday night. But why are we yakking when your kid needs a doctor?" No one is that *meshugge*, my mother says to herself.

"You're right," Trudy says. "Thanks much."

My mother hangs up the phone. I look at her expectantly. "If Trudy's kid is sick," she says, "your papa is in China."

The resort is far grander and larger than anything my father has imagined. There are tennis courts and handball courts, outdoor and indoor swimming pools, an archery range, a riding range, a lake for canoeing or even water-skiing. He has a room of his own because Bertha says they have to keep up appearances. The room is next door to hers.

The dining hall is immense. For appearance's sake, they sit with six strangers, rather than at a table for two. Dinner is a six-course affair. On the first night, when Bertha doesn't like the entrees on the menu, she asks the waiter to ask the chef to poach some fish. My father is astounded when the waiter says, "Certainly, madam." After dinner they watch the entertainment in a hall with at least five hundred people. My father is amazed to see Dean Martin and Jerry Lewis, live, right before his eyes.

Coming out of the show, Bertha waves to someone. "A business acquaintance," she says. My father keeps his left hand in his pocket. He has tried to remove his wedding band, but his finger is too swollen.

Later, when no one is in the hallway, my father slips into Bertha's room and spends the night. The next morning, Bertha insists on having breakfast in bed, which embarrasses him. "What do you care what the help thinks?" she says. She is thinking, Oh Ruben, I have so much to teach you . . .

The weather is brisk for autumn, so during the day they swim in the huge indoor pool, which is heated. Bertha puts on her rubber bathing cap and dives right in. She swims several laps before tiring. My father cannot keep up with her. "We'll have to get you some Geritol," she teases. Annoyed, my father wants to tell her that in a bathing suit she looks less like a woman and more like a German tank. After swimming, Bertha suggests they get a rubdown. It's my father's first. He has a new definition of *heaven on earth*.

All weekend Bertha says nothing about my father leaving my mother. But in the taxi from the Port Authority back to her place, she says, "When do you think the arrangements will be final?"

"Arrangements?"

"The divorce."

"I don't know. I have to see a lawyer."

"If you don't have a lawyer, I'll ask mine for a referral."

My father hates it when she *nudzhes* him. To change the subject, he asks, "Why are we going up Eighth Avenue?"

"It's faster. So you've discussed it with Chenia, then?"

"Not yet," my father says.

"Ruben! What are you waiting for?"

He doesn't know, really. He says, "This week the children go back to school. I'll talk to her."

"Very good." She takes his hand between both of hers.

"Your hands are so warm," he says. "Do you have a fever?"

"For you," she says. "I'm glad you let your mustache grow in."

At the entrance to her building, Bertha tells my father the doorman will see her up. She kisses him on the cheek. "Night night," she says. As soon as my father departs, the doorman says, "Mrs. Landau, a woman was here to see you at seven. She came back at eight. She didn't leave her name."

"Tonight?"

"Yes, Mrs. Landau. She asked if I knew when you would be back. I told her I wasn't at liberty to discuss anyone's plans."

"Thank you, Patrick. What did she look like?"

"A little taller than you, slender, brownish hair, I think. Shoulder-length."

"A long face?" Bertha asks.

"Yes, a very long face."

As they ride up in the elevator she reaches into her alligator bag and hands him five dollars. "I appreciate it," she says.

Going up the stairs with his suitcase, my father revels in the memory of his luxurious weekend. He wonders how much money Bertha actually has. She never worries about what things cost. The tips she leaves! He decides he'll wait awhile before he tells her not to overdo it.

As soon as he opens the apartment door he sees the kitchen light is on. He wishes my mother were already in bed. He wants to keep basking in the glow. "You're still up?" he says. "It's after eleven."

"Tomorrow is the kid's first day of school. I couldn't sleep." He looks *farmatert*, she thinks. Weary. "So tell me, how was Philadelphia?"

"What should I know? We stayed in the hotel for meetings."

"On Labor Day too?"

"Listen, I've had enough of the third degree—" Just then the telephone rings. My mother puts her hand over her breast. Bad news, she thinks, as my father goes to the hallway.

"Ruben, dear," Bertha says. "I just had to hear your voice."

After she hangs up, he says into the receiver, "You have the wrong number," and puts the phone down. *Go on*, he thinks. *Tell her.* As he walks into the kitchen, my mother turns out the light. "Time for bed," she says.

In bed my mother turns on one side and then the other. My father lies still, but he isn't snoring. "What's keeping *you* awake?" she says. "Your weekend was too exciting, *nu?*"

"Chenia, I want a divorce."

"No," she says.

"What, no?"

"I'm not giving you a divorce."

"I don't love you anymore," he tells her.

"I know. But you have a family to support."

"I'll support you. But I want a divorce."

"No."

"I can make it worth your while—if you make it easy for me."

"Forget it," she says.

"Chenia—"

"Forget it."

My mother falls asleep first. My father is awake till dawn, stewing.

At first I find school very boring. We're supposed to play a lot. Or stick Tinkertoys into each other. I'd rather read. We're also supposed to nap. I find it very hard to lie still and pretend to be asleep. And I get scolded when the teacher is teaching the alphabet, because I'm doodling. "I already know it," I tell her. "Well, in that case," she says, "maybe you'd like to recite it." After I recite the alphabet, she says, "Maybe there's something you don't know, so you better listen."

When she isn't teaching letters and numbers, I learn the names of different shapes: triangle, rectangle, square. Or different instruments. *Flute* is my favorite. I learn how flowers grow from seeds and how butterflies come from caterpillars. One day when the headmaster is in the room, I forget he's there and I look out the window instead of at the teacher. So much is happening on the street, with people and dogs and bicycles. Soon I am taken to the headmaster's office. He talks to me about why I don't pay attention.

"I can read already," I tell him.

"Is that so?" he says. He takes a book from the shelf. It's the one Cousin Sandy gave me, with all the fairy tales. "Read something from this page," he says.

It's not one of the hard pages. I read, *"A long time ago there were a King and Queen who said every day: Ah, if only we had a child!"*

"Indeed!" the headmaster says. "We'll have to see about a more advanced class for you." He asks a woman to take me back to my class.

"What's 'more advanced' mean?" I ask her.

On the day after Labor Day, while Barney is still asleep, Trudy reaches Bertha by phone. Softly, she says, "I want to tell you something I think will interest you very much."

"About Ruben?" Bertha guesses. "It's a little late. Ruben is divorcing Chenia to marry me. Got it?"

"To marry *you*? Hah!" Trudy says with all the aplomb she can muster. *Brazen bitch*, she thinks.

"It's a *fait accompli*. You shouldn't trouble yourself anymore."

"It's no trouble when your, uh, fiancé comes here to sleep with me," Trudy says. "He'll be over tonight, as usual. At eight. In half an hour, we're usually in bed." Trudy thinks she hears Bertha suck in her breath.

"Some ploy! I don't believe it for a minute," Bertha says.

"Well, if you get yourself up here tonight at eight-thirty, I can prove it. I'll leave the door open for you. Just walk right in."

There is a long silence before Bertha hangs up.

At seven that night, Trudy finishes feeding Hannah a huge bowl of oatmeal. In the oatmeal is a tiny bit of a sleeping pill, crushed to powder. Just after Trudy gets her into bed, my father arrives with cartons of Chinese takeout. "Aren't you going to lock the door?" he asks.

"Of course." She locks the door, waits for him to step out of the hallway, and quietly unlocks it. As soon as they're done eating, she's all over him. "I've missed you. Did you miss me?"

"You have no idea how much." His hands squeeze her slender waist.

At eight twenty-five they are lying naked on her bed. "Let me do you," she says to him. She strains to hear if there is someone at the door.

At eight-thirty, a casually dressed man emerges from the elevator, down the hall from Trudy's apartment. Hanging from a leather strap over his shoulder is a flash camera. Slowly he walks down the hall, looking at the apartment numbers. When he finds the Fleisches', he puts his head against the door to listen. Hearing nothing, he turns the doorknob. Carefully. The door opens.

My father receives a telegram at work: ALL MEETINGS OFF STOP DONT TRY TO CONTACT ME STOP THIS IS THE END STOP BERTHA LANDAU.

Telegram in hand, my father storms down to Mr. Gershenfeld's office. "I have an emergency," he says. "May I leave early?"

"Of course," Mr. Gershenfeld says. "Something happened?"

"My brother. A heart attack."

"I'm so sorry," Mr. Gershenfeld says, before he remembers. "I thought your brother lived in the city."

"That's right."

"I'm curious. Why would he send you a telegram here?"

"They were in the Catskills," my father says. "You'll excuse me, I have to hurry."

Outside, my father thinks of taking a taxi to Bertha's but decides it costs too much. Two buses and an hour later, he is asking the doorman if Mrs. Landau is in. "Do you have an appointment?" the doorman asks.

"Yes," my father lies.

"And your name?"

"Ruben Arnow."

The doorman consults his list. "I'm sorry, Mr. Arnow, your name is not down here."

"She forgot. Would you ring her?"

"I'm sorry, I can't do that."

"Bastard!" my father says.

In a fury, he storms down Fifth Avenue. How could it happen, his whole future, gone! Like that! In the wink of an eye! There is no doubt in his mind that my mother is responsible. Walking so fast, he doesn't see the truck that almost runs into him.

What did Chenia tell Bertha? he wants to know. That she won't give him a divorce? He could kill her, he thinks. Just strangle her.

He storms all the way down to Grand Central Station. Then he remembers the Western Union office there. At the counter he practices writing out his message to Bertha and finally decides on: I LOVE YOU STOP WHATS WRONG STOP PLEASE CALL ME STOP I WANT TO SEE YOU STOP RUBEN.

The Western Union clerk counts the words. "Eight over," he says. "That'll cost you—"

"Wait," my father says. He pens an abbreviated version: I LOVE YOU STOP WHATS WRONG STOP PLEASE CALL STOP RUBEN. Then he takes two subways home.

"How dare you! How dare you interfere!" my father screams at my mother. She is on her knees, relining the shelf of a kitchen cabinet. He leans over her. It's all he can do not to strike her.

"What are you talking about?" my mother says, moving sideways, out from under his angry face.

"You told her you wouldn't give me a divorce, didn't you! Didn't you!"

"Who?" she says. "I didn't talk to no one."

Ever since she returned from New Jersey, my mother has managed to stay busy. I imagine being busy has kept her from thinking too much. Being busy has kept her alive.

After taking me to school, my mother feels desolate. There is no reason to go on living, she believes, when you're so alone.

After my mother leaves me off, she stays downtown because there isn't time enough to go home and back again. She walks and walks to make the hours go by, and then she returns to the school to pick me up.

The kids spill out of the door, down the steps. Waiting with her are lots of Negro women in black uniforms, maids of rich people who can afford to send their children to private school without scholarships. The children wear beautiful clothes. Plaid wool skirts with matching hats. Corduroy jumpers. The boys have caps.

Today, when she sees me, my mother doesn't rush toward me. She watches. My blouse is half out of my skirt. My hair is wild; I've lost a barrette. I don't see her. I stand at the top of the stairs and look around, unsure of where to go.

One more year, my mother says to herself. If things aren't better by then, she'll kill herself. This time, she'll jump off a roof. And if she can't jump off a roof, she'll eat poison.

For the first two weeks of school, the sky is very blue. It's sunny, not cold. Hardly any wind. My mother walks and walks. Everyone seems to be in a hurry. Rushing to work. Rushing to shop. So useless, she thinks. What does it all matter? She passes a blind man selling pencils. She puts a coin in his pewter cup. She passes a Chinese laundry which is just below the sidewalk. She can see a slender little man pressing the shirts. How hard he works! And for what? For such a hard life. She thinks of her sister, the one who died long ago. How lucky she was! To get out of the whole thing.

Then the weather turns wet and cold. The hours drag. One night she consults my sister. "Where can I go to pass the time?" she asks. She doesn't really expect an answer.

"The museum," Mimi says. "The Metropolitan Museum of Art. It's just on the other side of the park. You can take a crosstown."

The first time my mother sees the outside of the Metropolitan Museum, she thinks it's large, all right, but not so interesting as the Cloisters. Skeptically she goes through the revolving door and into the Great Hall. She is a little ruffled by all the people. Such a busy place! But the Hall is grand! In the middle of the marble floor, she tilts her head back and gapes at the domes and circular skylights way up high.

Slowly she moves through some of the first-floor galleries. She falls in love with one Greek sculpture after another. She reads the placards but has no idea what many of the words mean. What is *Dancing Maenad* or *Sleeping Eros*? She has so many questions. For a fleeting instant she wishes she could ask Harry.

The two hours go like a minute. As she passes the circular desk in the Great Hall, she sees people taking brochures without paying. Shyly, she collects a few. On the crosstown bus, she looks them over. And then the size of the place begins to dawn. Even though she has never read a map in her whole life, she figures out that what she saw was the tiniest little corner.

She arrives at the school with twenty minutes to spare. Now she notices a couple of cars with chauffeurs who are also waiting. A gray-haired woman leaning against the wrought-iron railing strikes up a conversation with her. "You have a grandchild here, too?" she says.

"A daughter," my mother answers.

"Sometimes the late ones are not so gifted," the woman says. "You were lucky."

"*Kineahora*," my mother answers. It just falls out. "'No Evil Eye!' is just a superstition, like 'Knock on wood,'" she tries to explain, but it's too complicated.

"How quaint!" the woman says. After that, she is quiet.

Now my mother is kicking herself. It doesn't matter what the woman thinks of *her*, but she shouldn't get the wrong impression of her daughter. Like that movie *Stella Dallas*, so long ago, before she was engaged, even. That Barbara Stanwyck, how she could break your heart! My mother feels sick in her stomach, but as soon as she sees me coming down the steps, my reddish-brown hair flying, my jacket buttoned crooked, the white collar of my dress bunched up against my neck, her heart lifts.

Cut off from Bertha, my father turns to Trudy, but ever since Barney changed his schedule at work, Trudy hasn't been able to see him. When she suggests they meet by the river one Sunday morning, my father gets excited. Then she says she's bringing Hannah and he should bring his kid along, too. He feels too defeated to argue.

There's nothing really there, by the river, but I find it an interesting place. First of all, there's the Hudson River, where Henry Hudson sailed in his ship called the *Half Moon*. My brother says they think he landed at Spuyten Duyvil, which is the tip of Manhattan. My sister calls it *Spite the Devil*. In school they tell us about the Indians and how they traded twenty-four dollars of wampum beads for all of Manhattan. Then the Dutch people came to live here. My teacher doesn't know where the Dutch people went, though. Or the Indians. I get a little aggravated because no one ever tells you the whole story.

Waiting for Trudy, my father takes me for a walk between the road and the river, beside a rocky bank where men and boys fish. Today there's a girl fishing, too. My father peers at her over the top of his glasses and calls her a tomboy. He can't explain what the *tom* part means. "It's just a word," he says. "Better you should learn to tell time." He shows me his wrist-watch.

"Nine to ten," I say.

"It's a quarter to, or you can say, it's fifteen to ten."

"How can a quarter be fifteen?" I ask.

"It just is," he says.

I think there's also a torture called *drawn and quarter.* In the torture, *quarter* means "four." All the time now I get more and more confused.

On the other side of the grass, where the wildflowers grow, a train comes by, tooting its horn. There are so many cars we get tired of counting. We wave and wave. Walking by the river, we hold hands. His is warm, and he squeezes mine from time to time, but never so that it hurts.

Soon we see Mrs. Fleisch with Hannah. Mrs. Fleisch has her big smile on. I think it's too big because she wants us to like her. "Go play," she says to Hannah right away. I would rather hang around there, but my father becomes a copycat and says, "Go play."

Hannah and I run around the grass. I tell her I'm the cow-girl, like Dale Evans, and she's the squaw. I don't think she understands. Anyway, it doesn't matter. I let her shoot me dead with an arrow.

Then I blow the gray fuzzy stuff off the dandelions. Taking their clothes off makes me feel peculiar, but I like doing it. Each time I blow, I make a wish.

My father and Trudy sit on a bench facing the river and the Palisades of New Jersey. "What a long face!" I imagine Trudy says to him. "Problems with all your women?" She wants to tell him how, lying on top of him, she could hardly believe her eyes when she looked up. There was the man pointing the camera at them. Covering my father's forehead with noisy kisses, she used one hand to shield his eyes from the flash. She reached down for him with the other. That he never knew what was happening is some miracle. At the least, a credit to her powers.

Seeing Trudy's knowing smile now, my father realizes that she is to blame for his change of fortune. "What did you tell Bertha?" he demands. "Tell me, damn you!"

"Oh, look at you," Trudy says. "That's why I wanted to meet here. Here you wouldn't dare hurt me. I told that cow you could marry her for all I care, but I won't give you up."

My father stares, incredulous. A million dollars he's probably lost. He looks away. Little boats are bobbing on the dark blue waves. He feels as if a load of cement is pulling him down under the water.

"What is it? You're thinking about all the money you lost?"

"Don't be ridiculous." *A million dollars.* He feels sick. He wants to push her over the rocks and into the river—a fleeting thought that shocks him.

"Ruben, don't be angry. I did it because I love you."

She cajoles and flatters him until he gets the sense that she really cares. He tries to resign himself. At least he still has Trudy. And he won't give up on Bertha Landau. Not yet.

Just as we're getting ready to go home, Trudy says, "Don't look now! There's Barney." A man with a crew cut is walking pretty fast toward us.

My father steels himself. He is ready to punch Barney out if he has to, but Barney says "Howdy" and pats my father where his big arm muscle is. He asks Hannah, "What did you do this morning?"

"We played cowboys," she says.

"Cowgirls and Indians," I say.

Barney walks along with us, between my father and Trudy. "You came all the way to the river to see us?" Trudy asks him.

"I missed you." Then Barney grabs her, leans her way back, and kisses her. Trudy starts to sputter, then she gives in to it. Let Ruben see, she thinks. The competition will do him good.

M y sister meets my mother and me at the door when we come from downtown. Her eyes are red, and her face is swollen.

"What?" my mother says, all alarmed. Her thoughts fly in all directions.

"Sofie. She had a stroke last night and died in her bed." My sister shakes with sobs. After my mother pours her a glass of milk she calms down.

"The best way," my mother says. "To go like *that*."

"Like what?" I say. "Where's she going?"

"Shut up!" my sister says.

"To die quickly," my mother says. "Without pain."

I think about the rabbit in our class. I wonder if they gave Sofie an injection.

"But she was all alone," Mimi says. "I wish I could have been there. To say good-bye, at least."

"She was an old woman, *nu*? I know you helped her a lot." I imagine my mother can't help feeling a twinge of envy. "Drink your milk."

My sister gets angry. "I hardly did anything. I wish I'd done a whole lot more." She runs into the bedroom and slams the door. She stays in there and doesn't come out for dinner. My mother finishes the glass of milk.

Later I eavesdrop as my sister talks to her friend Suzanne. "She was so alone. I didn't know her brother died. If I knew, I would've gone to see her right away. I could kick myself."

When it's time for me to go to bed, I open the door. She sits up on her bed. Her eyes bulge like a frog's. "I was so selfish," she says. She pulls at her hair. "I hate myself," she says. She keeps pulling her hair.

"Stop it!" I say. "Stop hurting yourself."

"The first four-year-old in first grade!" the head of the school tells my mother. "On a trial basis. If it doesn't work out, she can go to kindergarten and still be a year ahead. Is that all right with you, Mrs. Arnow?"

"The older kids, they won't take advantage?" my mother says.

"We'll keep close tabs on the situation," he assures her. He explains about uniforms and where she can go to buy them.

"Write it down for me," she says.

"It's very simple," he tells her, but when she insists, he gives in. Maybe the father has the brains, he thinks.

The uniforms cost twice as much as my mother expects. More than dresses she buys for herself. She hates to do it, but she calls up her sister to ask for a loan. "Darling," my Aunt Ruchel says, "I'm thrilled to pieces at the news."

My mother feels guilty about all the money she spends on carfare and the cups of coffee she drinks while waiting for me. She cuts down on groceries. She hardly ever buys meat anymore. Her daughter needs clothes. Her son needs shoes. Although they've hardly spoken since that day my father came home early, accusing her of something, who knows what? she decides she has to talk to him about what it costs to send me to school.

"Why does Devorah have to go downtown?" my father asks.

"I'm surprised you say such a thing."

"All schools are the same. Reading, writing, arithmetic."

"You talked lately to your daughter?" my mother says. "What she's learning, she wouldn't get in just any school. What's the matter with you? You think for an ordinary kid I would *shlep* her back and forth? I'm worn out."

"No one's forcing you."

She shakes her head. "Why, because you didn't have much education, you want to keep her so little?"

"Don't be ridiculous."

"Already she knows more than we knew at ten years old, even twelve," my mother says passionately. *"Farshtaist?"*

"How much school does she need? She'll grow up, she'll get married, she'll have babies . . ."

"Zei nit kein vyzosah!" Don't be such a damn fool! "To wash and iron clothes like me, she don't need brains. Ask Gershenfeld, Should the kid go to private school? If he says no, it's no." My mother is only bluffing. She has decided that no matter what, if she has to take the clothes off everyone's back, I'm going to be educated. She wants me to be at least as smart as, smarter even than, Harry.

My father sulks. He slams doors and drawers.

She gets an idea. Every night now, she serves noodles for dinner. On the third night, my father blows up. "Noodles again?"

"Noodles from now on," she answers. *"Tsu gezunt!"* To your health!

A few days later she finds more money in her household allowance. After that, things are much easier. She can walk around the museum without a head full of worry.

Though my days are much longer now, my mother doesn't mind. She has the routine down. After she drops me off, she takes the crosstown bus. On Madison Avenue, she sits at the counter in a coffee shop until the museum opens.

She starts to attack the museum systematically, room by room. She keeps a little notebook, and after she gets tired of walking, she sits on a bench in one of the halls and writes down what she liked especially. She brings along a sandwich for lunch and eats it in the cafeteria with a glass of water. Then she takes the crosstown bus back to the school to pick me up.

She doesn't know how it happens, but one morning she wakes up and thinks only about what she is going to see at the museum that day. Gone are the questions: Why should she get up? Why should she go on? Gone are the thoughts of killing herself, and how to do it. Rain is beating on the windows, but she doesn't care. She hurries to the bathroom to brush her teeth.

By the entrance to the river, my father buys me peanuts in the shell from a little refreshment stand built into the cliff below Inwood Hill Park. I enjoy crunching the shells with my teeth and popping out the peanuts. My father says it's too much work.

We're there at ten, but by ten-thirty Mrs. Fleisch hasn't shown up. I tell my father what I learned about Henry Hudson looking for a way to get to the Orient, but my father isn't very interested. He's left his glasses at home, so he squints at his watch and keeps asking if I see Mrs. Fleisch.

The sixth time he asks me, I say, "Over there."

He gets all excited, happy-excited, until I say, "There's Mr. Fleisch."

"What? Are you sure?"

I point across the street. Mr. Fleisch is coming through the shadow of the arch that covers the whole street. The top of his head looks like a clothes brush. My father grabs my hand so hard, I feel the ring on his finger pressing into me. We go up into the park, which is like a forest. I want to ask why he's running away from Mr. Fleisch. Something tells me not to.

On the way home we stop at the Five and Ten. My father asks if I want to get a game. "Like what?" I ask, because games can cost a little money or a lot of money. He says, "Pick out whichever one you want." I really want the doctor's kit that my sister's friend Suzanne told me about, but that's not exactly a game. Finally I decide on Clue.

My father doesn't ask me to keep anything a secret. But somehow I know he doesn't want me to tell my mother about Mr. Fleisch showing up instead of Mrs. Fleisch. I don't know how I know.

At first my mother doesn't say anything about my new game. But after my father goes out, she says, "I didn't know it was Hanukkah already." I shrug. I've never fibbed to my mother. She says, "Okay, enjoy your secret." It's like a curse, the way she says it. All day I hear her voice in my head. *Okay, enjoy your secret.* I put Clue at the bottom of the bookcase, and I don't open it. I give it to Laura, my new friend from school, for her birthday. Then finally I get to play the game.

M y mother, brother, sister, and I are all home when the men come with Sofie's marble-topped chest. "It goes very nice there," my mother says, after my brother takes away the wrought-iron stand in the hallway. "Such a fancy place for a telephone." She pulls at the handles of one of the drawers. "It's locked?"

"I have the key," Mimi says. "I'll go get it." I trail after her and back.

"She locked away her important papers?" my mother says.

"I don't know. She never told me what was in it." Mimi turns the large brass key in the lock. She slides the drawer open. There are piles of used envelopes with canceled stamps. My sister thinks it'll make interesting reading. Idly she takes one envelope out. The flap opens. "Good God!" she says.

"There's money in there," Sheldon says.

"No kidding!" Mimi answers.

Soon we are all digging into the drawer and taking out envelopes. Each one is crammed full of bills. An inch thick. It's the same with the second drawer. In the third drawer there is also a box of old coins, but the rest is crammed with envelopes full of fifty- or hundred-dollar bills.

My brother starts to calculate. "Ma," he says. "I think we're rich."

"The money, it belongs to your sister," my mother says.

"I think Sofie wanted all of us to have it," Mimi says.

My mother stares for a moment, her eyes clouding. *"A leben ahf dein kop!"* she says to her. "A blessing on your head. What I did to deserve such a daughter, I haven't the faintest idea!"

At midnight my mother sits at the kitchen table. She sips a cup of cocoa and remembers the lifeguard who pulled her out of the water. Such a young kid! She can still see the freckles on his face. She wishes she had his name and address so she could thank him. She has to push away the thoughts of that terrible time . . . She starts writing a note to the social worker. She will ask my brother to help her with the English.

She hears my father on the stairs. He unlocks the door and walks in. He's dapper in a brown suit and rust-colored tie.

There's only the tiniest patch of gray hair on one side of his head. My mother realizes she hasn't noticed for a long time how handsome he is.

"You're up?" he says. "Can't sleep?"

"I waited up," she says. "I have such good news for you. I want a divorce."

Part Five

Ben Farber, the lawyer who looked after Sofie Vrebolovich, takes care of everything. He shepherds my mother through the cumbersome laws of New York State, designed to keep people legally bonded even when they no longer love each other. I imagine when the divorce finally comes through, my mother has mixed feelings. "Let's celebrate tonight," Ben says as we leave the office. I imagine my father at the other end of the long hallway, looking back at us, at me. I imagine that in spite of himself, he feels a pang of doubt. Regret, maybe.

"Are you happy?" Ben says to me, by the elevator. "No more arguments between your mom and dad. You said you don't like fights."

I want to ask him again how a piece of paper can stop people from arguing. Then I recall what he told me about the war in a faraway place. "Armistice," I say now.

"Silly," my mother says. "There was no shooting. But, I tell you, sometimes I was so angry—" Her eyebrows go way up. I see where she penciled them over to cover up the gray.

"Mrs. Arnow," Ben says, "I'd like you and you"—he pulls one of my pigtails—"to be my guests for dinner. And Mimi and Sheldon. Agreed?"

"What's to celebrate?" my mother says. "To think after so many years, the marriage, is *toyt*. Dead."

To cajole my mother, Ben jumps in front of her, his elbow grazing a passerby. "Look where you're going, moron!" the man barks. "Pardon me," Ben says, but moving sideways, he inadvertently steps on the shoe of a woman behind him. She yelps, they stagger backwards and collide with two clerks. Papers swirl in the air and spill onto the marble floor. The hubbub brings an elderly guard rushing over, but as soon as he sees it's Ben Farber, he says, "Ah, the *luftmentsh.*"

"His head is in the clouds," my mother explains, suppressing a smile. I imagine I feel a pang of jealousy when she pinches his cheek. "Why don't I make you some *latkes* tonight?" she says to him. "You're so skinny."

Ben's arm cradles her shoulder. "Mrs. Arnow, you would do me a great favor by dining out with me." I imagine it's all he can do not to give away his ulterior motive. He wants my mother to meet his recently widowed uncle.

I imagine the neighbors hanging out the window take notice of the black car that comes to pick us up, the uniformed chauffeur who opens the doors and helps my mother and my sister and me in. I imagine my brother sits next to him in the front, and on the way to the restaurant, asks him to stop at the florist. My brother buys an orchid corsage for my mother, which she pins above her bosom. We are all wearing new clothes. My mother's dress is a yellow silk print with matching jacket. Mine is blue velvet. My sister runs her hand against its nap. "It's like a dream," she says, "being able to buy whatever we want."

My mother's hand lifts up, then settles in her lap. "Money don't buy *naches.*" Pleasure from accomplishments. "Or *naches fun kinder.*" Pleasure from children.

"You make it sound like all this money is nothing," my sister says. "It's brought us lots of happiness."

"*Kineahora,* thanks to you know who," my mother says, meaning Ben.

"Aren't you forgetting someone?" my sister says.

"*Emes,*" my mother says. True. "Thanks be to the old lady, *oleho hasholem.*" May she rest in peace.

"And?" my sister prompts.

"And to my daughter, *kineahora*."

"Oh no," my sister says, "she's back to the Evil Eye."

"What's that?" I ask.

"Making with the compliments, you can bring the Evil Eye, *kholilleh*," my mother says.

"But what is it?"

My brother tries to explain, but I don't get it. "Whose eye is it?" I ask.

"Anyone's," he says. "You don't necessarily know. Isn't that right, Ma?"

"It could be anyone," she says grudgingly, "but let's not talk ourself into something. *Alevai*, may Ben continue to be so good to us, and you—" My mother pokes my sister in the chest. "You don't forget all he does for us—"

"Yes, Ma, he's a genius, a whiz at investments, as honest as Papa is crooked, he's the son-in-law you wish you had, if only he wasn't queer—"

"All right, enough," my mother says. *"Zindik nit."* Don't complain.

I actually remember some things about the dinner, how it was in a restaurant with dark-paneled walls and brass sconces that held lights with tiny black lamp shades, no bigger around than my mother's potato pancakes. I remember a white linen cloth, and getting my own menu to read as if I'm already a grown-up. There are other details my mother recalls, and which she will share with me. The rest I have to imagine.

Mr. Farber, Ben's uncle, is waiting for us, alone at a large round table. Before he stands up to greet us, I see the little bald spot on top. His hair on the sides is gray. The tie, my sister says later, is very expensive, and probably the jacket, though she isn't crazy about tweed. What I notice are the gray eyebrows, so thick and bushy, they look pasted on.

"Pleased to meet you," Mr. Farber mumbles. As we take

our chairs, he avoids looking at my mother. He knows why his nephew is hosting the dinner. He glances at me sideways, the way my mother does sometimes to see if I'm being good. Turning to my sister, he says, "The *mitzvah* girl, the lady of kind deeds. What you did for Sofie—"

My sister makes a dismissive sound. "I wish I did a whole lot more."

"I met Sofie," I tell Mr. Farber. "Her last name is Vrebolovich."

My sister gives me a look. She's told me before not to interrupt conversations, but I hate being left out.

Mr. Farber sits between my sister and mother. I sit between my mother and Ben. Next to Ben is an empty chair, then my brother and sister. Soon a man comes to the table, and Mr. Farber stands up again. He gives my brother a look, and he stands, too. The man is tall, with a big nose, and wild hair that sticks out all over. "Isaac Abrams," Ben says. "He's an art historian."

By the time the caviar and crackers arrive, my mother all but ignores Mr. Farber, spellbound by Isaac's discussion of an obscure artist, Gabriele Münter. "No one paid her much mind," Isaac says, "because she was a woman and the mistress of the famous Vassily Kandinsky."

"And she subordinated herself to him," Ben says. "He was her teacher before he was her lover, isn't that so?"

"Fortunately for us, he only influenced her work to a point. She was otherwise under his spell, even when he left her to go back to Russia—where his wife was. Münter didn't even know he was married until one day he sends for his belongings. She was a great admirer of Picasso's work. And of course, no one is as blatant, with the penises and vaginas in plain view—"

"Excuse me," Mr. Farber says prudishly, "I'm not used to such talk with ladies present—"

Ben taps his glass with a little spreading knife that I'm not supposed to call a spatula. "Has anyone besides my dear uncle been offended?" he asks. My brother looks at my sister, who shakes her head, her stare warning him not to say anything. "Uncle Sol, I'm afraid you're outnumbered," Ben says.

"This doesn't offend you, Mrs. Arnow?" Mr. Farber asks.

"*In bod zaynen ale glaykh*. In the bath everyone is equal. What's to hide?" she says. "Please, Mister," she says to Isaac, "you go on."

I imagine Ben's heart sinks, thinking of his uncle's disappointment with the woman who has no modesty, and of my mother's indifference to his matchmaking.

The meal is lavish. My mother oohs and aahs at all the side dishes, especially the creamed pearl onions and white asparagus. "So much is included!" my mother says wonderingly. My brother starts to tell her about à la carte, but Ben sidetracks him. "Shel, how're you making out on that car?" Ben explains to Isaac that my brother's hobby is souping up old convertibles. Their eyes lock, but I don't know what it means.

Bottles of wine come and go. Ben sneaks me a teeny sip, which tastes like cough medicine. From two glasses of Cabernet, Mr. Farber's cheeks get red. He tells my mother she has the eyes of a falcon.

"This bird, it's nearsighted?" my mother jokes. She sips the Cabernet and tries not to remember the last time she drank this kind of wine. In her mind's eye she sees the narrow bed in the furnished room, then wills the picture away.

"In Egyptian art, the falcon's eye is not only a symbol of sight but is coupled with the Eye of Horus," Isaac says, "around which was developed a whole symbolism of fertility."

"What's fertility?" I ask.

Mr. Farber does a double take. "How old is she?"

"You can ask me," I say. "I'm six. I'm in third grade."

My mother puts up her index finger—a warning to me not to boast. "Go ahead, explain her," she says to Mr. Farber. I decide she doesn't know what fertility is, either.

"Being able to have babies," Mr. Farber says, eager to be part of the conversation.

"Well," my mother says—her chin juts toward me—"this one was my last. Now is only hot flashes."

"Is it true what they say—the sex drive disappears with menopause?" Isaac asks. He peers mischievously at Ben.

"*Change of life* they don't call it for nothing," my mother says. "One day you think you're a woman, good for something besides cooking and cleaning."

"Good for what?" I ask.

She looks past me. "Just when you're thinking you're a really hot number, whoosh, the whole thing goes. You're a *shtekn*, a stick. You look at men like they're *behaimehs*, dumb animals walking around, some prettier than others." My mother, on her third glass of wine, cannot believe she is speaking so frankly, but she doesn't stop. "From the museum, I have all I need," she says. "*Emes*. When it comes to the Greek sculptures, *ai yi yi*. Who can compare?"

"Ah, a Hellenist," Isaac says. Ben generously explains *Hellenist*, even as he wonders if my mother is deliberately sabotaging his best-laid plans.

After coffee and dessert, Mr. Farber takes leave of us, singling out my mother. "It was a pleasure, Mrs. Arnow." A nod but no smile. He stops by the hatcheck to get his brown fedora. The girl titters at something he says.

Ben looks crushed. "I wanted this to be an occasion," he says.

"What for you worry?" my mother says. "The dinner, it was *kosher veyosher*." Perfect.

After a round of liqueurs, Isaac leaves, too, but not before he pretends to send a little smooch toward me. His hand still near his mouth, he turns to Ben. I make a noisy pretend-kiss back. Everyone laughs. When Isaac has gone, my mother says to Ben, "Excuse me for asking, this Isaac, is he more than a friend?" The look on Ben's face is hesitant. "*Bubbeleh*," she says, "such a brain, I could fall in love with him too." My sister shrinks back into her seat.

Later, in the rest room, I ask my mother a question that is burning in me. "If Ben and Isaac are more-than-friends, are they going to make babies?"

My mother laughs so hard, the tears come, and then I think she is crying for real, but I don't know why.

I imagine that back at the table, Ben has shared his now-dashed hopes with my sister and brother. In the car going home, my sister asks my mother, "So, what did you think of Mr. Farber?" My mother shrugs.

"Don't rush things," my brother says.

"What?" my mother asks.

"Mr. Farber is a widow," my sister says pointedly. "Ben was hoping—"

My mother sighs. "*Feh*, I'm a *getriknte floym*, a dried-up prune."

"What was Ben hoping?" I want to know.

"What's to hope?" my mother says. "Love, romance—*a nekhtiger tog*. Impossible. Maybe the *finster yor*, the dark time, is ending, but not altogether . . ." There is a silence in the car and for once I don't rush to fill it. After a while my mother says, "Like the shadow of the Boardwalk, it goes and goes. You're standing under, so you don't know what kind of day it is, outside. The sun so bright, it makes you blind."

"I thought there wasn't enough room under it to stand," I say.

"This one, a future lawyer, *alevai*. So exact." My mother fans herself. "It's hot, no?"

"No, Mama, it must be a hot flash," my sister says. "Tell us about Brighton Beach," she urges, before she remembers that strange story, how my mother wanted to kill herself.

"The Boardwalk, is like a fever when you're going. But under, where the sun never is, it can make you so cold. Chills it gives you, even on the hottest days," my mother says, and then she doesn't say any more.

After he moves out of our apartment for real, I imagine my father stays in the basement of his brother Yakob's house in Brooklyn. He is allergic to the two cats—named J.D. and J.P. after the tycoons Rockefeller and Morgan—but by closing the door, my father keeps them out of his bedroom and the closet-sized bathroom. *Pluses and minuses*, he thinks. On the plus side, the basement has a separate entrance. And his sister-in-law does his laundry in their new washing machine. "You want anything ironed, you send it out," she says. My father knows he is in no position to complain. He has a radio in his bedroom, and he can watch the swell T.V. upstairs in the living room. From the snacks Lilli makes at night—sandwiches, fruit, rugelach—he fashions most of his dinners. It costs him almost nothing to live, which is good, he thinks, because who knows how much Chenia will ask for alimony, not to mention child support.

On the minus side, my father is sick of the commute to Manhattan. And he's sick of Trudy's kid. She's old enough now to report his visits to Barney, so Trudy has to arrange for baby-sitters and make excuses to her husband why she needs them. My father and Trudy no longer have a place to make love safely. One night they go for a walk by the river and have sex on the grass. My father spends the next few days scratching the mosquito bites on his legs.

He still tries to contact Bertha, but her new phone number remains unlisted. The receptionist at her office says she will give Mrs. Landau the message, but Bertha never returns his calls. At work he daydreams about getting Bertha back. More and more it doesn't seem so important to get the rush orders filled on time. When one of the men at the Jewish Club talks about Florida, my father wonders if he would like living there.

A few days after the dinner, Mr. Farber calls to invite my mother to a concert. She's about to tell him she's too busy, but she wonders what it would be like. Also, she doesn't want to hurt his feelings. Even more important, she doesn't want to hurt Ben. She doesn't know why Ben has been so good to them. At first he wouldn't even take money for all the work he did, and now he'll take only a little, and only when she gets angry. She hopes he isn't helping just so she'll take care of his uncle in his old age. Many thoughts crowd her mind when she thanks Mr. Farber for asking, and says yes.

My sister is excited. My brother wonders if Mr. Farber is more interested in our sudden small fortune than in our mother. "You like him, Ma?" he asks.

"To tell the honest truth, I think he's a *mittelmessiger.* An average man. He's no *lebediker.*" An exciting person, she means. "So *nu,* we'll go see what it's about, this concert."

When Mr. Farber comes to pick her up, my brother and sister stand guard, like the lions outside the 42nd Street Library. Mr. Farber is bearing gifts, clued in by Ben, I imagine. For my brother, there is a big book on old cars. For my sister, a big book on Impressionist paintings. For me, a big dictionary, a grown-up's dictionary. He is sweating from the effort of carrying his load.

I stay up with my sister and brother, waiting for my mother to return. Close to one a.m., we think we hear her on the stairs. About to pull open the door, we also hear a man's voice. We strain our ears but to no avail.

Finally she comes in, flustered when she sees our expectant faces. She waves the program in front of us, as if to prove where she's been. "What he doesn't know about music!" she says. "So nice, the hall! A big piano, with a big orchestra. After, we went for Sanka and layer cake and two hours of talking. *Oy,* I feel so terrible. All the way back downtown, he has to take the subway now. He is *edel.*" For once, she doesn't translate.

.   .   .

One concert leads to another, and another. At first my sister and brother are impressed. Then they get suspicious. They ask Mr. Farber questions. They try to be subtle. I ask questions, too, but to show off: "What's a concert?" "What's a widower?" "Why do you want to go with Mama?"

I like the way he answers me, with a little teasing. "For what did I *shlep* a dictionary? Here, you know how to look up words, don't you?" Or, "Your mama is so beautiful, why wouldn't my ugly puss want to go with her?"

My sister wonders how long his patience will last.

My mother invites Mr. Farber for Sunday dinner. We are all dressed up to receive him. My sister carefully tracks his eye movements. Afterwards she pronounces Solomon Farber to have a crush on my mother.

"What are you talking?" my mother says. "We're friends only."

"Friends or more-than-friends?" I say.

"Friends. *Dos iz alts.*" That's all.

My sister reluctantly agrees. Two months into the relationship, according to her intelligence from the peephole, Mr. Farber still only pecks my mother on the cheek.

I imagine my mother believes it would be good for us to have a stepfather, a man who is kind and decent, and so very cultured, yet she harbors doubts. She calls her sister "just to say hello," and soon she is talking about why she can't let "what should happen, happen."

"But he's a nice man," her sister says.

"He's a nice man, but what's-his-name was also a nice man. I thought. And to tell the truth, I'm not attracted. I'm thinking I have to tell him not to waste his time."

"Don't tell him a thing," my Aunt Ruchel says. "Give yourself a chance."

Now when Ben calls to advise my mother on her investments, she doesn't stay long on the line. Each time, Ben asks if she's seen his uncle lately. And when she says yes, he says, "And so?"

"And what?" She feels guilty for not liking Mr. Farber more. She makes up excuses to Ben why she has to get off the phone. Once I hear her say she has blintzes on the stove. Afterwards she explains to me that lies are sometimes necessary.

"When?" I ask.

"Whenever," she says. "When you don't want to hurt someone."

"I never want to hurt someone. Can I lie all the time?"

"*Mach nit kein tsimmes fun dem!*"

I already know *tsimmes* is stewed prunes, but I can't figure out the rest of it.

"It's not to make a big deal of," my mother explains. "Lies and lies. When you're older you'll know the difference. Go read a book. A dictionary, I'm not."

I imagine my brother has given no thought as to what he'll do after graduating from high school. When Ben tries to interest him in college, my brother says he's not a student. He feels cooped up in the classroom. He doesn't say he cares only about cars and girls.

"I wish I was more like you," my brother tells his friend Donny. "You always got two or three girls on a string. Me, if I really like a babe, I say, Why kid around with someone else?" He hands Donny a wrench.

I am sitting on the stoop near the car they're working on, with a book in my lap, but it's more interesting to listen to them talk, especially if they don't know I'm listening. I turn the page even though I'm not done with it.

Donny steps away from the hood and lights a cigarette. "I don't get so involved. One gives me static, I got the others, dig?"

"That Liza from the Bronx, whew, some looker!" my brother says.

I know *looker* means "pretty," even though the dictionary only says "one who looks."

"In the dark, what do looks matter?" Donny says.

"And if it ain't dark?" my brother says.

"Hot dog!" Donny says, and whistles.

The next time I stop reading, Donny is talking about the Navy. "Whatever you's interested in," he says. "Engineering, auto-mechanics—"

"Auto-mechanics?" my brother says.

"Swear to God. They train you for a career. On their dime."

"Officer!" my brother says, in a very serious voice. "Reporting for duty, Sir! Yes, Sir! I'm here to train for ladies' man, Sir!"

"Don Sheldon Juan!" Donny says. "At ease!"

"Seriously," my brother says, "to be on a boat, I couldn't be that long away from girls."

"That's what they give you R&R for." Donny catches me looking at him. "R&R, rest and recreation," he says, for my benefit. Then to my brother he says, "And don't forget, there's the Waves."

I look up *recreation* and figure out they're talking about swimming.

A s they leave Lewisohn Stadium one night, my mother looks up at the canopy of stars, Beethoven's Piano Concerto No. 5 rippling through her ears. What would it be like, she wonders, to look down at the world from up there? Would everything be so little, so unimportant? Like her troubled heart.

Even before he says the words, she knows what's coming.

"Next week?" Mr. Farber asks.

"Better not," my mother says. "Don't misunderstand me, Mr. Farber. To know you is a blessing. But from all I went through already, my pulse don't beat nomore. *Farshtaist?* To feel something again, I don't think so. Not for anybody," she lies. She knows in her heart that the hate she feels for Harry could change in a minute to something else—not love exactly, but extreme wanting.

"I thought the same," Mr. Farber tells her, "and now I feel myself thawing, if I may say so, Mrs. Arnow."

"Mister, Missus, this is how we are with each other," my mother mocks, irritated she's let things come to a point where she will have to hurt him now. "Everyone's gone," she says anxiously, realizing they're almost alone in the vast, dimly lit stadium.

Mr. Farber takes no notice. "You don't like my company?" he says.

"Your company I like, but what I can offer you is the question."

"If I don't worry, why should you?" he tells her. "Look how beautiful the stars. The moon is cold, but it gives such lovely light."

A week goes by before Mr. Farber even thinks of calling my mother again, and only because he's been given ballet tickets by an associate in the importing business. I imagine he dials our number a few times but hangs up before anyone answers. Unused to being indecisive, he sounds out his nephew.

"She respects you," Ben tells him. "But that could be the obstacle."

"Since when is respect a drawback?"

Ben thinks of his relationship with Isaac. He admires him so much, it inhibits him sexually. "Chenia needs to see the beast in you," he tells his uncle.

"I should be a beast? This is the thinking of young people today?"

"Don't deny your animal nature, Uncle Sol. Chenia's very passionate."

"About art, I know. But I'm also getting her to like music."

"Her love of art, I should say her *obsession* with art—anyhow, Isaac says it's sublimation."

Mr. Farber hangs up, feeling even more confused. He thinks his nephew doesn't understand because he's homosexual, but maybe he has a point. After three months, it could be okay to kiss Mrs. Arnow—Chenia—for real. He invites my mother to the ballet.

Ballet. A magical word. She thinks, What's the harm if she goes? She wonders if it's like on *Ed Sullivan*, the dancers flitting so light, like butterflies. "Yes, thank you," she says to him, "on that evening I'm free."

Off the phone, my mother tells my sister, "Vera-Ellen I liked in that movie with O'Connor. Different from the Rockettes. Now with television—really, I could live without going. I don't know why I said yes."

"Ma! I wish *I* could go to the ballet," my sister says, studying herself in the mirror.

"So go, what's stopping you?" my mother answers.

"By myself?"

"Go with your friend Suzanne."

"She studies all the time. She wants to get a scholarship for college. She wants to be a doctor."

"*Mazel tov!*" my mother says.

"Medical school costs so much, she might not be able to go. Ma?"

"The answer is yes."

"If Suzanne—"

"I said yes."

"Really, we could help her?"

"If she needs? Of course. We'll talk to Ben to arrange it. And you? What do you want to be?"

"I want to study art, but I could also teach it." My sister pouts in the mirror, wishing she could look like Marilyn Monroe.

My mother nods but doesn't say anything, afraid to jinx the future. This is what she's been hoping for her older daughter, to become a teacher. *Alevai.*

"And you, Ma, what do you want?"

"To make up my mind for the ballet, to go, not to go—"

"Ma, Sheldon and me, we talked it over—"

My mother's stomach muscles tighten. "What?"

"If you want to marry Mr. Farber, we think it's all right. I don't think Devorah would mind, either."

"The little one would drive him crazy, *kholilleh*," my mother says. "Anyway, I hardly know the man. *Oy*, look at the dust on those books!" My mother gets the feather duster and swipes hard at the bookcase, from right to left, left to right. Soon there are clouds rising over the living room.

O n the long subway ride home from work, my father thinks how he'd like to stretch out on the bed and take a nap. He'd like to dream of something besides women who can't even sew straight seams, women who double-count their piecework to get more pay. Gershenfeld is getting so stingy he even keeps track of how many pencils and erasers he hands out.

At home, my father finds the cat sitting on his bed as if it's a throne. Irate, he scoops it up and flings it outside. The cat lands on a small, sharp rock. Its high-pitched yowl brings Lilli out of the bathroom, where she's been cleaning. "What have you done to J.P.?" she cries. The cat eludes her grasp and leaves a trail of blood. That night my Uncle Yakob steels himself and asks his brother to find his own place.

"You're right," my father says.

Surprised, my Uncle Yakob says, "I wish you well, and so does Lilli."

"The cat, it's okay?" my father says.

"The vet gave J.P. some stitches. He's on the mend."

"I'm sorry. I've been under a lot of pressure."

Uncle Yakob doesn't ask.

Over his wife Vera's objections, Arthur Vogel asks my father to stay with them until he figures out what he wants to do.

Before my father moves, he buys a box of Cuban cigars for his brother and a bottle of Chanel No. 5 for my Aunt Lilli. He buys a big fish at the fish store and has it boned for the cats. He can tell by the way Yakob nods at the gifts that he's made an impression. My father notes this new feeling in himself: satisfaction.

In the diner on Dyckman, Vera Vogel tells my mother, "It's only a temporary situation to have Ruben live with us. And we're not taking his side."

"How can *diner* be a place?" I ask. "I bet it's 'one who eats.'"

"Finish your cocoa," my mother says. "Go on," she says to Vera.

"I forget." Vera smiles at me. "You're still wearing the locket."

"You gave her so beautiful," my mother says. She touches her neck.

"Where's your necklace?" I say, remembering the gold heart with the middle part missing.

"I lost it," my mother says, with that voice that means she doesn't want to talk about it.

"Where?"

"I don't know."

"Bickford's?" I say. I have a flash of my mother throwing something before she threw the glass at Peter the Wolf. Was it the necklace?

"Anyhow I don't have to be concerned with how Ruben's getting along," my mother says, wondering why he didn't go to the rich lady with buckteeth.

As if reading her mind, Vera says, "Bertha's putting him through hoops, that one. 'Yes, Bertha,' 'No, Bertha,' 'I'll lick the floor for you, Bertha.' Oh, now I've said too much. She refuses to see him."

My mother shrugs. "*Alevai*, he should be well." Anyhow, she cannot take in the import of Vera's words, not when she is preparing to tell Mr. Farber—Sol, she corrects herself—it's over between them. Not that there was anything, she thinks, but maybe in his mind . . .

"Where are you?" Vera asks.

"At the ballet," my mother answers. "Tonight I am going with my friend Mr. Farber."

Vera's eyes light up. "Oh, you didn't tell me you're keeping company."

"*Keeping company*," my mother says. "That's a good expression."

For weeks after the performance, my mother rhapsodizes: "This Metropolitan Opera House, with the balconies going up and up to the sky, *ek velt*, out of this world. Downstairs, the men in tuxedos—one, he's in a mink coat, *ai yi yi*—and all the women, gloves to their elbow and such skinny dresses. Even before the dancers come out, I never saw, *oy*, anything so beautiful—" She rhapsodizes over the ballet: "And on the biggest stage, the pink gauze skirts like flowers; the love duet"—as she calls the pas de deux that made her cry—"how you can see every muscle of the men, their thigh, their *tokhes*, even."

"I want to see it too," I say. "When are you taking me?"

Meaning only to amuse him, my mother mentions my *nudzhing* to Mr. Farber. Soon the three of us are going to the ballet. "*Swan Lake*. There's a prince—" Mr. Farber starts to explain on the subway.

"I know the story," I interrupt.

"Excuse her, her sister already read her," my mother apologizes. When Mr. Farber says to her, "But I want you to know the story, too," she doesn't say I told her what I learned. She listens to the whole thing. Then she nods when he says, "You'll like it."

His presentation is so matter-of-fact, so plodding, neither of us is prepared for the ineffable beauty. We are so rapt, we nearly forget to breathe. Once, Mr. Farber rattles his program and my mother hisses, "Shhh!"

As soon as the curtain comes down at the end, I say, "I want to see it again. Take me." My mother doesn't even correct my bad manners. "Me, too," she says.

At home we hold my sister captive as we try to explain what it was like.

"The best part," my mother says, "is when the swan it's dying. This one," she says about me, "I see the elbows going up and down, in sympathy. She don't want the swan to die. I don't want the swan to die. A tear dribbles down my cheek." She doesn't say that she felt Sol's hairy knuckle gently *shmearing* the tear over her face. She doesn't say that this is the moment she thinks with him there is a future.

"What do I need him for?" Bertha asks her dog Silvey. "I have *you*, don't I! Don't I?" She kneels down and lowers her head practically to the Turkish rug to rub noses with the terrier. "Yeeess," she purrs, "I have my Silvey dear."

She rises and puts a linen hankie in her evening bag. In the mirror over the credenza, she primps and purses her lips. "It's all your fault," she tells the dog. "I just had to show you to Arthur and Vera. Yes, Sweetheart, Mama did."

She recalls ringing the Vogels' doorbell, with Silvey in her arms. How the door opened, and how it took a moment to register what she saw. It wasn't Vera or Arthur. It was Ruben. How could she have known he was there? All she'd wanted the moment before was to show the Vogels her new dog.

She recalls the long, silent moment that passed between her and Ruben, how he stroked the dog's withers, how she set the dog down, what the smell of his talcum was like as she buried her face in his shoulder . . .

"What do I need him for?" she asks Silvey in the mirror. Every day she asks the same question. Every day the answer seems to her further away.

"If I worked at night, we could see each other during the day, when the kid goes to school," my father says to Trudy on the phone.

"Mmm," Trudy says as she buffs her nails. "Did your boss go out?"

"He's in North Carolina. I do his job and mine—and for the same pay."

"You have time to call me," she says.

"What, you think I'm lying? So, what about tonight?"

Trudy is sorry she answered his call. He is starting to get on her nerves. "I couldn't get a baby-sitter," Trudy lies.

"Enough with the excuses, Trudy. I think you don't care no more."

"Ruben, if it's so easy to find a baby-sitter, you do it."

"You shouldn't have adopted Hannah."

"Don't say such a thing. She's the apple of my eye."

"And what am I? Anything to you?"

"Ruben, I care, I care. What do you want me to do?"

"Leave Barney." My father doesn't know why he says this. What would happen if she took him seriously? he thinks, but then he knows she won't.

"It wouldn't be right," Trudy says. "He's a very good daddy to Hannah."

Without saying good-bye, my father sets the phone down in its cradle.

Impatient at how slowly things are moving, Ben invites his uncle and my mother to his place for dinner, which he cooks himself. My mother has been to Ben's before, but still she can't get over it—the black and white furniture, the bathroom painted a deep red, the mirrored ceiling of the bedroom.

"How you learn to cook so wonderful?" my mother asks. The chicken breasts are stuffed with oysters and mushrooms. The corn pudding melts in her mouth. The salad has lettuce she's never tasted before, dark green and purple, and teeny shrimp.

"I know it isn't kosher," Ben says apologetically, "but being a sinner is good for the soul." He winks at Sol.

"You think this is true?" my mother says, suddenly very serious. "How can sinning be good?"

"Oscar Wilde says you only make progress through disobedience and rebellion." Ben rolls his eyes. "The way you're looking at me . . . Well, suppose you were perfect, and you did everything in your life perfectly. What would you learn from it? What kind of person would you be? You'd be insufferable."

"Insufferable?" my mother says.

Ben wonders to himself how Chenia can have a six-year-old with a vocabulary bigger than hers. "Obnoxious," he says. "A horrible person to be around."

"Yes, I see what you mean," my mother says. "But there are sins and sins—"

Sol exhales noisily through his nose. "Chenia, I can't imagine you sinning. Or worrying about sins." His smile is so peaceful, my mother thinks. There is no way he could ever understand what she's been through.

As soon as Ben has set down parfait glasses of chocolate mousse, the phone rings. "Oh Isaac," my mother hears Ben say. "I'll be right over." Ben hangs up and tells his guests he has a little emergency. "Stay where you are, the coffee is hot, I'll be back as soon as I can."

Before my mother can object, Ben is gone.

At the table Sol makes a tentative gesture of reaching for my mother's hand. He holds it, he rubs it. "So soft," he says before he lets go.

"Don't stop with the massage," my mother says.

Soon they are holding hands on the sofa. Sol removes his glasses and kisses my mother, not one of his usual quick pecks, but a long and lingering kiss. He does not open his mouth.

So sweet, my mother thinks. *This man is too good for me.*

After a few such kisses my mother says, "Tell me about your wife." I imagine she wants at that moment to put a wedge between them, but the story he tells is not what she expects.

Sol tells her that his wife was in pain for years, that she went from doctor to doctor, but no one could diagnose what was wrong. "After a while she went to a spiritist, to talk to all her dead relatives, which I thought frankly was *meshugge*, but she said it was the only thing that helped.

"Everything she ate, she said didn't agree with her. Every day I made concoctions for her special in the blender," Sol says. "She got thinner and thinner. I think she was depressed, who knew why? One day she collapsed on the bathroom floor. They said it was a heart attack. She was only fifty-two."

"You miss her a lot?" my mother asks. It's not an innocent question. She wants to know how much room there is in his heart—not for her, but for her children—in case, just in case things should develop.

"We were married thirty years. No children," Sol says. "You get used to a person after such a long time."

My mother says, "The bed after my husband is gone, it feels so big."

"For the ten years my wife was sick, we slept in separate rooms. My bed is a single bed, but now I'm used to it."

"Oh," my mother says. She looks at her hand, which Sol is rubbing again. "*A farshlepteh krenk.* Ten years is a long time for such a sickness. I wonder what it was. And you were good to help her."

"'In sickness and in health.' I wouldn't be honest if I said I didn't miss getting affection. I'm alone now, but in many ways I was alone then too."

Now my mother initiates the kiss. She opens her mouth, but Sol keeps his closed.

This time when Trudy asks my father to go with the group from Temple to Las Vegas, right away he agrees. Trudy is shocked. She expected him to say no. She expected them to have a big fight. She expected to tell my father they shouldn't see each other for a while. Now she has a problem.

"Your boss will let you go over Christmas?" she says.

"I've been there long enough. I'll take my summer vacation early."

Trudy brings him the flyer from Temple. "Let's stay at the better hotel," she says. "It's only five hundred extra."

My father feels as if a chicken bone has caught in his throat.

"If I go, I go first class," Trudy says. "And I want to see all the shows, no matter what they cost."

"All right, all right," he tells Trudy. Chenia hasn't asked him for any money yet, he thinks, and he pays the Vogels very little from his paycheck. It was even his idea to pay rent, so he doesn't feel so obligated. He wonders what it would be like to sleep all night with Trudy. He wonders if she snores. But the more my father considers the vacation, the more he worries. He knows if Bertha catches him, she will never take him back.

The headmaster of my school sends a letter to my parents, which my mother reads.

"Are you in trouble?" she asks me.

"No," I say.

"Then why do they want to see me?"

"I don't know."

"Are you sure you didn't do something wrong?"

"Like what?" I say.

"*A gezunt in dein pupik!*"

"*Pupik* is 'belly-button,'" I say.

"That's where your head is," my mother says. "Thanks for nothing."

My mother shows the letter to Sol. "What is 'social adjust-ment'?"

He tells her the school has concerns about the way I relate to others.

My mother laughs. She tells him about Trudy Fleisch's kid. "*Khas vesholem*, mine should be more like that one? *Nit heint, nit morgen*." Not today, not tomorrow.

I imagine this is Sol's first glimpse of my mother as rebel, one he cannot totally fathom. "They want you to call and arrange a meeting," he says. My mother makes a sound of distress. "Would you like me to do this for you?" he offers, knowing it's not pure altruism on his part.

My mother debates with herself for a few seconds. "I tell you, what I really want—you should come with me. You know how to talk to them with their big words."

"I'd be honored," Sol says.

Awkwardly my mother introduces Sol as her friend to the headmaster and to my teacher. "Friend of the family," Sol amends.

I imagine they deliver a litany of my sins: "Devorah constantly interrupts—the other children, the teacher, even during a fire drill. If someone is reading and gets a word wrong, Devorah blurts out a correction. She acts as if she's the teacher," Mrs. Blendheim says. She taps a pencil on her palm.

The headmaster says, "She was remanded to my office for disrupting the class. I had her write a composition acknowledging her behavior. May I read to you what she came up with?"

"Please," Sol says.

The headmaster reads aloud my story about a girl named Angela who promises to keep quiet but keeps breaking her promise. The first time it's to tell a boy to look out, before he falls into a hole. The second time it's to tell the class that the school is on fire. The third time it's to tell the teacher that his zipper is open. After that, the teacher is so grateful, he makes it Angela's job to tell people things whenever she wants.

My mother hoots when she hears about the zipper and

again at the end, when she hears, "'And Angela became the biggest buttinsky in the world.'"

"What you want?" my mother says to them. "You want to make her like everybody else? She could be dull like so many people"—she has to restrain herself from saying, "like you."

Sol immediately offers apologies. "Devorah means well, but we'll talk to her. It's only common courtesy, not to interrupt others." He thinks he will have to talk to Chenia too.

My mother says, "This is some special school, *nu*? For the talented, *nu*?"

"We're also teaching these talented children to live in a civilized society." Tapping the pencil hard on the edge of the headmaster's desk, Mrs. Blendheim says, "At home do you allow her to do whatever she likes?"

"No," my mother concedes, "I tell her something, she does it. She's like a grown-up, you know? My older girl and my boy, they weren't so good, but not so talented, either. The little one talks too much, *emes*. I let her, but not always."

"Is that it?" Sol asks. "That she's a buttinsky? She's not hitting or biting, she's not setting fires—"

"You have to realize," the headmaster says, "it's very disruptive in a classroom, especially when other children take their cues from her."

My mother takes her cue from Sol's chagrined expression. "Okay," she says. "The kid, she'll do better. But that story, it's good, *nu*?"

"It shows a manipulative sensibility," Mrs. Blendheim says. Sol interprets.

To hold in her anger, my mother keeps her eyes on Sol's placid face. "Maybe the little one, she's better to start over in a different class."

To her relief, the headmaster agrees. "We can try it—"

That afternoon my mother and Sol talk to me. They ask me why I interrupt the teacher.

"She makes mistakes," I say.

"Like when?" my mother asks.

"When she speaks French," I say. "She says 'mun-SIR' for *Monsieur.*"

"It's very embarrassing for the teacher to have a little girl tell her this in front of everybody," Sol says.

"I can't learn her anything?" I say.

"Not in front of the whole class. And if a girl or a boy in your class makes a mistake, you have to let the teacher do her job. I suppose you learned that word *buttinsky* from your mother?"

"No!" I say gleefully. "That's what Ben calls me."

"Well, suppose I took the pencil out of your hand and finished your story myself? Would you like that, Miss Buttinsky?"

"Is your story better?" I ask.

"You're incorrigible," he says, "and you can go look that one up."

Later my mother says to Sol, "So much I appreciate, your help."

"For what? For nothing."

"Being with me. Is so hard with the little one, doing everything by myself. My son and older daughter try to help, but you know what I mean."

"I would like to be a father to your children. Would you like to be my wife, Chenia?"

I imagine he has caught her at a very vulnerable moment. "Yes," she says, as surprised as he is to hear the answer.

B en offers to help Sol pick out an engagement ring, but Sol wants my mother to pick out her own ring. They decide to do it on a Thursday afternoon when I have Science Club after school. The Monday of that week my mother begins to get cold feet. She calls her sister in Jersey.

"He's too good for me," she tells my Aunt Ruchel.

"Believe me, I know you, you would do him a favor to be his wife."

"I don't know if I love him."

"What is love, my sister? More to the point, what good is love? Look at all the harm it does."

"There you have something," my mother says.

All day Tuesday, my mother chews on her situation. Can she love this man? Does it matter if she can't? Will he know? Is it a sin to pretend? What can she do for him? Round and round the questions go, keeping her awake that night. For the first time ever, she oversleeps. On Wednesday I am late to school.

After she drops me off downtown, she thinks of a way to test herself, to see if she is good enough for Solomon Farber. She takes a taxi back to Dyckman Street and Broadway. From there she marches straight into Magic Shoes, her heart drumming, and asks for Mr. Taubman.

It isn't excitement—a thrill at the thought of being near him. It isn't rage. The rage she had once, it almost makes her shiver. *Deigeh nisht,* she tells herself. Don't worry. It isn't like before, in the days when she wanted to come in with a knife, to leave a scar on him bigger than the one on her daughter.

After the clerk at the register buzzes him, Harry walks out between the customers trying on shoes. As soon as he sees her he stops, then begins moving again, slowly. He has gained weight, my mother notices. His face is fuller, he has a belly that pushes out behind the vest, like a pregnant woman. He doesn't look surprised to see her. He looks afraid.

When he's within hearing distance, she says, "What? You think I have a gun to shoot you?"

"You make a joke, Mrs. Arnow. Let's go outside," he says, taking her arm.

She shrugs her arm out of his grasp. "No, I just wanted to see for myself the *momzer.*" Bastard. She doesn't stay long enough to see Harry react. As soon as *momzer* is out of her mouth, she throws back her shoulders, turns, and strides out of the store. Outside, she hails a cab as if she's been doing it all her life.

Riding along the Henry Hudson Parkway, my mother marvels that Harry didn't look at all like a *baizeh kheiyeh*, a vicious animal. How she built him up in her mind! And he wasn't even so handsome as she remembered. He's just a man, she marvels. He couldn't help himself either.

M y father waits until the three men in suits leave his boss's office. He doesn't know who they are. He adjusts his tie and strides down to see Mr. Gershenfeld, surprised to find him at his desk with his face in his hands. Too late, he cannot retreat when Mr. Gershenfeld asks him what he wants.

"Time off over Christmas," my father says, "instead of next summer."

Mr. Gershenfeld strokes his beard. "That might be a good idea. That will give me time to figure things out."

"What things?" my father asks. Maybe Gershenfeld saw the unfilled orders that have piled up on his desk.

"I wasn't going to say anything so soon, but you've been a good, loyal employee."

"You're selling the factory?" my father guesses.

"Labor. Labor costs are killing me. We're moving to North Carolina. If you want to keep your job, I'll pay for the moving, and you can have a raise—only a small one, but it's cheaper living there than here."

"Moving," my father repeats dully. "When?"

"We're aiming for April. There are infinite details to be ironed out. Take your time, think about it. If you don't want to move, I'll give you an excellent reference."

"Thank you," my father mutters. He stands up, feeling dazed. Already he's forgotten the answer to his question.

"A man of your experience, you'll get something else," Bertha says to my father. She sets the teacup back in the saucer. "I've let it get cold."

"I don't know. I'm no spring chicken," he says.

"You're thinking of moving, Ruben?"

"Away from you? Never," my father fibs, "but Gershenfeld offered me a huge raise."

"That reminds me, I wanted to ask you. About your wife. Your ex-wife. You said you weren't paying alimony or child support."

"Chenia doesn't ask, I don't volunteer."

"But what are they living on? I happened to see Chenia step into a taxi last week, on Dyckman Street of all places. Last night she steps out of a car—you know, a private car service. Did she come into an inheritance?"

My father shrugs. "If someone died, I would have heard. I think her sister gives her. The husband has a good business." My father pats his thigh. "Here, Silvey. Here, boy!" The dog jumps into my father's lap and rolls onto its back so that my father can scratch its belly. "What kind of dog is this again?"

"Lhasa apso, it's a kind of terrier. I think Silvey needs to go out."

"I'd rather stay here with you," my father says.

"Ruben—"

"All right. I'm your slave."

My father goes to retrieve the leash, wondering why Bertha was in his neighborhood, so close to where Trudy lives, unless it was to spy on him. He consoles himself with the thought that she trusts him with Silvey. She's as crazy about Silvey, he thinks, as Trudy is about Hannah. What is it with women? For what did God give them the equipment to love men when all they care about are children and animals?

Opening the closet door, my father sees a wad of bills on the floor. He picks it up and tries to hear if Bertha has left the sofa. All is quiet. He thumbs through the wad. All hundred dollar bills, nine of them. He thinks about slipping the wad in his sock. Too risky, he decides. Then he thinks of taking one and returning the rest.

"Ruben!" Bertha calls out. "Did you find it?"

He comes into the living room. "This is what I found." He hands her the entire wad.

As soon as he has left with Silvey, Bertha counts the bills. When my father returns, she smothers his face with kisses. "Let's go have a really nice dinner with the money you found," she says. She takes a couple of bills and puts them in his pocket. My father wonders if there'll be enough left after the dinner to buy a new pair of shoes.

From the courthouse, Ben calls my mother, all excited. "Chenia, I found the perfect place for the party. An art gallery. New Year's Eve it won't be open, and it'll be a dramatic backdrop, to say the least. Isaac got it for us."

"What art gallery? Not the Metropolitan? It's too big. Or the Frick?"

As Ben has told Isaac, Chenia never ceases to surprise him with what she doesn't know. "A gallery, where paintings are shown to be sold. A painting and sculpture store," Ben says. "You must have seen them in Greenwich Village, only this one's on Madison Avenue."

My mother is quiet. She cannot imagine a party, least of all an engagement party, in a store.

"Well, at least see it before making up your mind. I just got a continuance on a case, so I could take the afternoon off to show you."

My mother has never heard Ben so miffed except when he scolds me sometimes for twisting his words. At such times my mother finds it funny, a grown man arguing with a child. Sol has told her that lawyers will argue with anyone, whenever they get the chance. My mother agrees to meet Ben at his office, and together they go to the gallery.

It's a store, like Ben said, she thinks, with a painting on an easel in the window. Inside it's wider than she pictured, and deeper, with very high ceilings. "We'll clear out the furniture, of course, set up the bar over there, or wherever you think . . ." Ben says, racing around. He's trying to help my mother imagine how it would work, but it's unnecessary. As soon as my mother sees these paintings that cover entire walls, with their crazy splotches of color, she hugs and kisses Ben with such fervor, he says, "Hey, save it for my uncle."

I n the week between Christmas and New Year's, my brother enlists in the Navy. My sister says he should wait to tell my mother, but he can't.

"With the party is enough for a nervous breakdown," my mother half jokes. "Now I can worry about you too. For how many years?"

"Four. I don't go in till I graduate in June. They'll even pay for my going to college, if I want." My brother is practically dancing in place with his news. "Don't worry, Ma, there's no war on."

"*Vos vet zein, vet zein.* What will be, will be." She can see my brother is excited. She feels a little sick, but she manages to say, "You'll leave a boy and come back a man. This could be all right, *kineahora.*"

"Ma, if you'd only stop already with the Evil Eye. Tonight I'll bring Delilah by the party, but we won't stay long, okay? We don't have a lot of time left together."

"As you want," my mother says. "I know, love has to come first."

Right away she calls Sol to tell him her son enlisted, surprised he thinks it's a good idea. "Today a high school diploma counts for nothing. At the very least he'll have a trade. Cars aren't going away in our lifetime, Chenia. Personally, I think he made a wise choice."

"I love you," she says. "Your good heart."

There is a strange sound on the other end of the line. A sniffle? She wonders if he's crying. "Solly?"

"That's the first time, Chenia. That you said it."

"Words," my mother says dismissively. *"Vifil kost a sho?"* What do they cost by the hour? "I mean it," my mother says. "On the head of my little one."

*W*hat a dilemma! my father thinks, about New Year's Eve. Bertha is already making plans, but how can he get out of seeing Trudy? One thing he has going for him: he can avoid a showdown with the two of them at the Vogels' annual party. The Vogels have gone to Florida. To escape the bookies, Vera told him.

Lately Trudy is driving him up a wall. After he got the days off for Christmas, she told him Hannah needed surgery, so she couldn't go to Vegas. A hundred-dollar deposit he lost.

On the phone today he pleads with Trudy. "Why don't you come over? I have this place all to myself. Don't you miss me?"

"Of course, but with all this medical treatment for Hannah, what can I do, Ruben? Anyhow, it's the Sabbath. We're going to services tonight."

My father cannot stand another moment without her. He takes the train, which he knows he shouldn't do on *Shabbes*, to go to synagogue in his old neighborhood. He does it just to catch a glimpse of Trudy.

She is there with Barney and the kid. The veil over her eyes from the black hat makes her seem mysterious. Her hips look bigger with the sash on one side. My father brazenly goes up to the Fleisches, intending to sit with them during the service. Barney greets him warmly, pats his back. "How is this one?" my father says, about Hannah.

"A-one," Barney says.

"Everything's fine," Trudy hastens to add.

"The surgery turned out okay?" my father asks.

"What surgery?" Barney says.

"On her eyes."

"Where did you get that idea?" Barney turns to Trudy, who looks down.

My father says he must have heard it wrong from the Vogels. He changes the subject to New Year's Eve and asks Barney if he's working.

"No, we're going to Las Vegas with the Temple," Barney says. "From there we'll fly to Palm Springs. Hannah's aunt will look after her. You look so surprised."

My father sees the rabbi emerge, but he cannot control himself. "Your wife and I were supposed to go to Vegas. Together. Ask her." To be sure that Barney knows what his wife has been up to, my father makes an obscene, unmistakable gesture with his fingers, and stalks out of Temple.

There is nothing left for him now, my father thinks, riding the subway back downtown. He must get Bertha to marry him. Then he can lead a comfortable life, free of worries about money. With all Bertha's meetings and committees, he'll have his evenings to himself, to do whatever.

Though he's not supposed to buy anything on *Shabbes*, my

father has a sudden craving when he gets to his stop. From the little candy store down the block, he buys Good & Plenty's. Going up in the elevator to the Vogels' apartment, he pops the black and pink capsules in his mouth, but his mouth opens and the candies spill out on the carpet as he sinks to his knees, sobbing.

Before the elevator door opens, he pulls himself together. In the hallway two men are standing in front of the Vogels' door. One of them says, "Arthur Vogel?"

"No, he's moved away."

"Sure," the other one says sarcastically. He removes his own glasses and puts them in his breast pocket.

"I swear to the Almighty," my father says. "I'm not Arthur Vogel. I'm Ruben, Ruben Arnow."

My father feels a terrific blow to his lower back. After he's down on the tile floor, the kicks and punches come, and a foot on his face, and then he blacks out.

A ll through the engagement party, Sol never leaves my mother's side, except to bring her drinks and *hors d'oeuvre*. So different, she thinks, from the New Year's Eve at the Vogels, when Ruben was always someplace else, flirting with the women. She recalls the horse face of Trudy and the buckteeth of the Landau woman. To push away the memories, she points to a painting on the wall. "Four thousand dollars, Ben said."

"You want it? I buy it for you," Sol says.

"You Sweet," she says, very loud, because the gallery is very noisy now, crammed full with lively guests. She loves seeing the people dressed up, eating, drinking, smoking, laughing. With Sol and me in tow, she moves through the crowd, introducing us: "My intended, my little one."

Never before have I seen her without a trace of melancholy.

"Now where are you bopping off to?" Sol says, as she rushes to the entrance. Of course we follow. My Aunt Ruchel is there and Uncle Isaac—"the other Isaac," my mother calls him now—and my Cousin Sandy.

"Rhonda couldn't come," my aunt says apologetically.

"My own daughter, you think she's here? Maybe later," my mother says. "So where is she?"

My aunt knows my mother means Millie. "Parking the car. She brought her husband, I hope that's kosher. *Bubbeleh*, let me give you a kiss." I think she's talking to me, but she means Sol. "We're thrilled to have you in the family."

"Mrs. Peisner, I appreciate it," Sol says.

"What's this Mrs. business? Ruchel to you."

And then Millie and her husband come in. "So stylish!" my mother pronounces, about her print dress, the blue of a peacock, and the broad-brimmed hat. Her husband has on a dark suit that looks too big for him; later we learn it's Uncle Isaac's. After my mother hugs Millie, Sol shakes hands with her, and then Millie pretends to try to lift me. She moans and groans as I giggle, and just when I think she's given up, she hoists me overhead. "Lord, is you heavy! You's too big to be a flower girl at the wedding."

"No!" I say. "I'm going to be a flower girl. It's a *fait accompli*." I love how they stare. I don't tell them Ben taught me the expression.

"Mrs. Arnow, ma'am, I'd like to cook for your wedding. And I'm not gonna be charging you."

My mother fiercely shakes her head no. "It's a small wedding," she says to Millie. "No bridesmaids, but you get anyhow an invitation. After all what you did for the little one—"

Seeing Sol's puzzled expression, Uncle Isaac says, "Chenia had a bad bout of pneumonia once. Devorah came to stay with us while Chenia was in the hospital. Our two families are like one. Right, Chenia?"

When my mother kisses my Uncle Isaac on the cheek, I know she isn't mad at him anymore. *Sinners can also be good people.*

No sooner does Millie set me down, a man passing by hands her an empty glass. *"Dummkopf!"* my mother mutters. Dumbbell. She grabs the glass from Millie. "Millie, what would you like to drink?" Sol asks. "And you, sir?" he says to Millie's husband, as Ben and his friend Isaac join us.

Then my brother shows up with his new girlfriend. I don't like Delilah, because she never talks to me. If I ask her a question, she'll say, "How long did you take thinking that one up?" but she won't answer.

Sol greets them with typical banter. "If she's Delilah, are you Samson?"

Delilah rumples my brother's hair. "It's already too short, and now it'll get mowed off in the Navy."

"But the hair on his chest will grow," Ben teases.

"I don't like hairy chests," Delilah says.

"Why not?" I ask.

"They're ugly," she says, looking straight at me. I think she's trying to tell me I'm ugly too.

"We know who isn't ugly," my brother says, giving her waist a squeeze. My sister says Sheldon likes Delilah because she's busty, but I think she's being silly.

After they leave, the five-piece band shows up and plays klezmer music. People are clapping and stomping to the lively rhythm, and soon dancers holding hands form circles within circles, some moving clockwise, some counterclockwise. Then I see my mother is dancing by herself in the very center. She's clapping her hands over her head, and I like just watching, but Sol makes me clap, too.

My mother's arms are high in the air now, and she kicks with her left foot to the right, her right foot to the left, before she takes a couple of steps, going in her own circle. After she goes round and round, she comes to get Sol, and holds hands with him as they kick. Sol looks uncertain, but my mother has never looked more confident.

Just then, my sister arrives with Robbie, her new boyfriend. They come and stand behind me, and my sister keeps saying, "Oh my God! I don't believe it!"

"She's cute," Robbie says.

"Cute?" Mimi says, incredulous. I know she feels mortified, but I don't care. It's the most wonderful thing, to see my mother dance.

Finally the music ends and there is wild applause and whistling. My mother applauds, too, thinking it's for the musicians.

My sister stays long enough to sample all the food, zeroing in on the miniature quiches. After she and Robbie are gone, my mother says to her sister, "What can I do about that one? A *fresser*, she eats and eats."

"Her boyfriend must like them Rubenesque," my aunt says.

"Rubens, the artist," Sol explains. "Even Degas's ballerinas are a little *zaftik*."

"I like the Expressionists," my mother says, "all the skinny people, their long faces." She glances at Sol. "And Picasso."

Sol takes my mother's right hand and brings it to his lips. "One more hour till the New Year," he says.

Lying in bed that night, my mother hugs the extra pillow. She is not in a hurry to go to sleep. Dawn comes as she thinks about how she got from there to here. What was it her mother used to say? *Got hit op di naronim.* God watches out for fools. She thinks about the party, about Solomon Farber. Such a *mekhaieh*—a pleasure—to be in his presence! she tells herself. *Passion, whatever it's good for, it ain't everything.*

Part Six

B efore I discover the necklace, I am certain that after my mother marries Solomon Farber, nothing interesting happens in her life. They are close companions, devoted to each other and to the symphony and ballet. "*Oy*, the passion in that Lenny Bernstein," my mother is fond of saying. Sol silently admires Margot Fonteyn, so strong yet feminine. My mother and Sol go for long walks in the city, and they travel, but only short distances—to the Poconos and the Adirondacks. When Sol proposes we go to Europe, my mother develops nightmares, because she is afraid of airplanes, especially over water. She becomes a sort of expert on plane crashes. "Nineteen fifty-five, I remember it," she might say in the middle of a conversation. "The plane went down, two planes that year, in the west United States."

In her nightmares, planes crash and people die, but not my mother—she becomes the rescuer. In one, she tries to pull a man into a rowboat; in another, she tries to catch a baby that falls through the air. In both she fails.

Sol gives up the wish to travel abroad and accompanies my mother to art galleries. She accompanies him to baseball games. They dine with Ben, they dine with friends, they look forward to all the occasions of family: the birthdays, graduations, weddings, *brises*, bar and bas mitzvahs, the seders, and even Thanksgiving.

My sister, tending toward plump, fights constantly with my mother over her diet. "These portions are huge enough for a horse," she complains one night. When Sol intervenes, my sister screams at him for taking his wife's side. For the first time ever, my mother slaps her.

At first I treat Sol as an extension of my mother. I ask him questions that dictionaries can't answer. I ask if he and Mama are more-than-friends, and when he says yes, I ask how can that be true, if they're not going to have babies. I love making him stutter. I ask how an atlas can be flat and also round, and after he painstakingly explains, I ask how they can both be accurate. Exasperated, he says, "The world is full of mysteries." This, I like to hear. I like the answers that are like puzzles.

Mostly, Sol's answers are so tedious that, halfway through, I regret asking the question. Sometimes I can tell he answers just to be polite. I know he'd rather be reading *The Wall Street Journal* while he sits quietly next to my mother, no matter what she's doing—ironing or sewing or polishing the silver they acquired as wedding gifts. "Sol would sit next to her if she was doing number two," my sister says.

On our outing to the Dyckman House, where a Dutch family lived once upon a time on their big farm, Sol has to remark on every tile and spoon. I get so bored I walk on ahead or linger behind, and then they get mad at me. Wherever I used to go with my mother alone, Sol now comes along. Under my breath, I mutter, *nuchshlepper.* Hanger-on. But not so my mother can hear me.

Even to grocery shop she waits till Sol gets home, no matter how irregular his hours. Sometimes he leaves his office early. Orders pile up for Japanese figurines and brass incense pots, ceramic salt and pepper shakers, elephants and palm trees—what my mother calls *tsatskehs,* meaning "things you have only to dust, what we don't need." The importing business is so good that Sol hires additional helpers. He tells my mother, "Frankly, one I hired so I'll have more time to spend with you."

He spends time with my mother at the A&P, where it takes forever to fill the basket. They have long discussions over which kind of cookie is best, and what brand. I ask if I can wait for them outside, but they always say no. I bring comic books to the store to read. I know Sol doesn't like comic books.

Sol comes with us even when we shop for clothes. I refuse to model for him, but my mother does. When we go to the beauty parlor, Sol *shleps* us back and forth. There I can't talk to my mother either, because she sits under a hair dryer and thumbs *House Beautiful*.

As separate as my mother's life has been from my father's, with Sol it's close to the point of what my sister says is suffocation.

"Is Mama really suffocating?" I ask.

"Mama has no room to breathe. Don't worry, not literally."

"Literally?"

"It's just an expression," my sister says.

I don't see my mother suffocating. If anything, she seems to breathe easier. She is *très calme*, I write in my diary. She no longer uses her sharp tongue, which I miss. Sol is now the comedian of the family, but there's no bite in his humor. When we move to a spacious apartment on West End Avenue, I think my mother lets go the last of her eccentricities: her fear of the Evil Eye.

Downtown, my mother and Sol become even more inseparable. My sister is able to make jokes about Mama and Her Shadow: "Her Shadow says it's time for dinner." "Her Shadow went down to the mailbox by himself." I feel my mother becoming a shadow as well, and the two of them slipping away from me.

After Sol becomes our stepfather, my father continues to telephone us on Sundays. He asks how my brother is doing in the Navy. He asks my sister how she's doing in school. He asks me if I still love my papa.

"Yes, Papa," I say, because that's the right answer.

"Better than your stepfather?"

"Yes, Papa," I say, but I don't really understand the question. I can't admit this vague longing I have for him, for his gruff presence, for the strength of his hairy arms around me. Is this what my father means by *love*?

With the help of my teacher, Miss Spinelli, I write a play that my fifth-grade class performs. Afterwards Sol hands me a bouquet of pink and purple flowers, but he doesn't say a single word, good or bad, about what he saw.

"What did you think, Mama?" I ask my mother.

"*Nu*, I should be surprised you do this?"

I'm struck by the notion that while they're standing right there, they seem to be behind soundproof glass.

Her arm through Sol's, my mother says Sol made reservations at a fancy restaurant.

"He knows you like fancy restaurants, Mama."

"Me? He did it for you."

"I want to eat at the Chinks on Dyckman. A combination plate, with pork fried rice." I know Sol won't allow us to eat pork.

My mother bops me in the head. "*Es brent mir ahfen harts.*" I have a heartburn.

"You're getting under her skin," Sol says. "Is it necessary? You're such an intelligent girl. Hours and hours your mother and I have spent discussing you. Yes, you. We don't know how to handle you."

"I don't want to be handled, thank you."

My mother shoves my shoulder. "You're right, but you should say it different."

Outside the Belevair School, I press my face into the flowers and inhale.

"You could thank him for the beautiful bouquet," my mother says.

"That's the conditional tense," I say to Sol, "when she means the imperative. Thank you. I never got flowers of my own before."

"Never *had*," he corrects. He seems eager to get us on our way, but I linger, relishing the attention of my classmates and their families. My friend Dina comes up to us with her parents.

"You're the writer I've heard so much about," Dina's mother says to me. "What a scream—that line Miss Hearts says about love! Remind me."

I recite, " 'Love is like bonbons. You can't tell if the center's going to be hard or gooey.' Then Mr. Flowers says, 'Or nuts— the kind you can break your teeth on.'" Sol's brow dimples. "It's a metaphor," I tell him, using a word I've fallen in love with.

"A joke, no?" my mother says.

"Yes, but it's also serious," I say.

"This could be," my mother says. Elegant in a black dress and fox stole, she's staring at my classmate's father.

"Delicious!" he says, looking directly at my mother. His mustache reminds me of Papa.

Nightly, I cover pages of my diary with just the word *Papa*, but it doesn't fill the emptiness. I make a conscious decision to wean myself from my mother and Sol. I no longer seek their attention. I don't ask them questions. Mostly I go limp and do whatever they want. I keep my thoughts to myself. It's easier than feeling excluded.

Before I graduate from Belevair, I am no longer an extrovert. I sit quietly in my classes. I don't volunteer answers. I get stomachaches when teachers call on me. I communicate mostly with my diary. In my diary I begin to imagine my mother's past.

I begin with the memories I have of things I can't explain. The Cloisters. Peter the Wolf. The red valentine's box that holds my mother's sewing needles and assorted buttons. The time I spent in New Jersey. I make up explanations, but the mystery remains.

M y vague longings to be close to my father dissipate when I realize the separation is permanent. He is moving to North Carolina. I learn this from my mother who learns it from Vera Vogel who tells it all to Sol: "Ruben decided he should move since Bertha Landau broke it off with him." My mother quotes Vera: " 'News travels fast. You wouldn't believe what he pulled at Temple. Little does he realize, Bertha's old schoolmate, she's sitting right behind them. It's fate.' "

"Consorting with a married woman," Sol says. "What could the man be thinking?"

He glances at me as if maybe he's said too much, but I can tell he doesn't really care. I've become for him just part of the mismatched furniture my mother *shlepped* from the old apartment.

"What is this, *consorting*?" my mother says.

Sol no longer stops to explain to my mother every little thing. He continues his thought. "In Temple, yet. Has he no sense of right and wrong?"

I see my mother looking out the window, far into the distance, between the Hudson River and the moon above.

I imagine my mother is seized with a sudden loneliness.

To fill her husband in on the *finster yor* has been her secret wish, but now she knows it cannot go. To tell him, the earth would open up between them. And for what? For the first time in her life, the ground under her feet feels solid. *Sol, solid*, she thinks. Such a perfect name! Yet something in her longs for danger, for the pull and tumble of the Atlantic Ocean, for a glimpse of a green fedora.

"Why is it bad for Papa to consort with a married woman?" I ask my sister. "The dictionary says it means 'associate with.'"

My sister informs me that *consort* means "to have an affair with."

"How do you know," I ask, "if it isn't in the dictionary?"

"Don't be silly. You learn words from hearing people use them."

"Ben says the whole English language is in the dictionary."

"Not curse words," she says.

"*Consort* is a curse word?"

"I guess you can call it that," my sister says.

She doesn't know how her offhand answer troubles me. I cannot believe my father would put his penis in Trudy Fleisch's vagina—in anyone's vagina, actually. I am even glad he is moving away.

The next time my mother mentions my father and Trudy, I tell her, "It's gossip, why do you want to believe it?"

"When you grow up—" she starts. I open a book and place it over my face.

My mother brings up my father a lot now, usually when she talks to Sol. Usually she is making comparisons. "The way you help with the dishes," she says to Sol, "Ruben would never."

She speculates about my father, how he's doing in the heat of North Carolina. "You think he likes his job?" she asks Sol.

"Why not?" Sol answers.

"The factory, it can get so hot. You think it's air-conditioned?"

"I doubt it."

"What's it like, this place, North Carolina? I know, you told me, it's hot, but what else?"

"It's very green. Rural. Mostly farms. The cities are small. People live in houses. They eat *trayf*. Bacon grease with everything."

"*Oy*," my mother says. Once I hear her use the word *umglik*, which I know means "unlucky."

At age ten I start seventh grade at Finestar Academy for Girls. Sol talks my mother into sending me there because "the school has backbone." I don't mind, because I find it easy and can use my time for other things. I correspond with a boy in France, only he's a figment of my imagination. *Mon cher ami*. Finally, when I get tired of answering myself, I turn my attention to writing a play for Valentine's Day, because the ones in the book are so dumb. In my play, Cupid is not very good with the bow and arrow, and makes a lot of mistakes.

I read everything I can about love, my sister's grown-up books, such as *Giant* by Edna Ferber and *Sister Carrie* by Theodore Dreiser, which is old but very good. I read parts of it over and over, and cry. In Sol's locked bookcase I see a book called *Sexual Behavior in the Human Female* by Alfred Kinsey. I use a bobby pin to open the lock, a trick I learned from my brother. It's the most amazing book. I ask my sister what *extra-marital* means. Soon my sister is also reading the book. So far, it doesn't mention love, but I think love has to do with it, anyhow.

From North Carolina, my father sends my sister and me presents at Hanukkah but forgets our birthdays. Once, he comes to New York for the week of Rosh Hashanah, and invites us to eat with him in a delicatessen downtown. "There's no deli where I am. I could go crazy for corned beef on rye," he tells me on the phone, "*meshugge* for kosher dill." My father, to my recollection, has never before spoken Yiddish. Though I feel anxious, I'm curious to see him again.

My sister, who is student-teaching art, simply refuses to go. "I just look at food and I gain weight. Besides, what do I owe him?"

Sol and my mother insist that my sister accompany me. "Whatever you think, he's your papa," my mother says.

"Two or three days a year," my sister says. "That's worth honoring?"

"From where you get such a smart mouth?" my mother answers. "For many years he supported you, he supported all of us. You think it's easy to work in a hot factory?" Unaccountably she begins to weep.

Shocked, my sister says she'll go, after all.

"Don't do me any favors," my mother says.

My father is not alone at the Formica table in the deli. Beside him is a woman in her late forties, with creased, bronzed skin and a smile that rivals Miss America's. At first I think my father has just told her a joke, but it turns out she's smiling at *us*, my sister and me, as we walk across the creaky wooden floor. She doesn't let go of the smile until after the introductions.

"Goldie is opening a Hadassah chapter in North Carolina. The first one in our city. There aren't so many Jews as here," my father explains.

My sister is on her best behavior. "That's very nice, Mrs. Chaffee," she says, and reaches for the bowl of pickles in front of us.

"Please, call me Goldie. So you're familiar with what Hadassah does?"

"Not really," my sister says.

Goldie leaves her tongue sandwich untouched as she tells us about Mitzvah Day projects and teaching the Midrash. "Our Temple has a *tikkun olam* project." I guess we look blank. The wrinkles in her tanned brow deepen.

I can't stand it. I have to ask her to explain *tikkun olam*.

She looks reprovingly at my father, who scrapes the last of the coleslaw from the pleated paper cup. "Repair of the world. To further Jewish identity, moral integrity, and social action," she says.

I have no idea what she means but it sounds interesting.

"You weren't bas mitzvahed?" Goldie says to my sister. Wrinkles fan out at the outer corner of her eyes as she smiles at me. "For you there's still time."

"Sol would like that," I say. My sister kicks me under the table.

While my father is in the men's room, Goldie tells us she has a grown-up son in college in Florida. "My husband passed, may he rest in peace, after a car accident."

"I'm sorry," my sister says politely. "Where did you and Dad meet?"

"I'm the bookkeeper at the factory. At first I wouldn't have a thing to do with him outside work"—she looks to one side, remembering—"I went to our boss, Mr. Gershenfeld. So everything would be on the up and up. And here we are."

"Where?" I say.

"I'll let your father tell you." But after he comes back, she keeps on talking.

Later, when we critique Goldie, my sister says, "Did Papa get two words in edgewise?"

"Did he even try?" I say.

"Should we tell Mama?" she asks. "Will she be jealous?"

"We'll tell her about Goldie's wrinkles and all the Jewish stuff."

"'Moral integrity,'" my sister sneers. "I think Papa puts up with that horseshit because she's so much younger than he is. Leopards don't change their spots."

I have at least a dozen questions to ask as we stand on a street corner, under a lamppost, but I choose the most important. "Why did Mama cry when you said you weren't coming tonight?"

"Menopause," my sister says.

"That was before, when she met Sol. She was always fanning herself."

"Oh, right," my sister says. "I hope she's not going crazy again."

"What do you mean?" In the pit of my stomach I feel queasy, but not from the pastrami.

"You know," she says, "from that time."

"What time? Tell me!" I say.

"When she went crazy."

Now I think I'm losing my own mind. "When did she go crazy?"

"Maybe you don't remember it. You were three or four. She went crazy, and they put her in a mental institution. That's why you went to Aunt Ruchel's."

"You're nuts! Mama had pneumonia then. Uncle Isaac said so, at the engagement party. I'll never forget it."

"That's what you think."

"I'll ask Aunt Ruchel," I say.

"Go ahead," she says. "But it's true."

A unt Ruchel says it's all a misunderstanding. "Your mother, she was worn out." The way she says it, I start studying my mother now for signs of insanity: how she looks, how she sounds, how she acts. Everything is normal, disgustingly so. She is as placid as Sol, and at least as boring.

For a memento, I make a list of my mother's former eccentricities: how she would talk to herself in Yiddish; how she would lose her temper in public places; how she was so afraid of the Evil Eye, she would throw salt over her shoulder, or spit, or stink up the house and our clothes with garlic.

I wonder now if she was crazy then and why I miss her the way she used to be.

"Y ou!" my mother says to me.

"What? I picked up my room already."

"I want to ask you something," she says. There is danger in her voice, but what could it have to do with?

"What, Mama?"

"Asia, where is this?"

"It's a continent on the other side of the world."

"What's this, *continent*? Like going to the bathroom?"

"I think that's *incontinent*. A continent is a land mass, there are seven in the whole world." I start to recite them, but she cuts me off.

"Show me," she says.

In Sol's den, I show her on the globe where we are and where Asia is.

"Where's New Jersey?" she asks. There is a new smile on her face, a wistful one. "I didn't have schools like you. And you, you don't know enough to appreciate. So, Asia, it's far, *nu*?"

"Why do you care where Asia is?"

"Solly's going. On business. He wants me to go, but the airplane, it takes all day and night. Crazy I'm not. You're smiling."

"No, Mama, you're not crazy."

The week before Sol's trip, my brother comes home for a weekend and right away notices my mother's long face. "You look like you're sitting *shiva*, Ma. Who died?"

"Such things you don't joke about, hear?" she says. "I'm worried about Solly's plane. My nightmares, the planes they fall from the sky. Or boom! one goes into the other. Now Solly wants to fly to Asia. A whole day he has to be in the sky, coming and going. We should both live through it, *alevai*."

"A thousand planes take off and land every day," my brother tells her. "Not just in airports. From our ship—they take off and land on the deck. They don't crash. It's very rare."

"It's the very rare I worry for, not the safe ones," my mother says.

No longer gangly, my brother has filled out just enough to make his leanness attractive. With his cap angled on his head, he looks like Frank Sinatra. He wants to talk about places he's been—Burma, Malaysia, Singapore—but Sol asks if he's learning a lot about auto-mechanics.

"I'm teaching *them*," my brother says. "About trucks."

"How can this be, you're not on a boat?" my mother says.

"Yes, Ma. We're military transport. We gotta transport everything—weapons, trucks, tanks."

"Fixing trucks—this makes a good living?"

"I don't know, Ma, but I like the Navy. Don't be surprised if I re-up."

"Reenlists," Sol explains.

"We may be going to Germany next month, it's just a rumor. Because of the Russians," my brother says, then remembers that Russia was where she was born.

Sol pretends to spit. "You couldn't get me there—"

Even my mother stares at this burst of passion.

"It's not as if I have a choice," my brother says.

"Please, I don't want to hear such words in connection with Germany," Sol says. "You'll excuse me." After he leaves the room, my mother tells us he lost all the relatives on his father's side in the concentration camps.

"You go by boat all the way there?" she asks Sheldon. "I feel better."

"Remember the *Titanic*? C'mon, Ma, I'm just clowning around. We have plenty of life rafts, God forbid anything." He puts his arms around her. "Flying is no big deal, Ma. I flew up from Virginia. And tomorrow I'll fly back."

"*Ver volt dos geglaibt!*" my mother says. Who would have believed it!

I imagine the very first meeting happens right after Sol leaves.

My mother is in a state approaching hysteria because Sol is in the sky, someplace over the water. All night she was awake, with the radio on. If the plane crashes, she figures she'll hear it on the news. After I leave for school, she has her coffee and a toasted English, and calculates that Sol still isn't on the ground yet in Asia. *The hardest part*, she thinks.

She puts on a new dress to make herself feel better, and medium heels so she can walk. Too restless to go to a museum, she goes to Broadway and heads south, without a destination in mind. She strokes the fox collar of her jacket, another gift of Sol's, *just because he felt like*, she recalls telling her sister.

On 72nd Street she sees a new store has come in, Magic Shoes. She stares hard—like a *yekl*, a greenhorn, taking in the sights. Still staring, she continues up the street, distracted finally by a plane passing overhead.

My mother looks up, and in the moment she is contemplating how it can possibly stay up there, her right shoulder collides with the right shoulder of a man not much taller than herself. Her heel catches on a crack in the sidewalk, and she goes stumbling forward, but the man grabs her from behind. She looks up, expecting the plane to fall out of the sky.

With his arms still on her forearms, the man glances up too. "Pardon me!" he says, and drops his arms. His glance follows hers to the pavement.

"*Oy*, my shoe, it broke," my mother says.

The man quickly stoops to pick up her heel. "There's a shoemaker around the corner, I'm sure he can fix it."

She meets the man's eyes, struck by his pupils, the color of caramel. She can't put into words how they make her feel.

While the shoemaker reattaches her heel to the shoe, my mother and the man sit in adjoining booths, a wooden partition between. She thinks it's strange for him to wait with her. The shop is very dark, his face in shadow when he introduces himself as Zeke Bialowski—Polish, he says. Already she forgets his last name. She doesn't tell him her name.

"I'm a salesman. Jewelry," he says, hoisting the black case off the seat to show her. "You live around here?"

"More uptown," she says. "You must be busy. You don't have to stay."

"I feel responsible. If you have lunch with me, I'll make it up to you."

I imagine that when she says okay, all she is thinking is that he'll keep her mind off Solly.

The steak house looks to my mother like a bar, the kind she went to with Harry. She wonders why he's come to mind now after such a long absence. Then she recalls the new store on 72nd. *Magic Shoes.*

"My husband, he's on an airplane to Asia. Right now," she says to Mr. Bialowski.

"And why aren't you with him?"

She shrugs, not wanting to tell him of her fears.

"You don't like flying?" he guesses. "I don't blame you. Remember when the two planes collided right over the skies here?" He shudders. "I wouldn't fly, except for my job. We're based in Frisco, but the business is here, Mrs. uh—"

"Mrs. Farber."

"Mrs. Farber, may I recommend the lobster?"

"Ah, you're not Jewish?" she says.

"Roman Catholic, but I've lapsed some." He laughs. "Too many sins to confess, so I go to the goditorium only once a year." My mother's expression is quizzical. "Goditorium— what I call church," he explains.

What a character! my mother thinks. "You're a big sinner?" she prods.

"Very big. Not murder, almost everything else. I like lying. It's creative. I cheat on my wife every chance I get."

"You're joking, Mister, no?"

He takes the matchbook out of the ashtray, moves his fist in a little arc, opens his hand. The matchbook is gone. "Now you see it . . . What about you, Mrs. Farber? Are you a sinner?"

She shakes her head no. *Not anymore,* she thinks.

"You're one of those faithful wives, cooking, cleaning, waiting for the old man to come home?"

"You make this sound terrible."

"Like death warmed over."

"What this means?"

"Barely alive. You don't feel like you're in a domestic prison?"

"Prison? I thanks God for what I have. My Solly, he's an angel."

"I hope not," Mr. Bialowski says. "Let's hope the plane landed safely."

A few hours later, when my mother is home again, Sol calls from Hong Kong. "What a long flight! Turbulent. We bounced around so much, the passengers applauded when we landed. Everything okay by you?"

She tells him how she bumped into a man and broke her heel.

"Here it's a shopper's paradise. You could buy all the shoes you want. They supply all the chains in New York now, like Magic Shoes—"

"Solly," my mother interrupts. She tells him she had lunch with this strange man. In her nervousness, she goes on and on.

"Don't faint when you see the telephone bill," Sol says gently.

"Solly, I love you," she says.

"That's good, because the trip may take a little longer. I may have to fly to the Philippines."

"Oh no, please—"

"Chenia, there's no danger. Repeat after me: There's no danger."

Dully, she repeats the words. But in her mind, she sees the blood-red sign on a white background: MAGIC SHOES.

Right away the phone rings again, and my mother picks it up.

"Mrs. Farber? It's Zeke Bialowski." When she doesn't respond, he says, "The man you had lunch with today?"

"Yes, yes, but how did you find me?"

"I'm a genius. I used the phone book. I'll tell you why I'm calling. I just happen to have an extra ticket to *Fiddler on the Roof.*"

"What's on the roof?"

"It's a Broadway play. *Fiddler on the Roof.* I'm sure you'll like it. It sounds like I'm flirting with you, but all I want is your company. Is that a sin?"

"I'm too old to flirt with," my mother says, "so long as you understand."

"To be honest, it's not my first choice, but I accept your frankness. You'll see the play with me? Eight o'clock. That gives you plenty of time."

My mother knows Sol wouldn't like her to go. At the same time, she knows if she explains it right, it won't cause any trouble. By Sol, she can do no wrong. "Mister, if I can pay for my own ticket, I go with you."

"I got the tickets from a distributor. They didn't cost me a dime."

"You're lying, no?"

My mother puts on a wine velvet dress that Sol picked out. And the pearls he gave her for her birthday—necklace and earrings. She likes how she looks but suddenly recalls her sister saying once, "Pearls are unlucky."

"*Umglik?* How can that be? All the famous actresses, the rich people, they wear the pearls," she told my Aunt Ruchel.

"What do we know about their lives? Myself, I wouldn't take a chance."

My mother sifts through her jewelry box. Nothing else goes so well. She considers changing the dress but now time is running out.

"Where are you going, Mama?" my sister asks. "Your lipstick's too red."

"*Oy vey.*" She swipes a tissue across her lips, and in a minute my sister is back with one of her dozens of lipsticks. Using her pinkie, my mother smears the purplish-red color on her small, heart-shaped mouth.

"It's perfect," I say. "You look very nice. Where are you going?"

"To fiddle on the roof."

"Pretty funny, Mama. Sol's gone one day and you're getting your sense of humor back."

Walking into the crowded lobby with Mr. Bialowski, my mother starts at a familiar silhouette, but it disappears inside the theater.

"What is it? Your husband?"

"Somebody I thought I knew. Maybe not."

Past the ticket takers, my mother is on high alert, and then she sees him. Harry is by the drinking fountain, beside a tall woman, her pale blond hair in thick swirls piled on her head. An interesting face. My mother's stomach churns. She can see why Harry would prefer the woman to her.

My mother's smile is feeble. "Where do we sit?"

After the usher seats them on a side aisle, my mother takes off her glasses.

"You're farsighted?" Mr. Bialowski says.

"My eyes, they need a rest."

I imagine in that moment my mother struggles between shame and longing. *Why this has to happen now?* she wonders. *I had a feeling something,* she thinks, about Sol's being gone.

Mr. Bialowski pokes the program at her. "Zero Mostel. They say he's terrific."

Reluctantly, she puts her glasses back on. She glances up as Harry and the woman go past them down the aisle. Harry glances back. "Chenia!" he blurts out.

My mother numbs herself as she introduces Mr. Bialowski to Harry, but not by name. "My second husband. The first one—" She sighs but doesn't finish.

Sympathetically, the woman crinkles her eyes. Forty-nine, maybe fifty, my mother guesses. Her neck has rocks of turquoise all around, each a different size. Her wedding band is plain.

Slowly my mother's gaze lifts to Harry's face as he says, "I'd like you to meet my wife, Claudia. You're a fan of musical theater?"

"After the program I tell you," my mother says. "The little one, she writes the plays now. Sol and I saw one—" She stops, realizing her mistake, but Harry doesn't seem to notice.

The lights flicker and Claudia tugs on his arm. "We better go, darling."

"A pleasure to see you again, Chenia," Harry says.

The theater lights dim, and my mother sits in a darkness of her own. *Darling.* The word slices through her belly. *Darling.* And this *grobyan* beside her, he sits through the introductions! It's all she can do not to run from the theater. To run under a truck.

In the spotlight, the conductor turns to face the audience.

Let him think what he wants, my mother tells herself. All that consoles her is that Harry believes she is with her husband. He should know she didn't die of love after all.

She joins the clapping, but before the orchestra sinks below the stage, my mother realizes she is not the only one who lied. She would bet anything that the tall woman is not Harry's wife.

At first my mother has to struggle to keep her thoughts away from Harry, but soon she's caught up by the music, the dancing, the costumes, the wonderful acting. Like a fever, they make her run hot and cold. The melodies lift her heart and break her heart.

In the lobby during intermission, she glances around but does not see Harry. *Darling.* She lets the word prick her again and again. She cannot figure why Harry would bother to talk to her. Was it to show off the woman? To make her feel small, less than nothing?

"So far so good?" Mr. Bialowski asks.

"It's very nice, this show," my mother says, playing down her feelings.

"Nice? It's terrific! Even at scalper prices, it's good."

"What's this, *scalper prices*?"

"Don't worry your pretty head," he says. "So who was the fellow? An old boyfriend?"

"I know him from the shoe store."

"He called you Chenia. That's your name?" After she nods he says, "My customers, they're Mr. and Mrs. No first-name basis, that's low class."

"I know him eleven years now," she says sharply.

He elbows her. "I wasn't born yesterday. There was electricity between the two of you. Am I right?"

"Excuse me, what are you saying?"

"Don't get your dander up!"

She laughs, a strained laugh. "He's a shoe salesman, that's all. You have a good imagination."

Can that be true? she muses. Since the little one wasn't born yet, is eleven years, she tells herself. Everything, her whole life, is like yesterday.

I imagine that as my mother leaves the theater she is exhilarated, yet full of yearning. *Sunrise, sunset.* Sweet and bitter. This is life, she tells herself—to see *Fiddling on the Roof,* and then to see Harry.

In the crush of people outside, she catches sight of Harry trying but failing to hail a cab. He returns to the sidewalk, where the woman waits.

Then, who knows how it happens, my mother is face-to-face with him, and he asks her, "What did you say your last name is now?"

She hesitates, wishing she could remember the long Polish name. "Farber," she says.

"You're still in Inwood?" Harry asks.

"Downtown," she says.

"Around here?"

"Not so far downtown."

"Mrs. Zeke Farber," Harry says, "very good."

"It's Sol," Mr. Bialowski says. "Zeke's my nickname."

"Sol Farber," Harry says. "I'll change our records—in the store." His voice is business-like.

My mother clutches Zeke's arm, feeling her knees wobble.

Minutes later, as Harry and the woman get into a taxi, Zeke says, "Shoe store, my ass."

"Mister, whatever your plan is, this is no way to talk to me. I think you *are* a devil, to tell him my name. Thank you for everything, but I go home now."

"Here, take my card," Zeke says. "I'm at the Roosevelt Hotel. At your service, anytime."

I imagine that she looks into his caramel eyes and knows now the feeling she couldn't say before. Sticky. I imagine that Zeke regards her confused, fearful expression, and finds her even more desirable.

In the cab, my mother wonders if she has a hole in the head. What is she thinking, that Harry will call her up and it will be as before? Even if she could love this man again, she thinks, she can never stop hating him.

The morning after she sees the play, she doesn't want to get out of bed. The covers are pulled over her head when I come into her room. "Are you all right, Mama? You're usually dressed by now."

"A headache!" she barks. "Leave me."

The next thing she knows, she is woken out of a sound sleep by the telephone. Her heart pounds. She knows it's about Solly, something terrible, but when she picks up the receiver and says, "Hello?" a familiar voice says, "Chenia?"

My mother puts the phone down and falls back on the pillow. "*Gottenyu!*" she says aloud.

As the phone rings again, she remembers a saying her mother made: *Me ken nit iberloifen di levoneh.* You can't outrun the moon. Wearily, she picks up the receiver.

"Give me a minute," Harry says, "and then you can hang up. All right?" When my mother doesn't answer, he begins talking. "For years I've looked for you. I wanted to apologize. Are you there?"

"I'm here."

"Did you hear me? I called every Arnow in Manhattan, in the Bronx, in all the boroughs. I even tried Fair Lawn, where I thought you said your sister lives, but I couldn't find you. Are you there?"

"I'm here." My mother thinks, *I'm not breathing, but I'm here.*

"I wanted to apologize. I know it was wrong what I did."

"What?" my mother says.

"To see you, you know, when I was in no position—" There is a pause, and then Harry says, "I'm sorry if I hurt you."

"*If* you hurt me?"

"I'm sorry I hurt you."

My mother's face crumples, but she will not let Harry hear her cry.

"Chenia?"

"I'm here."

"I didn't realize what I was getting into. You were some kind of lovely vision, there on the Boardwalk, dazzling my eyes like the sun at noon."

My mother squeezes the phone cord so hard, her nails dig into her palm.

"Chenia, don't say no right away. I'd like to see you. I have something for you, something I have to give you."

"A *frosk in pisk*," my mother jokes. A slap in the face, but she doesn't translate. "What?"

"I'd rather not tell you on the phone. Meet me tonight? Wherever you want."

At the bottom of the ocean, my mother thinks, but doesn't say. She is in such a tangle now, she has to see him, to get it all straight. "Where is best?" she asks.

D uring the week Sol is gone, my mother becomes moody, impatient, sharper-tongued—the mother I actually prefer. She yells at my sister, "For what you leave crumbs on the table overnight? Better the roaches can eat?"

"We don't have roaches here," my sister reminds her.

"So long as we're careful with the crumbs, *pisk*." Loudmouth.

My mother also becomes dreamy. She puts records on the phonograph, she stirs her coffee and stares into the distance.

One night she comes home and hums to herself. When I step out of the shadow, she's shocked to see me.

"What put *you* in such a good mood?" I say, which is what Sol would say.

"A movie. I forget the name."

"I didn't know you were going to a movie. I would've gone with you."

"At the last minute I make up my mind."

In the bathroom she's still humming, and now I have to know what movie she saw. I look through the newspaper. I wait a long time till she comes out of the bathroom. "Which theater?" I ask.

"Loew's. What do you want to know so much?"

I read her the name of the movies they're showing.

"That could be it," she says.

"It's two westerns. They put you in such a good mood?"

She shrugs. "I liked it, so sue me."

Other nights, when we ask where she's been, she has ready answers: She says she was shopping, she was walking around, one night she was with Ben. My sister and I know she is lying, but not why.

They meet in front of the Coliseum at 59th Street. He is waiting for her by a frankfurter cart. "Thank you for doing this," he says right away. "The restaurant I have in mind is five blocks from here. We can walk or take a cab."

"A taxi I would like," my mother says, because she is testing him. And anyway, she has worn high heels, not so good for walking.

Settled in the cab, Harry says, "You look wonderful. Very chic."

"My husband, he has good taste," my mother says, about the tweed suit.

"Your earrings, they gleam like real pearls."

"Of course they're real," my mother says. "From Solly." Quickly she says, "He likes *Zeke*. I call him Solly." She thinks she prefers Harry to be thinner.

There is a heavy silence until Harry says, "You'll appreciate this place we're going to. Lots of *ambiance*—atmosphere," he says.

"Here is, too," my mother says, making a joke.

The light is soft inside the restaurant. On each table is a white candle, its flames dancing yellow and blue. In the corner, a man in a tuxedo plays the violin, a romantic melody. My mother is beginning to think that Harry really is sorry for the trouble he made.

She studies the tiny tufts of hair on his fingers as they hold the wine menu. Once upon a time she could faint, thinking of his hands on her, but now—nothing. Harry orders and then the Cabernet arrives.

Lifting his glass, Harry toasts, "To precious memories, Chenia."

"*Oif mist iz geroten korn,*" she toasts back. It means "Corn can grow on manure," but she doesn't translate. She is curious what he wants to give her, but she only asks about his mother.

"She succumbed to a stroke a couple of years ago. Mercifully."

"I'm sorry. My mother, *oleho hasholem*, she passed away soon after we come to this country. My father, *olov hasholem*, he passed away before the little one was born. The little one, she's not so little. Such a mouth on her!"

"That's normal," Harry says, "to rebel against the parents."

"Solly's an angel," my mother says. She looks hard into Harry's dark eyes as if to say, Don't think I'm lying, Mister.

"Even so, it's an upheaval, living with a stepfather."

"This could be," my mother says.

"I'll bet she's a good kid. She just needs your approval."

"You think so?" my mother says hopefully.

"She was such an amazing child. A prodigy."

"Now you couldn't know her from a *nishtikeit*. A nobody. And by her, what isn't a joke?"

"Your husband, he has a sense of humor?"

My mother can't help it. She bursts out with, "This Zeke, this *grobyan*, he's not my husband."

"I knew that."

"You knew?"

"He's not your type. Where did you meet him?"

My mother tells him the story, about her shoe, about Solly flying.

"I understand," Harry says. "The woman I was with—"

"Not your wife," my mother says.

Harry smiles. "We're a pair, you and I. No, she's not my wife. My wife divorced me after she found out about you."

My mother is dying to ask, but the waiter sets down their plates, then the busboy brings water.

Finally Harry speaks. "The bill for Bickford's, for the damages, they sent it to Mr. and Mrs. Taubman. My wife opens it. She contacts Bickford's, gets the police report—" He shakes his head, as if he's sorry for himself.

My mother tries not to care, one way or the other.

"We had it out then," Harry continues. "She forgave me, until she found the umbrella. The one you gave me. Do you remember?"

My mother shrugs, but she recalls perfectly.

"How's your veal cutlet?" Harry asks. "This sausage is hot. *Mmm.*"

"To have an appetite at this time—" my mother says. She takes a small bite. "A little spicy but is okay, this. So go on, please."

"Remember the girl in the front of the store? We'd have coffee, get things off our chest—about my wife, about her boyfriend. One day—I think that was right after you came in the last time, like gunning for bear—Sylvia walks into Nasch's. Jilly and I, we're in back, laughing over something. Harmless, but that was the coup de grace—the final blow. She flew to Vegas and divorced me. But first, she made a lot of trouble for me in the store. I lost my job."

Harry stares intently into my mother's eyes. "After that I began to think about things, the cost of taking risks—"

"A person that understands his own foolishness isn't so foolish," my mother says, translating from an old proverb. "But what I want to know—"

"What?"

"Why you didn't tell me you were married."

Harry looks sheepish. "I thought you knew."

"*Meh ken brechen*," my mother says. "You can vomit from this."

"I was afraid you'd have nothing more to do with me."

"So you lied?"

Harry gives a half-shrug. "Let's say I tried to shade the truth."

My mother stares. "*Ich vil nit kein gedempts.* I can't translate exact but like this: I could do without the sauce."

"Like I said, Chenia, you were such a vision."

My mother wants to hear more, but Harry seems to be done. "So, you're sorry," she says dryly. "This is good to know."

The violinist is at their table now and asks what they would like to hear. Harry says, "'Dark Eyes,'" but my mother says, "No, not that one. *Fiddle on the Roof* something. You know this?"

The violinist plays a medley of tunes from the show.

"*Oy*, so beautiful!" my mother says. Music, dancing, art—she knows now why they exist: to make up for the troubles people have with love.

Harry smiles indulgently. "Your taste—it's very eclectic. A little of this, a little of that."

Whoosh, the time goes by like nothing, she thinks, when the check arrives. Harry takes something out of his pocket. Money, my mother thinks, but he says, "Open your hand."

Holding the necklace by the chain, he lowers the heart into her palm. "I had the chain fixed." When my mother looks vague, he adds, "You tore it off your neck and hurled it at me, in Bickford's."

My mother stares at the heart. *Coeur*, she recalls. She remembers my asking why there was a hole in the middle.

"Real gold," Harry says.

My mother nods. To her it's like a riddle: how something can be both real and false. This Harry, he's like a stranger. Looking at him across the table, she cannot imagine why she would ever kill herself over him. She drops the necklace in her purse. "Now where are you working?"

"I'm between jobs. I was an expediter for a shipping company, routing packages, tracing them when they got lost . . . Then my son, he got into a car accident, no insurance. The bills wiped out my savings. If I didn't know better, I'd think I was the victim of the Evil Eye."

"*Kineahora!*" my mother says automatically, but she has a fleeting thought: That curse she put on him—it took. *I take it back*, she says to herself. *Zolst nit visn fun azelkhe tsores.* May you not know of such troubles.

"A penny for your thoughts, Chenia."

"You have no job and you invite me to dinner?"

"I was afraid to let more years go by. Your name might change again."

My mother takes some bills out of her wallet. "Is enough?"

"Plenty," Harry says, and lays them on top of the check.

Out on the sidewalk, before he puts her in a taxi, Harry says, "I'd love to see the necklace on you. May I fasten it for you?"

My mother takes it from her purse and hands it over. After he secures the lock, he kisses her on the nape of the neck and squeezes her shoulders.

Electricity runs right through her, quick and sharp. Besides the physical shock, she is jolted by the thought that as a woman, she is not dead, after all.

"Been a pleasure," Harry says. "Thank you for accepting my apology."

"Excuse me," my mother says. "I listened, but who says I accept?"

In the taxi, my mother takes off the necklace and contemplates it. She cannot bring it home, even if she wanted to keep it. Where Ruben never noticed a thing, she thinks, Solly is the opposite. She rolls down the window, turns her back to it, and flings the necklace over her shoulder, into the Henry Hudson Parkway.

As she expects, Harry calls her in the morning. "Chenia!" he says. "I just wanted to see how you are."

She wishes she hadn't told him that Solly is in Asia. "Excuse me, I have company here."

"I'll call you later," he says and hangs up the phone before she can say, "Don't bother yourself."

My mother dresses and puts on her walking shoes because she doesn't want to be home when Harry calls again. In a coffee shop on Broadway, she orders a cup of coffee and cheese Danish at the counter. It's very interesting to see who comes in, where they sit, what they order. She sips another cup of coffee, and before she knows it, two hours have gone by. To her surprise, she finds she doesn't mind in the slightest being alone.

She continues walking down Broadway to Columbus Circle, but then she follows Central Park to Fifth Avenue and turns right, toward the stores. Soon her bladder is so full it feels as if it's bursting. Where can she go? she wonders. She stops a woman in the street to ask.

"A hotel's your best bet. Go over to Madison." The woman points.

On Madison, my mother sees it, the Roosevelt Hotel. She thinks if she laughs, she'll *pish* right there in the street. She hurries inside and finds the powder room in the lower lobby. On her way out she quickly scans the upper lobby, relieved not to see Zeke. It would be just her luck, she thinks. He would never believe she came there just to *pish*.

In Saks, my mother buys two new ties for Solly, so smart she wants to buy an armful, but it would make him suspicious. At the jewelry counter, she discovers a necklace like the one Harry gave her, but it's not real gold. Soon she's browsing in fine jewelry. "How much?" she asks the saleslady about a cameo brooch. "The old things I like better," she confides.

In spite of her resolve, my mother spends another evening with Zeke.

During the day she walks around town, the way she did when she was waiting for me in school. All she wants is not to be home when Harry calls. But whenever the phone rings, it's Zeke Bialowski. Better to lie to Solly about Zeke than to sin with Harry, she thinks.

"If you're game, we can have dinner and shoot some pool," Zeke says.

My mother takes it as a figure of speech, but after Sunday dinner they go to a pool hall, where Zeke shows her how to hold the cue stick, how to use the chalk. My mother, who has never studied math, is able to figure out the angles. She gets a kick out of seeing Zeke's astonishment as the billiard balls plop into the pockets. It pleases her even more when he gets irritable and says, "Beginner's luck."

At the end of the evening they sit in the corner while he drinks one glass of beer after another from the pitcher he ordered. She only sips from the first glass. This is what *pish* must taste like, she thinks.

"Tomorrow it's my last night here, then back to Frisco and the grind. How about you meet me at the Roosevelt Hotel at seven?"

"No funny business," my mother says, "I told you."

Zeke keeps my mother waiting in the hotel lobby for twenty minutes, but when he appears, he has a rectangular yellow box with him, chocolates from Schrafft's. He apologizes for being late. "I was on the phone, long distance." He expects her to ask, but she doesn't.

They dine in a fish place with an Irish name written in white on the green canvas awning. Zeke has two bottles of beer with his fried smelts and goes twice to the men's room. Hours go by before he insists on her having a slice of chocolate layer cake. Although it's too late to be having dessert, my mother thinks, she enjoys every bite.

Then, seemingly from nowhere, a deck of cards appears in his hand. "Now you see it . . ." The deck disappears.

My mother laughs.

"Now you see it . . ." He fans the deck over the table. At first the pictures seem to be abstract. My mother squints. "Put your glasses on!" Zeke instructs, which she does.

My mother is flabbergasted. On the first card a naked man is lying on a bed. Hanging over him are breasts as big as cow udders.

"*Gevalt!*" my mother says, and shoves away the deck.

Zeke sweeps up the cards, and again they disappear, only to reappear, this time as a perfectly ordinary deck.

My mother feels as if she's going to jump out of her skin. As if Zeke has read her mind, he snaps his fingers. Suddenly there is a card, mid-air, with a woman in a black bra and garter belt, her mouth over a man's penis. Is she going to swallow it like a sword? My mother cannot believe her eyes. She turns to Zeke. He's shuffling the deck now, as if it's nothing special. *That people do this*, my mother thinks. She can't get over it.

Afterwards as they walk up the street, he talks a little loud. Later she doesn't remember a thing he said.

On 57th Street they walk crosstown, and then, past Fifth Avenue, my mother sees the horse-drawn cabs lined up by the park.

The next thing she knows, the driver, who's wearing a top hat and a fancy gray coat with a flared bottom, helps her up into the cab. There's a smell of leather and something else she can't identify. She finds it thrilling when the horse begins to trot down the big street along Central Park, cars on either side of them. She thinks of a time when she was a little girl in the old country. Where were they going in the carriage, all dressed up? And then she recalls the funeral of her sister. *Oleho hasho-lem.* May she rest in peace.

Soon the carriage turns into the park, where only an occasional lamppost lights the darkness.

Zeke is quiet for once. My mother can hear the *clopCLOP* of the horse and some kind of humming from the trees. At first it's pleasant, and then she gets anxious. "It's dangerous in the park, no?"

"If you was on foot, I would say, 'Run for your life.' Who's gonna contend with a horse?"

Now my mother feels foolish.

Zeke slides closer, the moment she's been dreading from their first night out. She jumps when he puts his arm around her. She wants to push it away, but she's afraid of making him angry. He squeezes her shoulder, once, twice. She sits very still, frozen with expecting the worst. The *clopCLOP* of the horse is like a drumbeat now, hypnotic.

Then she gets the strength, who knows from where, to shrug off his hand. "Mister," she says sharply, "if you touch me again, I'll scream bloody murder."

"Relax, will you!" As if nothing at all has happened, he says, "To beat the morning rush I have to get up with the birds. It's one thing for birds to fly—"

My mother stares straight ahead into the darkness, hardly daring to breathe until she sees the street lights again. As soon as the driver has helped her down, she hails a cab beside them. The box of Schrafft's she's left behind.

Two more days, she says to herself, and Solly will be back.

At home, she takes off her clothes, puts her suit in a pile to take to the cleaners. Everything else goes in the hamper. She fills the bath, extra hot, and runs the soap all over herself.

My mother knows it's crazy but she wishes she could tell Solly about the deck of cards. She can imagine his disgust. She, too, is disgusted, but with herself, more than with Zeke. Anyway, by now she's decided she can't tell Sol anything at all.

She recalls the pictures on the cards and feels astonished at her reaction. *A lebedike velt*—lively things are happening—in her own love pocket. She never knew such a thing was possible, to get that kind of feeling from pictures! She doesn't want to, but then she does. She reaches down to touch her *knepl*, and keeps touching, until what she calls *the miracle* happens.

And then I am knocking on the door. "Mama, there's someone on the phone for you."

"Who?"

"A man, I didn't ask. He said he's going to wait."

"*Ai yi yi*," my mother says. "What now?"

"Where've you been, Chenia? I've called day and night."
"Is it your business?" my mother says on the phone to Harry.

"No, but I felt very bad after I saw you. Here I was, trying to apologize, and you paid for the dinner. I'm in such financial straits now. I have debts. Serious debts. They've repossessed my car—took it back—because I couldn't make the payments."

"That so?" Her fingers twirl the sash on her quilted satin robe.

"Anyway, I want to get things square between us, to clean the slate—"

"What, you think my life is some chalkboard you wipe and make all clean?"

"That's not what I meant," Harry says.

"Excuse me, but what you said."

"Chenia, I kept that necklace all those years, hoping to see you again—" He talks and talks. Soon my mother doesn't even hear the words, just the sound of his voice, which is deep and rich, like an announcer on the radio.

"—let's go tomorrow, to the Cloisters. For old times' sake."

All she has to do is say no. Then she thinks, Maybe if she sees him again, she could better understand the whole thing. Anyway, she won't go with him anywhere else, and what bad could happen in the Cloisters? It's been so long since she's seen it. Sol doesn't care for it. "Too Christian," he said when she asked why.

"Okay," my mother says to Harry, "what time I meet you?"

My mother takes the bus up, a long ride she's always enjoyed till now, when it feels endless. They meet at the subway entrance on Fort Washington Avenue and walk together into the park. Harry looks good in a turtleneck sweater under his tweed jacket. Like a professor, my mother thinks.

Though it's a beautiful fall afternoon, there aren't so many people around. Then she sees the sign on the front door of the Cloisters: CLOSED.

"You!" she rails at Harry. "You get me here for nothing? You do this on purpose—" She balls her hand into a fist and is about to strike his chest, but she notices how he looks almost sick, like a dog someone kicked. She drops her hand. "I'm sorry, I lose my temper," she says.

"I'm not sorry," Harry says. "I was beginning to think you'd been lobotomized."

She loves how he explains this new word to her.

"When I saw you at *Fiddler*, you looked like the serene Madonna herself, but the fire is still in you, Chenia. Ah, cha-Chenia," he croons.

After she leans back against the sign, his arms encircle her, and he presses his mouth to hers.

Her lips feel as if they're melting, but Harry pulls himself away. "Now I'm sorry. I'm truly sorry. I couldn't help it," he says, then he's kissing her again, their tongues circling. When they come up for air, they walk to the bench where she used to sit with me.

The view is different now, with new buildings below, maybe a housing project. She stares till she gets her fill, and when she glances back to the low stone wall, she's startled that the stroller isn't there. Then she notices Harry patiently waiting.

He holds her head between his hands and kisses her some more. It's as if they were back on the Boardwalk, how it was in the beginning, with the sun in her eyes. "I want you, Chenia," Harry says in her ear. He tugs her hand and leads her into a thicket nearby. They sink down on the brown grass.

"For this I will go to hell," my mother tells him. "Whatever bad happens to me now, I deserve it. So long as it's not my children, *kholilleh*."

"Foolish Chenia, nothing will happen."

"*Hob rakhmones*," my mother says. Have mercy.

The pleasure is like before, although her feeling for him is different. This, too, is new, to enjoy making love with someone you're not sure you like. To tremble and pant with a man not your husband, and feel no guilt—she cannot understand this, or herself.

Afterwards, holding hands, they sit on the bench again and talk, almost like old times. Harry tells her so much about himself as a boy in Rumania, how his family expected him to be a doctor. "My mother, God bless her, had this dream that I would cure people from terrible diseases."

"From love," my mother says, but he doesn't smile.

Hours go by, and then they walk around the bluff. The gray water is pink along the Jersey shore. The sun is blood red. They stand quietly and watch the wafer drop into the mouth of the Palisades. My mother feels as if she's in a trance. She doesn't want to admit it, but she's happy, so happy she wouldn't mind to die right this minute.

At the entrance to the elevator that leads to the subway, Harry says, "Chenia, I hate to ask. You've no idea how much I hate this, but I'm in a bind."

"What?"

"Could you—would it be possible if—if you could lend me some money?"

"How much?" She thinks she has maybe thirty dollars in her bag.

"Two thousand."

"What?"

"Even a thousand."

"What do you take me for?" She answers her own question. *Yekl.* Greenhorn. No matter that she wears nice clothes and lives in a swanky building. *Yekl.* The word should be carved into her chest. She laughs. "That's what you wanted from me? Money?" Her laughing gets louder and alternates with crying. She tries to stop but she can't. "Such a joke . . ." she says.

"You're getting hysterical," Harry tells her, thankful that no one else is around.

She keeps laughing and crying. From a distance she hears a sound like hiccoughing, but she is powerless to stop. Even when he slaps her, she doesn't stop. He slaps her harder. He shakes her, until she comes to.

She feels exhausted, and frightened. *A krenk*, she thinks, about how she acted. A sickness. Over Harry's shoulder is a *shtik* of moon in the darkening sky, the tiniest piece. A cold light, Solly said once. She blows her nose and moves toward the subway entrance.

"It's not what you think—" he says.

"Don't come with me, Mister," she warns.

As she descends the stone steps, she thinks, *Yeder barg-aroif hot zein barg-arop.* Each way up the mountain has its way down.

Pressing the button to summon the elevator, she knows something seems different. Is it the doors? They were dark, but now they're shiny, like aluminum. The elevator arrives, the doors open. No one is inside. It's self-service now. The operator is gone.

On her ride down to the subway, my mother regrets she can't say hello and good-bye to that nice Negro man. It would be good to do that, she thinks, before she throws herself in front of a train.

For that night, my sister has made reservations for us—my mother, me, and her—in a Viennese restaurant on 72nd Street. It's the last night before Sol is due back, the last chance, Mimi thinks, for us to have Mama all to ourselves. The reservations are for seven o'clock, which my mother knows, but at seven, she is not home.

Mimi calls the restaurant to change the time.

"Make it eight-thirty," I say, and she does.

While we wait, Mimi plays the piano, a spinet that Sol bought for himself after my mother begged him: "Do yourself a little something." Mimi never plays when Sol is there because he likes only classical. Tonight Mimi plays, pop tunes, show tunes. She doesn't sing on key, but she sings along anyhow. Over and over, I hear, "'Can't help, loving dat man of mine . . .'" An hour goes by, then another.

Sol calls us from Idlewild when he lands. "I'll be home in two hours," he tells my mother. "I can't wait."

An hour later, my mother is already in the lobby. She paces the marble floor as she debates with herself: to tell, not to tell, what to tell. She doesn't know why she is still alive.

The train was coming when she got to the platform. She started running toward the edge, ready to jump. Only at the last second did she think: I should kill myself for a *vantz*? For a louse, a bedbug?

When Sol's taxi pulls up now, she runs into the street and trembles as the door opens. She is sure Solly will take one look and know everything. But he only looks glad to see her. His eyes shine as he presents a bouquet of tiny pink roses. *"Pupiks,"* she blurts out. Belly buttons. "You adorable—"

He reaches into the backseat to get his bags. "Oh, I forgot," he says, as he slams the taxi door shut with his backside. "Go into my breast pocket."

My mother takes out a tapestried box. "I have a present for you, too. Upstairs. Not such a beautiful box as this."

"It's from Hong Kong," Sol says. "Open it."

Hugging the flowers by their stems under her arm, she manages to open the lid. Inside the box, on a bed of red silk, is a chain with a golden heart, completely solid.

Part Seven

My mother wears the necklace for a few days, and then it disappears, even from my memory. Her twenty-five years with Solly are happy ones—on this, even my sister and I agree. Of course there are sorrows. *Ven nit di shein, volt kein shoten nit geven*, my mother says. If not for the light, there would be no shadow.

My brother, who remained in the Navy, is killed at the age of twenty-seven, saving someone from a falling winch. I still have one of his postcards, a grainy photo of a sailor dancing with a hula girl. "Guess where your bro is now?" he writes on the back.

While my mother continues to grieve over her son's untimely death, I'm consoled by the thought that Sheldon led the adventurous life he wanted. My sister disagrees. "You were too little to know what he went through. After Lenore's abortion, he was never the same. *Hartsvaytik*, as Mama likes to say." Heartsick. "The Navy was just his escape."

I drop out of college to marry foolishly, a man like my father, charming and selfish. Four years later, after I abort our child, the marriage ends. I return to school to get my bachelor's. I go to graduate school. My mother says it's the happiest day of her life when I get my Ph.D. On that day, I feel very sorry for Sol.

My sister marries a successful executive who provides a huge house and swimming pool for them, only he isn't around when she has her first miscarriage. She has three more, until finally she gives birth to twins. My mother learns not to say to me, "And you? When is your turn?"

By then I am already living with Jack Wisenfeld, a lawyer who specializes in copyright law for artists and musicians, none of whom has made him rich. From the very beginning our relationship is as comfy and enveloping as an old robe. We get married only because Jack wants to have children. Ironically, we spend years trying to conceive and a small fortune on *in vitro* procedures that fail to work. Long after we're accustomed to being childless, the Fates reverse their course.

And when Isaac Abrams goes to Italy to study art, Ben follows, abandoning his law practice. He is nearly disbarred for unprofessional conduct. On his return, we learn that the investments he made for us have become largely worthless, except for some real estate and Treasury notes. The debts Jack and I have incurred trying to get me pregnant wipe us out, but he says he feels no animosity toward my cousin. Between uncle and nephew, however, is a wide rift. It takes years for my mother to reconcile them. "Which is more important," she tells Sol, "the money or what Benny did to bring us together?"

During that quarter of a century, if my mother and Sol have endured any grief not caused by the death of loved ones, I cannot imagine it.

Today I stop at my mother's apartment to bring her over to our place for dinner—a Friday ritual that begins after Sol dies of a stroke. My mother is eighty-six now and getting frail. I am on the cusp of forty, and seven months pregnant.

I find her in a cotton smock, rummaging through the famous chest that Sofie gave my sister. "You're not dressed yet, Mama. What gives?" I ask.

"I just remembered, an old bankbook. Before we moved here."

"That was a long time ago. Are you sure?"

She waves her bony arm at me. "From long ago I remember everything. Don't ask what I did yesterday." Suddenly she slaps her thighs. "In the bottom drawer. In the bedroom. You go look. I get dressed."

The drawer is crammed with brassieres. I remove it from the bureau and overturn it on the bed. Out falls the passbook, from a bank probably no longer extant, yet it may be possible to trace its assets. I try to slide the drawer back into the bureau, but something is in the way.

Carefully I lower myself to the floor and bend over as far as my beach ball stomach will permit. There is a wad of waxed paper wedged in the groove. I remove it and am about to toss it when I hear a slight rattle. I unwad the paper and slip the necklace out, then I go find my mother in the bathroom, where she's combing her fine white hair.

"Mama, I found the bankbook, and this." I stick out my hand. "Isn't this the necklace Peter the Wolf gave you?"

"*Meshuggeneh*, that's from Sol."

"Why is it in waxed paper?"

She shrugs. "To keep it clean."

I laugh. "Why isn't it in your jewelry box or one of the little velvet boxes?"

"What difference?" she says. "The money in the bankbook, for you to save—" She points to my bulging stomach. "Should I wear the green dress?"

"Really, Sol gave it to you?" I ask. We both know I mean the necklace.

"You, with the memory," she says, "you don't remember? Solly, who else?"

"But you never wore it."

"Yes, a couple times—"

"You didn't like it?"

"Something happened I wanted to forget. Each time I put this necklace around my throat, I'm thinking things—"

"What things?"

"Not today," she says.

For our annual visit to the cemetery, my mother wears the heart Sol brought back from Asia a quarter-century ago, but she refuses to talk about it.

Before we ride out to Beth El, we gather at my sister's condo in New Jersey. As usual, my sister is not ready on time. While we wait, my husband, Jack, plays billiards downstairs with Ben. In the massive living room, I tell my mother the story of Madame Bovary, which I am teaching this quarter. Then, hoping to get the story of her necklace, I ask, "What is love?"

"'What is love?' *Zol ich azoy vissen fun tsores*," my mother says.

"*Tsores*, 'troubles,'" I say.

"She's learned a little something." My mother looks toward the ceiling. "I think like this it goes: I should know as much about troubles as I know what you're asking. Your brother, *olov hasholem*, he knew about loving."

"How can you say you don't know what love is? What you did for Sol—"

"Who wouldn't? Solly, he was an angel. *Olov hasholem*." May he rest in peace.

"Did you love Peter the Wolf?"

"Who?"

"C'mon, Ma. Harry from Magic Shoes."

"What's to remember about that one?" she says.

"This," I say, indicating the faint scar on my cheek.

"I don't know what you're talking," she says. "Go see if she's ready."

I go up the circular staircase. Near the top I hear my sister say, "I'm the guilty one, then. Lock me away. Feed me bread and water—"

Elihu says, "You don't even know how irresponsible you are."

I retreat down the stairs. My mother looks like a bolster in the middle of the S-shaped sofa, which is at least twenty feet long. "She's almost ready? I'm afraid for you going up and down," she says. "You'll break the water."

"They used to think that, Mama. Now they think exercise is good for pregnancy."

"So far along?" she says dubiously. "*Pssshhh.* Anyhow, that Madame LePage—" She corrects herself. "Bovary. For her, real love was not enough."

"Why don't you come teach my class?" I banter.

"You make fun of me."

"*Maman, pas du tout.*"

"What for, you ask what is love—" She rubs at a spot on the purse in her lap. "Don't be too blind, you. You have Jake—a *mentsh* like my Solly. I told you how it was with him? In the beginning?"

"Not all of it." I don't mind if she repeats herself. Sometimes she adds details I haven't heard, and anyway, I am fascinated with the retracing of her past—our past. Consumed by it, Jack says.

She fingers the golden chain around her neck. "Solly, the moment I see him, my heart turns to stone. With suffering I have enough already. Solly, he tells me later, he makes up his mind right away he wants me, but children his wife never gave him. 'I don't know if I can accept someone else's,' he tells me." She squints. "You look so surprised."

"That explains a lot."

"What means this?"

"Everyone agrees Sol was a prince, but accepting him as a father was so hard. I always thought it was *my* fault."

"What he didn't do for you—more than any father. And you, you wouldn't let him adopt you. 'Why's she so angry?' Solly said over and over."

"Mama, forgive me—"

"It was very hard on Solly." My mother fumbles with her purse, and it falls to the floor. She ignores it, and returns to the story of their courtship. "What to do? For me, was already too late. The hot flashes come like crazy—"

"That I remember. But Mama, at the restaurant, you didn't even know Ben was matchmaking—"

"Restaurant? That came later. First was at Ben's—"

"No, the first time was at a restaurant," I argue. "Let me ask Ben." Before she can protest, I call down the stairs. "Ben, can I lure you away from The Shark a moment?"

"Yo! Any excuse will do," Ben shouts, and runs up the stairs. Puffing a little, he says, "Jack is demolishing me. While you're working on your definitive guide, I bet he sneaks off to pool halls. What's up?" Bending down to pick up my mother's bag, he almost knocks the glass top of the coffee table clear off its base. "Go ahead, laugh at the *klutz*!" he says, smoothing an abundant shock of white hair. He has aged beautifully. My mother's biggest fear, next to my not giving her a grandchild, was that in the era of AIDS, Ben wouldn't age at all.

"You were the matchmaker between Sol and my mother, right?" I say.

"Guilty as charged."

"Their very first meeting, where was it?"

"Sofie's funeral."

"Ben!" I whine.

"Being pregnant has sucked out your memory cells," Ben says. "Sol had to hold you when they lowered her casket into the ground, remember?"

"What are you talking about?" my sister says, trailed by

Elihu as she descends the stairs, in a smart navy dress that hides twenty excess pounds.

We put the question to her as to where Sol and my mother first met. Elihu answers, "Even I know. I heard it so many times. A fancy restaurant."

"Right!" I say.

"Right!" my sister says.

"*Rashomon*," says Ben, who is a movie buff. "The point being, Truth is a matter of perspective."

My mother shrugs. "What difference where? Remember what you like."

In the car, my mother sits in front beside Jack. Apropos of nothing, she says, "Believe me, this meeting, is at Ben's apartment," and then she falls silent, watching the scenery whisk by, like so many memories.

At the cemetery we walk in pairs, Elihu and my sister, Ben and me, Jack and my mother trailing behind. Elihu leads us in prayer, and we place pebbles on the headstones of Sol, my brother, and my Uncle Isaac.

During the extended discussion of where to have lunch— mostly between Elihu and my sister—I stroll along a row of headstones, and go commune with my brother. "Aren't you going to weigh in?" Elihu calls out.

"A hundred sixty and rising," I joke. "Don't worry, I'll eat whatever."

"Lucky you," Elihu says to Jack, "being pregnant doesn't make her high-strung."

"She is already," my mother says.

Jack blows me a kiss, a signal to let my mother's remark pass without comment. He puts his arm around Elihu's shoulder and gets him to step away from the group. When they return, Elihu announces we're going to Three Corners. "Lots of salads," he tells my sister. "Something for everyone."

Ben rides with us to the restaurant. "You're such a diplomat," he tells Jack. "I personally wanted to knee Elihu in the groin—contrary to my usual proclivity. He *is* a hunk. I won't say what I'd do to Mimi, but it starts with *L.*"

"Give her a fat lip?" my gentle husband says.

"That starts with *F*," I point out. "Liposuction, am I right?"

"Actually, I was thinking lobotomy, but yours is delicious," says Ben.

I glance at my mother, who by now is usually asking us to explain ourselves. She is turned to the window and humming faintly.

As soon as Jack pulls into the parking lot of the restaurant, I spot my colleague's car. Elihu and my sister have parked and are already walking in the front door, so we cannot go elsewhere. All I can think about is how to avoid having my husband meet my ex-lover.

Inspired, I say, "Go on, you three, I've a kink in my leg."

Jack lingers, but I become insistent. "Honey, I'll uncramp in a moment. Go order me some apple juice. Please. I'm dying of thirst."

"I'll bring it out to you," Jack says.

My show of impatience is born of fear. "Jack, for God's sake, will you go inside and wait for me for three lousy minutes?"

Now Ben does the arm-around-the-shoulder routine with my husband.

Once inside the restaurant, I immediately locate my colleague who's with a woman—no surprise! I walk over anyhow, enjoying the alarm on his face. Even if I allowed myself to feel something at the sight of his irregular features, the intense eyes, the beard grown a little wilder, I don't know what it would be.

"Look who's come to the boonies," I say, a reference to our mutual love of the city. "My family's making our annual visit to the cemetery. What's your excuse?"

"Katya lives nearby," he says. "This is our colleague Devorah."

He doesn't say in which department Katya teaches. Dressed in clothes made to be worn wrinkled, a print scarf knotted at the nape, silver and onyx earrings, she's obviously a poet. I don't ask. Perhaps with her olive skin, she is the archetype of the poem he used to recite to me in his office, "The Nutbrowne Maide."

Confident he and Katya will not stop now at my family's table, I bid them "Enjoy!" and waddle away, queasy from the sight of breaded clams heaped on their plates and the odor of cooking oil. Before I see my family, I can hear their animated discussion over what to order. I limp a little as I approach and by my smile signal to Jack that all is truly well.

"So what happened to that man?" my mother asks. We are in her bedroom where I am helping her sort out her accumulated papers.

"Who?"

"That man," she says. "The one you—"

"He's still at the college. I see him at faculty meetings."

"That was him—at the Triangle?"

"Three Corners, Mama. You're so amazing!"

She shrugs. "The leg business, you made it up?"

"Yes, Mama."

She sighs. "How this ended?" Never before has she asked about him. She only knows he exists because in a weak moment, I sought her advice.

Waiting for me now to tell her how the relationship ended,

my mother studies some photos. "Here's when you took horse-riding lessons."

"I never took riding lessons. I don't remember ever being on a horse."

My mother shoves the photo at me. In it, I am nine or ten, and wearing a riding habit. "You told Sol you spend the time better reading books. I think you hurt his feelings. It wasn't the first time. You didn't appreciate—"

"I grew to appreciate him. To love him. Really, Mama. I was too extreme for him. You were, too, but he didn't know it—"

My mother sticks her hand up. "So tell me," she says, "how this ended."

I tell her how one morning I am in a tiny, crowded cafe on campus. I hear one of the students mention my colleague's name, and I learn that he is sleeping with their friend. Same place. Different hours. I learn that he also recites to her from "The Nutbrowne Maide" . . . *For in my mynde of all mankynde I love but you alone.* The irony of this line strikes me even as I knock over my café au lait on the messenger.

"You never see him again?"

She is rapt as I tell her how I had to fight the impulse to see him. "Like a junkie craving crack. Finally I call him. We meet—a restaurant in the East Village. Where did people in other centuries have their dramas? You know, Mama, before there were restaurants?"

She laughs. "That's a good one," she says. Her eyes narrow, as if thinking back. "To tell you the truth, I didn't think you and Jake would make it through."

"I don't know how Jack put up with me that year. I despise what I did. Really. Jack deserves a better wife." When my mother doesn't rush to agree, I pat her hand appreciatively. "So how come you're asking about him now?"

As usual, she takes a circuitous route. "Your sister, she's very different from you."

"All she wants is for Elihu to spend more time with her. Jack spends all the time with me I want. I don't spend enough with him."

"This I know," she says.

"Nice that my mother and husband talk about me!"

"You're *kvetching* or you're angry?" She doesn't wait for an answer. "Sometimes I wonder, why my own life is like this. Now I see: This craziness, from one generation to the next, *nu*? My own *mameh*—I told you this—all the time she's laughing. Such a personality! Then one day, I'm seven years old maybe, whoosh, she stares blank. Now I know—your *bubbeh*, she was *hartsvaytik*."

"Heartsick," I blurt out, because the word has stuck. "Ben says passionate love is always obsession. Funny for him to say, huh? After the way he threw over his law practice for that Isaac."

"Isaac," my mother says dreamily. "Now there was a man . . ."

There are many boxes to sort at my mother's. Always I use the time to fill in more of the gaps from our past. I learn that my father wrote poetry—not something I could have imagined or can easily believe. I learn that years after he moves to North Carolina, Trudy Fleisch apologizes to my mother. And that my mother bought a car for Mr. Mangiameli.

"To make my own self feel better," she says. "For a year I couldn't sleep, thinking of how your papa broke his crutches. Later, when we move already here, I run into him on Riverside Drive. He's sitting on a bench, making circles with the pencil around the advertisements. For a car. He says, 'What I like I can't afford, and what I can afford I don't like.'

"This gave me such a laugh. 'Mr. Mangiameli,' I say, 'I know the feeling.' We get to talking. I get to asking how much is this car he likes. 'Allow me,' I say. 'It would do my heart a lot of good after what happened.'"

"That's so touching, Mama. I don't know if I actually remember him or it's that you talked about him. His face is thin, right? His eyes sunken in—"

"That's him," my mother says. "He looks a little like you-know-who." Her expression is mischievous.

"My colleague?"

"'My colleague,'" she mocks. "Mr. No-Name."

It occurs to me that my mother doesn't even realize she never calls us by our names, except Jack, and even then she changes it to Jake.

"Mr. No-Name, I forget how you meet him," she says.

"In California, at a convention. I didn't know we taught at the same school. He wasn't wearing his badge—see, 'Mr. No-Name' is perfect for him. I was drinking with a group of professors from Berkeley, and they invited other people to join us. Where else, at a restaurant! Then he invited us back to his hotel room for a drink. He was very witty. He loved reciting poetry and he was good at it. Everyone else left after a while, and I was still there—"

"So back in New York," my mother interrupts, "how you can meet him without Jake knowing?"

"Good question, Mama. It was on campus, in his office. You've seen my office. It's like that, with even more books."

She nods. "You didn't feel cheap?"

I shake my head no. *Excited*, I recall. "Sometimes I wished we could go see an opera together, stroll in Central Park . . . Is that how it was for you, with Peter the Wolf?"

"Why you keep calling him this?"

"I don't know. It's easier than calling him Harry. I knew it was supposed to be a secret, so I made it like a fairy tale—"

Her breast heaves. "What was I thinking, to see him at this

time? I told him, 'The little one, she understands too much.' *A shtik naches*, you never made a breath at home."

"Breathed a word," I correct. "But I sure blabbed at the police station. They almost took me away from Aunt Ruchel."

"*Takeh?* Sometime you tell me the story. Now I'm too tired. Tell me just one thing, you miss this guy?"

I know she doesn't want to hear the truth, but I don't want to lie to her. Not now, when we're growing closer than we've been since I was little. "I miss the passion," I say.

"*Oy vey*, I'm so tired." She shoves a mound of papers back in a drawer. "Thank you—all what you help. You take me to your place for dinner now?"

I don't say that Jack and I were planning to see a movie this evening. Perhaps she thinks it's Friday, which is our regular night with her. "Sure, I'll take you anyplace you want."

"*Alevai*, to the hospital, if you deliver."

"I'm not due for a month," I remind her.

"I know. You asked. I answered."

In the middle of the week my sister calls, although we call each other only on weekends. She is fifty now, menopausal. Her twins are in graduate school. After they were born, she never returned to teaching art. I made tenure before I even thought about having a child. It's strange to think of my nephews almost grown when I'm about to become a mother for the first time.

When Mimi calls now, I guess it's about Aunt Ruchel, who lives in a retirement home not far from her, but I'm wrong. "Mama doesn't sound good," she tells me. "She says she hurts all over."

Miffed my mother has kept this from me, I say, "What do you want me to do?"

"I'm in Jersey," she says. "It's easier for you."

"You don't have a job. I'm teaching an extra class because I'm taking fall off. I'm not exactly able to run around with this protuberance."

"*Protuberance?* Does that mean what I think it does? A lump, right? You call your baby a lump?"

"Swelling," I say. The pause is long, and I know she's contemplating an insult. "Mimi, take a joke. At least 'Swelling' is more colorful than 'You.' That's the only name Mama's ever called me."

My sister ignores my whine. "Take her to the doctor. I have a feeling."

My sister is uncanny with her feelings. "You scare me," I say.

"I'm scared, too. I can't help it."

L eaning against the doorjamb of my study, which is fast turning into a nursery, Jack asks if he can come with my mother and me to the doctor. On his corny T-shirt from the American Bar Association meeting, it says, ATTORNEYS SUCK, and below it, ALL THEY CAN. That's just like Jack, to knock the profession that feeds him. "I love your irreverence," I tell him.

"I don't think it's part of Mom's definition of *mentsh*."

A good human being, my mother means—someone you can lean on and he won't collapse, unlike my first husband.

"Why don't you just take her?" I say. "Do we need redundancy?"

"Don't you want to be there?"

"Be logical, Jack. She enjoys being with you more than me, and there's nothing I can do for her, medically." I shift my beach ball away from the computer keyboard and aim it toward the doorway, where he is still lingering. "You can come in," I say. "The computer doesn't bite."

His arms move as if playing a theremin. "I detect electronic waves, an invisible barricade. Seriously, why wouldn't you want to be with Mom?"

"To get the bad news? I can wait a few hours. Why?"

"I see the logic, Devorah, but it sounds—very inhuman."

"Say it the way my mother says it, Jack: 'Such a brain you got. Don't you have a heart?'"

I imagine my mother leaning on Jack's arm, walking from her apartment to the elevator, then out to his car, which is double-parked. "You took the time off from your customers?" she says to him.

"For days off, I charge them double," Jack jokes back. He tells her, "Devorah had to teach. The University's not thrilled she's taking fall quarter off."

"Jake, you don't have to apologize for my daughter. Doctors make her nervous. That imagination of hers—she can make the littlest thing so big."

The seminar on romantic motifs in nineteenth-century keepsakes goes well. After the bell, my students huddle around me, trying to suck up more. I imagine their lips glued to my nipples, and behind them, a line of students awaiting their turn to be fed.

In the class that follows, I get tangled up in words. I misunderstand some questions, I get peeved at others. My back is killing me. Then Mr. No-Name peers through the window of the door. He holds his fist to his ear with thumb and pinkie extended. I nod. What does he want? I wonder. My stomach lurches, but it isn't on account of the baby. All across my field of vision are zigzags of flashing lights.

I cancel the second class and take a taxi to the clinic. My mother is already with the doctor, but Jack is in the waiting room. I plop down beside him. "I don't know if it's guilt or concern," I say.

"Whatever," he says. "Mom will be glad to see you."

An hour goes slowly by. The zigzags keep me from being able to read. When the flashing lights finally vanish, I try to keep my thoughts away from Mr. No-Name, but they gravitate to him like shavings to a magnet.

At last my mother emerges from the corridor. She seems a little thin, though not a whole lot different from last year. She shrugs and says nothing about her appointment. Jack and I trade eye-rolls. "I'll be back," he says quietly. I know he's going to buttonhole the doctor.

"Jake told me something I never knew before," my mother says.

"What?"

"Sitting here waiting, he makes the time to pass. He tells me about Brooklyn. The Indians. The Canarsees?"

History is Jack's new hobby, not to mention giving my mother the attention he thinks she lacks from me.

"Yes," I say. "They were in Brooklyn before white people."

"Jake told me the name they called Coney Island," she says. "What?"

"'Place without Shadows.' Imagine."

My mother is in the rest room when Jack returns with his report. He shakes his head. The doctor has his suspicions, and orders X rays and a bone scan. Inside me, my mother's grandchild kicks furiously.

What the doctor calls hot spots are signs of bone cancer. For a long time my mother has ignored the pains in her pelvis, her hip, her shoulder. Now the cancer is well advanced. She refuses to undergo radiation. Jack and I think she decides wisely. My sister is not totally certain.

Two Sundays in a row when we are supposed to take her to the museum, my mother doesn't feel well enough to go. I bring my laptop over to her place and sit by her bed, practically the whole day. Occasionally as we talk, I bristle, but I no longer argue. That's one of the things about having a parent whose existence you stop taking for granted. You can no longer be yourself around them. You become a nicer person, but more like a stranger.

Another week goes by. Jack says we should move the chair with the pull-out bed into my study. It's the bed Ben sleeps in when he comes over for dinner, has too much to drink, and winds up playing chess with Jack all night. We cram the computer into a corner of the living room. We bring my mother to stay with us.

On the phone, my sister has a fit. "We have lots more room here," she argues. "And Mama likes the view of the Hudson."

"What?" I say, incredulous. "She doesn't, quote, 'give a fig for the river.'"

"Devorah, she told me herself. She loves the view."

"The skyline, I'll bet. More to the point, you're too far from her doctors, from the hospital. From civilization, actually," I say. "I think you better get over here."

"What are you telling me, Devorah?"

"The doctor said it could be two months, it could be a year."

"So why do you have to think the worst?"

"I don't mind being proven wrong," I say. "When are you coming?"

"Are you going to call Papa?" she asks.

"Why?" I say.

Our father has been in Florida for fifteen years now. I call him on his birthday and on Father's Day. Today, though it's neither occasion, he isn't surprised to hear from me. "Goldie and I just came back from the clinic," he says. "I had an angioplasty. You know what that is?"

I think he should be talking to Elihu, whose business is medical supplies. They would have more in common than my father has with the rest of us.

"Papa, I'm calling to tell you about Mama."

"Yeah? You're still in New York? They couldn't pay me to come back."

I tell him about my mother. I give him the prognosis.

"The doctors, they're always wrong," he says. "Maybe she'll live for a long time."

"Let's hope," I say. "Anyhow, I thought I should tell you. The doctor says she's dying."

"What can I do from here?" he says. "Who knows what they can come up with? This angioplasty, it's incredible—" I imagine he is still talking after I put the phone down.

I call my cousins, Sandy and Rhonda. We decide not to tell their mother. Aunt Ruchel is eighty-five now. She sold her home after Uncle Isaac had a series of heart attacks. They came to my sister's fancy wedding, and a week later he was dead.

Sandy runs a chain of day-care centers now, and Rhonda still plays tennis, the amateur trophies accumulating on the shelves of her den, beside an oil painting of Millie that Uncle Isaac commissioned.

In it Millie wears a large-brimmed picture hat and a gauzy dress in soft turquoise. She's younger looking than I remember, handsomer, with walnut-colored skin. Her sturdy arms rest along the arms of the rocking chair, which I don't recall she ever sat in. What draws me to the painting again and again is her expression. *I'm unknowable*, it says. Somehow the painter, whoever he—or she—was, resisted the temptation to simplify.

A few years after Millie moved with her children to South Carolina, she and Aunt Ruchel lost touch.

Just when I wonder if my mother will last the week, she gets out of bed, puts on a nice dress, makes and pours coffee, which she brings to Jack while he shaves. "Today I don't lay around," she tells him.

I overhear him say, "Mom, you want to go to the museum?"

"Ja-ack," I call plaintively.

"Devorah, come out, come out from your ivory tower. They have wheelchairs. You want to be wheeled around, Mom?"

The gleam in her eye is telling enough. Jack takes the day off and hires a car service. He doesn't tell her he'll have the car wait the whole time, in case she suddenly needs to leave the museum.

"We had a wonderful day," my husband says tonight as we lie in bed. "The Egyptians, the Expressionists—"

"For a long time she liked the Impressionists. Mimi's sappy influence."

"Two hours' worth, and then we went to the cafeteria. She hardly ate, but she swallowed a little apple juice. Loved the wheelchair." Jack quotes her as saying, "'Jakela, if you ride your baby around half as nice, the kid will be *gebentsht*.'" Blessed. To myself, I can't help it, I say, *Kineahora*.

"Don't be jealous." He puts his hand on my stomach. "Whatever happened with the two of you, she loves you, Devorah. She doesn't know how to express it."

"I've been trying," I say.

Jack takes my hand and kisses it. "I know, but I tell my clients, 'Between the lines doesn't count.'"

"Between the legs does," I say, a come-on that results in some fine lovemaking, even if we have to forgo intercourse.

Afterwards I lie awake, musing on his words about my mother. *Whatever happened with the two of you.*

As I brush her hair I ask my mother if she would like to tour Brooklyn. We have an account now with the car service.

"Listen," she says. "Don't make it so much fun. It's easier to let go when the world is *ipish*." When it smells.

"C'mon, Mama. What's your pleasure?"

She seems annoyed at having to answer. "All I want—I don't know if I'm going to live long enough to see your little one. *Alevai.* You asked me."

"If there was anything I could do to make this baby come sooner . . ." Although she knows she's dying, we never talk about it directly.

"Your Aunt Ruchel," she says suddenly. "So many times she saved my life. And yours too."

"You want to see her? Say it, Mama."

"I said it," she claims.

I call the retirement home and ask them to give my aunt a message. She can't hear well on the phone. They tell her to wait for us in the lobby, else she would be in one of her friends' apartments, playing mah-jongg.

The driver of our hired car takes us along the Henry Hudson Parkway to the George Washington Bridge. The air-conditioning makes my mother shiver. Reluctantly the driver turns it off and rolls down the window.

"I bet you don't remember. You stood on my lap the first time we crossed over," my mother says, her white hair fluttering in the breeze.

"You're right, but I remember what you told me—the river doesn't compare with the ocean. Wouldn't you like to see the ocean again?"

"This could be," she says, and dozes off.

Aunt Ruchel is very happy to see us. In her white slacks, print blouse, and white cardigan, she is indistinguishable from dozens of white-haired ladies who sit in armchairs, in the spacious, air-conditioned lobby. After much back-and-forth over which place is best, we sit under an umbrella by the outdoor pool where no one swims. "The only drawback," my aunt says, "is being around so many old people. Like flies they go. Every day they carry out someone—"

"Aunt Ruchel," I interrupt, "they have good programs here at night?"

She shows us a calendar with the different activities—music, lectures, bingo. On the back are the daily menus. "They don't cook like Millie," she says wistfully. "You remember her?" she asks me.

"Even without seeing that portrait Rhonda's got, I picture Millie clearly—"

"Tuesday I went with Jake to the museum," my mother interrupts, perhaps afraid I'll say something indiscreet.

"He's working, no?" my aunt says.

"He took a day off for once," my mother says. "Look at Benny, he's supposed to be retired, but lawyers, they always work."

"Not Jack," I say. "He's the only attorney I know who lacks ambition. He's hoping to become a judge."

My aunt gets the joke, but my mother says, "By my daughter this is a fault. Let me tell you something." She points at me. "The way you work all the time, you're lucky Jake comes home at night."

"If he's that unhappy, he's never told me."

"When would he tell you? Even when you're home you're at work."

I'm stung, of course. Not by the charge, which is true, but by the confidence she and my husband share. I retreat for the balance of the visit.

When we get up to leave, my aunt kisses my mother on both cheeks, as usual. Usually my mother only clasps her sister's forearms. This time my mother covers her sister's face with kisses. Aunt Ruchel holds her, looks over my mother's shoulder at me, searching for the explanation. I walk away. I imagine my face looks puckered, like one of those dolls made out of dried apples. I'm trying to hold back the tears. I fail.

For the next few days my mother gets out of bed only to go to the bathroom. Thanks to my brother-in-law, she has state-of-the-art pain management, where she can press a button on the pump and give herself morphine. She uses it sparingly. Unable to bear the thought of my mother in pain, my sister encourages her to use it more. Selfishly I keep out of it. I don't want my mother to succumb just yet, to let go.

I am home with her all the time, now that the quarter at the University is over. "Mama," I've taken to saying, "put your hands on my belly." I want her to feel the baby kicking. Seven days to go. I know that waiting for the baby to be born is all that keeps her alive.

Tonight, though the air-conditioning is working overtime, it's too hot to talk to anyone. I let the machine take phone messages while I suck orange Creamsicles, my latest craving. My mother has been asleep for hours. At the computer I research paradigms based on the myth of Herodias, the sensual mother of Salome. Unnamed in the Gospels, Salome lives in her mother's shadow.

It's late when Jack comes home. I hear him rummaging in the kitchen, then he's on the phone, but I can't hear what he's saying. I decide he's had a bad day. Still, when Jack comes into the living room without a word to me and turns on the T.V., I don't give an inch. I say, "Honey, I'm working."

"Honey, I'm relaxing," he says, mimicking my tone. "Do you want me to go to a bar to watch the Mets?"

Certain he'll back down, I say, "Do you want me to drive to campus?"

"First you took over the extra bedroom. Now you've taken over the living room," he says. "Do I live here?"

Although Jack and I occasionally snipe at each other, scoring points by being witty, on a humid summer's night wit goes by the wayside. Insults fly.

"You jellyfish," I say. "You pretend you're fine, and now the real truth comes out—but not from you. No, I have to hear it from Ben and my mother. You're the one who turned things upside down to accommodate her."

"'High crimes and misdemeanors,'" he says. "So file for divorce."

"Your excessive kindness—it reminds me of Sol's. I have to wonder what it's covering up."

He winces.

A gotcha! I think. "Damn it!" I say suddenly. It's my bladder. I run to the bathroom, not quite in time. I clean myself off, avoid looking at my swollen body in the mirror.

Feeling unlovable does nothing to abate my temper. The argument resumes. In the midst of the shouting I suddenly detach. I hear my snide tone. I see Jack's gentle eyes, sending out the equivalent of deadly laser rays. "Wait, wait," I say. "Darling, stop! What is it?"

He fishes out his white handkerchief, waves it, accepting the truce, but not a hug from me. Reluctantly, the words come out: "Checked your phone messages?"

"No." I feel myself flush. Jack doesn't have to say any more.

"It was an accident," Jack says now. I'm about to say, Yes, it was, I didn't mean for my colleague to call, but Jack's saying, "The light was flashing—the tape was full. You know how I goof up those goddamn—" His eyes bore into mine. "You didn't tell me you're presenting a paper."

I process the information. I decide that Mr. No-Name is giving me a pretext to attend the spring conference that he's chairing on the West Coast.

"Did you delete the message?" I ask Jack.

"No."

"What?"

"I answered it."

I imagine the end of my marriage. I imagine our child being passed back and forth between us. I imagine growing old alone and bitter. But I don't ask. I take the advice that Jack has given as a lawyer: Never ask a witness on the stand a question to which you don't know the answer. This is what saves me. For once I keep my mouth shut.

Elihu and my sister come to the city to have dinner with us. The plan is to eat out, if my mother's up to it. "Nothing ethnic," my sister says. She doesn't mean Chinese.

The overpriced Mandarin restaurant affords us a more leisurely meal than the noisy hole-in-the-wall that Jack and I prefer. Lethargically my mother pushes noodles around on her plate. Jack and Elihu carry the conversation, arguing over whether Governor Cuomo could win if he ran for president. Elihu argues, "His drive isn't strong enough."

"So wanting makes it so?" my sister says.

"I wouldn't underestimate force of will," Elihu replies.

"Well," my sister says, "I'll just sit down and wish with all my heart I hadn't found those *letters*—" Her la-di-da tone is new.

My mother perks up her ears. Elihu whispers something to Mimi, then stalks off to the men's room. My mother says to her, "You went looking for trouble, or you find the letters by accident?"

"What difference!" my sister barks. "You think you know someone for twenty-five years, and one day you learn you don't know a thing!"

Calmly, my mother says, "Not so long ago *I* found some letters."

Chopsticks or forks suspended mid-air, we wait for her next words.

"From the Philippines," she says.

I let out a breath, assuming it's just letters Sol wrote to her from his many trips to Asia over the years, but then she says, "From a woman. A child by Sol she has. Imagine!"

Jack stares at me, obviously wanting me to say it isn't so.

"*Emes,*" she says. "What for you all look at me? I still love him. He loved me. Things happen. Life is not so, how you say, uncomplicated."

Now Elihu is back and my sister flies off to the bathroom. I waddle after her, needing time to recoup from these revelations.

I hear Mimi in the stall next to mine, sniffling. I flush the toilet, wash my hands, comb my flyaway hair, and wait. Finally my sister emerges, oddly more beautiful than I've ever seen her. No longer is her face a mask of creamy skin and perfectly made-up features. For once, she looks vulnerable.

"Is it a fling, or does he have serious intentions toward her?" I ask.

"I don't care, I want a separation." She reapplies her lipstick, sucks in her cheeks. Even with too much weight, she turns heads. And anyhow, I tell myself, it's not the weight that made Elihu unfaithful.

"He only agreed to come tonight because I begged him," she says. "I want Mama to think everything's normal."

"Mama's way ahead of us, kid," I say. "She's done it all, knows it all."

"What are you talking about?"

"The man in Magic Shoes."

"What about him?" she says.

"You don't know Mama as well as you think you do," I say.

"What the hell does that mean?" my sister says. "Oh, I get it, you found things, going through her stuff. Or is it your overactive imagination, Devorah?"

I hesitate for a moment. I want to tell her I've made it my business to know. More than my business. My obsession. I want to know everything about my mother. But if I tell her this, Mimi will ask me why. For why, I don't have an answer.

"Too much French literature," I say with a Gallic shrug.

As if nothing has happened, we finish our plates, read our fortunes aloud to each other, promise not to let so much time go by before we get together again.

Jack drives us home and gets my mother to sit for a change in the back with me. "What he's looking for," she says, "he won't find."

"Who?" Jack asks.

"Who? Her husband, that's who. 'If you chase unhappiness, look out—before you catch it.' *Kholillah*. You hear me, Devorah?"

"Mama! You used my name."

"What?"

"You said, 'Devorah.'"

She shrugs. "It's your name, *nu*?"

"But you never call me that. You told me once when I was little—using names tempts the fates. Or maybe you said the Evil Eye."

"I don't know what you're talking," she says.

I lean forward and poke Jack in the shoulder. "Isn't that true?"

In the rearview mirror he catches my eye and winks, but says nothing. That's Jack, considerate to the nth degree. I feel shamed by his goodness.

There is a hearty kick in my stomach. "That's right," I tell the baby. "Don't be reticent like your father. Feel free to express yourself."

This time my mother places her own hand on my stomach. But when the baby kicks again, my mother is fast asleep.

My mother is dusting the blinds when I get home—a good sign, of course. I hand her the mail I've picked up from her building, my father's squarish envelope on top, his right-slanted script easily recognizable.

"Papa," she says. "You told him?"

"He asked how you were," I lie.

Above a basket of daisies on the front of the card are the words TO CHEER YOU. She pronounces the verse inside "nice" and hands me the card, signed, "Ruben & Goldie." A postscript says, "Regards to Mimi and Devora."

"He spelled my name wrong," I say.

"Spelling you get from my side, even if I don't know many words." She studies the postmark on the envelope. "Fort Lauderdale, is by the ocean?"

"You miss the ocean? We can visit Coney Island."

"Enough with the ocean. To here," she says, her hand under her chin. "For one thing only I would go, the Parachute Jump."

"I remember when it closed down," I tell her. "Too bad none of us ever got to ride on it, unless Sheldon did. Maybe he did—with Lenore."

"I went," she says. "One time."

I try not to blurt out, Tell me. Ever since learning my mother is dying, I'm almost as eager for news of her past as I am for the birth of a new life.

She stands at the window overlooking Riverside Drive and the Hudson, her back to me. "First I'm swimming to the ocean—" She tells me again about the lifeguard, but the next part is new. "The police, they want me in Bellevue, but the boy—I see his freckled face—he makes a lie to save me. An accident I swim so far, he tells them. He don't say I begged him, 'Let me drown.'"

She turns around to face me. "What?" she says, as I give a start.

"Nothing," I say. But I think it's a contraction. A week early. Superstitious, I don't dare to hope. "Go on, Mama."

"*Es tut mir vai.*" It hurts me. Refusing the pump, she sits at my desk, in the swivel chair. I sit on the bed, which she has already made up.

"Later I wake on the beach," she recounts, "sand on my tongue. My bathing suit, is dry. *Veys mir*, I'm burning from the sun. The strength, *oy*, is out of me. I stumble like a *shikker*. Later on the Boardwalk, a sailor, he comes by. Not a young one in a middy blouse, but more my age, with a stiff cap."

"An officer," I say.

"'Game for the Parachute Jump?' he asks me. These funny words. Maybe he's kidding. 'Sure. Okay, why not?' I tell him. I was even thinking maybe I could fall off, *mirtsishem*." God willing.

"What a ride! The sailor, all he wants is to take advantage, his arm around me, under my armpit, like so, so his fingers can feel my bust. But I forget everything as we go up. Up and up. The view, is open all around, like an elevator—no walls. From there, the Boardwalk so small, and my *tsores* like grains of sand on the beach. Nothing in the way, I'm going right to the sky over Brooklyn. *Ek velt.* Out of this world.

"The top of the parachute hits. Bom!" She gestures with her hands. "It bursts open, the biggest umbrella, the light so soft coming through. Whoosh! We drop. Right through the air we push. How can I explain? The air, is thicker than regular, with all the salt. I can feel it going against us."

My mother leans over to pat my large belly. "Soon you're pushing too."

The phone rings. I know it makes her nervous if I don't answer, so reluctantly I go. "*C'est toi*," I say to my colleague, careful not to betray a flutter.

"Actually I called to wish you luck, Devorah. On the birth. I mean it. I want to give you this amulet I picked up abroad—a crowned figure sitting on a sea horse. She's a Siren, but indisputably Diana, moon goddess, protectress of women in childbirth. She's also used to protect against the Evil Eye." He's heard a lot from me about my mother.

"I'll be glad if my mother doesn't stuff the bag I've packed for the hospital with garlic," I tell him.

"I wish she would," he teases, before urging me to attend the conference.

When I return to my mother, she is humming. "What is this song?" she asks. "I remember it from the Boardwalk." She hums it again.

"'No, no, they can't take that away from me,'" I sing.

She sings, "'The way you wear your hat, the way you danced till three—'"

We look at each other for prompts. I sing, "'The memory of all that—'"

Together, we sing, "'No, no, they can't take that away from me.'"

When my mother wakes, I bring two tablespoons of pistachio ice cream, in a large bowl so the portion will look even smaller. More than that makes her full just to look at, she says. My contractions are more frequent now but not all that intense, and nowhere near ten minutes apart. I'm trying to remember where Jack went. I can't decide whether to tell my mother yet. I'm afraid of overexciting her. I pretend to go for a glass of water. I get my watch and look at Jack's calendar. Something is scrawled on it, something I can't read.

"Devorah!"

I hear my mother's cry, a feeble cry. I run as best I can. Her eyes are wild. Her mouth is open.

Please, please, I think. *Not yet. Not now.*

"I have to go," she says. "Hurry."

She means to the bathroom. I breathe out. I help her up. She leans on me heavily. We stagger more than we walk. In the bathroom I help pull her dress up and her panties down. She leans on me the whole time, then I help lower her to the toilet seat. "Pshhh," she says, echoing the stream. After she wipes herself, I help her up. Again she leans on me as we pull up her panties and pull her dress down over them.

"You're so good with *pish*," she says. "How did you learn to be so good with *pish*?"

"I'm *kvelling* with the compliment, Mama." Bursting. I realize that because of her fear of the Evil Eye, I've been starved my whole life for compliments. There in the bathroom, I suddenly have to ask. "Mama, are you sorry you had me?"

My mother doesn't answer directly. "Move me back," she says.

This time she lies down. I arrange the pillows for her and wait for her answer. I'm sick with disappointment. She *is* sorry she had me, I decide, and she doesn't have the courage to tell me. I jerk as another contraction comes.

"The baby?" she says. Her eyes light up.

"I think so. But it'll be a while."

"You have a nice picture of me to show your little one?" she asks.

"Yes, Mama. Lots of nice pictures."

"Don't cry. I want to tell you something. I never told nobody. Not Solly. Not my sister. Not even your Jake." I try to lean forward. "The week I was gone, I slept under the Boardwalk," she says. "You want to hear this now?"

"Yes, Mama. Everything."

"*Nu*, the Boardwalk. Where else could I go? No money, nothing. The whole week I'm there. How I got so cold. The bums, they're living there all the time. We sleep one next to the other to keep warm. Twice I got raped—"

"My God, Mama, you went through such hell—"

She shakes her head. "You want to know what hell is? I tell you. The guilt for not loving Solly enough. My *aveyreh*." My sin. "What happened under the Boardwalk, I deserved it. *Emes*." True.

"Mama, how could you even think that?" I try to embrace her, but she stiffens.

"Now is different. An affair at that time—with heaven comes hell."

"Mama, I'm so sorry—"

She shrugs. "Why should you be sorry? All I want to know is, Why are you so angry at me?"

Just as I'm about to tell her, she nods off.

The contractions are erratic, and infrequent. I don't mention them to Jack when he comes home for dinner, Thai takeout, and says he's going to a meeting. Selfishly, I want my mother to myself. I boil potatoes for her and put them in the Cuisinart with milk and butter. Casually I ask Jack where his meeting is. The funny look he gives me says I don't trust him. I pat my stomach. "Just in case," I tell him, and he looks relieved.

My mother goes to bed right after what she calls dinner, a teaspoon of mashed potatoes, a few sips of Ensure. "Wake me up if anything."

I sit by her bed as she sleeps. I don't work on my laptop. I turn my mother's words over and over in my mind. *Under the Boardwalk. Raped.* I try to imagine that terrible week. I try to imagine her over the years, silently suffering from her *aveyreh*. My imagination fails.

What I remember is her faraway look. How often she seemed distant, cold even. Times when I would search for what I had said or done to upset her. Times I tried to dig further into the past for an answer that was always out of reach. I massage my belly, as if to reassure my baby that things are okay.

My mother opens her eyes. "So, tell me. What this anger is," she says. "First make my pillow." She presses on the pump.

I adjust her pillow. I help her sit up a bit. She is actually half reclining. She takes my hand and holds it, something I remember her doing only when I was a child.

"Compared to what you went through," I begin, "it isn't important—" *If it were some other time, if my mother weren't dying . . .*

"Tell me," she says. "The moments are dripping through."

I stare at the hollows in her cheeks where there used to be fat and flesh. "Don't you think I missed you?" I begin. "I was barely four years old. I spent virtually every minute with you, up until you dumped me on Millie. And when you came back it wasn't the same. I never trusted you after that. Or anyone, as Wally could tell you. As Jack can tell you."

I jerk and involuntarily take my hand out of hers. I place it on my belly.

"More pains now?"

"Some. Nothing like yours. Then when you married Solly, I was shut out. He turned you into someone different. I missed you, the real you." My fingers try to locate the scar on my cheek.

"What me?" she says.

It shames me to say that at this moment I imagine throttling her, my hands around the loose flesh of her neck. I don't believe the cancer has caused her to forget.

"You became so bland. Like mashed potatoes. You used to be eccentric, full of verve and temper. 'Like a dragon,' Ben once said, 'breathing fire.' Then you became Mrs. Sol Farber. You didn't yell, you didn't scream anymore. Yes, Sol. No, Sol. Let's make everything so pretty, Solly."

"For this you're blaming me?"

"You vanished on me. I never stopped loving you, but when you married Sol, it was worse than your disappearing into Brooklyn. Ever since, I've been trying to find you, or at least a shadow of you."

I see her searching her memory. I look at my watch. I make a mental note to process her reactions later. Now it's too much. The contractions are twelve minutes apart. Such a morbid subject we're on, I think. I should drop it. I fear it'll somehow contaminate the delivery. But I can't help it. *The moments are dripping through.*

"Mama, I love you. I wanted to know you loved me back."

"That's why you're angry with me? You think I didn't love you?"

"Love has to make itself known," I say. "Even when you were here, you were nowhere around."

"Look at me, *bubbeleh*. Tell me, does your *mameh* love you?"

I hesitate.

"When I got the pneumonia," she says. "The social worker, she figured it out. The one thing I had to live for."

"What?"

"What?" she says, incredulous. My mother raises both her hands in the air as if addressing the gods. "My daughter asks me, 'What?'"

I crumple up with the next contraction. "Mama, you better be here when I get back from the hospital. I'm going into labor."

I'm in the hospital several hours when Jack shows up, looking grim. He says Ben is with my mother. He is torn between wanting to tell me she's holding her own and what he thinks is the truth. He makes the right decision. He says, "I think it won't be much longer."

Later, when we tell the story, again and again, we disagree over who had the idea first. Probably we think of it simultaneously: to induce the baby. The doctor isn't moved by my appeal to do this for my mother's sake. "It's not medically indicated," he says.

I recall my sister's friend Suzanne, who is an obstetrician on the East Side and used to catering to rich women. Jack calls Mimi to get Suzanne's home number. Mimi heads for Manhattan. Jack calls Suzanne and explains the situation. Suzanne advises him. Jack tracks down my doctor in the cafeteria and talks to him in a calm, knowing way about hypertonic labor. Jack suggests bringing in a consulting physician. The doctor explains all the risks and finally agrees to induce.

My husband, who faints at the sight of a pinprick, waits outside as I go into active labor. He misses the miraculous moment, but not by much. The little wrinkled creature and I stare each other down. She wins with only one eye open. Then she opens the other to hypnotize Jack. Suddenly I am ravenous.

After our daughter is cleaned up, we wait till she has rooted awhile at my nipple, then Jack wraps her in a pillowcase. No one sees him leave. When the baby is discovered missing, I try to reassure the nurse. I imagine she thinks I killed my daughter and put her body in the medical waste bin. It's so ludicrous I laugh, and of course the more I laugh, the more agitated she becomes. Soon there is a whole cadre of official-looking people around my bed. They even call in a shrink. "Two hours," I tell him. "If she's not back, summon the police." Finally I get through. I can see it on the face of a nurse. It goes all dreamy. "That is the sweetest thing . . ." she says.

According to Jack, my mother holds our daughter for a few minutes. According to Ben, it is much longer. Both agree that she says, "I can't tell who she looks like." Ben says, "She does major *kvelling*. A look I haven't seen on her in thirty years."

Mimi asks her what she thinks of the newborn, maybe fishing for comparisons with her twins.

Ptooh, ptooh. My mother spits, but there's so little saliva it disperses into the air. Then she says she's tired and hands the baby to my sister. My sister returns the baby to Jack and drives them back to the hospital. They're greeted by the police, but after Jack explains, the hospital decides not to press charges. On campus I become the talk of my department.

For the next twenty-four hours my baby sleeps most of the time, and so does my mother, who is being watched by Mimi during the day. She calls me once when my mother's awake and puts her on the phone.

"Mama," I say. "I love you."

"I know," she says.

"And Mama, Sol never felt for a moment you didn't love him."

"You think so?" she says, her feeble voice rising hopefully.

In the middle of my second night at the hospital, I bundle up my baby, sign us out, and we take a taxi home. Jack doesn't hear us come in. He's asleep on the sofa, in jeans and a T-shirt. I'm sure he's worn out, caring for my mother. He wakes briefly, gently taps our daughter's nose, then mine, puts his head down and begins to snore.

The baby and I sit in the room where my mother sleeps, where my daughter will grow into a little girl who hears stories about her grandmother. In the dark, I listen for my mother's breathing. From time to time I nurse my baby. Such a good baby. She doesn't cry. I think she knows we need to be quiet. Perhaps I doze off. The room lightens, I open the blinds slightly. The sky is gray, then golden over the Hudson. Behind me I hear nothing. I know before I turn around to look. I don't see my mother's chest rise and fall.

With my baby in my arms, I go to the bed. I lay my daughter down beside my mother's still body. I kiss my mother's cold hand. I kiss her cold forehead. I smooth her hair. We will name the baby for her, I imagine telling Jack. Perhaps he will suggest it first. I pick up our daughter, cradle her in my lap. We wait beside my mother, until Jack comes to get us.

I imagine my mother finally at peace. *Alevai.*